PRAISE FOR THE MANHATTAN PROJECT

'Paul McNeive takes a very real worldwide medical problem and turns it into a disturbingly plausible thriller that builds to an edge-of-your-seat climax. Altogether a compelling read!'

Robert Goddard, author of *The Wide World* trilogy

'With an extraordinary, original and well-researched plot, contemporary themes, action, twists and turns, *The Manhattan Project* has all the ingredients of an international bestseller.'

Glenn Meade, *New York Times* bestselling author of *The Romanov Conspiracy*

'With a plot as fast-paced as the writing – bioterrorism meets big pharma – and a storyline stretching from Japan through the Middle East to the USA, *The Manhattan Project* is a cracking debut thriller. Guaranteed to be read in an all-night sitting!'

Paul Carson, author of *Inquest*

'*The Manhattan Project*, a brilliant debut novel, starts as a slow-burn and quickly ignites into a fast-paced biological disaster facing the citizens of New York.'

John McAllister, author of *The Station Sergeant* trilogy

'For anyone who likes their books big, blistering and utterly compulsive, this is the read for you. It is explosive, addictive and ultimately very satisfying. There's a new boy in town – at last an heir to Tom Clancy.'

Doreen Finn, author of *My Buried Life*

THE MANHATTAN PROJECT

PAUL McNEIVE

BLACK & WHITE PUBLISHING

First published 2018
This edition first published 2019
by Black & White Publishing Ltd
Nautical House, 104 Commercial Street
Edinburgh EH6 6NF

1 3 5 7 9 10 8 6 4 2   19 20 21 22

ISBN: 978 1 78530 240 4

With thanks to Hozier for kind permission to
reproduce lyrics from 'Better Love'

A CIP catalogue record for this book is available
from the British Library.

Typeset by Iolaire, Newtonmore
Printed and bound by CPI Group (UK) Ltd, Croydon, CR0 4YY

For Kate, Megan, Killian and Michael

'Now I am become Death, the destroyer of worlds.'

J. Robert Oppenheimer, 'Father of the Atomic Bomb'

PROLOGUE

HIROSHIMA – SATURDAY 6 AUGUST 1945

The world was going to change today – and he was going to change it. Tom Ferebee, the bomb aimer on the *Enola Gay*, was drenched in sweat. His shirt stuck to his back as he tried to concentrate.

'Shit,' he said under his breath, as a drop of perspiration ran off his forehead and clouded up his bombsight. Every bombing run was a nerve-jangling experience, but right now, twenty-six thousand feet over Hiroshima Bay, he was feeling the pressure. *Nearly there now.* He had been chosen for this mission as a member of one of the most experienced bombing crews in the US Air Force. This bomb would be dropped from twice their normal bombing altitude, for their own safety. They were on a northwesterly course from their base on Tinian Island. About sixty seconds to go, he thought.

'Yeah, there's the river, where it splits into seven channels. Definitely Hiroshima,' he heard the navigator reassure the pilot through his headphones. He watched the grey grid of buildings and streets unfolding slowly below him and noticed ant-like movement on the ground. Tom could normally detach himself from thinking about the consequences of the bombs he dropped, but on this occasion, he couldn't help wondering who those people were. *What are they thinking, right now, in the last few moments of their lives?* For now, just thirty seconds or a mile or so from his target, he knew that those people had no chance.

The knot in his stomach tightened. He blinked away another drop of sweat as the four massive engines around him droned closer to history. With five seconds to go, some miles away to the left, he noticed three white lights flashing brightly skywards from the ground. Flash, flash, flash. Unusual, he thought. One second later, the crosshairs on his bombsight were centred over the target coordinates and he gave the order firmly and clearly –

'Bomb away.'

Twenty-five feet behind him, Deak Parsons, hunched over the bomb bay, pulled the lever in his right hand. 'Bomb away.'

The giant B-29 Superfortress bomber, suddenly freed of the weight of her deadly cargo, bucked upwards as Paul Tibbets, the pilot, banked away from the drop zone. The first atomic bomb to be used against civilians, nicknamed 'The Little Boy' by the crew, dropped two hundred feet or so, lazily turned its nose downwards and headed towards a city of four hundred thousand people. Aboard the *Enola Gay*, the twelve crew members watched the city below them through their windows, in tense silence. Tom Ferebee swept a pale blue shirtsleeve across his brow. He had a mixed-up feeling, not knowing whether he had just finished something or just started something. For some reason, a picture of his wife and baby son flashed through his mind.

*

Thirty-one thousand feet below the *Enola Gay*, and now perhaps five miles away, Saina Yohoto was also sweating as she ran behind her three children, pushing them in turn higher and higher on the three park swings. 'Higher! Higher!' the children shouted and squealed with delight. The morning sun reflected off the three metal swings and flashed upwards towards Tom Ferebee in the *Enola Gay*. Suddenly, disaster, as the youngest child, Tsan, five years old, slipped under his seat restraint and shot forward, falling heavily on to the concrete in front of his swing. His mother darted around the swing, instinctively using her right arm to fend off the empty swing seat, which was now coming forward again. Her little boy Tsan was face down on the ground and had begun to scream – a child's scream of pain and shock. As she bent down to hug her son, Saina Yohoto was illuminated by a dazzling white light and her long black hair was lifted by a warm wind, which quickly became too hot. She ducked and shielded her young son as a fireball swept over the park wall. Two seconds later, the screams of the young mother had joined those of her youngest, who lay beneath her, face down on the ground.

★

Now seven miles away and at thirty-five thousand feet, those on board the *Enola Gay* peered downwards in amazement. Tom Ferebee's intuition was right: they had just triggered a disaster, which would have deadly repercussions, seven thousand miles away. Decades later. Everything had changed.

PART ONE

LIGHTING THE FUSE

1

MANHATTAN – THE PRESENT

The old man didn't deserve what happened.

Down around Piers 34 to 44 on the southern end of the island, there are still some old warehouses and fish markets, just a few blocks from Broadway and Wall Street. These sheds have probably escaped redevelopment because of the elevated highway running overhead. If anyone dared to attempt a remake of *On the Waterfront*, this location could be their set.

In his empty factory building, Abdel Moamer had nothing much to do, so he decided to start lunch early. While he was unfolding the greaseproof paper, which his wife had carefully wrapped around his sandwich that morning, a gun appeared around his office door.

'Get the fuck out of my office, you bastard. I'm too old to be frightened by your type,' snarled Abdel Moamer.

His visitor's response was to point the Colt 45 at the old man's face.

'You're mad. What do you want? I'm calling the cops.' Abdel made a defiant grab for the telephone, but the gunman chopped his hand down on his thin arm, almost breaking it.

'Aaargh, you shit!' The old man winced in pain and doubled up, cradling his arm.

'Such a pity, Abdel. I do not want to cause you unnecessary pain. Get up now and walk out to the factory floor,' said the stranger in a low, cultured voice. Abdel Moamer raised himself slowly out of his chair, wincing as he heard a crack from his artificial hip.

'Abdel, quickly please,' said the man, waggling his gun.

Abdel Moamer assessed his options. Unfortunately, it had been many years since anyone else had worked in this place. There was no one here to help him now.

'Turn around,' came the calm voice from behind as he reached the factory floor.

The old man turned. For a second he thought of his beloved wife, Nina, singing as she cooked in their cosy kitchen at home. *Would she be all right?*

The gunman pulled the trigger and a .45 bullet crashed through Abdel Moamer's forehead at approximately 1,500 m.p.h. It exploded out the back of his skull, spraying a large chunk of Abdel's brain onto the steel vat behind him. His body crumpled backwards, falling partially under the steel container. A pool of bright crimson spread across the white tiles. His executioner bent to remove his victim's wallet and Rolex watch.

In Abdel Moamer's office he pulled open the desk drawers and threw a few handfuls of files and documents onto the floor. He then walked back around the pool of blood, pushed open a fire exit in the side wall, closed it behind him and strolled down South Street. He put his leather gloves into his coat pocket as he melted among the pedestrians on Market Street, making sure to avoid the traffic cameras on Manhattan Bridge.

★

When the call came over the radio in the unmarked Ford Crown, Detectives John Wyse and Michael Cabrini were halfway across Brooklyn Bridge, returning to the station, where Wyse had a potentially career-changing meeting scheduled with his boss.

Wyse, the younger of the two, had joined the Fifth Precinct station three years previously. Last year he'd been paired up with Cabrini, whose partner had retired.

'Pier 34, John, that's gotta be us,' said Cabrini, flicking on the siren and flooring the accelerator. Wyse hit the switch on the dash to activate the strobe lights in the front grille and rear window.

''Bout five minutes, tops,' he advised the dispatcher. 'Uniform's already there,' he told Cabrini, who was squeezing between two artics on the bridge.

'Easy, Mike,' he groaned and shut his eyes as the bridge narrowed and the two trucks began to close up. Cabrini dropped into second, rammed his foot down and shot through the gap. Wyse sighed and Cabrini raised his eyebrows to his pal.

'Assertive driving, John,' Cabrini explained, with a twinkle. 'Everyone in Italy drives like this!'

Cabrini powered into South Street, where they could see a uniformed cop moving back a cluster of onlookers by stringing crime scene tape across the kerb. Cabrini pulled over behind the group and jabbed at the brake, causing the tyres to screech and the rubberneckers to turn around to gawp at them.

★

Thirty minutes later a routine murder investigation was underway. The late Abdel Moamer was being photographed from a variety of angles and a forensic team was dusting the office and the fire door for prints. Cabrini was in his element.

'Looks like he went out the fire door,' he said. He looked down at the distorted shell case in a plastic bag in his hand. 'That's a .45, just one shot. Make sure we get a list of any potential witnesses. And someone go round the back, pronto, and collect all the CCTV.'

'On it,' said one uniform, moving for the door.

'And don't forget the traffic cameras on the bridges. Brooklyn and the toll,' Cabrini called after him.

'I got it.'

Detective John Wyse glanced at his watch and cast an anxious last look at Abdel Moamer's body. The old man was lying flat on his back, his eyes wide open in a futile stare. He almost appeared to be trying to read a brass plate, riveted close to the bottom of the steel vat. *Manufactured in Sweden by Alfa Laval*, declared the plate, through freckles of blood. Wyse noticed that the dead man wore an expensively tailored suit. Even in death, Wyse thought the man had the face of a kind grandfather. *Poor guy*. An instant later, his mind flicked back to his own problem.

'Shit, Mike, I'm late for Connolly,' he said, pointing at his wrist.

'Yeah, okay, bud, I'll stick with this; you go. We'll catch up later.'

'Okay, Mike, see ya,' said Wyse, spinning around. 'I'll find a ride back.'

'And good luck,' called Cabrini at his buddy's back.

★

Back on South Street at the front of the warehouse, there was still a cluster of locals hanging about, joined now by a couple of reporters and photographers. John Wyse left a voice message on Sergeant Connolly's phone to say he was running late. He was looking around hopefully for a cab, when he got lucky. Paul Carter was coming out of the warehouse and heading for the tape.

'Paul. Hey, Paul,' Wyse called.

Carter turned around and waved.

'You goin' back towards Forty-Seventh?'

'Yeah. Need a ride?' replied Carter, slapping Wyse's upturned palm with his own.

'Sure do. I'm late for a big meet with Connolly.'

'No problem, car's over here.' Paul Carter's black 3 Series BMW was parked just a few yards down the street. Carter turned the ignition and muted the radio.

'So, whaddya make of all that?' he asked, inclining his head at the warehouse as he pulled out onto South Street.

Wyse shrugged, glancing at his watch again. 'Routine one-off, I'd say, no biz for you guys.'

Paul Carter was a psychologist, one of three criminal profilers based at the NYPD's Park Row headquarters, also in the Fifth Precinct. The profilers turned up at most of the homicides, in case they were linked to one of their investigations. Wyse knew Carter casually from drinking beers after shift, but hadn't worked a case with him. Carter was in his early thirties with shoulder-length curly hair and an easy smile. He was one of those laidback guys who could look cool in a tuxedo or a T-shirt, without trying.

'Yeah, I'd say you're right, John. Looks like the old man surprised a burglar. Drug deal gone wrong maybe. No psychological profiling requirement likely.' Carter took a left into Market Street.

Sometimes, down at Harry's Bar, some of the older guys with a few beers on, would try and wind up Carter, mocking his profession. One memorable night Carter had finally retaliated by taking twenty dollars each from Cabrini and nine other detectives by correctly guessing seven of their ten star signs. 'Party tricks,' he'd winked to Wyse later. 'Half of them are easy guesses. The other half have forgotten that they bought me a drink here on their birthdays last year – now they're paying me to tell them their star sign!'

Wyse had laughed. He liked Carter.

'So, what's with this big meeting with Connolly?' Carter asked him, carefully overtaking a delivery truck.

'Uh, make or break,' groaned Wyse. 'I've pretty much decided to resign.'

'Wow, that's pretty radical – you not enjoying it?'

'Dunno. I mean, I love the Force and all that, but it's all becoming a bit, you know, same old.' Carter nodded and stopped at a red on Center Street.

'Take that homicide,' Wyse continued, jabbing his thumb back in the direction of South Street, 'I'll lay any money it was some coked-up local kid. We put enough pressure on our snitches, we'll have the guy within a month. I'm not gettin' a buzz any more. Feel like I should be doing more.'

'I gotcha,' said Carter, turning right at the courthouse into Chinatown. The Fifth Precinct station was another couple of blocks ahead on the right.

Wyse kept talking. 'Sometimes I get sick of all the violence. You know, like the whole world just seems to be getting crazier and crazier. You wonder where the hell it's all gonna end up. When I was growing up I was taught to always do the right thing, that the good guys always win out in the end. These days I'm not so sure. There seems to be an awful lot of bad guys getting the upper hand. I mean, how the hell do you try and deal with someone who'll walk into a concert and blow up a load of young girls? And themselves.'

Carter was shaking his head, tight-lipped. 'I know. It's next to impossible,' he said. 'Problem is, you're fighting an idea, not a war. And, it's almost impossible to identify the tiny percentage of people who might be radicalised. From the outside, they're living totally westernised lives: same clothes, same dress, same lifestyle – even drinking alcohol.'

'You're right,' said Wyse. 'Hopeless. But then I think, well, what better place could I be than here, trying to do something about it?'

Carter nodded. 'Like it's your duty?'

'Suppose so,' said Wyse.

'Can I take a punt here with ya, John?' asked Carter.

'Sure,' said Wyse, puzzled.

'Just bear with me. You got brothers and sisters?'

'Yep, one of each,' replied Wyse, seeing images of Jess, an architect in Malibu, and Larry, a coder in Silicon Valley.

'Okay, well I'm going to bet that you're the first-born, the eldest,' said Carter. 'Am I right?'

'Right in one.'

'Well, I'm guessin' that's why you're unsettled. There's a few leadership genes sparking there that ain't gettin' an outlet.'

'Whaddya mean?'

'See, it goes like this. In those crucial early years, the first-born gets lavished with attention. The parents simply have more time. Then number two and number three come along and suddenly there's less time for all the kids. But Mr First-Born had the head start, the special treatment.'

'So, what's all that mean?' asked Wyse, growing interested.

'So what happens next is, kids start growing up and playing together. But guess who's always the boss? Guess who decides what game to play? Then guess who makes up all the rules?'

'The first-born,' ventured Wyse, seeing the light.

'Exactly. So, from the time they're a toddler, the first-born feels their own confidence and authority. And uses it.'

'So?'

'So, that's probably why you joined the police. First-borns are attracted to jobs where they're in authority. Where there's clear rules. Like policing. And teaching.'

'Aah, I see,' said Wyse.

'First-borns also tend to have a strong sense of duty,' continued Carter, squeezing into a space on Elizabeth Street in front of the station, 'but the bigger picture is that about eighty per cent of high achievers, the people who rise to the top leadership roles, in business, politics, you name it, are . . .'

'First-born? No kidding.'

'You got it, man. You've got some leadership genes goin' on there and they're not finding an outlet, cos you're curtailed within the police force's set way of thinking.'

Wyse nodded. It made sense.

'It means "pathway", you know, "leader", in Latin,' Carter continued. 'Most pioneers, over-achievers, even the guys who walked on the moon, were first-born. I'd say you were born to find a new path and inspire people to take it,' he finished, switching off the engine. 'So, I suggest you look at something that gives you a chance to lead, take decisions and inspire others to follow you.'

'Heavy stuff,' said Wyse, 'but makes sense.' He shook Carter's hand and headed up the steps into the station, calling over his shoulder. 'Thanks for the advice.'

'You're welcome.' Carter smiled, locking the car. 'And John,' Carter called after him.

'Yeah,' said Wyse, turning.

'When you have kids, make sure they all feel special!'

'I will. Thanks again,' said Wyse, laughing, as he hurried inside to find Sergeant Connolly.

2

TOKYO – THREE MONTHS AGO

Tsan Yohoto sat at the head of the polished mahogany table, fifty-six floors above damp streets packed with evening commuters. The spectacular view over the Tokyo skyline had become shrouded in low cloud and Yohoto noticed the air-conditioning unit clicking off as the boardroom cooled naturally.

Sitting opposite Tsan Yohoto were the ten directors of Yamoura Pharmaceuticals, the third largest drug manufacturer in the world. Yamoura had been a small company after the war but had grown dramatically since the 1970s. Its growth was spearheaded by the brilliance of Tsan Yohoto. Every new product launch and every merger and acquisition promoted by Tsan Yohoto had been successful. He had been the youngest-ever board appointment at the age of thirty-six. He had become chief executive, or *daitoryou*, at the age of forty-three. To most Japanese, Yamoura Pharmaceuticals meant Tsan Yohoto.

The finance director was droning on about a proposal to take over a small company that had come up with a vaccine for the Asian bird flu. But Tsan Yohoto's mind had wandered elsewhere – something that happened more frequently these days. He was back with his most vivid memory, one that had been seared into his brain at the age of five.

He was sitting up in front of the swings and his mother was beating his back. Why? His mind spun with shock and pain. He screeched at the hot agony taking over his body. Tsan's mother Saina, kneeling over her little boy, finally beat out the flames on his red jacket. She pulled her screaming child to her breast as she turned around to look for her seven-year-old twins, a boy and a girl, Kendo and Lita. The sight that assailed her eyes was too much for any person to take in, let alone a young mother. Kendo and Lita's charred bodies were still on their swing seats, still swinging gently backwards and forwards, backwards and forwards, their hands fused with the metal chains. Most of the skin had been burned from their bodies. Their small white teeth shone in a mad smile through the black mess that had replaced their faces. Small yellow flames worked their way lazily through what remained of their hair. Tsan felt his nose and mouth filling up with the smell of roast meat. He felt himself gagging. All was quiet, except for the creak and groan of the chains on the swings. Backwards and forwards.

Saina and Tsan Yohoto lay on the concrete in front of this macabre scene, some five miles from the drop zone. They had been spared the worst of the bomb's subsidiary fireballs. Tsan hugged his mother tighter. He could hear his mother's heart pounding wildly, even through her screams and the creak of the swings. Backwards and forwards, backwards and forwards. Backwards and . . .

The image began to fade and Tsan Yohoto realised he was caressing the black and white photograph of Kendo and Lita, which he always carried in his inside jacket pocket. The photograph helped him remember when he had felt really happy. Before the bomb had taken away his family and his very soul. He rubbed his eyes as he found himself slowly becoming aware again of the finance director's voice, droning towards the end of his long report:

'And so, I propose that we proceed with the purchase at nine hundred million yen and enter due diligence.'

Around the table a series of nods and grunts granted the approval required and Tsan returned to his daydreaming.

'Tsan, Tsan, my beautiful boy!' His mother was holding him tight. He had woken again, screaming, from the regular nightmare.

'Mother, Mother, I can see the swings,' he cried.

'Tsan, Tsan, we must be strong, we must be strong. My beautiful boy.' She stroked his scarred face and eventually soothed him back to sleep.

After the bomb, Tsan and his mother were taken to the Fujama hospital in Tokyo, where they stayed for four weeks, before they returned to view the wasteland that had been their home city. His mother, a nurse, worked long days treating survivors of the explosion.

Both mother and son had suffered burns to their hands, their backs and to the tops of their heads, but the blackness had flaked away to reveal healthy skin beneath and both were left with just mild scar tissue. Tsan had one distinctive scar, in the shape of an arrow, just below his right temple. Every time he looked in the shaving mirror, his scar reminded him. If he didn't look away quickly enough, he could smell roast meat.

Tsan Yohoto's father was dead, his body burned to a crisp in a street near their home, a mile from the park where Saina had taken her children to play. Almost every human and building within a five-mile radius of the drop zone had been obliterated. Conversely, there was a high survival rate in the suburbs, between five and seven miles from the city centre.

'Aieee, aieee,' the mournful screaming continued, day after day.

The young mother and son were moved to a dormitory in a converted schoolhouse, near the clinic where Saina Yohoto worked. The school buildings were crammed with survivors, the broken remnants of life in Hiroshima. The adults spent their days sitting around the radio in the corner of the dormitory and the little boy, Tsan Yohoto, listened to their cries of anguish. He did not understand that the war was now over, that Emperor Hirohito had surrendered. But as he listened to the adults, he understood that all the trouble had been caused by 'the bomb'. 'The bomb' had killed Kendo and Lita and his father. 'The bomb' had killed the little baby next door. 'The bomb' had killed his friend, Mr Horunda, who swept around the swings. 'The bomb' had killed them all. 'The bomb' had been dropped by the Yankees. And Tsan knew that, one day, when he was big enough, he was going to kill all the Yankees in return.

★

His mother's decision to return to Hiroshima had cost them dear as, six months later, the government realised that the radiation which saturated the region was damaging the survivors. Within weeks of the bomb, cancerous growths and a plethora of heart-breaking deformities in newborn babies confirmed everyone's worst fears. Tsan's mother was ordered by the Atomic Bomb Commission to return to Tokyo, to continue her work with survivors of the Hiroshima and Nagasaki bombs. Two years later, following testing, Tsan's mother knew that her body and that of her son had been affected by the radiation. The fallout had caused an invisible but catastrophic genetic mutation and they were among the tens of thousands with compromised immune systems and at risk of developing leukaemia. For many years Tsan's mother ensured that they were both checked for any abnormalities. Long after his mother's retirement, Tsan had availed himself of the facilities of the Yamoura laboratories to continue those checks. His mother had been lucky – she was still healthy at ninety-five years of age. Unfortunately for Tsan Yohoto, his last tests had shown an increase in cancerous cells. Leukaemia would kill him – and probably not too long into his planned retirement.

In Tokyo, Tsan had grown up with his mother's stories of

life at the hospital and the pitiful attempts to treat the victims of Hiroshima and Nagasaki, the agony of the daily dressings and the ravages of infection to burnt skin. Tsan wanted to learn more, especially about the great new antibiotic called penicillin, which was helping to save so many lives.

'Help, help, save me,' laughed Saina Yohoto, in the sitting room of her Tokyo apartment. It was two years after the bomb. Tsan and his 'new brother' Horto had jumped out, growling, from behind the door, wearing masks and pretending to frighten her. Horto had been badly burned at Hiroshima, and all of his family killed. Saina had brought him home from the burns unit to live with her and Tsan. Horto's mask was real – a thick canvas balaclava, with holes cut for his eyes and for what remained of his nose and lips – which he had to wear on his face, twenty-four hours a day. The aim was to smooth out the scar tissue on Horto's face. He had a spare one to allow the usual one to be washed, and Tsan wore that one when they were pretending to be monsters.

Tsan loved having Horto in the house. Horto was one year younger than him and he never talked, but he was his best friend. Tsan gave Horto half his toys and his favourite model aeroplane, because Horto had nothing. Horto slept on a mattress on the floor of Tsan's tiny bedroom but Tsan often let Horto have the bed. Tsan became Horto's defender, too. He'd put his judo skills to good use with a flurry of kicks and punches to the shocked faces of the many boys stupid enough to mock Horto's mask.

When Tsan was nine, Horto fell sick and died. For some reason, Tsan couldn't cry. His mother told him that Horto had contracted cancer from the bomb.

Saina hugged her son, gently stroked the scar on his temple and whispered, 'Be brave, my son, be brave. We must be strong. Strong for everyone who has died. We who survived must make our lives count.'

Tsan prayed that Horto would be able to find his brother and sister in the afterlife and that Kendo and Lita would look after him there. Once again, the bomb had brought sorrow and pain into their lives. Every night he imagined the time when he would be clever enough to take revenge on the Yankees for dropping the bomb. *I will find a way to do it.*

★

After he left school, an insatiable interest in chemistry and genetics propelled Tsan Yohoto's graduation as the top student at the Genetic Engineering Faculty at Tokyo University. Within weeks he had his first job as lab technician, number L-149, at Yamoura Pharmaceuticals, the company which was to become his life.

A shaft of sunlight broke through the cloud and lit up the boardroom. Tsan Yohoto heard the air-conditioning unit recommence its hum. He looked at the faces around the table. These were his most trusted friends and confidantes. He had appointed all of them to the board (after he had cleared out the deadwood), and all shared his intelligence and ambition. Together they had created a multinational giant with over fifty thousand employees and with manufacturing plants, research and development facilities and distribution networks in almost every country in the world.

His closest friend and ally was Lumo Kinotoa, who was seated on his right. Kinotoa had almost matched his rise through Yamoura and had been Tsan Yohoto's first appointment, as his *skikaisha,* or chairman. He was known in business circles as the 'Silver Fox', because of his shining head of silver hair and his cuteness. The two men had grown close over the years, drawn together by their passion for chemistry, their drive to succeed and their strongest common bond – Lumo Kinotoa's family had been wiped out at Nagasaki.

'The suspense is killing us, Tsan,' said Kinotoa, with a grin.

The board members smiled. They had reached the last item on the agenda – listed as 'Tsan's Tsumori' or 'Tsan's Plan'. Now a very fit man in his seventies, of slight build, immaculately groomed and with jet-black hair and wire-rimmed spectacles, Tsan was due to retire in two years. Some months ago, he had advised the board of his wish to head up one last project. This, he said, would mark his retirement in a fitting manner. He had in mind a humanitarian initiative on a grand scale – perfectly appropriate for a healthcare company. The project, he advised, would be loss-making initially, but the PR benefits would be far reaching.

The chairman turned to his left. 'Tsan,' he asked, 'are you ready to tell us of your grand plan? The directors' bets are on an Ebola-related project!'

Tsan Yohoto smiled. 'No, Mr Chairman,' he replied. 'But please allow me some time on this at next month's meeting.'

Lumo Kinotoa returned the smile. 'Certainly, Tsan, of course.'

Lumo Kinotoa was the only other person at that boardroom table who knew what Tsan Yohoto was really planning. And the devastation that those plans would mean for the Americans.

3

SAITON – TWO MONTHS AGO

Near the small village of Saiton, sixty miles north of Tokyo, Yamoura Pharmaceutical's chairman, Lumo Kinotoa, was hosting a 'chess evening' in the reception room of a villa he normally used at weekends. The beautifully restored house was on a site of thirty acres, with surrounding woodlands providing privacy. Security personnel manned the gate and patrolled the boundaries. Kinotoa's passion was military history and his chess evenings involved anything but chess, but he enjoyed the cover story, given the strategic planning that took place at these ever-more-frequent meetings.

'Gentlemen, your attention please,' said the silver-haired Kinotoa as he tapped the table with his pen. To his left sat Tsan Yohoto. Across the table was the thin-faced Dr Juro Naga, a renowned consultant in biochemistry and lynchpin of the Atomic Bomb Casualty Commission, established by the Japanese government after the bombs at Hiroshima and Nagasaki. Beside Dr Naga sat Kazuhiro Saito, president of the Woko Corporation, the largest producer of computers in Asia. A jovial, overweight man, in his early seventies, he was an expert in branding and international marketing. His family had been killed by US Marines on Saipan when they overran the island to use it as a launch pad for the bombing of Japanese cities. All present were double-digit millionaires, many times over. All were at the height of their powers, nearing the end of their careers, but capable of allocating large sums of personal and corporate capital to their 'special projects'. All shared the common bond of having suffered the loss of their families to the Americans and all nurtured a deep desire to exact a fitting revenge, for the suffering and shame inflicted on their people.

The Japanese hosts all wore expensively tailored, dark suits with sober ties, as the business of the Chess Club was conducted in a formal and serious manner. An antique chessboard with hand-carved ivory pieces sat at the centre of the highly polished table. Although they had met regularly around this table for over twenty years, on this night the atmosphere was particularly charged.

'Gentlemen,' repeated Kinotoa, 'let me extend our warmest welcome and thanks to our friends, for making the journey here.'

He made a half turn and bowed to the two Arabs who were seated at the end of the table. 'It is indeed an honour to finally meet such long-standing friends and allies.'

The visitors nodded graciously and both acknowledged the tea, which Kazuhiro Saito poured for them.

Kiyo Arai, a tall, well-built Arab in his mid-fifties, with brown eyes and a greying beard, was one of the most wanted terrorists in the world. He had travelled to Japan with Kazuman Tokash, another of al-Qaeda's most senior members. In contrast to Arai, Tokash, also in his mid-fifties, was of a stocky, powerful build, with a thick black beard. Their journey, which had begun in southern Afghanistan, had been a dangerous one. If tracked, they could have been assassinated by either US or Saudi agents.

On this occasion, however, such was the importance of the message from their friends in Tokyo, that their leader, Najeed Shammas, had instructed that the trip should go ahead. Al-Qaeda had produced passports and travel documentation which would pass scrutiny by the nosiest of airport security officers. And so it was that, wearing shortened and darkened hair, trimmed beards and with their eyes re-coloured by contact lenses, the two, posing as Saudi Arabian businessmen, had travelled undetected to Tokyo, via Kuwait.

'Thank you for your welcome, my friends,' beamed Kiyo Arai, 'and indeed the pleasure is entirely ours to meet such old and trusted friends. How can we ever forget your help in Kenya and Tanzania?' Arai was referring to the bombing of the two US Embassies in August 1998, which killed two hundred and fifty-eight people. Arai had personally armed the devices for both attacks. The Chess Club, as he knew them, had helped with reconnaissance information from the embassies – carried out by a Japanese tourist with an apparent enthusiasm for photography.

'Yes,' added Tokash, 'your loyal support in the Jihad against the Zionist pig Yankees has been most generous. These are good days for the fatwa. Muslims all over the world are uniting to fulfil Shaykh bin Laden's instruction to kill all Americans. The glorious success of 9/11 has struck fear into the hearts of the Americans. Now they waste billions trying to stop us striking again – but they cannot. Our sleepers abroad have had great success with shootings – Sydney, Tunisia, Toronto, the train bombs in Spain. And we have exacted full justice on Paris and its damn cartoonists.'

'Not to mention the gays in Orlando,' said Arai, with a smile.

'And our Jihadi brothers have found a new use for trucks in Nice, Berlin and the UK,' added Tokash.

Despite Tokash's words, Yohoto suspected that some of the attacks he referred to had been carried out by lone IS fanatics. IS was putting most of its efforts into attacks on America's allies, in Europe and the Middle East. Yohoto might consider allying with IS in the future, but for the moment, al-Qaeda had the longest established network of radicalised 'sleepers' in the United States. And these sleepers were just what he needed.

'So, what is this important plan, which has brought us here tonight?' asked Kiyo Arai, his voice buzzing with excitement. Lumo Kinotoa nodded towards Tsan Yohoto. Yohoto, wearing his trademark black suit with a pale blue shirt and navy tie, was caressing the photograph of his dead brother and sister. He stood up to address the meeting.

*

'My good friends,' said Tsan Yohoto. He spoke in a low voice and made positive eye contact with all those sitting in front of him. 'It has been my privilege to work with you in helping those who fight the Yankee murderer. But I am growing older. Soon I will retire and my effectiveness will diminish.' He paused and then began again in a clear, firm voice. 'It saddens me to say it, but we must accept that all our efforts have failed.'

The visiting Arabs tensed in their chairs. This was not what they had expected to hear.

Yohoto continued. 'Yes, it is true we have had some splendid successes – most notably with our Muslim friends. But look at our losses compared with the Americans. We have managed to kill a score here, a score there. The very best successes were the 9/11 killings – but still, we are like a wasp buzzing around an elephant – an intermittent annoyance. Think, gentlemen – at Hiroshima – one hundred thousand people wiped out, and thousands died of resulting cancers. At Nagasaki, fifty thousand killed, seventy thousand seriously injured and thousands died in agony years later. Think, gentlemen, hundreds of thousands of lives ruined in just three days and with just two bombs.'

He dropped his voice. 'Yet, we deal in numbers in the low thousands.'

And then, more pointedly for the benefit of the visitors, he raised his voice again.

'How many thousands of innocents were murdered in the carpet bombing of Iraq?' he asked. 'And after the bombs they murder thousands more by denying access to medicines through their satanic sanctions!' His voice grew louder still. 'Now, they disgrace themselves, murdering Muslim leaders with their cowardly drones.'

Kiyo Arai interjected quietly. 'Great sacrifices have been made by those who fight our cause,' he said. 'What more can we ask people to do? We are many years from having our own atomic bombs. We are fighting very rich, very powerful forces. We have dedicated our lives to the fatwa. We are training fast and building our network of activists across the world. How can we inflict greater damage on our enemies?'

'This is exactly where we have failed,' replied Tsan Yohoto. 'We have not, as the Americans say, boxed clever. We have directed our efforts into bombings and shootings against well-defended targets. Even where we succeed, the American losses are small. Then they tighten security further and make the next attack even more difficult. We have not looked at the bigger picture. Until now!'

All those around the table sat to attention, riveted. Tsan Yohoto, well practised in presentation and public speaking, measured his delivery. He knew that actions and images were more powerful than words, in communicating his message. He moved closer to the top of the table and chopped his hand down.

'As a boy, in Tokyo, I studied judo,' he continued. 'Judo means *the gentle way*.' He became more animated. 'Judo taught me to be fast and efficient in my life. Judo taught me that the best way to defeat your enemy is to identify his greatest strength and to use it against him. For many years I have studied the American culture and I have learned how to sell them more and more medicines.'

Tsan Yohoto leaned forward.

'A people of blatant contradictions,' he continued. 'Yet, like all humans, like all animals, they are driven by certain basic instincts.' He focused his delivery now on the Arabs. 'For the American people, that instinct can be captured in one word – greed. The Americans want to buy the best of everything that they can. They call it the American dream. They look for good value and then they will buy even more. And they are obsessed with desirable brands. And they want everything *now*. This applies to automobiles, fashion, TVs, phones, computers, food and credit. And medicines. No matter if the American suspects that what he's buying may not be the best thing for him to have – if he wants it, he buys it. Take the example of food. The Americans, despite the best healthcare information available, consume vast amounts of food. Every type of food they can think of, and faster and faster. Two out of three meals in the US are eaten outside of the home. Why? Because it's faster and cheaper. And so, they keep consuming. Over thirty per cent of Americans are clinically obese and have diabetes from consuming too much sugar.'

Yohoto struck the table again.

'Yet, many more Americans are wealthy but underweight – they are dieting fanatics – low fat foods, low sugar foods, low fat *and* low sugar drinks, diet supplements, vitamin supplements, protein supplements. And when the fat people and the thin people become sick, they run to their doctors and their drugstores. And whatever they think will make them better, they will buy. They have integrated the sale of medicines with the sale of everything else. Their drug stores are located in food stores, for convenience. Some US hospitals even provide "drive-thru" flu jabs. They are a nation addicted to consumption. This wealth, this greed, this desire to consume, this love of advertising, is in fact their greatest weakness.'

Tsan Yohoto paused. The attentive silence in the room was broken only by the quiet ticking of an old grandfather clock. He pushed his wire-rimmed spectacles back up onto the bridge of his nose and continued with passion.

'And this cycle, gentlemen, lies at the heart of our plan. In America, many scientists are convinced that they are heading for a public healthcare disaster of catastrophic proportions.' He looked around the table, catching everyone's eye before he continued.

'What we are going to do, my friends, is to make that catastrophe a certainty. We are going to turn the Americans' own culture against them. We are going to market them to death!'

4

THE VILLA AT SAITON – TWO MONTHS AGO

Tsan Yohoto moved away from the table and stood beside a black metal flipchart holding large sheets of heavy paper. He paused while Kazuhiro Saito refilled the cups of tea. Both Kiyo Arai and Kazuman Tokash were independently forming the view that they were experiencing the start of something special – certainly something different.

'And so,' continued Yohoto after the short break, 'over the past decade I have conceived this plan and prepared for this day. One major part of the plan is already in place, but we need the help of some of your al-Qaeda operatives in Manhattan to help in the execution.'

Tsan Yohoto turned over the flipchart cover to reveal a simple diagram of interconnected boxes. He faced the visitors.

'Let me explain our plan to you,' he said. 'It is on a grand scale. But, like the best plans, it is a simple one. It will deliver us the deaths of at least two million Americans in two years.'

*

MANHATTAN – THE PRESENT

Detective John Wyse slid onto a barstool at Harry's Bar on Canal Street and somewhat wearily responded to the high five offered by his buddy, Detective Michael Cabrini. Its red booths, low lighting and good music made Harry's, just a couple of blocks from the station on Elizabeth Street, a favourite eating and drinking spot among the station's police officers. Importantly for the sports fans, due priority was given to the Giants games on the big screen, and they served a knockout homemade burger and fries. Cabrini had overseen the departure of Abdel Moamer to the city morgue, the famous blue-tiled building surrounded by hospital blocks on First Avenue, or Bedpan Alley as it is known by New Yorkers. Once the crime scene at the warehouse had been preserved, Cabrini knew just where to catch up with his partner.

'Well?' asked Cabrini, having sensibly allowed Wyse enough time to savour the first cold mouthful of Miller. 'How'd it go with Connolly?'

'Bad news, pal,' replied Wyse, 'looks like you're gonna have to put up with me for another two years. He talked me around again.'

'Way to go, buddy,' responded Cabrini with a grin. 'I'd hate to have to watch the Giants games on my own. Hey, Harry,' he called out to the elderly owner behind the bar. 'Two more beers and a couple of your best burgers – we're celebrating.'

Wyse took another swig of cold beer. 'You finish up on that shooting?'

'Yeah, vic was some old Libyan guy. Used to run a chain of restaurants from that place. That's where they used to store ingredients 'n' stuff, did some cooking there. Then his nephew bought out the business and he kinda retired. Looks like he disturbed a burglar. His wallet was taken and his office was trashed.'

Wyse nodded.

'I talked to his wife. Sez he kept the old factory, even though they don't use it much now. Sez he used to get dressed up every day and go down there, to his office, just for somethin' to do.'

'Shit. That's kinda sad.'

'Yeah, well sad ain't on my agenda right now. Lesson to us all is enjoy every day. Hey, Harry – what time's the game starting?'

Cabrini clapped Wyse on the back and then leaned over, prodded him and spoke furtively in his ear.

'And don't look now, buddy, but two of the cutest office workers on the island just walked into the bar – this looks like our night!'

Wyse smiled to himself. *How could I ever have considered leaving all this?*

*

Two miles away, the light was fading as the man dressed in black walked to the stern of the Staten Island ferry. He was wearing his black leather gloves again. He looked around to make sure no one was watching, then leaned over the railing and felt a few drops of spray on his face. He slid his hand inside his jacket pockets and carefully dropped a Colt 45, a wallet and a Rolex into the Hudson River.

So far, so good, he thought, as he watched the wallet surrender to the inky black water.

*

'Excuse me, girls,' said Detective Cabrini, as he approached the two attractive arrivals in Harry's Bar, with his notebook open and pen poised. 'My colleague and I,' he said, pointing his pen at Wyse, 'are conducting a lifestyle survey. Would you agree that any man who adds a smiley to the end of a text is probably gay?'

The two women took one look at Cabrini's mock-serious expression and at Wyse's uncomfortable pose on his barstool and burst out laughing.

Ten minutes later, Wyse and Cabrini, each fortified by four Millers and a Harry's homemade burger, had managed to chat their way into joining the two advertising executives in their booth. Wyse usually let Cabrini, who had a black belt in wisecracks and chat-up lines, take the lead with the small talk. Cabrini's approach had worked, but it was becoming clear there would be no short-term result with these two women – who were doing a better defensive job than the Giants were on the big screen.

Wow, thought John Wyse, there really is something special about this girl – Anna. It's not just her gorgeous accent – is it an English one? Or is it simply that she's turned down the invitation to go on to a nightclub?

Anna had long shiny hair, green eyes and a smile that lit up the whole bar. He loved the way she crinkled up her nose when she laughed. *Something playful, or innocent, about it.* He plucked up his courage again.

'Maybe we could go out for a drink sometime, when it's quieter?'

'Yes, maybe,' she teased. Although maybe she was interested, because she added, 'Call me.'

'What's the name of your agency again?' asked Wyse, kicking himself for forgetting.

'Dynamic Communications,' said Anna, 'we're in the Paramount Building, overlooking Times Square.'

'I'll call you,' said John Wyse. And this time he knew that he would.

⋆

SAITON – TWO MONTHS AGO

'Sayonara.'

'Ma'a as-salamah.'

At the Japanese villa, the Chess Club meeting was breaking up with much deep bowing, in the Japanese style, by the Arab visitors, which Najeed Shammas had insisted they practise. Such civilities were particularly important to the Japanese, he had advised.

Kiyo Arai was concluding the conversation.

'So, we will expect to convey our final approval and cooperation in two weeks' time – in the usual manner,' he said.

'In the meantime, we will make enquiries about this restaurant owner, Abdel Moamer, to see if his background makes him a suitable person to enlist,' Tokash added.

The group was edging closer to the front door, when Lumo Kinotoa suddenly tensed, and whispered in Tsan Yohoto's ear. Yohoto inwardly cursed himself. *How could I have forgotten part of the plan?*

'Gentlemen,' he interjected, 'before you go, I have omitted one small but important detail.'

The group paused in the elegant hallway as Tsan Yohoto continued.

'In order to maximise the impact of our plan, we need the services of another two of your volunteers in New York. Their involvement will be important, but I think low risk, and they can remain undercover once we have achieved success.'

Kiyo Arai raised his eyebrows. 'And what type of people do you need?'

Yohoto couldn't prevent himself smiling. 'What we need are the services of good, fit, curtain swishers.'

Both of the Arabs hesitated. 'Curtain swishers?' repeated Arai, wondering if his excellent grasp of English had failed him on this occasion.

'Yes,' said Yohoto, 'curtain swishers,' and with his right arm he mimed the action of rapidly opening and closing a large curtain.

'I understand,' said Arai, 'but why?'

Yohoto's explanation brought them as far as the hall door. Kiyo Arai threw back his head and laughed.

'Curtain swishing,' he bellowed. 'First you want to take over a restaurant chain, now it's curtain swishing! It's not on the syllabus in our training camps, but I'm sure we can help.'

After a further series of clasped handshakes and much bowing and smiling, the Arabs left through the front door and darted to an S Class Mercedes, where a chauffeur was holding the rear door open. Despite the heavy rain, Arai could not resist turning for a final wave – followed by an exaggerated miming of the swishing of a curtain. Much laughter rang out around the porch as the sleek black car scrunched away on the gravel.

5

PAKISTAN – TWO MONTHS AGO

The autopilot on the white Airbus added another five degrees of flap, as the Gulf Air service from Dubai to Karachi descended gently earthwards. In window seat 2A, Kiyo Arai was deep in thought as he watched roads and buildings slowly take shape on the approach to runway 27 at Jinnah International Airport. The travel and stress of the previous two days had been exhausting. He found himself tensing up again as they approached airports; he knew they were always the most dangerous point. And, by returning via Pakistan, they would add a hard four days' drive onto their journey. However, the chances of detection were far lower here than with a flight direct into Khwaja Rawash Airport, Kabul, a hot spot for surveillance by international anti-terrorist organisations.

Pakistan – a troubled land of one hundred and seventy million people. Kiyo Arai had long been fascinated by the tumultuous history of the country and its waves of conquerors over the centuries, from the Persians to Alexander the Great to the British. The national motto of this Muslim-dominated land is 'Ittehad, Tanzeem, Yaqeen-e-Muhkam' (Unity, Discipline and Faith). Kiyo Arai had often found this amusing. Discipline and faith were undoubtedly in strong supply for Pakistanis – 'unity', however, was hardly the best word to describe this nation's history of uprisings and assassinations.

The newly reformed Republic of 1991 had shown close support for the Taliban regime in Kabul. On the other hand, somewhat confusingly, Pakistan had also been a long-time ally of the US and that link had strengthened after the 9/11 attacks, when Pakistan cut links with the Taliban. The country had been rewarded with an instant increase in US aid – to the tune of four billion dollars. Ironically, some of those millions were most likely invested in Pakistan's nuclear weapons programme – the rapid development of which had reignited tension with India and further destabilised the Greater Middle East region. It was help and support from northern Pakistan, together with one thousand five hundred miles of mountainous borders with Afghanistan, that had helped Osama bin Laden lead his American pursuers a merry dance through almost impenetrable villages and networks of caves. After the assassination of bin Laden in the town of Bilal, Najeed Shammas had emerged as a fanatical new leader. His first instruction had been that the al-Qaeda leadership would revert to living in the remote caves, which had proved undetectable for centuries.

Experienced al-Qaeda recruits from the northern tribes would now be assisting Arai and Tokash on their journey from Karachi to Najeed Shammas's base.

The steward in a sky-blue uniform flashed Kiyo Arai a courteous smile as she took their empty water bottles and checked Kazuman Tokash's seatbelt in the seat beside him. Their papers for this last airborne leg of the journey presented them as travelling to attend a sale of Pakistani wall-coverings, which they were interested in buying for an apartment development in Dubai. The documents in their briefcases included brochures for the exhibition, delegate registrations and hotel bookings. Once outside the airport, they would abandon that cover and disappear into central Karachi, from where their al-Qaeda network had arranged lorry transport into the mountains of Afghanistan.

Kiyo Arai reflected on the last few days. He had been struck by the simplicity of Tsan Yohoto's strategy. The plan was low risk from an al-Qaeda point of view, yet the potential damage to the Americans seemed enormous.

Below him, buried in the fuselage, bundles of cables executed the closing sequence of electronic instructions from the Airbus's flight management system and the giant aircraft settled gracefully onto the hot tarmac. The plane taxied to stand one and Arai and Tokash waited until almost half of the plane's passengers had passed them to exit through the front door. Another big advantage of the Airbus flight was that the sheer number of passengers put increased pressure on the customs and immigration officials, who would be less likely to delay lengthy queues with overzealous enquiries. The two men collected their black Samsonite cases from the bright and efficient baggage hall and again, apparently randomly, joined the growing queue for Passport and Immigration control, with about half the Airbus passengers ahead of them.

The passengers represented a good selection of Asian society, Kiyo Arai mused, as they shuffled forward. A strong showing of Pakistani, Indian and East-Asian businessmen from the first- and business-class sections, almost all dressed in navy or black business suits, with a good selection of turbans, similar to his own. Most of the queue behind them was made up of Pakistani construction workers from the massive building projects in Dubai, returning home on family visits, with a sprinkling of noisy tourists from all corners of the globe, in a selection of bright shorts and shirts.

Nonchalantly pushing an industrial cleaning machine along the best polished floor in Karachi, an agent of the Pakistan Secret Service pressed a small black button on the handle of the polisher and filmed the passengers in the queue.

Sitting on an uncomfortably high stool inside a glass-fronted kiosk was police officer Imran Hassan, who was six hours into his shift and had already cast his eyes over maybe five hundred faces and passports that day. He had perfected an expression of intense seriousness, which belied the fact that he was more interested in surveying the occasional cleavage displayed by an incoming western female, than he was their passports. He shifted on his stool and waved through another three dark suits as the radio concealed on his desk advised him at low volume that Pakistan was now sixty-seven without loss in the one-day match against Bangladesh.

As Kiyo Arai neared the kiosk, he became more and more nervous. This policeman hadn't stopped any passenger in the last thirty or so, and Arai knew he would be likely to make a bit of a show of examining someone's papers soon. As Pakistan's first wicket fell to a fast inswinger, Imran Hassan decided to use the break in play to display the importance that his police force placed on security matters. Two impressive Arab businessmen in black suits with white turbans were next to approach. He assumed an expression of deep concentration and, instead of waving the first passenger through, Hassan smiled and asked to see the man's passport. The passport had the well-creased cover of a frequent traveller and declared its owner to be a Saudi national by the name of Amar el Rashtin. Hassan studied the multiple immigration control stamps and visas to the rear of the passport.

'Good morning, Mr Rashtin.' He smiled as he studied the face looking in at him, which was identical to the one peering up at him from the passport photograph. 'And what is the purpose of your visit to Pakistan?'

The tall Arab in front of him smiled confidently and replied, 'I am here to purchase wall coverings and rugs, which are being displayed at a sales exhibition at the Karachi Marriott Hotel. My colleague and I are developing apartments in Dubai and we find that your local products are superb.'

The Arab added, 'With any luck, we will find some free time to watch your excellent cricketers.' Imran Hassan passed the passport through the scanning device and the screen told him that the passport and its owner were of no interest.

'I hope your trip is a great success.' He pushed the documents back towards the Arab and waved him and his colleague through.

Then, 'Damn and blast it,' he muttered as the radio commentator advised that Pakistan's number 2 had just been caught in the gully.

*

CENTRE STREET, LOWER MANHATTAN – THE PRESENT

'One dollar sixty-five,' grunted the surly cart vendor on the busy sidewalk, not lifting his eyes from his magazine, as Detective John Wyse picked up a bottle of sparkling water. It was unseasonably warm, which wasn't helping his throbbing hangover from last night's drinking with Cabrini. He wasn't used to dealing with this level of alcohol.

'Have a nice day,' Wyse replied sarcastically as he dropped the coins on top of a pile of newspapers. He gulped down the cold liquid as he walked the last few blocks to the station. The strengthening smell of Chinese food affirmed that he was getting closer to Elizabeth Street. As usual, a couple of NYPD cars were squeezed in against the kerb outside the station, leaving just about enough room for a truck to pass on the narrow one-way street. The old, white-fronted, four-storey building looked like a disused shipping office; but for the stars and stripes flying proudly from the front wall, a tourist would never know that this building was the heart of the Fifth Precinct. Wyse dragged himself up the steep steps, under a crumbling portico that declared that the building had been built in 1881. The faded blue timber doors opened straight into the public office with its old bare floorboards and the background smell changed from curry sauce to disinfectant. The walls were covered in public notices – mostly in Chinese – and police department flags. Pride of place was given to a photograph of the group of officers from the Fifth who had assisted at the World Trade Center, lined up on the steps outside the station.

Wyse waved at a few of the officers sitting behind the old wooden desks in the public office and climbed up the squeaky stairs to the second floor, where his desk was in an open plan area used by detectives. He smiled to himself as the previous night's events came back to him. Cabrini, as usual, had drunk about six more beers than was good for him and had spent the last hour before closing asleep in one of the booths. He had, however, entertained the whole bar with his Mick Jagger moves, as he pumped out a succession of Stones hits from the jukebox. Wyse was an accomplished guitarist, but he would never be able to match Cabrini's theatrics on air guitar. Soon, he and the two pretty girls had joined in. Wyse had spun the sexy dark girl, faster and faster, to 'Brown Sugar', while Cabrini focused on the redhead.

'Shit,' he gasped and fumbled in his wallet. A smile spread across his face as a Dynamic Communications business card fell out into his hand – for written across it, in a handwriting that wasn't his own, was the name Anna, and her cell number. *Yes*, he thought. He hadn't felt the same instant connection with a girl since Lisa. And he'd messed up there. He would definitely call Anna.

*

PAKISTAN – TWO MONTHS AGO

'Son of a dog,' snarled the driver of the white Volkswagen minibus as he braked suddenly to avoid a wobbling cyclist.

He'd been told to take his passengers as speedily as possible to their rendezvous point at the al Kolad warehouse in the industrial area on the northwest edge of Karachi. Allah be blessed, he thought as he contemplated the disastrous consequences if he had hit the cyclist and drawn police attention to himself and his important passengers. Seated beside him, his al-Qaeda superior, Mohammed el Karbour, grimaced. He straightened his turban and contented himself with a stern frown at his driver, as they continued to weave dusty trails through the heavy traffic. He knew his comrade was not to blame. At least five cyclists a week were killed in Karachi.

'A long way from first class with Emirates,' muttered Kiyo Arai to his travelling partner, Kazuman Tokash.

Tokash grunted and raised his eyes to heaven, but both men were grateful and respectful of the help being provided by their top Karachi unit. Sweating profusely now in the back of the non-air-conditioned van, Arai slid his briefcase, with his false passport and documents supporting his recent impersonation of a Saudi businessman, under the worn rear seat, as arranged. Tokash did likewise. These would be destroyed by the driver to remove any connection between them and their trip to Japan.

'Ten more minutes, gentlemen,' called el Karbour as they entered an area of low-rise factories and warehouses with cheap asbestos roofs cracked from the relentless heat. Once at the al Kolad warehouse, the plan was that they would hand over their business suits, shirts and shoes to the local unit, who would provide them with the simple robes and sandals of an Afghan lorry driver and his assistant. Together they would take an empty lorry on an apparent return journey to Kabul, Afghanistan. The road was a long and lonely one, with little traffic. The main excitement would be the possibility of a passing NATO patrol, though they should take little interest in two Afghan locals, with convincing paperwork, driving an empty lorry. Once at the foothills of the mountains, they would turn northwest and start the three-day climb into the mountain range separating Afghanistan from Pakistan. At the mountain village of el Dohh, they would be contacted and taken to whichever of the mountain camps Najeed Shammas was using, for he changed location at least once a fortnight.

The white van pulled slowly through the open gate in a broken-down chain-link fence and drove around the building to the open roller-shutter door to the old warehouse. Arai groaned as he stretched his back and stepped gladly into the shade of the interior.

'Brothers, it has been an honour to help you,' sparkled el Karbour as he took his passengers' clothes and handed them bottles of reasonably cold water. Arai looked around the dusty warehouse and wondered if the staff had been purposely kept away for the day.

'Thank you, indeed, my friend,' he replied as he and Tokash began pulling on the robes.

'There are two boxes of food and water under the front seats of the truck,' said el Karbour, 'and ten gallon drums of diesel in the back. I can offer you a cell phone which I know to be untraceable?' he added.

Arai shook his head. 'No, my friend, we have no need of a cell phone. In three or four days, we will be back in contact with our brethren.' Arai was well aware that a mobile could be tracked and his position triangulated by American satellites. He was not going to take any risks.

'And are you certain that you will not join us for a meal or to bathe?' asked el Karbour.

'Very certain,' said Tokash, and he bowed his head in appreciation. Both he and Arai knew they were still at risk here, outside their normal territory, and in the company of local al-Qaeda. 'The sooner we get moving the better,' he added.

'The truck?' queried Arai.

El Karbour ushered them to the rear corner of the warehouse and, with the driver's help, removed a grey tarpaulin from a dark blue Tata truck.

'It may not look great, but mechanically I can vouch for her myself,' said el Karbour. 'No air-con, but in Pakistan we leave the windows open,' he added with a grin.

Arai smiled. He and Tokash embraced their hosts. Then Arai stepped up into the truck as Tokash took the passenger seat and put the map on his knees.

'Turn right at the gates and follow the sun,' called el Karbour. 'After two miles, there is only one road and no more turns until you reach the mountains.'

Kiyo Arai waved and smiled as the Tata's engine burst into life at the first turn of the key and he eased the truck out of the warehouse, passed through the open gate and turned right.

'Allah bless them,' said el Karbour to his colleague, as they stood side by side in the yard and watched the cloud of dust grow small in the distance.

'I do not know who they are,' said the driver, 'but today, my friend, I feel that we have been in the presence of great men.'

'You speak the truth, my brother,' said el Karbour as he turned and began to pull the giant loading door closed. 'May Allah bring them every blessing and good fortune in whatever work they are doing.'

*

TOKYO – TWO MONTHS AGO

Tsan Yohoto was sitting in his magnificent corner office on the penthouse level of the Yamoura Pharmaceuticals headquarters. The vertical blinds on the large windows cast a grid pattern of shadows across the office. He was listening to Kazuhiro Saito going over the meeting of the Chess Club.

'I was very impressed,' said Saito. 'They were even smarter than I'd imagined them. I mean, you have to admire a handful of men living in caves, with a few satellite phones and laptops, giving the Americans the run-around. I am more certain than ever that they are the perfect partners. Let us hope that they can recruit Moamer – the restaurant owner – or his partner.'

'They seemed fairly confident about that,' replied Yohoto, who was carefully polishing the lenses of his spectacles with a tissue. 'I suspect they have their ways. But let's not count our chickens,' he said, 'nothing can happen without Shammas' go-ahead.'

'Absolutely correct,' said Saito, 'but my instinct is that it will be all systems go.'

'In the meantime,' said Tsan Yohoto, 'we must continue to challenge, test and perfect our plan. I have again today, with the help of Dr Naga, rechecked all my formulae.'

'And you are still adding your own DNA?' asked Saito, grinning.

'Yes, indeed. A signature twist of the family DNA makes our

revenge even more personalised. Are you absolutely certain that your marketing strategy is perfected?'

'Yes, it is ready to be implemented,' said Saito. 'I have taken personal responsibility for every detail. Never before in my marketing career have I had an almost unlimited budget for a campaign. Yet, I have taken great care that every part will add weight to the impact on the New Yorkers. As my legacy, it will be seen in world marketing as the most effective campaign for decades. We will make Coca Cola and Nike look like amateurs!'

Yohoto smiled. 'How quickly can you start?' he asked, replacing his spectacles on his nose.

'On the assumption that we get positive news from Afghanistan, I have already arranged a meeting with Dynamic Communications in Manhattan, on the tenth of April. You will brief them on a major new product launch – with a very generous budget. They know to give this campaign top priority, that we want their very best healthcare marketing specialists on the job and that we are prepared to pay overtime rates for quick results. If we allow them, say, six weeks to devise straplines, logos and artwork, and to book advertising space and celebrities –'

'Which celebrity are we going to use?' interrupted Yohoto.

'That's one aspect I'll leave to them – they know best who can best influence New Yorkers on their home patch,' replied Saito.

'You're certain that we need to take the extra time to involve celebrities?'

'Yes, Tsan,' continued Saito, 'without a doubt. America is obsessed with celebrities. Using celebrities to endorse products has been part of American culture since the creation of the Hollywood movie star. John Wayne could persuade men to buy boots or a truck – because he was big and strong. Women believed that they would look like Marilyn Monroe, just by using the same face cream as her.' Yohoto smiled.

Saito stood up, shook his friend's hand and said, 'Trust me, Tsan. Every part of this marketing plan will wreak havoc on New Yorkers.'

Tsan Yohoto accompanied his companion as far as the elevator lobby and then returned to his office. He pushed a blind to one side and gazed out across the skyline of downtown Tokyo. He felt a tingle of nervous excitement. *So soon now. Can I really go through with this?* As he looked out over the soaring office towers and apartment blocks, he thought of his home city of Hiroshima, levelled by the bomb. He thought of his father. He thought of Kendo and Lita on the swings. *No, must keep going.*

6

AFGHANISTAN – TWO MONTHS AGO

'This reminds me of my boyhood days,' said Kazuman Tokash, breaking a silence that had lasted for two hours.

'How so?' asked Kiyo Arai.

'The drone of the engine, the never-ending road, the dust. On the farm where I was raised, twice a year we took the village truck and drove our produce to the market at Kabul. My father never let me drive – even though the journey was two days in each direction.'

'I remember that truck,' said Arai, his eyes fixed dead ahead on the narrow tarmac roadway.

'Yes. The elder tribesmen realised we could get better prices at Kabul, so, between the families, we bought an old Bedford truck – ex-British Army stock from India. An early form of communism, perhaps!' he added with some amusement in his eyes.

Arai shifted down into third gear again as the truck began yet another long steep climb. Although spring heat would soon be on its way, snow still covered Afghanistan's highest peaks – though none could compete with the majesty of K2 on Pakistan's side of the border, second only to Mount Everest in height. Arai flipped the wiper stalk to clear the film of dust building up on the windscreen. They fell silent again, each to his own thoughts.

Darkness was falling on the third day of their drive as the dependable Tata trundled into the dusty square at the centre of the village of el Kohl. Sitting on a creaky wooden bench in the long shadow of the minaret on the village mosque, Ibram el Swahalid took careful note of the expected arrival of these very important visitors. As instructed, he confirmed that there appeared to be no other passengers in the truck and he would now stay in his position to make certain that no strange vehicles followed the Tata into the village.

Kiyo Arai took in the familiar village scene with its market stalls and whitewashed buildings. Groups of men sat on benches around the square with horses tethered nearby and two heavily veiled women were walking slowly past displays of bright, intricate rugs. A handful of cars, trucks and jeeps were scattered around and a group of children kicked up dust as they chased one another in circles. Kiyo Arai's pulse quickened as he stopped the truck under a large canvas awning.

To a casual observer, the white awning was to keep the sun's rays off a selection of vegetables in timber crates. However, its real purpose was to ensure that neither the truck's registration, nor its occupants, could be photographed by a passing satellite. Arai was confident their journey had been undetected, but he would go to every extreme to ensure that not one possible clue might be casually given away by complacency, although they were safer in the mountain villages than in any urban setting. All the villagers had, since childhood, witnessed many enemies and traitors being tortured to a slow death in the square and none would ever forget the agonised screams of those unfortunates who begged for death to end their suffering. The idea of placing agents among the villagers was just not an option. Everyone was known and strangers stood out a mile. Only locals could speak their own very particular dialect of Dari or Pashto.

'Salaam, salaam,' muttered Mukhtar el Maswar, the el Kohl village mullah, as he embraced first Kiyo Arai and then Kazuman Tokash. They entered the stone building beside the awning and allowed their eyes to adjust to the low light.

'Greetings and great thanks to you, mullah, and your tribesmen for your help on our journey,' said Arai.

'Please come and sit,' replied el Maswar, smiling and gesturing to a low table, surrounded by brown cushions and creaking under the weight of a vast selection of cooked meats, fresh vegetables, breads, dates and jugs of cold water.

'Thank you again, my friend, for your hospitality,' said Arai as they lowered themselves onto the big cushions. In accordance with tradition, the mullah, as host, washed his hands first and dried them on a clean towel. The bowl of water was then passed around to the right and only when Kiyo Arai, to the mullah's left, had dried his hands, did the Mullah invite them all to take salt and begin the meal. They ate in silence as the mullah and his two senior tribesmen repeatedly replenished their guests' plates and drinking pots and allowed them to fill their bellies and relax. Mukhtar el Maswar had been the mullah, or chief of the tribe, for over twenty years and his ferocious devotion to al-Qaeda was his strongest instinct. He was trusted wholly by Najeed Shammas and had helped bring al-Qaeda colleagues to and from his secret locations many times before. He had known of Arai and Tokash for many years and was in awe of their abilities. He knew he didn't have the education or skills to wreak havoc on the west in the way that Arai and Tokash could, but he was proud to play a role in assisting these men.

'I hope your journey was a worthwhile one?' asked the mullah, with a raised eyebrow.

'Yes, indeed,' replied Arai, wiping his mouth precisely with a white cloth napkin. 'We are anxious to report back to our leader – is he far away?'

'Luckily for you, no. I am sure you have done enough travelling for the moment. A day's horseback trek will get us there.'

Kiyo Arai felt a wave of relief.

'We will leave at dawn.'

*

Arai and Tokash slept in a sparsely furnished bedroom to the rear of the old stone building. They were roused just before first light. They washed and changed into the fresh robes which their hosts had left out for them. After a good breakfast of cereals, bread, fruit and tea, they went through the back door into a rough stoned yard, surrounded by buildings and stables. Waiting for them was the mullah, Mukhtar el Maswar, sitting astride a magnificent white Afghan steed, a good sixteen hands high. A hunting knife in a brown leather scabbard hung from his waist and a shining AK-47 was fastened to the saddle, within easy reach. Two other bearded and turbaned tribesmen were also mounted, loosely holding the reins and also with AK-47s to hand. A third man, with an easy strength, helped Arai and Tokash mount their horses, which had water bottles and panniers filled with meat and bread, and Kalashnikov rifles strapped to the saddles. With the mullah leading the way, Kiyo Arai clicked encouragement to his horse and squeezed his heels into its flanks. The group made their way out of the yard to a dusty trail, leading ever higher into the mountains.

*

MANHATTAN – THE PRESENT

'Good afternoon – Anna Milani.'

Why does the phone always ring just when I've taken a bite of a hurried lunchtime bagel?

Anna knocked over the remains of a strawberry smoothie when grabbing the phone. *Blast.* She quickly threw a couple of paper napkins over the spreading mess.

'Hi there, it's John, remember me? *Brown sugar, you make me feel so good?*' At the other end of the line, John Wyse sang the chorus of the Stones classic.

'Of course, I remember – it's only been about twelve hours! What a to-do.' Anna's head still throbbed. She had never intended that her last-minute decision to go for 'just one drink' after work yesterday with Cindy would end up with her falling exhausted into a spinning bed at 3 a.m.

'So, are you missing me already?' chirped Wyse. Inwardly, he groaned as he heard himself say the line and realised that it sounded like a Cabrini chat-up classic on a bad day.

'Not sure yet, concentrating on staying awake, not saying anything too stupid to a client and trying to keep a bagel down.'

'What a night . . .'

'Sure was,' she replied. 'How's Mike?'

'He'll live. Just after you left, me and Harry, the owner, got him awake and into the back of a cab. Last I saw of him, he was collapsing face down on his bed. You know the annoying thing is he'll breeze through the station any moment, with more energy than the whole division put together and talkin' about some new bar downtown which just has to be checked out after the shift.'

'Yep, I can just see it.' Anna giggled as she neatly diverted a tide of strawberry smoothie from drowning her mouse.

'Either that or he won't show up at all. So, you got home OK?' asked Wyse, trying to sound thoughtful and concerned.

'Yeah, no problem. Me and Cindy shared a cab and looked after each other. How 'bout you?'

'Yeah – just fine. Once I got the big baby to bed I got home, hit the sack and slept like a log. Not feeling too good today though. Apart from meeting you . . .'

Anna smiled. 'That's nice.'

Her desk at Dynamic Communications was in the middle of an open plan area of about five thousand square feet on the eighteenth floor of the Paramount building on Broadway and West 43rd, with a spectacular view into Times Square. She felt more like a New Yorker every day and her oldest friends in Leeds teased her about how she had so rapidly lost most traces of her native accent, apart from the odd giveaway turn of phrase. She caught Cindy's eye, pointed at her phone and gave her a big 'thumbs-up'.

'So, will we do it again?' asked Wyse, his heart skipping.

'Yes, love to,' said Anna, 'but on one condition . . .'

'What's that?'

'Not so much alcohol.'

'That's a deal. Maybe we could go for a meal?'

'Yes, I'd like that,' Anna replied. 'Perhaps in a week or so. I'm really busy at the moment.' (Always keep them anxious, was Cindy's advice. Never appear over-eager.)

'Okay,' said Wyse, puzzled as to why he would have to wait so long. Was this a brush-off?

'So, why don't you give me a call next week and we'll fix something up?'

'Sure thing,' said Wyse, wondering if this was going the way he wanted.

'Thanks, John. Talk to you then,' breezed Anna.

'Okay, see ya.'

'And, John,' she said, 'I really did enjoy last night. You're great fun,' she added, concerned now she might have overdone the hard-to-get bit.

'You're welcome. Talk to you soon then,' Wyse finished, feeling a bit better now.

Anna put her phone back down on her desk, pleased with how she had handled that. Cindy had taken Anna under her wing and had mentored her through Manhattan's social scene. Some of Cindy's instructions on 'how to get a man', with complicated combinations of low necklines, 'open' body language and 'when to laugh' protocols, were a bit much for Anna, but Cindy had a streetwise sassiness, which Anna knew she lacked. She definitely wanted this tall dark cop with the deep blue eyes to call. Despite all the usual male bravado, her intuition told her there was a gentler, shyer and more thoughtful person inside those very good looks. Maybe even a little bit of vulnerability.

'That was him. John,' she said to Cindy, across the passage. 'Asked me out.'

'Awesome,' said Cindy, smiling. 'Sounds like you played it well.'

Cindy turned back to her screen. *Huh. I really fancied that guy, John. But, of course, I ended up having to fend off the overweight drunk. I'm getting tired of playing second fiddle to Miss Goody Two-Shoes there. Might be time to make sure she messes that one up. And then I'll have a slice of John, all for myself.*

★

AFGHANISTAN – TWO MONTHS AGO

In the equine world, experts will argue over whether US- or French-bred horses are best for speed on the flat, or whether Irish- or English-bred will get you around most reliably over fences. But all experts will agree that, when it comes to strength and surefootedness, the mighty Afghan mountain stallions are world-beaters. And so it was that Kiyo Arai and Kazuman Tokash, both natural horsemen since childhood, had little to do except stay in the saddle, as the steeds beneath them picked their steady way up the steeply rising stony tracks. From time to time the blue sky was interrupted by large flocks of waterfowl migrating northwards. The birds' shadows, flickering across the rocks, caused their calm horses no alarm. As they came within ten miles or so of the cave complex, the riders knew that every step was being carefully observed by hidden al-Qaeda sentries.

Kiyo Arai and Kazuman Tokash were in familiar territory. Both had been born over fifty years ago, in small mountain villages near Badakhshan, close to the highest peak in the area, the Nowshak, which rises to 24,500 feet. Their fathers had struggled to make even a spartan living from a handful of animals, from cultivating unyielding soil and fishing the many rivers that flowed down their mountain. They refused to take the easier pickings available from producing hashish and opium on the lower slopes. The easy export of those crops, along old caravan trails protected by the Taliban, had seen Afghanistan become known as the world's 'cocaine kitchen', but their families wanted no part of that. Their mothers worked long hard days, struggling to feed and clothe their children and supplementing the meagre family incomes by weaving rugs and tapestries in the finest Afghan tradition.

But what the boys were rich in was education. Continuing a tradition that started in the seventh century, the Taliban ran a Madrasa school in their village. The boys were expected to work hard, and work hard they did. Kiyo Arai and Kazuman Tokash had been classmates since the age of seven, in their small, stone-built school. At their fathers' sides, they had learnt the arts of horse riding, hunting, fishing and survival in the wilderness. But they were most happy in their classroom, hanging on their teachers' every word.

The Taliban teachers filled their pupils with passion for their country, their people and their religion. The boys swelled with pride as the teachers told them of their forefathers who had risen to arms, century after century, to protect their people from infidels and invaders. Apart from providing education and organising the shrines and religious ceremonies, the Taliban also administered all social services in the region.

Now, in the twilight, the mullah pulled gently on his reins as the five riders hesitated before entering a clearing between steep rocks on four sides. At the centre of the clearing was a grey canvas awning, suspended over four timber poles, close to the entrance to a deep labyrinth of caves. A team of horses was loosely tethered to one side and a dozen or so chickens pecked at the ground inside a roughly wired timber enclosure. Under the awning, six or eight men sat cross-legged on rugs and cushions. All of them were smoking peacefully from long ceramic pipes. As the riders paused to take in this sight, one of the men rose and stood to face them.

Over six feet three inches tall, he was a commanding figure in pristine white robes, his dark grey beard flowing across his chest. He had well-defined features and large, intelligent brown eyes. Najeed Shammas smiled broadly as he waved his visitors into the camp.

7

AFGHANISTAN – TWO MONTHS AGO

Two stoves had been lit at the entrance to the cave complex. The mullah and his tribesmen had departed for the return journey to el Kohl, having been rewarded with a solid meal and the thanks of Najeed Shammas and the most senior leaders of al-Qaeda. Dotted around the mountainside, for perhaps ten miles in every direction, heavily armed tribesmen continued to keep a careful watch on every pathway towards their camp near the summit.

The group had eaten a meal of couscous, lamb and vegetables, and now Kiyo Arai and Kazuman Tokash were going over every detail of their journey to Japan, with the four other men, seated on a twelve-foot by twelve-foot rug, under a star-filled sky. Mohammed al Katah, of thin, wiry build, wore a heavy dark beard that failed to fully conceal the many deep scars to his face caused by a rocket fired from a Soviet helicopter. He had personally been involved in training the nine hijackers for the 9/11 attacks. Baddar Attabar Mussan was another Afghan veteran. He had studied engineering and computer science at Hamburg University and had later received intensive training from US experts in intelligence and counter-intelligence techniques in the early years of the Soviet invasion. He delighted now in putting that expertise into effect against the Americans.

Seated to Shammas's right was Aswan bin Tolawar, another wealthy Saudi who had been a boyhood friend of bin Laden's. A small, intelligent-looking man, he had shared bin Laden's spiritual values and he too had turned his back on the excesses of a western lifestyle, which he saw as corrupting his country. While he had no official title in the Army Council, he was recognised and valued as Najeed Shammas' most trusted confidante.

The men had been talking now for four hours. Baddar Attabar Mussan was taking notes and asking careful questions in order to spot any possible slip-ups in procedures or compromising of their cover. The leader, Najeed Shammas, knew of the Chess Club and Tsan Yohoto, but these more human descriptions enthralled him, such as Tsan Yohoto's habit of touching an old black and white photograph of his deceased brother and sister.

Arai and Tokash had taken them through the details of Tsan Yohoto's plan. 'In fact,' Arai had concluded, 'if you will forgive the familiarity, Najeed, both Tokash and I saw strong similarities between yourself and Tsan Yohoto. You are both men of great intelligence and power, strategy and execution.'

'This great plan,' said Shammas, 'seems almost too simple to be true! I had expected a new series of attacks on western targets. Instead, I find that we are required to simply recruit one restaurant owner, one van driver and two, what did you call them?'

'Curtain swishers,' repeated Arai.

There was a long silence, broken only by the echoing screech of a distant vulture. Remembering Tsan Yohoto's judo moves, Arai said, 'Yohoto says it is all about turning your enemy's greatest strength against him. Before your enemy realises what is happening, it is too late.'

'It is an extraordinary plan,' said Shammas in a low tone. 'So little risk for us and yet maybe two million Americans killed by their own excesses.'

Shammas paused and looked at the faces of Mussan, al Katah

and lastly his old friend bin Tolawar. Each in turn looked him in the eye and gave a solemn nod. Shammas turned to his chief of intelligence, Baddar Mussan.

'Baddar, how long to recruit this Libyan restaurant owner?'

'Two, three weeks perhaps, allowing one week for background research.'

Shammas turned back to Arai and Tokash. 'My friends, I thank you again for your great work and for your advice. Tell our Japanese friends that we will return their support of many years. We will be proud to play our part in this great plan!'

★

SAITON – THE NEXT DAY

At Lumo Kinotoa's villa, the Chess Club had gathered for a Wednesday night meeting. Tsan Yohoto, Lumo Kinotoa and Kazuhiro Saito were sipping tea and chatting quietly, yet the air was filled with expectancy. At almost one minute past 9 p.m., Eastern Pacific Time, Kinotoa's satellite phone, which was placed on the table beside his teacup, emitted the familiar high-pitched double bleep of an incoming text. Everyone sat in silence as he thumbed his way into his inbox. Lumo Kinotoa read aloud:

'The club is delighted to join in the chess game and has begun preparation. More information next week.'

Kinotoa looked up and met the excited gaze of his colleagues. 'Gentlemen,' he smiled, 'it's all systems go.'

PART TWO

IGNITION

8

AFGHANISTAN – FIVE WEEKS AGO

The chief of al-Qaeda intelligence, Baddar Mussan, had been busy. From his bank of battery-powered computers and satellite telephones he had sent out coded messages to a sleeper cell in Manhattan and to one of many operatives in Tripoli. From his mobile base in the caves, with his single aerial elevated through a fissure into the clear mountain air, he could maintain almost instantaneous, unobtrusive communication with the al-Qaeda training camps throughout the region and with a myriad of sleeper cells based in western Europe and the US. How ironic, he thought, that the very satellites, which the US are using to try and find us, are also carrying our messages to volunteers in their own territory. The secret to not being discovered, he knew, was to keep his communications restricted to short electronic bursts of coded, apparently meaningless messages, which would be mere drops of water in an ocean of electronic email, text, satellite and cell phone communications in the region. He knew to keep the messages short to prevent US intelligence getting any fix on transmissions from suspicious locations in the mountains. The camouflage was further deepened by the layers of hundreds of messages sent by dozens of al-Qaeda-affiliated students in the universities of Karachi and Kabul. Most of these deliberately contained key words such as 'bomb', 'bin Laden', 'al-Qaeda', 'terrorism', 'twin towers', 'fatwa', etc., which were electronically tagged by US National Security computers and added to the vast pile for agents to follow up. Most never were.

The first outcome of Mussan's messages was a burst of photography at locations in Manhattan, New Jersey and Tripoli.

*

NEW YORK – THREE WEEKS AGO

New York, concrete jungle . . . was playing on Takar el Sayden's car radio as he pulled out of the yard at his food production unit on Basin Street, New Jersey. He accelerated hard to get ahead of a looming forty-foot articulated truck as he started the drive home from the industrial hub of factories and warehouses that cater for the population of the five boroughs of New York.

The sun was shining and life felt good for Takar el Sayden. He had arrived in the US in the 1990s with fifty thousand dollars and a young wife. His father had helped him by buying out his uncle, the main stockholder in Quick 'n' Tasty, a small restaurant chain with six outlets and one depot. The old man had retired and Takar had brought new energy and vision to the business. Fifteen-hour days cooking in the small factory, and a cleverly expanded menu, had seen Quick 'n' Tasty grow quickly over ten years. Takar now owned a chain of two hundred and fifty-two eat-in and takeaway restaurants in New York. He had learned the real estate game rapidly too and, after just one or two mistakes, he had discovered that fast food had to be situated very, very close to busy people. That was why he located his stores beside office buildings that housed companies with younger staff profiles, and beside schools and crèches, where stressed-out parents collecting their kids could be easily tempted to take a shortcut to the day's main meal.

Yep – life was good. The money rolled in and they had their five-bedroom detached house near the coast in New Jersey, with plenty of space for his wife and two beautiful young daughters. The only setback had been the recent murder of his uncle Abdel, during a burglary at the original Quick 'n' Tasty factory. A kind old man, Abdel had been a great help to Takar.

Takar and his wife Tasha sometimes talked about selling up one day and going home to Libya, before the children got too old. But, for now, there was work to do, dollars to make. Takar's multiple gold rings clinked as he drummed his way across the steering wheel and into the chorus. It was on the word *York* that Takar el Sayden felt the cold pressure of the muzzle of a gun in the back of his neck as a voice whispered in his ear, 'Turn the fuckin' radio down and keep driving.'

Takar el Sayden's heart froze but he kept his composure enough to lean forward and turn the volume knob to the left. As he did so, he risked a glance in the mirror and caught a glimpse of a swarthy complexion under short, black, tightly curled hair.

'Just take my wallet, my car, no problem, but please don't shoot me,' he pleaded, realising he was close to soiling himself.

'Shut up and drive where I say,' was the response. 'Act real cool, and you'll be home eating dinner with your lovely wife and children in a couple of hours. With your wallet *and* your car. Now, take the West Shore Expressway towards the coast.'

Takar el Sayden gulped. He tried to breathe deeper and slower, but it didn't help much.

'You can take my rings too, man,' his voice croaked. 'They're solid gold, real valuable. No problems, just take them,' he pleaded.

'Shut the fuck up,' snarled the voice. 'Keep the damn rings. Just drive. Here, take the next left, towards Bakersville.'

Terrified, Takar swung left and, after following blunt instructions for another twenty minutes, pulled into a deserted boat yard a half-mile outside Bakersville on the New Jersey coastline. The place looked like a scrapyard for boats, he thought, and then he noticed a few newer models to his left, suspended around their keels on purpose-built stands. He was aware that he was sweating heavily. *Christ, this looks like a scene from some kind of gangland murder. What the hell?* In all his business dealings, he'd stayed away from any trouble with gangsters or protection rackets.

'Pull up over there, beside that blue boat,' said the low voice in his ear. 'And don't try anything stupid.' The speaker emphasised the point by increasing the pressure of the pistol in Takar's neck. Takar groaned as he killed the engine. The swarthy man, his hand inside his jacket pocket, stepped out of the back, opened the front door and slid into the passenger seat.

The new occupant of the front of the car looked to be in his mid-fifties, of lean build and average height, with a small moustache and some scars on the side of his face. He was dressed in black. The feeling was growing in Takar el Sayden that this was no ordinary stickup.

'Takar el Sayden,' the man said, as he looked Takar straight in the eye. 'I am a member of al-Qaeda and we need your help.'

A shiver of fear ran deep through Takar el Sayden. He knew all about the strength and influence of al-Qaeda, not least in his home city of Tripoli. *But what the hell do they want from me in New York?*

'Takar,' the man repeated, 'we know all about your family, and your background. We know that your family has a strong love of Islam and that you must be outraged by the sufferings of Muslims at the hands of the Americans.' The man was right that Takar had been raised in a devout family, but it was also true that his attention to his religion had dissipated steadily as he chased the mighty dollar in New York.

'I'll get to the point,' the stranger continued. 'Friends of ours need your assistance in Manhattan. You will be helping with an experiment. Our friends wish to see how many of your burgers they can sell to New Yorkers in two years. Your restaurants will be re-branded as BurgerFantastic. Your prices will be about half those of your competitors.'

Takar el Sayden gulped. Even under this pressure he wondered how the hell these guys expected him to turn a profit from selling half-price burgers.

'My friends will make a top advertising agency available to you and a marketing budget of one hundred million dollars.'

El Sayden's eyes bulged. One hundred million dollars!

'You will make your money by selling burgers in vast quantities,' the man continued, 'and you keep all of the money. My friends do not want any share of it.'

Takar el Sayden swallowed hard again, his brain was spinning. *What the hell is this all about?*

'Also,' the man went on in his monotone voice, 'my friends wish to add a new ingredient to the sauce on your burgers. Call it research. We understand that the sauce for all of your restaurants is manufactured overnight at the facility where I, ah, collected you, Takar?'

Takar nodded and added, his voice squeaky, 'The vans deliver the sauce and all the supplies to the stores before 6 a.m. each day.'

'Yes, this is where we need your direct help,' the man said. 'Every night, as part of the experiment, you must add a bag of a secret ingredient into each vat of sauce as it is blended and before it is put into the containers for each restaurant. The ingredient is completely harmless, I promise you. It will cause no harm to your customers and it has no taste or smell. Every week I will bring a new supply to your depot and check how you are doing. You must never test this powder and you must never tell anyone else about our arrangement. This arrangement will continue for about two years and when the experiment is over you will be paid five million dollars for your help. If any difficulties should arise along the way, you have our word that you will be given ample notice and assistance in bringing your family back to Tripoli. Waiting for you back there will be your five million dollars. Our friends are generous, but also serious. You have our word.'

Takar el Sayden needed no convincing about the power and

influence of al-Qaeda. All his instincts told him that this was a man to be listened to.

'Takar, the recent demise of your uncle, who started your business . . .'

Takar's eyes widened as a deep chill ran down his spine.

'That was no burglary. That was to show you that we are serious. So, will you be of assistance to my friends?'

Takar el Sayden nodded, then squeaked out the word, 'Yes.'

His bladder failed him as the stranger left, satisfied that he had a suitably motivated new recruit in New York.

9

MANHATTAN – THE PRESENT

'Pharmaceutical medicine has become the single greatest danger to the health and safety of the American people – and the Food and Drug Administration has become the single most dangerous organisation in North America. You know, we're about the only country in the world that allows advertising of prescription drugs? What's more –'

'Aw come on, that's outrageous,' Mandy Callaghan interrupted and made an appealing face to the interviewer on Manhattan WNYC 93 FM's drivetime show. 'The drug companies are developing new products all the time to help the people out there listening to this show – products that can prolong and enhance their lives.'

'You're lying to the people. You're inventing new diseases so you can boost profits. We're overusing medicines and you won't tell us about the side effects because . . .'

'Andy, you just have to withdraw that,' Mandy retorted calmly. 'I'm prepared to be civil . . .'

John Prosser, the show's host, sat back in his chair and sipped from his mug of hot coffee. Great stuff, leave 'em at it. Two minutes to the weather and traffic. Then I'll take a few calls from the public . . .

Andy Hawkins was continuing, 'Last year, over twenty billion dollars were spent on pharmaceutical marketing in the US alone, more than twice what's spent on research and development. The pharmaceutical industry, which generates revenues of over four hundred billion dollars, has become the world's most profitable stock market sector. And the doctors are its dealers . . .'

John Prosser touched the icon on his screen to instantly broadcast the sponsor's message to about two million New Yorkers. 'Yessee guys, it sure is hot today in the Big Apple, but it's getting even hotter here, in the studio, where we are talking about the power of advertising by the big drug companies. Are you being manipulated into buying medicines that you don't need? On line two, we've got Gina Diaz. Hi, Gina, you're live on Drivetime, what's your comment please?'

'Hi, John, great show.'

'Thanks, honey.'

'What I'd like to ask is: what's the point of the drug companies spending all this money advertising prescription drugs that you can only get if your doctor prescribes them?'

'Great question, Gina; guys?'

Mandy Callaghan got in quickly. 'Hi, Gina, it's really all about sharing knowledge about these great products. You know –'

Andy Hawkins interrupted with a snort. 'That's complete bullshit, Mandy. Gina, the answer to that is simple. Us ordinary New Yorkers are busy, we're stressed, we're tired. We're being bombarded with advertising promising us miracle cures for tiredness, headaches, lack of energy. Course we're gonna go for it. We can all identify with those symptoms. We recite them back to the doctor and we tell him the name of the drug we need to cure it. And it works! Research shows that seventy per cent of doctors will write that prescription, cos in the background the drug companies are manipulating the doctors with other tricks.'

'Thanks, Andy; thanks, Gina,' interjected John Prosser. He could see over twenty calls backing up on his screen. *Got to keep the pace up*. The producer was holding up three fingers behind the soundproofed window.

'And on line three,' said the host, flicking at his screen, 'we have a Manhattan medic.' *Doctor Wilson*, his screen told him.

'Hi, doc, which side of this do you come down on? Are we being conned or are the drug companies being unfairly canned?'

'Hi, John, thanks for having me on.' The doctor's deep, calm voice filled their headsets. 'I have to say, John, it makes my blood boil to hear people suggest that doctors can be influenced into writing unnecessary prescriptions. In my twenty years' experience in New York, I can say I have never heard of one case where it was proven a doctor had acted improperly. Doctors invest many years in learning how to help sick people and they're out there doing it twenty-four seven.'

'Thanks, doc, thanks for joining us. And on line two . . .'

The tension in the radio studio at WNYC 93 was rising.

'... and on average, patients over fifty-five years of age, with high blood pressure, are now living five years longer than they did in the nineteen-seventies, and that's all down to research and development and education initiatives by the pharmaceutical companies,' Mandy Callaghan said, managing to get in a nice strong piece on behalf of the pharmaceutical manufacturers. 'There are grandparents out there now, playing with their grandkids, who would not be alive today, without knowledge about the helpful medicines that are now available.'

Time for some conflict, then, the host thought.

'Well, one lady who doesn't quite share your views is journalist Megan Thomson, who has been writing in today's *New York Times*. Line one, Megan, what on earth is Sinclear?'

'Hi, John. Well, Sinclear is the name of an antibiotic originally made for sinus infections by Daleroc, one of the world's largest drug manufacturers . . .'

'And what's the problem, Megan?'

'Sinclear was approved by the FDA in 2012, but soon afterwards there were reports of liver damage and deaths among patients.'

'Uh-oh,' grunted the host as Mandy Callaghan began shuffling through papers on the table.

'So,' continued the journalist, 'the FDA investigated and issued Daleroc with a serious warning. However, that's not all. Now, FDA investigator Angela Nelson is saying that Daleroc had evidence that its safety study of its antibiotic contained fake data, but that they submitted it to the FDA anyway.'

'Wow, heavy stuff, tell us more,' prompted the host.

'So now, Nelson and two other government investigators have been subpoenaed to testify before a fifth government inquiry into Sinclear. Ross McParland, the first FDA investigator to handle Sinclear, said that when he tried to get permission to probe Daleroc on fraudulent data, he was blocked by senior FDA officials.'

'Heavyeeee' – Prosser, genuinely surprised, accentuated the word. 'Mandy?' he said quizzically to an uncomfortable-looking Mandy Callaghan.

'Yes, John. Well, I'm not familiar with every detail of the case, but I know that the Daleroc president, Dave Agar, has testified that the company submitted its data in "good faith".'

'Megan?'

'Unfortunately, John, it gets worse. The FDA are saying that several physicians hired by Daleroc falsified data in its 2010 study. One doctor is now serving a four-year sentence after pleading guilty to fabricating results. According to Nelson at the FDA, the Daleroc study, and I quote, "contained all the hallmarks of illegitimacy, including forged signatures and altered results".'

'Sounds like there's more to come out of that one, Megan?'

'Yes, John, we'll be keeping a close eye on how it develops.'

'Okay, folks, we're heading for the bottom of the hour. Last comments, guys? Mandy?'

'John, the people out there can have full confidence in their medicines and in their doctors. You can trust your tablets.' *She'd wanted to make sure she finished with that line.*

The producer was circling his hand in the air, urging a finish to the item. John Prosser got the message. *Hope I've got the balance right.*

'Andy, last few words?'

'You know, John, perhaps the most effective way I can warn people about what's going on is to encourage everyone to log on to Havidol.com.'

'What's that, Andy?'

'In order to prove how this drug advertising works, Justine Cooper, a journalist, set up a spoof website for a disease she invented called Dysphoric Social Attention Consumption Deficit Anxiety Disorder, in the style of a pharmaceutical company, supposedly to educate the public about the terrible effect that DSACDAD is having on their lives.'

'Sounds quirky, Andy. If you can't beat 'em, join 'em?'

'Well, pretty much. The drug to treat the disease is called Havidol, afafynetyme HCI. Lots of newspapers and magazines carried her spoof press releases, thinking they were real. John, the website was flooded with enquiries for Havidol.'

'So, what was her point, Andy?'

'Her point was that anyone can market like the drug companies market. And they all missed the big clue.'

'What was that, Andy?' said the host.

'The name of the drug, John.' He enunciated the words slowly. 'Have it all – and have a fine time!'

The presenter laughed. 'Nice one, Andy, thanks again to my guests, let's go to the news.'

And, at that, the producer gave a big double thumbs-up through the window.

★

FIFTH PRECINCT STATION

'Listen up, guys.' Sergeant Connolly had called one of his briefing sessions in the open plan area on the second floor. Later that day, John Wyse would muse over the coincidence of Connolly's timing.

'Quiet please!' Connolly hollered – and he got the room's attention.

'OK, guys. Homeland Security has renewed the Orange Level warning – that's a continuing high risk of terrorist activity in the city. Make sure you read the emails. You can see yourselves from the type of attacks we've been getting that we're facing shooters and bombers who don't care if they die too. It's real tough to defend against, so I want everyone keepin' their eyes open for *any* suspicious activity.'

There were a few grim nods around the room.

'There's a pattern of young middle-eastern males,' Connolly continued. 'A lotta the shooters wear combat-style gear, black baseball caps. Sometimes masks. Often have backpacks with bombs and more ammo. Some of these newly radicalised guys have hardly seen a gun before, but it doesn't take a genius to cause mayhem with an AK-47. But some of 'em, like our pal who tried to bomb Times Square, have had al-Qaeda training. So, like I say, be careful and . . . eyes open.'

★

Two hours after Connolly's briefing, John Wyse was driving south on Park Row, approaching One Police Plaza, headquarters of the NYPD, where he'd arranged to have a coffee with David Carter, the profiler. He was interested in hearing more of Carter's advice on his career path. The traffic slowed to a halt between City Hall and One Police Plaza and Wyse noticed a group of four tourists on the paved area outside HQ. One of them raised a camera to take a photograph and a police officer strode forward from the gate and put his hand in front of the camera.

'No photos of the building, sir.'

Wyse heard an outbreak of car horns behind him. Just in time he stopped himself from hitting the gas and rear-ending the car in front of him, which hadn't moved. In his mirrors, he could see that a large white truck had stopped, maybe twenty yards behind him, and hadn't closed the gap. The driver appeared animated, twitching around in the cab and jabbing away at his phone. He was a young guy. Black jacket. Black baseball cap. He gave Wyse a bad feeling.

Suddenly the truck engine roared, the driver spun the wheel and the truck mounted the kerb. Wyse was already jumping from his car, watching in horror as the four tourists turned towards the noise. The uniformed officer had barely got his gun out of his holster when the truck hit the group, tossing some of them sideways and crushing the officer beneath its massive wheels. The driver gunned the engine again and headed straight at the barriers guarding the entrance to the complex. He hit the gates hard and they buckled. But held. The driver threw the truck into reverse. *Once more and I'll be in.*

As the driver braked and shoved the truck into gear for another assault on the gates, Wyse raced alongside, his Smith & Wesson in his hand. He ran around the front of the truck and as it surged forward again, he steadied his wrist with his left hand and clustered eight rapid shots through the windscreen. The engine noise faded instantly and the truck rolled forward into the gate, which buckled, but held firm. Wyse leaped up onto the cab, ready to fire again, but the bloodied head hanging backwards told him this danger, at least, was over. Then he noticed a packed rucksack on the seat beside the dead driver. A wire hung from it, connected to a remote-control device. Wyse jumped down. Police officers were rushing from all directions, guns drawn. The shriek of sirens filled the air. Wyse holstered his gun and held his badge out in front of him.

'Driver's dead. Probable bomb in the cab. Could be explosives in the back too. Call the bomb squad.'

Then he walked slowly away from the scene as officers

established a cordon and paramedics checked the five crumpled bodies on the plaza for signs of life. It was clear there weren't any. Wyse sat on a wall and rubbed his face with his palms. He was jangling with adrenaline. *Shit. This day just got complicated.*

★

HARRY'S BAR, MANHATTAN – THAT NIGHT

When John Wyse walked into Harry's Bar, Manhattan, he received a standing ovation from the large group of cops gathered there. Cabrini steered him onto a stool at the bar, and his back soon stung from all the slapping. Drinks appeared in front of him from all directions.

'Great work, buddy, proud of ya,' said Cabrini, hugging him tight. 'Everything go okay?'

'Yeah, no problems.' Wyse filled him in quickly on the hours of procedural interviews and statements he'd been making since he shot the truck bomber. He'd eventually won the argument to keep his name out of the media. A group gathered around, keen to shake Wyse's hand and get an inside track on the day's drama. The truck driver was a twenty-two-year-old US citizen from Dallas, whose parents had been immigrants from Pakistan. The rucksack had indeed contained a bomb, and the back of the truck was packed with explosives too. When sitting in the traffic, just before launching his attack, the driver had posted the familiar suicide bomber's video on Facebook, filmed in front of an IS flag, and denouncing America for its role in the Middle East.

'They reckon his plan was to detonate the bomb up close to the Police Plaza building,' Wyse added. 'There was enough explosive in the truck to bring the building down. Coulda killed hundreds. And made a mess of City Hall too.'

'Freakin' rag heads,' said a bleary-eyed Detective Smith. 'We should chuck the whole lot of them out.'

'Yeah. And then build a wall,' threw in Detective Williams.

Wyse sighed. 'Not sure that's the answer, guys.'

'Try tellin' that to that cop's wife,' snarled Smith, every line on his face a challenge. 'Six months pregnant.'

'And those four tourists. Germans. Crushed by a truck on freakin' vacation. Makes me sick. Fuckin' Muslims,' added Williams.

'We're talkin' about a tiny number of bad guys here,' said Wyse, shaking his head and then swigging a drink. 'And what they're doin' is nothing to do with Islam. There's billions of Muslims, great people, who want peace just as much as us.'

Smith shook his head. 'Nah. Too soft, John. We gotta defend ourselves. We should go over there and bomb the hell outta them.'

Wyse was about to ask, 'Over where, exactly?' when he realised that further discussion was pointless and he changed the subject.

'Hey, Mike, what's your odds on the Giants for Sunday?' he asked.

10

MANHATTAN – THE PRESENT

John Wyse pressed the 'down' button in the back of the yellow cab and gratefully gulped some slightly cooler air as it struggled in the window. Another hot Manhattan day, more humid than usual for spring. *Why do I always seem to get a cab without air con, just when I need to stay cool?* It had been a stressful few days since he'd shot the truck bomber, dealing with the suits in internal investigations, while making sure his name didn't get into the press. He was looking forward to this first date with Anna and the last thing he wanted was to arrive with a sweaty shirt. Or late.

He leaned forward to peer through the windshield and cursed the kaleidoscope of angry red brake lights blocking their way. The cab was making slow progress in heavy evening traffic on Church Street. Anna had been delighted with his suggestion that they have dinner at Emilia's, in his view the best Italian on Union Square. Good start. Wyse sat back on the shiny, slippery seat and glanced at his watch for the umpteenth time. 7.05 p.m. *Fifteen more minutes oughta do it – even at this speed.*

He made himself take the time to absorb the sights around him. The sidewalks were crammed with armies of office workers, heading for the subways or bars. Red stars on Macy's bags fought for attention with the black and silver of Bloomingdales and the pale blue Tiffany & Co. branding, as shoppers stepped around tourists heading for the shows on Broadway. Early evening diners, some in suits, some in sweats, were making for the restaurants in Chinatown and Little Italy. Within one hundred yards or so, those looking for faster food could choose between McDonald's, Subway, Burger King, Dunkin' Donuts, Pret A Manger or Quick 'n' Tasty. Starling-like flocks of yellow cabs dived between red sightseeing buses, jaywalkers and roller-bladers, as they competed for inches with the world's largest collection of white vans. Sirens screamed and horns hollered as pedestrians pushed their way past stubborn cars at every traffic light. Every pole was a godlike octopus, bristling with commandments: No Standing, No Stopping, Lane Ends, Buses Only, Truck Route, Don't Walk.

Wyse grunted. He remembered how awed he'd been at the scale and energy of Manhattan when he moved here. His work-place was these streets, as they pulsed relentlessly with the throb of commerce. It was a prize posting and one he'd thought he would never tire of. But, for the last year or so, he had felt a growing emptiness; a feeling that something was missing in his life. And he was growing tired of the violence that seemed to follow the job around. His father had been a career man with the Bureau and had all the contacts to ease a transfer to the FBI and a posting in Washington. But, for the moment, he'd let Connolly persuade him to stay. *Maybe I just need to settle down, get married, have kids.*

He tipped the driver with the remainder of the twenty-dollar bill and walked quickly through the open door of the restaurant. Massimo, the white-haired *maître d'*, was ready, as always, with a cheery smile and a warm handshake.

'Signor Wyse, what a pleasure to see you again.'

'Thank you, Massimo, you're looking well.'

'Ah *grazie, grazie*. It's the good food you know,' Massimo said with a wink.

'I hope I'm first here?' Wyse asked, looking around.

'You are, Signor Wyse, and I have the best table in the house ready for you.'

Massimo, who was a legend in the Union Square district, knew well that John Wyse was a police detective. The job did bring a certain range of perks.

'Thanks, Massimo,' said Wyse, as he sat at the table facing the door and accepted the leather-bound menu.

'*Grazie*, a pleasure always.'

John Wyse scanned the antipasti, one eye on the entrance. He had just reached Emilia's selection of salamis, olives and mozzarella, when his eyes were drawn to the woman walking through the door. She stood close to six feet tall. She had thick black, shoulder-length hair. She was wearing a beautifully fitted white cotton dress, which seemed to glow in the evening sunlight streaming through the doorway behind her. She was stunningly beautiful.

Christ, thought Wyse, as he began to stand. Normally women look better when you're drunk – not the other way around. He waved and she caught his eye and waved back. He noticed the admiring glances from both men and women seated at other tables as Anna followed Massimo to the table.

'Hi, John.' She leaned over and pecked him on the cheek.

'Hi, Anna, nice to see you again. You look awesome.'

'Thank you, you're looking pretty good yourself.'

They both laughed as they sat down.

Wow, John thought, those amazing green eyes. Like a Persian cat's. Sultry, deep, intelligent. He could look into those eyes for ever . . .

Massimo broke the spell. '*Signore e Signora*, a glass of champagne, with my compliments?'

'Oh yes, please.' John smiled.

'Gorgeous, thank you,' said Anna.

They clinked glasses. John looked at his companion again. There was that cute crinkle of her nose as she smiled. *Christ*, he thought again, *don't mess this up, John!*

Anna returned his gaze and he smiled, then broke away to look down at the menu, almost shyly. He was gorgeous, but she detected a genuine softness.

Don't mess this up, Anna.

11

YAMOURA BOARDROOM, TOKYO – 6 APRIL

'Bring on the recession, I say,' said Lumo Kinotoa, with a twinkle in his eye.

The board members looked up. They were chatting about the Nikkei and the world economy, during a tea break.

'Nothing like a good recession to boost sales of drugs,' continued the smiling chairman. 'People without jobs always get sicker!'

'Ha ha, very good,' laughed Tsan Yohoto and there were chuckles around the table. The silver-haired chairman called the meeting back to order for the last item on the agenda.

'Now, Tsan,' he said, 'we are all looking forward to hearing of your Grand Plan. Are you ready to tell us?'

'Yes, thank you, Chairman,' said Tsan Yohoto putting his glasses back on. 'Please feel free to refer to the paper which I have left on the table for each of you. But first, please have a look at the screen.'

He pressed a button on a remote control and a large white screen was lowered from the ceiling at the end of the room. Tsan Yohoto started into another presentation, which, as always, he had practised carefully. His board members would have approved a few notes written on the back of an envelope, but Tsan wanted to take no chances. He spoke emotionally about the tens of thousands of Africans who were dying each year from a whole range of infections, from pneumonia to bowel infections to kidney infections to gonorrhoea – because they did not have the basic medicines to fight the bacteria. The presentation was heavy on close-up shots of starving black babies and skeletal women carrying children long distances, in the hope of getting medical help at a field hospital or clinic. The images included a heart-breaking slow-motion video of dying babies, accompanied by a soundtrack of Peter Gabriel's 'Don't Give Up'. The last image on the screen was the face of a beautiful little black girl, sitting on her mother's grave, with her arms outstretched in an appeal to the camera. The music faded and the lights came up slowly. There was a long silence. Tsan Yohoto could see that many of the board members had tears in their eyes. Someone sniffled and blew their nose. He chose his moment.

'Gentlemen, all they need is an antibiotic. Simple cephalosporin tablets. My plan proposes that we multiply our production of cephalosporin tablets fiftyfold and give them free to the people of impoverished African nations. The cost will be maybe ten million dollars, but the PR will be invaluable. Most importantly, it is the right thing to do. For this, my last strategic recommendation, I ask that you support me in saving the African people from diseases that do not have to kill them.'

'I'll propose the motion,' said the chairman.

'I'll second,' said the finance director swiftly.

The board members added their rapid approval. The motion was passed unanimously. The production director was instructed to boost manufacturing of cephalosporin immediately. The chairman rose to his feet and began to applaud his chief executive, Tsan Yohoto. One by one, the directors also rose and joined in a standing ovation to their leader and to this, his last great initiative. Tsan Yohoto waved an acknowledgement of their applause and thought of his mother, Saina – she would be so proud to see him now. With a teary eye, Lumo Kinotoa managed a wink to Tsan Yohoto.

The plan was moving forward. Perfectly.

12

PARAMOUNT BUILDING, MANHATTAN – 10 APRIL

'Oh, yes, good morning, Mr Yohoto, good morning Mr Kinotoa,' chirped Sonya, the bubbly receptionist at Dynamic Communications. 'Victor and Katie are ready for you.'

I should hope so, thought Tsan Yohoto, considering all the money we've handed them over the years.

'Please take a seat, they'll be with you in a moment.'

The visitors sat into an enormous white leather couch and took in the expensive minimalist lobby with its central water feature. Lumo Kinotoa, the Yamoura chairman, who had not visited Dynamic's office before, stood to examine a framed print of the famous skyscraper. The narrative down the side told him that Jack Benny, Elvis Presley, Frank Sinatra and many others had performed in the theatre on the ground floor. Just as he learned that the building had hosted the Alan Freed show and had brought the phrase Rock'n'Roll to the world, the door burst open and out came Victor Dezner and Katie Keller, the two founding partners of Dynamic Communications.

'Gentlemen, you are most welcome,' they said in unison.

Not surprisingly for someone in their business, Victor and Katie had long perfected the civilities of greeting Japanese business guests and there was a drawn-out sequence of stiff bowing and handshaking as Tsan Yohoto introduced Lumo Kinotoa and business cards were ceremoniously exchanged.

'Come in, come in,' said Victor as he flounced his way ahead of his best clients and into the main offices. Victor Dezner wore tight black trousers and a tight black poloneck that accentuated his slim frame. The typecast dress code was topped off with a pointy chin, a neatly trimmed beard and longish sideburns. Kinotoa had long ago formed the impression from telephone conversations that Victor Dezner was gay, and now decided that he had been right.

'The team are all waiting to meet you in the boardroom,' sparkled Katie. 'We are super-excited to hear about this new product!' The advertising executives ushered their guests into a large boardroom, dominated by a shiny chrome table, flanked by chrome and black leather chairs.

'Mr Yohoto, Mr Kinotoa, let me introduce you – this is Mark Reynolds, Head of our Healthcare Communications Team.'

The thirty-year-old, in a black suit and with spiky black hair, launched into his rehearsed procedure of deep bowing.

'And this is Arlene Thomas, who works alongside me on print media communications, stakeholder education and outdoor advertising.' Arlene, a young woman from Harlem, in a very tight pair of black leather trousers and black Armani T-shirt, joined in the greetings.

'And last, but not least, this is Anna Milani, who looks after our celebrity endorsements and product placement. Anna, this is Mr Yohoto and Mr Kinotoa.'

Anna stepped forward, beamed an enormous smile and bowed respectfully to these important clients. As they shook her hand, both Yohoto and Kinotoa were struck by the woman's natural beauty. The ritual exchange of more business cards took another minute or so.

'Sit down, gentlemen, please,' said Katie, as Victor filled everyone's glasses with Perrier water and pushed forward bowls of exotic fruit. 'Gentlemen, we can't wait to hear about your exciting new product. We're so looking forward to getting involved.'

Tsan Yohoto and Lumo Kinotoa settled into two seats at the centre of the table and the attentive executives sat around the table, facing them. Tsan Yohoto jiggled a floating cube of ice in his Perrier with his right index finger and started.

'My friends, together we have had many great years of success in marketing our drugs into the US – enormously helped by your skilled advice and dynamic campaigns.'

The beaming Victor Dezner almost burst with pleasure.

'We have decided to rebrand and relaunch one of our existing products on a global scale. We are convinced that creative marketing and pricing techniques can guarantee even greater sales. We are going to pilot this campaign in Manhattan. If it proves successful, as I'm sure it will, we will be asking your team to roll it out across the world.'

Victor began to stroke his beard furiously.

'Also,' Yohoto added, 'as you know, we want to start this campaign as soon as possible.'

'But how long will the FDA approval take?' asked Katie.

'We don't need it,' said Yohoto. 'This drug has long been approved by the FDA – all we will be doing is rebranding, repackaging and promoting it more heavily.'

'Oh, superb,' interrupted Victor. 'So, we can get straight on it.'

Tsan Yohoto frowned. He wanted to proceed in an orderly fashion.

'Firstly,' he said, 'the drug is used to cure a whole range of problems from bowel and urinary tract inflammation, to sore throats, ears and sinuses. It has been in successful use for many years. However, our ongoing clinical trials have also shown that people taking the drug are finding it helps alleviate headaches and gives them more energy. Some consumers also find that they lose weight and generally feel fitter. It will be some time before we have full long-term data to prove these side effects clinically, but in the meantime, we would like to get the campaign underway.

Our advertising needs to find a way to highlight these beneficial side effects and yet we do not want to overstate them and draw the FDA down on us, before we have the full clinical back-up.'

'Absolutely, absolutely,' nodded Victor.

'For once, we come to you with our own brand name chosen,' continued Yohoto. 'The drug will be called SuperVerve.'

'Brilliant!' Victor exclaimed.

Tsan Yohoto continued. 'We envisage targeting the health conscious, who are trying to cope with a busy lifestyle here.'

Doesn't leave many out in Manhattan, Katie thought.

'We have a marketing outline for you, for a saturation coverage campaign, to include TV, radio, print media, social media, bill-boards, websites, celebrity endorsements – you name it. We want to throw everything into this pilot programme and see which works best.'

'No problem,' said Victor, leaning forward to assure Tsan Yohoto of his undivided attention.

'Absolutely,' said Katie. 'We can get the guys started straight way. Arlene?' she said, raising a quizzical eyebrow.

'Yep, I'm on it,' said Arlene. 'We'll have a logo, strapline and branding fully detailed and costed, read to roll out as soon as you need.'

'Anna?' Katie enquired.

'Yeah, I'm good to go. I'll start thinking about a suitable celeb-rity to front the campaign for us. Sounds like a sports personality who has successfully battled a weight problem and gone on to greater heights. Or perhaps a supermodel with kids and a busy life.'

'Or both?' said Yohoto, impressed with Anna's suggestions.

'Why not?' she said. 'But these celebrities don't come cheap.'

Katie broke the pause. 'Mr Yohoto, can I assume that there will be some new high credibility medical endorsement of the product?'

'Yes, indeed, Katie, that is already commissioned and you will have a paper within a week or two.'

'And do you want us to set up a programme of Continuing Medical Education for the doctors?

'Certainly, Katie. That's an important part of the strategy,' Yohoto replied.

Lumo Kinotoa interjected. 'Or, as we call it – educating the doctors to continue prescribing our drugs!'

Everyone laughed.

'So, when do you see us launching?' asked Victor as he took a sip of water.

'We have set a target of six weeks from now,' replied Yohoto.

Victor coughed out a mouthful of mineral water.

'What – what – six weeks?' he gasped, as he frantically dabbed his poloneck with a tissue. 'That's impossible!'

'Impossible is not what we came to hear,' said Yohoto quietly. 'By the way, did I mention that our budget is one hundred million dollars over the next two years?'

Victor's eyes bulged. 'No, not yet.'

'This campaign is particularly important to us, which is why we have allocated that budget. We want your media buyers to negotiate the best rates for us – and, of course, your agency takes its normal fifteen per cent commission. With the same commission for the global rollout. So, can you do it, or should we be talking to one of your competitors?'

'No, no, no,' said Victor as he jumped up and began to shake Yohoto and Kinotoa's hands. 'Take it as done. You have my word.'

'Excellent,' smiled Tsan Yohoto as he and Kinotoa stood to say their goodbyes. 'And when can I expect to see a first draft of the marketing plan for our consideration?'

'Three days, three days,' said Victor. 'We're starting right now. Absolutely.'

13

WASHINGTON – 11 APRIL

'And, there we have it,' Professor Alan G.F. Milton proclaimed, finishing with a trademark flourish across the bottom of his diagram on the board. 'The A to Z of ear, nose and throat infections in the twenty-first century.'

Polite applause rang out around the lecture hall at Washington University, where the final year medical students were reaching the end of their first term.

Bit of a show-off, thought a student in a middle row as he shoved his notes into his bag. Still, you don't get to be a world authority on anything without being able to sell yourself.

Professor Milton acknowledged the applause with a wave and pushed back a few locks of blond hair from his face. People had often told him that his hair reminded them of Robert Redford. His chair at the university was a reasonably lucrative and prestigious one and he made sure that he fulfilled his requirements to personally deliver six lectures each term. Now a fit and well-groomed fifty-four-year-old, life was good for Professor Alan G.F. Milton. Despite the couple of unfortunate incidents with some particularly attractive final-year students over the years, his ever-loving and adoring wife Sylvia continued to provide him with a comfortable and secure home life. They had even survived that mix-up with the au pair at the holiday villa in France, when he certainly hadn't intended to encourage the girl's advances. Sylvia had forgiven him his dalliances and they were well able to work around her only condition that he would no longer provide tutorage to undergraduates at their house.

Christ, if she only knew the half of it, Professor Milton had often thought to himself. But with each passing year, and with his wandering eye and hands slowing somewhat, the risk of any further catastrophic disruption to what was a satisfactory marriage seemed to diminish. Sylvia, despite his disappointment at what he saw as her low sex drive, had provided him with two fine sons, both now practising as lawyers in Washington.

Professor Alan G.F. Milton had enjoyed the money that flowed from private practice and the lifestyle that went with it. In 2010 he'd earned over one and a half million dollars, his best year to date. But the pressure of work was severe and he had jumped at the offer of Professor of Otolaryngology, the ear, nose and throat speciality at the university, with its promise of less stress, longer holidays and plenty of admiration from colleagues and students. What he hadn't fully reckoned on were the difficulties that went with surviving on a salary of three hundred thousand dollars, plus a few fees from the medical lecture circuit and some small-scale research work. The mortgage on the country house had still not been cleared and the boys' college fees had hit hard. He and Sylvia found it hard to eliminate the luxury lifestyle items to which they had become accustomed. Suddenly, money had become a new source of tension between them.

Then, out of the blue, one chilly December day, he had received a letter from one Tsan Yohoto, chief executive of Yamoura Pharmaceuticals in Tokyo. Mr Yohoto had expressed enormous admiration for Professor Milton's research papers and had complimented him on the high standard he had established for medical graduates from the university. Mr Yohoto was particularly interested in Professor Milton's speciality in the ear, nose and throat area; a field in which Yamoura worked tirelessly to help the many people around the world suffering from pain and discomfort. Coincidentally, Yamoura was organising a high-level medical convention in Hawaii in mid-January, where leading international specialists would share their knowledge on how to help unfortunate people with sinus, throat and lung complaints. Mr Yohoto was wondering if Professor Milton and his wife would like to attend the conference at the Sheraton, for five days. Professor Milton would be invited to attend a workshop at the convention and Mr Yohoto would also be honoured to host Professor and Mrs Milton at dinner on the second night. Attached to the letter was a brochure on the hotel and an itinerary for the five days, which included dinners, sightseeing trips, complimentary use of the hotel spa and, Professor Milton noted, first-class flights. Sylvia had been most impressed at the news and he had emailed their acceptance that day.

It had been a magnificent trip. Yamoura were excellent hosts. Nothing was any trouble. The dinner with Mr Yohoto had been a highlight. They had never enjoyed such good food and such fine wines. Mr Yohoto had turned out to be extremely knowledgeable about the whole area of ear, nose and throat infection. He was convinced that there were many people suffering chronic headache and discomfort, but who were undiagnosed – owing to a lack of knowledge of this complex speciality. Professor Milton couldn't agree more. Mr Yohoto had suggested that Professor Milton might help them with some further research in the area, as he was one of the world's most eminent experts on the subject. Again, Professor Milton couldn't have agreed more. He had almost fallen off his chair when, a week after they returned, a letter had arrived from Mr Yohoto asking that he further research the subject and report on the high level of missed diagnosis that was due to lack of information on the topic. For a fee of a quarter of a million dollars. Professor Milton was also encouraged to involve any other of his leading medical contemporaries, who were like-minded in their desire to see cutting-edge healthcare information made properly available. For his work in coordinating any other supporting contributors, he would be paid a further quarter of a million dollars and his contributors would be also paid directly by Yamoura at up to one hundred thousand dollars per head.

Professor Milton had contacted three of his contemporaries in universities around North America and they had pooled their knowledge and research data on the level of undiagnosed bronchial and ENT infection. They pointed out a whole range of symptoms, which merited the earlier use of medication, in a paper that was published widely in medical journals throughout the US and in *The Lancet* in the UK. They had spoken at several conventions on the topic and the medical community agreed that this was a problem that was not receiving proper recognition at GP level. A series of guidelines was put forward which advised doctors to instigate aggressive intervention at an earlier stage of diagnosis. Indeed, patients presenting with coughing and headache symptoms, on two occasions, should be treated over a period of up to one year, to eradicate the condition entirely.

Yamoura Pharmaceuticals had been delighted with the work and had issued payment of six hundred thousand dollars to Professor Milton, which included a further hundred thousand-dollar bonus. He had paid off the outstanding loan on the country house and had bought Sylvia a convertible BMW. Even better was promised when Professor Milton accepted an annual retainer of one hundred and fifty thousand dollars to make himself available for occasional consultation to Yamoura, and to attend their annual convention.

Doctors' surgeries around the world were bombarded with glossy leaflets on the new level of concern at this increasingly prevalent illness and the suggestion that this was a result of a fast-moving and stressed-out twenty-first-century lifestyle. The leaflets suggested that climate change and deterioration in air quality had greatly increased the numbers of people at risk. It happened that the leading drug for the treatment of these problems, Davratin, was produced by Yamoura Pharmaceuticals. Sales of Davratin increased by 325 per cent in the year after Professor Milton's findings and stayed at that level, adding approximately five hundred million dollars to Yamoura's annual profits.

Everyone was delighted. The only irritant had been the carping of a couple of crank doctors in Australia, who questioned the research findings and pointed out that lowering the threshold at which the medication should be prescribed, to two periods of occurrence, had brought at least ten million people, previously thought of as suffering tension headaches, into a new category requiring prescription medication. But these snipes were swiftly drowned out by a deluge of articles that approved Professor Milton's conclusions.

*

'How are you, my dear friend?' The phone call to Professor Milton's house had come at about nine on a Friday evening. The voice on the other end of the line was that of Tsan Yohoto himself.

'I'm great, thank you, Tsan, and how are you?'

'Beginning to feel my age, I'm afraid,' replied Tsan Yohoto.

'Ah, unfortunately, the evolution of medicine has not yet found a pill to halt the advance of time.'

'Yes, indeed, but we have had some great news from our research and development team.'

'Oh?' replied Professor Milton. He had an idea that this call was going to end up swelling his bank balance.

'Yes,' continued Yohoto, 'extraordinary really, somewhat of a fluke. One of our teams has discovered some very positive unexpected benefits from patients taking our cephalosporin antibiotic tablets . . .'

'For throat and sinus complaints?'

'Yes, of course. And for bowel inflammation, bronchitis, soft tissue infections, you name it. We have carried out significant trials and there is no doubt that patients are reporting increased energy levels and alleviation of headaches.'

'Really?'

'Yes, and what's more, there is definite evidence of suppression of the appetite. Many overweight patients are reporting long-term weight loss and improved general health after a few courses of cephalosporin.'

'How fantastic!'

'We have amassed considerable clinical evidence from our trials in Japan. What we would like you to do is to assemble a small team of US experts who will review our research material and advise us whether you think these results are reliable.'

'With pleasure, especially if –'

'Also, because all our trial patients have been Asian, can you please give us an opinion on whether these beneficial side effects are likely also to benefit westerners?'

'Because of the difference in diet?' asked the professor.

'Exactly,' continued Yohoto. 'We are planning a major relaunch of our cephalosporin brand in the US and I believe we can bring better health to the American people. Especially to those who have trouble losing weight or who have low energy levels.'

'Marvellous,' said Professor Milton. He paused. 'So, what's the next step?'

'We're so excited about this breakthrough that we wish to relaunch our brand in six weeks or so.'

'Six weeks!' Milton said, and the surprise in his voice was genuine.

'Yes. We have stepped up production already here in Tokyo. Will you be in a position to chair a panel of experts to review our research and to have your findings in, say, four weeks?'

'Four weeks, but –'

'In recognition of this demanding timescale, Professor, if you can meet the deadline, your own fee will be a minimum of five hundred thousand dollars. A further five hundred thousand dollars will be made available to the experts you select. And if you thought our success-related bonuses in the past generous, I can assure you that a successful relaunch of this product will see all previous figures surpassed. I envisage a potential bonus for your good self of at least two million dollars.'

Professor Milton had to steady himself with a hand on the fireplace.

'Do you think you can be of assistance, Professor Milton?' Yohoto asked, in a tone that suggested there would be no second chance.

'Absolutely, Tsan, my friend. It will be an honour to be involved in such a major project, bringing such benefits. I am humbled.'

Tsan Yohoto smiled to himself. The words 'humbled' and 'Professor Alan G.F. Milton' did not sit naturally together, in his experience.

'Excellent,' replied Yohoto. 'Will you consider consulting Professor Kolsen in Dallas?'

'Almost certainly,' replied the professor, sensing that would be the favoured option. Both the professor and his caller knew that Professor Kolsen at the JFK Memorial Hospital in Dallas was on a healthy retainer from Yamoura Pharmaceuticals for ongoing advice on product development. He was also on various FDA panels for approving drugs.

'And Dr Anton Cook in Toronto is a renowned expert in the field of weight loss and lifestyle illness,' said Professor Milton. Milton knew that Dr Cook was also on the Yamoura payroll.

'Oh, a superb choice,' chimed Yohoto, 'yes, that sounds like a powerful team. I can assure you that our clinical trials have been exhaustive and carried out to the most stringent standards. All the research work will be couriered to your home by tomorrow evening. Perhaps you would let me know in a week that everything is in place?'

'Absolutely, Tsan, absolutely. I'll call you late afternoon. Asia-Pacific time,' he added, reminding himself that Tokyo was thirteen hours ahead of the east coast. He caught a glimpse of himself in the large mirror over the fireplace and smiled.

'Thank you, Professor. It is so important for us to have the top medical brains in the world helping us with our research.'

'Oh, my pleasure, Tsan,' purred the professor. 'We'll speak again next week.'

'I look forward to it. Goodbye, Professor.'

Professor Milton ended the call. Then he turned and delved into the drinks cabinet. If ever there was a good reason for that bottle of vintage Bollinger, this was it. 'Sylvia, Sylvia,' he called out into the hall. 'Come here, honey – we're celebrating!'

14

MANHATTAN – 12 APRIL

The Al Jahada Mosque is one of the oldest mosques in New York. The grand dome over the central prayer hall and its tall minaret dominate Side Street in the Bronx, which is mostly made up of low rent but settled apartment blocks. There was an air of quiet calm about the street.

The two Muslims were sipping organic tea and chatting with a group of their fellow worshippers, as was the normal routine after the *salat* or daily prayers. It was usually the most devoted worshippers who stayed on for these discussions, which increasingly centred on the sufferings of fellow Muslims in Iraq, Syria and Palestine.

Ibrahim Fallah approached the two, quietly and calmly.

'My friends, will you join me in the courtyard for a moment?'

Neither hesitated and a minute later the three were standing at the Qibla wall, which faces Mecca, in the tradition of the very first mosque, Mohammad's house in Saudi Arabia.

Ibrahim Fallah spoke in a low and serious voice.

'I have a request from most important friends in al-Qaeda. They ask for the help of two volunteers who are well immersed in the ways of life in New York. The work will involve some research activity in the city's hospitals. I am assured that this activity is low key, but very valuable. There is no question of you causing any damage or harm to any people.'

The two facing him nodded solemnly.

'There will be no risk whatsoever of breaking any laws. The volunteers will be asked to visit New York hospitals, dressed as a maintenance crew to test how well the curtains around the beds in the wards are working.'

Two sets of eyebrows shot upwards in surprise.

Fallah shrugged. 'I know, I do not understand it myself,' he continued. 'But it is not our place to ask questions. The most important factor will be absolute secrecy. I am told that the hospitals will be busy and it's unlikely that anyone will question you. It is better that we do not know any more detail. This work will continue for a few hours each day, for perhaps a few weeks. Then you will be relieved of your task and you will hear no more about the matter. I am assured by very senior al-Qaeda superiors that this work is most important and that great thanks will be due to the volunteers who carry it out.'

Fallah paused and held their gaze.

'So, can you offer your assistance?'

Both immediately nodded their confirmation. This was indeed a great honour.

'When do we start?' asked one.

'The full instructions will not be confirmed for at least another year,' replied Ibrahim Fallah. 'In the meantime, you must prepare thoroughly and discreetly. You are asked to familiarise yourselves, in detail, with the location and layout of every hospital in New York. The location of nearby loading bays and travel times by van between the various hospitals. Pretend you are visiting the hospitals and get a feel for where the security guards' offices and the nurses' stations are located. And don't risk attracting any attention to yourselves. You have plenty of time.'

'We will start tomorrow,' the two assented.

'Excellent,' Fallah declared. 'We will not discuss this matter again until I have further instructions.'

After they had respectfully embraced Ibrahim Fallah, the two left the mosque through a side door near the *minbar*, the pulpit from which the Friday sermon is preached.

Hospitals? they were both thinking, bemused.

'Looks like we need a satnav,' said one to the other.

★

SECOND AVENUE

'For gawd's sake!' the woman screamed. 'You're wrong! There's no way I'm pregnant. Just no way!'

Outside, in the busy doctor's waiting room, a dozen or so patients overheard the voice, caught each other's eyes in embarrassment and lowered their heads deeper into the dogeared magazines.

'Just no way, doc, can't be.'

The receptionist leaned over and turned up the volume on the background music. The soothing tones of Mahler swirled around the room, but the woman's voice continued and then they heard her collapse into a fit of loud sobbing, punctuated with curses. A tense five minutes passed before Dr Peter Phillips gently led Mrs Claudia Riccini, a forty-two-year-old mother of six, through the waiting room and out to the front door. Dr Phillips caught the amused expressions on the faces in the room and fought the urge to smile too.

Christ, what a day. There can't be many jobs worse than this.

At 9 a.m., after a coffee and bagel at the Quick 'n' Tasty diner next door, he had started the day by lancing a septic boil in the anal passage of a two hundred and fifty pound, sixty-year-old woman. That had been followed by a procession of complaints about coughs, phlegm, psoriasis, stomach problems, irritable bowels, lack of energy, unhappiness and finally some counselling for Mrs

Riccini, following a fifty-dollar examination and pregnancy test. *Which she hasn't paid for*, he realised.

'Christ,' he sighed, but at least it was lunchtime and he had seventy-five minutes before it all started again.

The busy practice, close to the junction of Second Avenue and East 23rd, catered mostly for office workers in the area. They also got plenty of business from the School of Dentistry across the street. He had six partners in the practice and business was booming – if a little hectic. There was an AppleDay pharmacy next door, which was convenient for the patients.

'Dr Phillips,' his always cheerful receptionist Elaine called to him at the door, 'don't forget you've got Bob Sanders for lunch.'

'Oh, yes, I nearly forgot – thanks, Elaine.'

That was good news. Bob Sanders was his favourite of the many drug company reps who visited frequently. This would be a welcome break from the day's hassles. Bob was great fun and the two men shared a love of golf. It was Bob Sanders who had brought six of the doctors from his practice, plus their wives, on that incredible trip to the Ryder Cup at the K-Club in Ireland. They had flown on a luxurious corporate jet, together with a further fifty or so doctors, and had been treated like gods for the entire week. There had been a presentation to the doctors on the Thursday morning on some new research findings and by lunchtime they were eating prawns on the terrace of a corporate marquee, watching Phil Mickelson choose a three wood on the eighteenth. The next four days had been just heaven, golf every day for the real enthusiasts and the wives had been taken on shopping trips into Dublin city centre. It had been the trip of a lifetime and hadn't cost him a dollar. Just a pity that the Europeans had kicked their ass for the Ryder Cup but hey, you can't have everything.

He glanced back into the packed waiting room.

'Yes, doctor, you've finished your list,' said Elaine, predicting his next question.

Phew, he thought. And, sure enough, there was Bob Sanders, waving out the back window of a cab, which had just pulled up outside the clinic. He waved back as he stepped out the door.

'See you later, Elaine,' he called over his shoulder.

A perfectly grilled John Dory and a beautiful bottle of chilled Pouilly-Fumé surely deserved more respect and attention than they were getting at the best table in Salvadori's, the fine Italian restaurant on the corner of Second Avenue and 81st. But Dr Peter Phillips was laughing so hard that he found it hard to catch his breath as the tears rolled down onto his napkin. 'Stop, stop, for God's sake, stop,' he begged Bob Sanders, who was reliving some of the highlights from the trip to Ireland. One particularly intense doctor from Detroit had become uncontrollable after a few drinks and all sorts of funny events had ensued.

'No, wait,' said Bob. 'Then on the Friday, he decided to go on the trip to see the Book of Kells in Dublin. He's so hungover, he missed the bus by an hour. So, he calls a cab at the hotel and asks the driver to take him to see Kells. So, the driver takes him on a one-hour drive into some village called Kells in the middle of nowhere.'

A burst of Pouilly-Fumé shot out Phillips' nose as he exploded again with laughter. He now had a serious pain in his side. 'Stop, stop!' he begged.

'No chance,' said Bob, 'so then, apparently he gets out of the cab in the middle of this village and asks this old guy on a bike where can he see the Book of Kells.'

'No, no, stop . . .'

'So, the old guy tells him he's going to need bionic eyesight to see it from here, cos it's one hundred miles away back in Dublin!'

'No, mercy, please,' begged Phillips, doubled over in his chair, tears rolling down his cheeks.

'Okay, okay,' said Bob, 'let's eat.'

They allowed the conversation to lapse and concentrated on the succulent fish.

Bob Sanders, one of Yamoura's highest earning medical reps in Manhattan, lavished attention on Dr Peter Phillips' clinic on Second Avenue and maintained a file on every doctor there, including information on their families, birthdays and hobbies, which he used to plan how to reward and incentivise them.

'So, how's biz?' asked Bob, having given his guest a chance to enjoy the food and recover his composure.

'Just great, Bob,' said the doctor, sitting back from the table. 'Gets better every month. Sometimes I think even the good Lord couldn't have healed the numbers we deal with. And you?'

'Yeah, really good,' nodded Bob as he beckoned the waiter for the dessert list, 'and it looks like I'm gonna be getting busier.'

'Why's that?'

'Well, news from Tokyo is that there's gonna be a big push on one of the antibiotics. By some lucky break, the research guys have discovered new beneficial side effects. They've got some top US doctors reviewing the clinical reports and, if they verify it for here, apparently we're going into overdrive on production. The New York reps have been told to make it their priority product – so pressure's on me to get the sales up.'

'What's new?' Phillips grunted as he studied the menu, toying between the crème brûlée and the banoffee.

'Nothing new, just same old pressure. But if we can hit the targets there's talk of the mother of all trips to the Olympics in Tokyo in 2020. Yamoura are going all out on it, it being the home city and all that. They're talking a week-long trip and all best seats. Let's hope we're all there, Peter,' said Bob as he refilled his guest's glass.

'Wow, I'm sure the guys at the clinic would love to be in on that one,' said Phillips. 'Please keep us in the loop.'

'Sure thing. I'll drop in all the research stuff when it's ready. Maybe you can tell the guys all about it?'

'You got it.'

'Here's to Tokyo, buddy,' said Bob, raising his glass.

'To Tokyo,' responded Dr Peter Phillips as they clinked glasses.

The waiter availed himself of the opportunity to take the check and the Yamoura Pharmaceuticals credit card that lay on the white linen tablecloth.

15

NEW JERSEY – 13 APRIL

'Goddamn it,' cursed Takar el Sayden as he slammed his fist into the metal up-and-over door on his double garage. He pressed the button on his Lexus key fob and the electric motor whirred into life and the large door began its slow journey upwards. As it passed eye level, Takar noticed three dents in the door caused by the gold rings on his right fist. Everything had been going so well. And now, his world had been turned upside down.

The call to his cell phone had come at about ten the night before. He had instantly recognised the low calm voice as belonging to the man who had hijacked him in his car a few days ago. The stranger was going to call to his office at the Quick 'n' Tasty production facility tomorrow morning at half nine. He was to follow the man's instructions and no harm would come to his family. He had an impulse to call the cops, but he dismissed the idea as madness. He knew exactly the calibre of people he was dealing with. The cops could never protect his wife and kids here in New York – let alone his parents and family in Tripoli. His proud uncle, Abdel Moamer, had probably tried to face down these bastards and been mercilessly shot. Takar el Sayden slid onto the cream leather seat of the Lexus and the engine purred into life. As he drove down the driveway, he waved to his two girls, Farah and Jasmin, who were already out playing on the swings.

'Bye, Daddy, love you,' they called and blew kisses. He blew kisses back through the open window.

Goddamn. Goddamn.

The silver RX accelerated smoothly into the New Jersey morning traffic. For once Takar didn't turn on the radio. He needed to think.

The new Quick 'n' Tasty production facility was in a 1980s industrial park near Newark airport and Takar was very proud of it. He'd taken over this business with just six restaurants in Manhattan, all down near the financial district. His menu of home-cooked chicken, lamb, pizza, pastas and salads had been an instant success. He'd found himself meeting a growing demand for good-quality food, freshly cooked and served quickly. He soon realised that New Yorkers didn't like waiting around for anything. He got upset when people described his restaurants as 'fast food'. He liked to call it 'quick service'. He was even more upset when McDonald's, Burger King and all the rest also abandoned the 'fast food' tag and began calling themselves the 'quick service' industry. No matter, because, whatever he called it, Takar el Sayden had the formula just right, as testified by the long lines of hungry customers for his tables and at his takeaway counters.

With the financial backing of his father in Libya, he had opened a seventh restaurant on Pie Street. A month later, he opened two more restaurants on Wall Street and then things really took off. Quick 'n' Tasty restaurants spread rapidly through Manhattan and Takar el Sayden and Tasha worked twelve-hour days and often longer in the early years. As the chain mushroomed, the cash rolled in.

The other big step forward had been in 1994. They were at sixty or so restaurants and each restaurant was preparing its own food each day, in its own kitchen. Takar knew that this was inefficient – the whole process of each restaurant ordering in its own supplies as they needed them was a logistical nightmare and his accounts department was overwhelmed trying to handle all the different suppliers. Takar and Tasha knew they had to centralise production and minimise the number of suppliers to strengthen their buying power, and then to deliver to each restaurant from a central depot. He remembered the day well, 10 June 1994. He'd spotted an advert in the real estate section of *The New York Times* – a big pizza making company out by Newark had gone bust and a liquidator had been appointed. The advert read:

> **LIQUIDATORS SALE**
> Modernised food production facility approx. 100,000 sq. ft. On three-acre site. Full inventory of one-year old food production equipment.
> **PRICE $14M.**

Wow, he thought. It's too big, we can't afford it. But we gotta have a look.

Tasha went with him and it blew them away. It had everything they would ever need, from cooking equipment and utensils to huge stainless-steel machines for preparing meat, commercial peelers and ovens. There were vats for blending sauces, cheeses, you name it. Almost for the hell of it, they had offered nine million dollars. He couldn't believe it when the liquidator had come back to say they had a deal. That June, 1994, New York was in a state of distraction – the Rangers had just won the Stanley Cup, the soccer World Cup Finals and the World Gay Games were both on in Manhattan and O.J. Simpson had just been arrested. With the summer vacation looming, the bank wasn't going to let a cash deal slip through its fingers. He was in business.

The Newark facility had proved a huge success. The more restaurants Takar could open, the more food he produced. Most of the production happened overnight and the delivery vans went out with the food from about 5 a.m. They invested in a computerised system that connected the production facility to every one of the restaurants. Every time a till rang up a sale of a chicken breast and fries, a salad, or a sandwich, the system registered the sale on the inventory back at base. Each night the computer calculated and printed out instructions on exactly how much food needed to be delivered to each restaurant, and when. Takar el Sayden loved that production facility and he took great pride from walking around it, watching all the food being prepared. The party they threw when they got to one hundred restaurants went on for three days. Then, because the vans were travelling to Manhattan from Newark, it made sense to open some restaurants along the way in New Jersey, and that success had prompted their expansion out into the Bronx, Queens and Brooklyn. Today, two hundred and fifty-two outlets – bigger in the region than KFC, Wendy's and Taco Bell and gaining fast on Subway, McD's and Burger King. Fifteen years of creating the American dream and now this damn stranger was screwing with his life.

He pulled into the car park at ten to nine and was soon at his desk in his modest office on the first floor. There were two green chairs for visitors and the walls were covered with framed food industry awards and pictures of Takar's family. He was nervously drinking his second cup of coffee when his secretary buzzed to say he had a visitor – 'A Mr Ali.'

'Send him up, please,' said Takar, noticing that his voice nearly cracked.

The door opened and Takar instantly recognised the same man who had appeared in his car the other day – the middle-eastern appearance, the thin black moustache and those pock marks on his face. He was carrying a large briefcase and he offered a polite smile but no handshake as he sat down. Takar was glad. He didn't want to shake hands with this man.

'Good morning, Takar,' said Ibrahim Fallah.

'Look, what the hell is this all about?' Takar whispered, spinning the rings on his fingers around in circles, one by one.

'Relax, my friend,' said Fallah.

'I'm not your friend,' Takar hissed through clenched teeth.

'True, Takar, true, but it is better that you do not become my enemy.'

Takar fell silent.

'Again, I assure you that no harm will come to you or your family, if you follow my instructions.'

Takar nodded slowly.

'Your business has been a great success and it is about to go from strength to strength. As I said, you will be rebranding your restaurants as BurgerFantastic.'

Takar flinched. He couldn't have thought of a worse name.

'A bank account has been opened in your name, using your passport, at the Bank of America branch at 1109 Wall Street.'

Fallah handed over four pieces of paper from his briefcase. One was a copy of the photograph page from his passport. *Jesus, how the hell had he got that*? The next two were copies of his home electricity and gas bills. *For chrissakes!* He felt the hairs standing up on the back of his neck. The fourth was a copy of a bank statement in his name. His eyes nearly popped out of his head when he saw that there was only one entry – a deposit, made two days ago, of twenty million dollars. What the hell was going on?

Fallah spoke again, quietly and calmly. 'There will be a bit of change to your daily routine, but in two years or so everything will return to normal. Remember, my superiors are simply conducting an experiment. They want to see how many burgers you can sell. The more you sell, the better things will go for you.'

Fallah held his gaze and Takar nodded again.

'And, we will make it easy for you because we are giving you as much money as you need to market your new brand of burgers. And you are to sell them cheaply, to help your sales. You can keep all the money that you take in.'

Fallah took another bound A4 document from the briefcase and pushed it across the desk.

'This is your marketing strategy. You are to visit the offices of Dynamic Communications at Broadway and West 43rd – Times Square. The contact details are on the back. Call them in advance. Ask for Victor Dezner or Katie Keller. The brief explains the launch of BurgerFantastic, where your outlets are, your pricing policy, low price deals, promotional offers, super-size deals – the whole lot. As you know, your target consumer wants good-quality produce served fast. You are simply continuing to target your usual market: office workers, parents who are too busy to cook a home meal, younger people looking for a tasty lunch. Tell the agency you want to launch in six weeks. They'll bitch and moan but tell them you have a two-year budget of a hundred million dollars and that if they can't help you, you're going straight to Saatchi & Saatchi. They'll do it.'

Takar nodded again and stayed silent.

'Pay them everything they need from your new account,' Fallah said. 'When it starts to run short, let me know. I'll be coming here to see you every week – same time.'

Christ, this is like a bad dream.

'The only other thing you've got to do,' Fallah said, 'is to continue to visit your production facility here, every night, as I know you do anyway. Every night, you must empty a bag of this powder into each vat of the sauce that goes on the burgers. Do it before the sauce is blended, to make sure it is mixed through.' He took a clear plastic bag of white powder from the briefcase and put it on the desk. 'If anyone asks, you can say it's a secret ingredient – just like McDonald's, eh?' Fallah raised an eyebrow and looked almost amused.

'Yeah – just like McDonald's,' said Takar tersely. *Allah, what is going on?*

'I will bring you these bags every week,' said Fallah. 'As soon as it is time to start. I assure you, it is harmless.' He pulled open the top of the bag, put his finger in and scooped out a thin line of powder. He ran his tongue along his finger and took the powder into his mouth. 'Try some,' he offered, holding the bag out.

Takar poked his finger in, crooked it around some of the powder and dropped it on to his tongue. It was tasteless.

'Every night, without fail, one bag in each vat of sauce.'

Takar nodded sullenly.

'And, in two years, I disappear, you never see me again and life goes back to normal.' Fallah opened the briefcase again. He slid a brown A4 envelope on to the desk.

'Go and meet the marketing consultants and I will see you here next week. Thank you for your time.'

Fallah stood and, as he went out the door, he paused, looked back at Takar and said, 'The weather here is much better than in Tripoli.'

Then he disappeared.

Takar turned the envelope over in his hands. He hesitated, then opened it and pulled out a set of black and white 8x6 photographs. The first three were of his girls, Farah and Jasmin, at a birthday party in a friend's garden. The next three were of his father, mother, sister and brother. They were sitting around a circular table, outside a restaurant, which he recognised. They were all laughing as his father blew out candles on a cake. It was his father's birthday yesterday. The umbrella over the table was up to protect the party from the rain.

'Bastard,' whispered Takar as a shiver accelerated down his spine.

16

HARRY'S BAR, MANHATTAN – 17 APRIL

'Two Millers please, Harry,' called Detective Michael Cabrini, as he hoisted himself onto a barstool beside John Wyse. It was just before 6 p.m. and after a hot, hard day, deskbound in the station, Cabrini's suggestion that they go for a beer had been a welcome one.

'It's okay, buddy, I just got one,' said Wyse, pointing to his almost full bottle.

'Nah, don't worry, bud, that won't take long.' Cabrini's constant habit of buying drinks for people who already had one was beginning to annoy Wyse.

'Hear you've got one of the Fenuccis talkin'?' said Cabrini.

'Yeah, I think we've got enough to go to the DA.' They were referring to a recent breakthrough Wyse had made on a drugs bust he'd been working on. 'How you doin' on the shootin' in that old factory?' asked Wyse in return.

'Brick wall, man,' said Cabrini with a shrug. 'Dead ends everywhere. Don't know where to look next.'

Wyse took a mouthful of beer. As far as he knew, Cabrini was lead detective on three unsolved murder cases that were starting to pile up on his desk. The other day he'd heard a couple of detectives talking about Cabrini losing his touch.

'Hey, man, you seen that good-lookin' chick again?' asked Cabrini, with a grin.

Wyse smiled. 'Sure have.'

'Where'd you go?'

'Took her for dinner at Emilia's.'

'Woohoo – way to go!'

'Yeah, the works. She looked stunning. You should see her dressed up.'

'So, what happened?' asked Cabrini.

'Well, we had a great meal. Massimo threw in some free champagne. We talked for about four hours. Her about the advertising business and her exciting clients. Me givin' her the old macho lines about "New York's Finest".'

'You old smoothie.'

'Yeah, it was real nice. She's only been in New York a few years – grew up in the UK somewhere.'

'So, your place or hers?'

'Neither.'

'No way!' Cabrini's face fell. He drained his bottle. Wyse hadn't finished his, but Cabrini was already looking for Harry for two more.

'No – it just didn't seem right to suggest anything. There's something special about this girl, buddy. I don't wanna mess it up by rushing things.'

'Hey, how's that cute redhead friend of hers? Askin' for me I hope?'

'Cindy? She wasn't mentioned. Don't think there's anything doing there for ya.'

Cabrini shrugged. 'So, when you seein' her again?'

'Don't know yet. She's busy on some project. Said not to call for a few days.'

Cabrini made a face. 'Just playin' hard to get, I'd say,' he suggested, almost finishing his second bottle in three gulps. 'Harry, two more please, when you're ready.'

'You might be right.' Wyse shrugged. 'Any event, I'm gonna call her, say Thursday, Friday.'

'If I was you,' said Cabrini, 'don't call for about a week. Give her a dose of her own medicine. She'll come runnin'.'

A pause as they both took a mouthful.

'Then again,' said Cabrini, 'who am I to be advising on women?'

'You hungry?' asked Wyse, clocking his friend's downcast look.

'Yeah, sure, thought you'd never ask.'

Wyse called for a couple of menus. Cabrini was slugging back his beer and Wyse had two on the counter in front of him, yet he felt under pressure to order another round to suit Cabrini. Mike had a heart of gold, but his personality gradually changed as his drinking got a hold of him. Wyse took a deep breath. 'Hey, Mike, don't take this the wrong way, but I'm startin' to think that maybe you're hittin' the booze a bit heavy.'

Cabrini's face reddened and his eyes narrowed.

'Aw, piss off, John. For gawd's sake, you sound like my ex-wife. Surely a guy can relax after a hard day's work?'

There was an embarrassed silence. Wyse hesitated; he wasn't sure what to say next.

'It's just, you know, Mike, you gotta be careful. I've heard it said in the station that maybe it's startin' to affect your work.'

'Aw, for fuck's sake, John, no way,' said Cabrini, jumping up. 'Who the fuck is sayin' that? I'll beat the crap outta them!'

'Hey, easy pal, sit down, take it easy.' Wyse put his arm around his friend's shoulder and eased him back onto the stool.

'For chrissakes, John,' said Cabrini, jabbing his thumb towards the other end of the bar. 'Look at them. Smith, Williams, Garcia – they're just the same. Jeez,' he sighed, 'ten years of listening to shit about drink from my wife and now *you* start. You know, if she hadn't gone on about it so much, I woulda drank less!'

Hmmm, thought Wyse. You can't argue with that kind of logic. 'Sorry, buddy, just tryin' to offer some advice.'

'Well, that kind of advice I can do without,' Cabrini shot back.

'And what about that time you fell asleep at that party in Queens, and I had to put you in a cab, Mr Preacher?' Wyse partially remembered that event all right, from a couple of years back, and still squirmed when he thought about it. He'd made sure it never happened again.

The two detectives sat silently facing Fox News on the TV, something about Syria. Wyse eventually broke the silence. 'How are things with Liz anyway?'

'Goddamn bitch,' snarled Cabrini. 'Out there in the house in New Jersey, breakin' my balls with maintenance payments and now she's threatenin' to stop me seeing the boys. It's not as if I get a chance to get out and see them much as it is.'

'What's happened?'

'Just shit. Collected them last week and took them to the Yankees game. Great day out, havin' a blast with the boys, then who do we meet in the car lot on the way out, only Graham Slater – remember him?'

Wyse nodded – Slater had been a popular detective who took early retirement.

'Turns out he lives out near Liz's place, so we arranged to stop for a coupla beers. Talk about old times, you know?'

Wyse could guess what was coming.

'So, we stop off, have a few beers, burgers and Cokes for the boys. Then when I drop them back, Liz turns into a raving monster. Sez I'm too drunk to be driving the boys around, the bitch. Wants to control me. So, she's shoutin', I start shoutin', the boys are cryin'. Next thing she's threatenin' me with barring orders. For chrissakes. You can't win.'

Wyse could picture the scene.

'And now *you* start.' Cabrini was reddening as he stood up again. 'I'm sick of all this. I'm goin' somewhere a man can have a beer in peace.' And he turned on his heel and banged out the door.

Wyse's shoulders dropped as he let out a deep breath. *Phew, hit a nerve there. Hopefully, he'll have calmed down by tomorrow.*

He ordered a spaghetti bolognese from Harry, took a swig of beer and looked back at the TV. The Defense Secretary was warning Russia that the US government would not stand by much longer if Russia continued to support the regime in Syria.

17

18 APRIL

'You're past it, Pops, don't flatter yourself,' said the waitress to herself, in the busy dining room of the Hay-Adams Hotel, Washington, four blocks from the White House, as she carefully topped up three glasses of claret. *Christ, if this blond guy touches my arm and winks at me one more time I'll smack him one.* But her instincts on maximising tips won out and she fluttered her eyelashes and said a flirty 'Thank you, gentlemen' as she turned away with a wiggle of her hips. Professor Alan G.F. Milton followed her curvy walk with an admiring gaze and then returned to business.

'So, Oscar, Anton, what do you think?'

Professor Oscar Kolsen and Dr Anton Cook had made flights earlier that day from Dallas and Toronto respectively. Professor Milton had reserved a corner table where they could chat discreetly. At the other end of the dining room, the elderly pianist faked enthusiasm in his rendition of 'The Girl from Ipanema'. The discussion hadn't been proceeding quite as smoothly as Milton had hoped.

'I'm not entirely sure, Alan,' said the Dallas professor, raising his crystal glass to take a sip of claret. 'It all looks a bit flimsy to me.'

'These weight loss findings after taking cephalosporin antibiotic,' added Dr Cook. 'Surely if someone has a bowel inflammation, the weight loss is down to being sick? Some patients naturally lose their appetite for weeks after being ill. And wouldn't people say that they have more energy, as they are recovering?'

'I don't doubt the veracity of the data,' said Professor Kolsen gravely. 'I'm sure we can trust the research results of these Japanese doctors. And yet . . .'

'Oh, one hundred per cent,' affirmed Milton, pushing his blond locks back off his forehead. 'Yamoura operate to the highest standards worldwide – they have their reputation to uphold you know.'

'Of course, of course,' Kolsen nodded.

'And really, they're not asking us to challenge the core findings of the research,' added Milton, a little anxious now. 'Just to add our opinion as to the possible positive effects of cephalosporin on general health. And they want us to confirm whether we feel the findings are as likely to hold true for Americans as for Asians.' Professor Milton paused, then added, 'They're very concerned, you know, not to use any data which hasn't been thoroughly challenged on every front.'

'Well, I suppose,' said Professor Kolsen, 'with suitable caveats.'

'And the fees are incredibly generous,' said Dr Cook.

'I'm comforted by the fact that they seem to be interested in new beneficial side effects of an established antibiotic,' continued Professor Kolsen. 'We're not being asked to promote a new drug and if any doctor wants to prescribe cephalosporin because he thinks it has some new benefit, then that's "off label" prescribing. It's each doctor's decision and no comeback to us. It sure as hell won't help with all this resistance to antibiotics that's building up, though.'

There was a tense pause for thought. Professor Milton knew that the next few seconds were vital. The pianist moved from Ipanema to Copacabana.

'Well, all right then, let's have a go,' said Kolsen.

'I agree,' said Dr Cook. 'Yamoura have been great friends to us in the past and I trust them implicitly. The deadline's tight, though.'

'Very tight,' agreed Professor Kolsen.

'Terrific. Well, let's get started tomorrow then, gentlemen,' said Professor Milton. 'We'll formally review their data. Anton can address the weight loss findings. I'll look at the overall beneficial effects on health, energy gain and so forth.'

'And I'll give an opinion that the findings should hold true for westerners,' said Kolsen.

'Excellent, gentlemen. Can you let me have your papers in, say, three weeks max?'

Kolsen and Cook nodded their agreement. All three raised their glasses and clinked them together over the centrepiece candle.

'To Yamoura Pharmaceuticals,' said Professor Milton, as the pianist slid into 'Ain't Misbehavin''.

'To Yamoura Pharmaceuticals,' his esteemed colleagues replied.

*

Ibrahim Fallah smiled to himself as he killed the engine of his five-year-old brown Nissan Versa. It had to be the best possible car for going unnoticed. Discretion was everything. He was parked in the rear yard of the New York Metropolitan Library on Fifth Avenue, close to the Metropolitan Museum of Art. He turned the key in the back door and went into the office that came with his job as chief librarian. He changed out of a loose-fitting cream suit and back into his more familiar black jacket and pants and put on his turban.

The contacts over the years from his old comrades in al-Qaeda had been most welcome and he had been glad to assist in this new battle, the fatwa against the Americans. He had been the contact man in New York for Mohammed Atta, one of the 9/11 hijackers, and had recommended that the hijackers of Flight 93 should stay at an airport hotel the night before the hijackings, in case of any traffic delays that morning on the New Jersey Turnpike. And, now, he found himself energised by these new instructions from Afghanistan. Nothing should be rushed. No chances taken. Absolute secrecy would be the key to success.

As he stepped into the public library, he noticed the large sign hanging on chains over the centre of the room ... *Silence Please.* His smile widened into a grin.

*

PARAMOUNT BUILDING, TIMES SQUARE – 20 APRIL

Victor Dezner of Dynamic Communications was slowly pushing a cashew nut around the edge of his writing pad with the manicured nail of his right index finger. There was silence in the boardroom.

The tense silence continued as Katie, Mark, Arlene and Anna watched the nut successfully take a tight ninety-degree turn around the top corner of the pad. Eventually, Victor Dezner looked up.

'We can do it, guys – we just have to.'

'I feel like I've put us under such pressure,' said Katie.

'You did the right thing, honey. There was no way we could let a new client with a hundred million dollar budget walk down the street to Saatchi's.'

'The funny thing is,' said Mark, while he topped up his glass, 'not only do the Yamoura Pharmaceuticals and the restaurant jobs have the same launch dates, but there's a lot of overlap on the activities side of their marketing plans.'

'How so?' asked Victor.

'Well, not only do both products seem to be targeting the same consumer sectors, there's even a strong locational overlap for where they want to focus branding activity. It looks like we're gonna be creating clusters where lotsa people are buying SuperVerve tablets – and burgers!'

'So, you can do a bit of cut and paste from the Yamoura plan to impress this new guy with your speed,' said Katie teasingly. They all laughed.

'On the ground,' Mark continued, 'we're gonna have huge pressure on billboard locations and neon advertising. What's the story with print media, Arlene?'

'We're in reasonable shape,' she replied. The ambitious young professional was responsible for advance buying of advertising space. One of the cornerstones of the agency's success had been taking a ballsy approach to advance media buying in the most popular newspapers and magazines.

'It's gonna be real tough for full-colour advertising at this short notice, but I'm gonna pull every trick in the book. And all the online advertising can be done quick enough.'

Arlene's colleagues were convinced. She had a hard-earned reputation for always delivering the goods.

Victor Dezner turned to face Anna Milani. 'Anna, how are we on the celeb for SuperVerve?'

'Aye, we're okay. It's crazy notice but we've got a budget that makes a lot of problems, like, disappear. I've talked to some of the leading agents – I'm thinking a sports star. I think you're going to be happy. I'll let you know.'

'Sounds good. What about product placement?'

'Well, I'm talkin' turkey with the networks about some subtle brand integration in primetime slots. We're looking at about four hundred K for visibility in two episodes of a top five ranked show. And we're at about three-fifty K for a three-second visibility on a shelf in a judge's dressing room in one of the talent shows. I'll get a deal.'

'Nice one, Anna,' said Katie, 'can't wait to hear more.'

'And,' Arlene chipped in, 'the medical info seminars for the doctors are pretty routine at this stage. We'll throw big money at the production and staging and include some really valuable giveaways.'

'Okay, ladies, thanks,' said Victor, feeling better by the minute. 'With a little luck, I think we can pull off the BurgerFantastic launch too. The storefront signage was a challenge for us, but I've found a company who can do it pronto. So that's taking shape.'

'All right, team,' said Katie, wrapping up. 'We've put our heads on the block, and it's time to deliver. Let's pull the ideas into two smoking hot presentations and let's go wow some clients.'

18

20 APRIL – 6 P.M.

Wyse and Cabrini pulled up outside the Fifth Precinct station.

'What time you knockin off, John?' said Cabrini.

'Gonna try and get away a bit early. I'm seeing that girl again. Anna. Remember the two girls we met at Harry's?'

'Sure. Way to go, man. Give her one for me, won't ya?'

'Huh. It's taken ages to get her out on another date,' said Wyse, starting to open the door.

'Just a sec, John,' said Cabrini, putting a hand on his arm.

'Sure,' said Wyse, a bit puzzled. There had been a tension between them since he'd challenged his partner over his drinking.

'Eh, I've been thinking about what you said the other night. About me drinking too much, and all that.'

'Okay.'

'And first I want to apologise to you. I shouldn't have reacted like that. Guess I was a bit wound up. I know you've got my back.'

'Always, Mike,' said Wyse.

'Well, I want you to know that I appreciate you saying those things. It probably wasn't easy. And you're right. I *was* drinking too much. So I'm gonna dial it back, new regime, get a bit healthier.'

'Hey, glad to hear it, man. Way to go.'

'Bring it in, man.' Cabrini leaned over, and they did the quick male hug with the backslapping.

Cabrini's new regime didn't quite last a week.

*

20 APRIL – THAT NIGHT

'You're what?' said Wyse, laughing.

'Jiggered!' Anna replied, laughing too. 'Sorry, it's an expression from back home. Means tired, exhausted. I've never seen it so busy at work.'

John and Anna were having dinner at an organic restaurant in midtown. Her choice. Turned out she was vegetarian. It had taken three calls over two weeks to get her back out on a date. It seemed like she kept trying to put him off, and he'd very nearly given up. But he needn't have worried because once again there was that strong, easy connection and the conversation was flowing. Like all New Yorkers, they'd chatted about the attempted truck bombing, but Wyse wasn't mentioning his role in the drama. They'd had all the superficial chat on that long first date, but now there were a few layers peeling off.

'Yeah, I think about Adam every day,' she said, her eyes moist. 'He was just so gorgeous. So brave. He never complained.' She was telling him about the death of her younger brother from leukaemia. 'Just eight he was.

'I think it's one of the reasons our family moved to New York,' she went on. 'You know, like, fresh start and all that. And I'd just finished my marketing degree, so it seemed like a big opportunity.'

Wyse had been telling her about his family too. 'So, it was definitely Dad's influence that got me interested in being a detective, but the music all came from Mom's side.' He had played down his prowess as a guitarist.

'I'd love to come and see you play sometime. When's the next gig?'

'Uh, they're sporadic. I'm not in a band any more, just didn't have the time for it. But every now and then I hook up with them. Or sometimes I sit in on a blues/jazz session. Keeps me in practice.'

As the conversation deepened, Wyse found himself mesmerised by Anna. She was a natural beauty, but seemed unconscious of it. She was intelligent and down to earth and she made him laugh. Then, inevitably, the conversation got to previous relationships.

'There was a couple of guys back home, but nothing special,' she said. But she managed to ease a bit more out of him about Lisa than he expected.

'Yeah, I guess it was serious all right,' he said. 'She moved in with me and she was talkin' about getting engaged and stuff. Everyone seemed to assume we were going to get married. I guess I did too, for a while. Anyway, I just wasn't ready for it. I had this feeling that I wanted to do a whole lot more with my life. Problem was, I wasn't sure what.'

Anna nodded.

'Anyway, it took an earthquake to finish it off.'

Anna's eyebrows arched.

'Yeah, the earthquake in Haiti happened. The Force was sending down teams to help out, and I wanted to go for a year. Really do something useful, you know? So, big row. She moves out and, six months later, she's engaged to another teacher at the school. Lucky, cos now I've met you.'

Anna laughed and took his hand. Wyse returned her gaze then broke away to take a sip of wine.

'But the irony of it all was,' he continued, 'I never even went in the end. One minute I thought I was going, next thing my boss, Connolly, blows a gasket and won't let me. Said I was showing too much intuition for catching bad guys here. At least that was encouraging.' He shrugged.

'I actually thought hard about quitting,' he said. 'This is gonna sound soppy, you know, but . . .'

'Go on,' she encouraged.

'Okay, so I was walking down Park Avenue, thinking maybe I

should do a job where you don't get the worst parts of humanity thrown at you every day.'

'Yeah?'

'And there's this nice old church, near the top, and as I'm goin' past, I hear this singing. A choir. So, I go in and sit down. Then this priest gives a sermon, all about compassion. Caring more for others. Doing your best to help. That kinda stuff.'

'I hear ya.'

'Something about it hit home. So, right there, I decided to stick with the police and give it my best.'

'Aaah, that's nice.' Anna squeezed his hand.

'Thanks.' Wyse smiled. 'So that left just me and Glenda.'

'Eh, who?'

'Glenda. Tall, leggy blonde. Stays in my apartment a lot.'

Anna's face fell. Where was this going?

Wyse took pity. 'Just kidding. Glenda's a dog. A lurcher. Kinda like a greyhound. Leggy blonde.'

'Aaah.' Anna smiled. 'I love dogs. But, where'd you get the name Glenda?'

'Old man in our block, who owned her, told me it was because she was kinda ladylike. It fits. You'll know what I mean when you meet her. When he died she was being sent to the pound so I took her in. A few of the neighbours help to look after her, but she sleeps most nights with me.'

'Glenda!' Anna laughed. 'You had me jealous there for a minute. I'm looking forward to meeting her.'

'She's a character all right. Butter wouldn't melt in her mouth, but she's despatched every cat that dared to walk through the yard beside the apartment block. Trained killer, doesn't bark or give them a chance. Hits fifty miles an hour once a day and sleeps for the rest of it.'

Anna raised her glass and Wyse clinked it.

'To Glenda,' she said.

'To Glenda,' he replied. 'The world's first energy-saving dog.'

19

SAITON, NEAR TOKYO – 4 MAY

'Congratulations, gentlemen,' said the thin-faced Dr Naga as he raised a glass of premium Courvoisier in the direction of his fellow Chess Club members. All present raised their glasses. 'To the success of the Plan,' said Dr Naga.

'To the success of the Plan,' they chimed and each savoured the warm glow of the brandy as it slid down their throats.

'We are underway, gentlemen. This is a great day,' said Tsan Yohoto. 'Here's to the successful completion of the project.'

'The first draft of the marketing plan for the SuperVerve tablets has come in from Dynamic Communications in New York,' said Kazuhiro Saito, handing around printouts of the report. 'I have made a few small changes, but it is very much along the expected lines.'

'And the great Professor Milton has the two experts from Dallas and Toronto on board,' added Tsan Yohoto.

Lumo Kinotoa nodded. 'Excellent. Also, the Yamoura production director has organised that the SuperVerve tablets are twice the labelled strength – he thinks that it's to keep import taxes down on the African side, and won't question it.'

Tsan Yohoto removed his wire-rimmed spectacles and began

polishing the lenses – usually a signal that he had said his piece and was clearing space for others.

'And so, to be clear,' said Kazuhiro Saito, 'what exactly remains to be done now – and when is our launch date?'

'Well,' said Dr Naga, 'Kazuhiro, Tsan, I believe you plan to visit Dynamic again to sign off on the marketing plan?'

'Correct,' said Kazuhiro Saito, 'and in particular I want to give them instructions on some hot spots for the outdoor advertising, where we want to create clusters of consumption. I have an email from Victor Dezner at Dynamic. He's saying they can definitely make our launch date and he's asking if we are available for dinner on the evening of their presentation to us.'

Tsan Yohoto and Dr Naga both smiled. Their many years of experience in dealing with the west had told them that the mighty dollar could move mountains when it came to meeting deadlines.

Dr Naga winked. 'A celebratory dinner. Sounds nice. Have a nice glass of wine, for me.' He glanced around the table. 'So, with everything proceeding according to plan, we should be launching to the public in, say, four weeks?' he asked with an upturned eyebrow. 'That would make it the beginning of the month?'

'The first of June it is,' said Tsan Yohoto firmly. 'And then we sit back and watch the Americans dig their own graves.'

20

NEWARK – 4 MAY

'I'm sorry, Takar, but this was never the plan.' Milly Davis was distraught and frustrated.

'I'm sorry too, Milly, but please just give it a try,' pleaded Takar.

'No way, I'm out. If I wanted to run a fast food burger joint, there's a whole lotta places I can work.'

'But we're going to keep the quality up, Milly; we're just going to add in beef burgers. And we've got to sell much bigger volumes if we're gonna keep this business growing.'

'It's selling out, Takar,' said Milly, wiping away a tear. 'I wish you luck, but I won't be part of it.'

Takar el Sayden was not a happy man. That morning he had called a meeting of his five hundred or so staff at manager grade at the Newark Clarion Hotel and, with the assistance of Arlene Thomas from Dynamic Communications, had made a PowerPoint presentation on the rebranding of his restaurant chain to BurgerFantastic. The official line to staff was that they would be undertaking a big expansion programme. The plan was to increase their market share and the number of restaurants to four hundred within two years. This would create a whole new level of Area and Regional Managers and the best performing restaurant managers would be promoted to that grade. Then Arlene Thomas took over and went through a mini version of the plan that Dynamic Communications had presented to Takar a few days earlier.

'Guys, this is our new storefront and logo,' said Arlene as a selection of computer-generated images of newly branded BurgerFantastic outlets appeared on the screen. There would be "supersize me" offers and toy giveaways. 'Best of all,' said Arlene, 'we're going to launch with a "buy one, get one free" deal.'

Most of the managers were thinking the same thing. How the hell is Takar going to make money outta this?

Takar took over again for the finish. He knew that he had to appear confident in front of the sea of faces before him.

'Guys, I know you will all support me in this. I rely on you folk to keep up the standards in your own restaurants. This is a big strategic move; it opens up massive opportunities for all of us. The most important thing is that, while all your restaurants are going to be way busier, all you managers stay on your same percentage cut of turnover. So, you're all going to be much better off.'

This brought an enthusiastic ripple of reaction from his audience.

'So, the more you can sell, the more you're gonna make.' A spontaneous round of applause. 'So, let's go kick McDonald's ass.'

A cheer.

'Let's kick Burger King's ass.'

A louder cheer.

'Let's knock Wendy's and KFC outta the park!'

An even louder cheer. They were beginning to enjoy this.

'Let's go put BurgerFantastic all over the Big Apple,' finished Takar el Sayden with reasonably convincing passion.

There was a roar of approval, and a standing ovation from the managers.

*

Takar el Sayden sighed as he sat back in his chair in the quiet of his office later that day. Milly had been the first of four of his longest-serving managers to resign that day. They had joined up with him because of their interest in freshly cooked, wholesome food and had seen his move today as selling out, joining the burger bandwagon. He couldn't blame them.

Well, at least the rest of them seemed happy enough, in the end. *But what about me?*

Takar el Sayden absentmindedly rotated the gold rings on his left hand in turn. These al-Qaeda guys were messing with his business. Messing with his life. The contractors had already started fitting the new red and yellow BurgerFantastic plastic signs to his storefronts. And, tomorrow morning, that motherfucker was due to come back with his bags of powder. Takar slammed his fist down hard on a paper clip on the desk.

Goddamn it. Where would this nightmare end?

★

THAT EVENING

'Hey, John.'

'Oh, hey, Anna.' John Wyse was on the couch in his neat two-bed apartment on Eldridge Street, picking out some blues chords. He was on the eighth floor of a red-brick 1970s block. Most of the detectives from the Fifth lived on Staten or in Brooklyn, but Wyse felt it was worth the extra rent to be closer to the action. His heart skipped a beat when he heard Anna's voice. 'Didn't expect to hear from you for a while. Everything okay?'

'Yeah, sure, John, but I am, like, buried in work. Never been busier. I'm still at the damn office.'

'Wow, sorry to hear that,' said Wyse, glancing at his watch. *Jeez, 10 p.m.*

'Nah, it's okay, just suffering from sleep deprivation and cabin fever.'

'You're jiggered then, I guess?'

She laughed.

'We're working on this huge presentation to these Japanese clients. Only five days to go – so it's manic. It's big stuff though, I'm enjoying it.'

'So, any chance I can take you out and offer a distraction?'

'Well, I'd love to, John, but not till after this presentation's done. Actually, that's why I'm calling.'

'Oh?'

'Yeah – you see, the company's taking these clients out to dinner, night of the presentation. And I've been asked along. I guess we're hoping we'll be celebrating winning the contract.'

'Great.'

'Yeah, it is. It's the two partners, plus my boss, Mark, and just one other associate, so it's kind of a big deal to be asked.' She sounded excited.

'Wow, that's great.'

'Yeah, thanks. Anyway, we've been asked to bring along our partner, or whatever. So, I'd love if you'd come along with me?'

'Yeah, I'd love to.' John's heart fluttered. 'When is it?'

'The tenth. Thursday evening. Drinks at seven. Dinner at eight. Posh place called Le Cirque.'

'Cool – count me in.'

'That's great. Hey –'

'Yep?'

'You got a good suit?'

'Yeah, sure,' he said.

'How good?'

''Bout as good as my Japanese. And my karaoke.'

Anna laughed.

'But don't worry, I'll rise to the occasion.'

A broad smile spread across John's face as he picked up his guitar again.

'You hear that, Glenda,' he said. 'Hot date.'

Glenda cocked an ear, looked at him with one half-open eye, grunted and returned to sleep.

21

DYNAMIC COMMUNICATIONS, TIMES SQUARE – 10 MAY

These beautiful women – but so tall! thought Kazuhiro Saito, the Chess Club's marketing strategist, as he thanked a six-foot blonde in a short white skirt and very tight white T-shirt, who was leaning over to pour his coffee.

'You're welcome.' Sonya smiled as she straightened up. 'I hope you have a great visit with us today.'

Sometimes Saito wondered if it was a deliberate policy to parade sexy women at their presentations as a distraction. He refocused on the PowerPoint presentation. Victor Dezner was in full flow.

'Gentlemen, thank you for this opportunity to share our vision for SuperVerve with you today.' The visitors nodded an acknowledgement as Katie handed out silver folders with the Dynamic Communications and SuperVerve logos on the cover. Victor continued.

'Inside your folder is an executive summary of today's presentation. At the back of the report is a ten-page spreadsheet, itemising expenditure, broken down into the main activities.' The visitors nodded respectfully.

Victor went on, 'The stakeholders we will be educating are the doctors and the public. Winning the physicians' minds is absolutely the key to winning market share.'

'Agreed,' Saito said. He'd given them the SuperVerve name and about half of what they wanted in the plan. *Still, better let them add their bits.*

'We believe that this plan is a sharply focused, high impact campaign, designed to deliver branding recognition and key positioning.'

Give me strength, thought Saito. Another hour of buzz words and he'd go mad. Still, they were the best in the business and had produced results before. He leaned back in his seat as the campaign was rolled out.

Sensing the tension, Katie Keller decided to move things along. 'Let's skip forward to our flowchart slide,' she said. 'This really pulls together all the activities and timelines on one page,' she said, moving swiftly through the slides.

She clicked on the mouse, and kept clicking.

'Activity Four – TV advertising – we've made the storyboards for TV, radio and printed media advertising. We know you're gonna love it. Production can start immediately – studio time is booked. We can be "on air" in ten days.

'Activity Five – Outdoor Advertising. All billboard and neon sites are confirmed bookings. Ready to go in ten days when the artwork's finished.

'Activity Six – PR: all the press releases for the medical journals, newspapers and magazines have been drafted. We're using plenty of good quotes from Professor Milton's group for the medical publications.

'Activity Seven – Celebrity Endorsement. Anna?'

'Yes,' said Anna Milani. 'I'm glad to say that I'm in serious negotiations with Christopher White's agent.'

Kazuhiro Saito raised a quizzical eyebrow.

'He's exactly what we need,' continued Anna. 'Christopher White is this year's leading scorer for our basketball team, the New York Knicks. He's a hero; a legend. Nice clean image. Good-looking guy. Speaks well. Turns out he had some stomach problems a few months ago and for the right money he might be more than happy to talk about SuperVerve and how it got him back shooting baskets.'

'Nice one, Anna,' said Mark.

'Absolutely,' said Victor.

'Well,' said Anna, 'I think he'll give us a lotta bang for our two million bucks.'

'Wowee, that's a lotta stomach problems!' said Mark and everyone laughed on cue.

Anna continued, 'I'll keep you in the loop. And I've firmed up terms for product placement on a couple of network TV series, and some reality TV options – perfect for our demographic. I've also got a great panel of social media influencers lined up.'

Katie smiled. 'Okay, thanks, Anna, great work. Finally, Activity Eight.'

Arlene Thomas took over. 'Interaction with the public. We'll be rolling out a comprehensive campaign of patient information sessions at doctors' clinics and hospitals over the next year. We'll get some good convincing patients involved to talk about the great changes in their life since taking SuperVerve. Then we've got a big educational conference for the doctors. It's a lunchtime event at a top Manhattan hotel, hosted by Professor Milton, Professor Kolsen and Dr Cook. There'll be lots of information, excellent food and wine and some real good gifts for attendees.'

Victor Dezner turned to face Kazuhiro Saito and Tsan Yohoto, square on.

'Gentlemen, it has been a great pleasure working with Yamoura in designing this campaign. We believe it's a winner. Absolutely. It's going to create a buzz for SuperVerve like no other. We're absolutely ready to launch. Are you?'

Kazuhiro Saito couldn't help himself. 'Absolutely.'

*

LE CIRQUE RESTAURANT, EAST 58TH STREET – THAT EVENING

John Wyse made sure he was early. He jumped out of a cab outside the Beacon Court development at 6.45 p.m. Anna had told him that the restaurant was off the central courtyard. He spotted his reflection in the glazed archway and stopped to straighten his tie, for the umpteenth time. *Yeah, not too shabby, John.* He'd decided to buy a new suit. Navy, with a faint pinstripe. The salesman had easily convinced him to set it off with a new white shirt and a plain blue tie. Silver cufflinks and polished shoes completed the picture. He hoped Anna would be impressed. He knew how nervous she was about this big client. *I wonder if they got the deal?*

His eyes widened when he walked into the spectacular glass and steel bar area. They widened even more when he spotted Anna striding towards him, looking like a supermodel. *Wow!*

'John, hi, John.' She looked like she was about to explode with happiness and good news. She threw her arms around him. 'We got the deal, we won the contract!' she almost squealed in his ear, as she squeezed him tighter. He could smell the champagne on her breath.

'Brilliant! Congratulations.'

'Wow, and check you, Mr Businessman!' she said, stepping back and looking him up and down. 'I'm impressed. You look fantastic.'

'Thanks, you too.'

'C'mon,' she said, taking his hand, 'I'll introduce you to the guys. The Yamoura guys will be here soon.' She led him over to the famous levitating glass bar, where the group from Dynamic Communications was standing around the end of the counter.

'Victor, Katie,' Anna addressed the partners first, 'this is John Wyse.' Wyse shook hands and smiled at Katie, her husband Trevor, and Victor Dezner (who had decided not to bring his husband – just in case the clients weren't impressed).

'Pleased to meet you, John,' said Mark Reynolds, and he introduced his girlfriend, and Arlene Thomas and her boyfriend.

'Shhh, here they are,' said Victor Dezner, spotting their Japanese guests in dark suits, coming through the revolving door. 'Discretion for the moment.'

John Wyse spotted Yohoto and Saito; one small and thin, the other quite fat. A picture of Laurel and Hardy flashed through his mind.

After another round of introductions, Tsan Yohoto and Kazuhiro Saito were handed glasses of champagne.

'Formal celebrations upstairs,' said Victor Dezner, as everyone clinked glasses.

★

'Ladies and gentlemen.'

In the private dining room on the mezzanine level, Victor Dezner had stood up to make the after-dinner speech. Katie Keller had spoken about the importance of *celebrating with friends*, before the tuna takaki starter. Over the lobster poached with lime and celery purée, Mark Reynolds had got in a good line about how Dynamic saw Yamoura Pharmaceuticals as *partners* rather than *clients*.

Victor Dezner finished by proposing a toast and everyone got to their feet.

'To our great clients and friends, Yamoura Pharmaceuticals. Thank you for trusting us with your business. To Tsan and Kazuhiro – thank you for your friendship. And, finally, to Yamoura Pharmaceuticals, Dynamic Communications and the success of SuperVerve.' Everyone smiled and clinked glasses daintily.

'To SuperVerve,' said John Wyse, raising his glass to Anna.

'And,' Victor called, over the buzz of conversation, 'to make sure everyone gets to meet everyone, for the coffees, I suggest that all the men from Dynamic move a place to the right.' There was a cheer, and laughter, as the women sat down again.

John Wyse moved to the other side of Anna and found himself sitting with Tsan Yohoto on his right.

'Mr Yohoto,' he said, as the waitress filled their cups, 'what a lovely dinner.'

'Oh, yes, John, superb. And call me Tsan, please,' he said smiling, and making strong eye contact.

'Of course. Tsan.'

They both laughed, then Tsan Yohoto leaned towards him, put his hand on Wyse's arm and lowered his voice.

'You must surely be the luckiest man in New York, to be dating the beautiful Anna,' he said, nodding discreetly in Anna's direction. Wyse noticed that Tsan Yohoto's intense brown eyes kept constant contact with his own.

'Won't argue with you there,' said Wyse, feeling proud, 'she's absolutely gorgeous.'

'And very good at her work, too,' added Yohoto. 'We have been most impressed with her contributions to our marketing plan.'

'I have no doubt, Tsan.' *Must remember to tell Anna that.* 'I wish you great success with your new launch.'

'Thank you. And what line of business are you in, yourself?' asked Yohoto.

'I'm a detective, Tsan. NYPD, based outta the Fifth Precinct. That's downtown, it's –'

He wasn't able to finish, as Tsan Yohoto started spluttering and coughing into his napkin.

'Are you okay, Tsan?'

A few of the other guests had noticed the commotion, but Tsan soon caught his breath again.

'Yes, yes, thank you, sorry, coffee went down the wrong way.'

'Can I get you some water or something?'

'No, no, I'm fine thank you. It's okay. We should be getting back to the hotel. Tomorrow we fly home, and Dynamic have a lot of important work to do.' Tsan Yohoto cleared his throat and stood. Kazuhiro Saito followed his lead.

'Victor, Katie,' said Yohoto, 'everyone, you have been magnificent hosts. Thank you for your hospitality. But, unfortunately, we have an early start in the morning.'

Everyone around the table stood up and the goodbyes commenced.

'John, thank you, a pleasure meeting you,' said Tsan Yohoto, offering his hand.

'My pleasure, Tsan,' said Wyse, firmly shaking his hand. 'Please let me know if I can ever be of help.' And he handed over his card, with its gold NYPD shield embossed on the side.

'Thank you, so much . . . Detective Wyse,' said Tsan Yohoto, looking at the card. 'I will.'

Wyse noticed that Yohoto wasn't making eye contact any more. Almost subconsciously, it struck him as odd. It was one of the first things he was trained to look for, when interviewing a witness or suspect, a sudden change in the pattern of eye contact. It usually meant that the interviewee was uneasy, or had switched away from the truth. *Bit unusual, but probably means nothing. Maybe he's embarrassed about choking on the coffee.*

Everyone went back downstairs, and after the Japanese guests had been ushered into their limousine, Victor Dezner suggested a last celebratory drink in the bar.

*

'I'm so sorry, John, but I'm exhausted, and I've just got to be back in the office by 7 a.m.'

John and Anna were holding hands as they shared a cab uptown. He'd suggested that they stop off at his apartment.

'Sure, honey, I understand.' But he was disappointed.

'You were fantastic tonight. Thank you so much. You really did me proud. They were all saying how nice you are.'

'Oh, well, I aim to please,' he said, tickling her wrist with his finger.

'Well, you were great. How did you get on with Tsan Yohoto? I couldn't believe it when you ended up next to him!'

'Oh, nothing much, wasn't much time. Bit of a strange fish

really. At first he was all, you know, touchy-feely, best buddies. Then I told him I was a detective and he was like a turtle disappearing into its shell.'

Anna laughed. 'Maybe he has a few unpaid parking tickets?'

'Huh.' Wyse smiled. 'I dunno. Just got a funny feeling about him, not quite sure what it is, bit shifty or something. But he did say how impressed they were with you at your presentation.'

'Really?' Anna's eyes lit up. 'Wow, that's awesome!'

They fell silent again as the cab made another two blocks. Wyse's instincts about Tsan Yohoto gnawed away at him. Something didn't seem quite right. Maybe he was after Anna? *I'll have to keep an eye on him.*

'You know,' Wyse said, 'I heard someone say that they have about fifty thousand employees, all over the world?'

'Yeah – thirty-six countries, apparently.'

'And Tsan Yohoto runs all that? From Tokyo?'

'Yessir! He's the Bill Gates of the pharmaceutical world.'

'Isn't he kinda old to be running a big corporation like that?'

'Suppose so, but they work much later in the east. There's a Chinese guy, runs Hutchison, one of the biggest companies in the world, and he's eighty-nine. Anyway, Yohoto is retiring in a couple of years.'

'Isn't it strange that a guy running a company like Yamoura would be so involved in the detail of one product launch?'

'Never thought of that. I guess some bosses are real, like, hands on. Anyway, the amount of money they're gonna be pumping through Dynamic, he can have as much detail as he wants.'

Wyse grinned. 'So long as he's not lookin' to get too close to you.'

Anna laughed and punched his shoulder. 'No chance, detective. Okay, this is my stop.' The cab had pulled up outside her block. 'Thanks again, John,' she said, pecking him on the cheek, 'you really were brilliant.'

'My pleasure.'

'And you won a prize,' she said, handing him one of the two Le Cirque presentation boxes of chocolates.

'Even better.' He blew her a kiss.

'Night, John, I'll call you, soon as I get a chance.' She blew him one back.

Wyse sat back in his seat. *Well done, John, good job. That went well. Feeling pretty good. Warming up nicely.* Finally getting to open his top button and loosen his tie felt good too.

22

MANHATTAN – 17 MAY

Ricky Morgan jumped out of a cab outside Fitzpatricks Hotel on Lexington and signed an autograph for the doorman on the way in. His agent had set up a meeting with some advertising woman. Thirty minutes later and the meeting wasn't going well for Anna Milani, who was upping the money and the charm.

'I'm sorry, miss, but I'm not gonna advertise eatin' burgers. It's not the right message. The young kids need to be eatin' less of those, not more.'

'But as part of a balanced diet, Ricky, they're perfectly healthy,' countered Anna. *Shit. This isn't going as easily as I hoped.*

'Let's take a time-out here, guys,' said Ricky's agent, Max Sherry. 'Anna, would you mind giving us a few minutes?'

'Sure, no problem. I'll grab another coffee in the lounge.'

As soon as Anna left the room, Sherry got stuck into his client.

'Ricky, are you freakin' losin' it? She's at one and a half mill and you're comin' over all preachy! There's more money in her, let's not lose this.'

'Don't wanna do it, Max. It's not the money. I'm a footballer. I'm supposed to be some kinda role model for kids Why don't you get me something better to endorse?'

'Ricky, what if you get injured? You'll be on the scrapheap. You can't afford to turn down opportunities like this.'

'It's not for me, Max,' said Ricky, standing and making for the door. 'That lady's nice. Tell her it's nothin' personal, but I don't like her product. I'm going to visit my mom.'

Sherry found Anna in the lounge and broke the bad news. 'I'll work on him, Anna. Give me a week or so.'

*

TOKYO – 17 MAY

The gentle scent of a lilac bush enveloped the wooden bench in the beautifully maintained gardens of the Nashima nursing home. Saina Yohoto closed her eyes, inhaled deeply and let the relaxing fragrance fill her senses. It was late afternoon. Tsan Yohoto and his mother Saina always chose this bench for their chats during Tsan's visits, even though her tiny feet could barely touch the ground after Tsan helped her onto the seat. His routine was to visit his mother almost every day, on the way home from the Yamoura headquarters. He missed their chats when he was away on business trips and so he made certain to call her daily when abroad. He loved his mother more than anything in the world. They had been through such horrors together in Hiroshima and had survived. He had never even contemplated maintaining a relationship with a woman. That would distract him from his devotion to his mother. And any children might inherit his susceptibility to leukaemia. Most importantly, a woman in his life would distract his attention away from executing his revenge on the Yankees.

'Tsan, my beautiful son,' said Saina as she gently stroked the arrow-shaped scar below his temple. 'Tell me, how are your tests?' She was referring to the regular tests they both had carried out to monitor any growth in cancerous cells.

'All good, Mother, thank you, no problems.'

Saina Yohoto was not so sure. 'I think you have lost a little weight. Are you eating well and getting enough rest?'

'Yes, Mother, thank you, I'm fine.' Tsan Yohoto was lying. He had known for over a year that the number of cancerous cells in his body was increasing exponentially. Leukaemia was going to kill him, and probably not too long into his retirement.

'And how is your flying? Have you been anywhere nice?'

'Yes, Mother, mostly along the coast and out to the islands. Perhaps you would like to come up with me for another trip some day?'

'Yes, I would like that, Tsan. Someday soon, when I am feeling strong.'

'Well, in another couple of years I will retire and we will be able to spend much more time together.'

'That will be nice, Tsan,' she said, still stroking her son's scar, 'but please take care of your health. I am a little worried. Sometimes I think that perhaps you do not want to trouble your mother with all that is inside your head?'

'Please don't worry, my beloved mother,' said Tsan, taking her hand. 'Everything is perfectly normal.'

⋆

In her tiny kitchen in the Bronx, Ricky Morgan's mother was breaking the bad news to her shocked son.

'I didn't want to tell you and upset you. It's some kinda myeloma they call it. Blood disease. The doctors are sayin' I need stem cell treatments. Quickly. But that costs a fortune and I haven't kept up the insurance since your father hightailed it outta here.'

Ricky hugged his mother tight. 'Don't you worry, Mom. I'm gonna make sure that you get the very best of everything.'

⋆

Anna was at her desk in Dynamic Communications where a long day at work was turning into another long evening. She was under pressure to tie up a second celebrity in case Ricky Morgan couldn't be talked round, but she was tired and her mind kept drifting. She found her thoughts turning to John, and she didn't really want to stop them. Thinking about him gave her a lovely warm feeling, and a tingle of excitement. She had been so proud of him at the dinner at Le Cirque. She was looking forward to seeing him again. She yawned and shook her head to clear the daydream. *C'mon Anna, back to work.* She was trawling through the player lists of top-flight NFL clubs when she got the call.

'Anna? Max Sherry. I talked him round. Two mill, we're in business.'

Anna's pulse quickened but she told herself to keep her cool.

'Let's just go over the details of the deal again to make sure everything's clear.'

Five minutes later, it was all agreed.

'Thanks, Max. I'll email you the contracts within an hour. Great doing business with you.' Anna disconnected the call and punched the air. *Rock 'n' Roll. Nice one, Anna.*

*

Tsan Yohoto was savouring the last mouthful of fillet steak and onions, which had been prepared for him by his housekeeper. He ate slowly, and alone, as he did most evenings, in the dining room of his luxurious penthouse on the top floor of the Suzaru Building. His apartment was in Tokyo's upmarket Roppongi district, about a mile west of Tokyo Harbour. Tsan downed the good French claret and carried his plates and cutlery into the kitchen. He switched on the dishwasher and went into the study, his favourite room. The walls were covered in shelves laden with medical textbooks. The few remaining spaces were taken up with framed certificates of medical qualifications and photographs.

Visitors' eyes were usually drawn to the photographs of a smiling Tsan Yohoto shaking hands with a succession of US Presidents. All had been taken in the Rose Garden, alongside the Oval Office at the White House. Those on the Yamoura board knew that their donations guaranteed more receptive ears for Yamoura and the other pharmaceutical industry lobbyists in Washington. It was very important to maintain the status quo.

Tsan sat in his handcrafted leather chair and booted up his computer. As he waited, he thought again, momentarily, of his mother, Saina. How he loved her. How he admired her for her strength and courage in raising him after the bomb. It worried him sometimes to think that she might not approve of every aspect of his plan, his revenge. But, as in all conflicts, it was always the 'little people', the ordinary folk, struggling to survive, that suffered the most. The politicians who led their people into disaster, generally survived. And the Americans had shown no mercy for his family, or his people. Just three days after Hiroshima they had dropped another atomic bomb on Nagasaki. That was cruelty heaped upon cruelty. No. *No mercy.*

He went to earthcam.com and paused over a choice of thirteen webcam views of Manhattan. He clicked on 'Times Square' and a second later he was looking at a live, high-definition view of Times Square, from a camera positioned over Broadway. He watched the crowds of people crisscrossing the square, the white vans, the yellow cabs, the enormous signs. He wondered if these people even knew they were being watched, from all over the world. He picked out one man, carrying a briefcase, who stopped to take a call on his cell phone. *I wonder who that man is? I wonder if he has a wife and children? I wonder where he lives? I wonder if he'll be one of the many who are going to die?*

Using his password Kendolita2, he logged into the Yamoura Pharmaceuticals intranet. His computer pinged and a pop-up alerted him to the publication of a new Warning Letter on the Food and Drug Administration website. He clicked on the link and was soon at the heart of one of his favourite websites. *God bless America and her freedom of information.* He smiled to himself. And there it was. A copy of a Warning Letter to Australe-Forsyth Pharma, saying that its advertising of its arthritis drug, Deleton, was misleading, that its promotional materials aimed at the elderly were misleading and that its Safety Presentation was misleading. Australe-Forsyth was being asked to discontinue its advertising. Tsan Yohoto grinned as he exited the site. His competitors were all playing the same game. The FDA would react too late. The key to success was getting the message out, fast and strong.

He then opened an email from the Yamoura marketing department with an attached PDF press release for his approval.

YAMOURA PHARMACEUTICALS MOVES TO ERADICATE DEATHS FROM BACTERIAL ILLNESS IN SUB-SAHARAN AFRICA

Yamoura Pharmaceuticals today announced plans to provide free supplies of its cephalosporin antibiotic tablets to governments and famine relief agencies in sub-Saharan Africa.

This benevolent strategy is the brainchild of the Yamoura Pharmaceuticals Chief Executive, Tsan Yohoto, who has headed the leading multinational for over thirty years.

Mr Yohoto commented, 'In the twenty first century, it is a crime that thousands of men, women and children die every year in Africa from treatable infections. Septicaemia, bronchitis, pneumonia, skin infections and gonorrhoea are now just as dangerous as the famines. Their deaths can be prevented by a simple course of antibiotics. Yamoura Pharmaceuticals can stand by no longer and we will provide the African governments with free cephalosporin antibiotic tablets until this problem has been resolved – once and for all.

The release finished with a stock head and shoulders photograph of a smiling Tsan Yohoto and the standard corporate information on Yamoura.

One note that caught his eye was from the Finance Department. It had estimated the cost of the initiative at fifteen million dollars. As is normal procedure for companies listed on the stock market, any significant company announcements were sent in advance to Yamoura's own stock market advisors. Tsan noted a remark from their top financial analyst, approving the announcement and adding the opinion that their stock price on the Nikkei would probably rise by at least one per cent after the announcement – based purely on good PR and media exposure. This rise alone would more than cover the cost of the cephalosporin production in the first place, the analyst commented.

Tsan chuckled to himself. *Maybe we should have thought of this years ago – giving away free drugs.* He typed a message approving the immediate issuing of the press release and clicked *send*. He sat back, sighed and closed his eyes. Suddenly, he could see Kendo and Lita's burned bodies on the swings. He could smell roast meat. He clenched his fist and snapped out of the memory. He took the old black and white photograph of Kendo and Lita from his jacket pocket and studied their smiling faces. His eyes filled with tears. *Don't worry, brother and sister. Everything is going according to plan. No one can stop me now.*

23

MANHATTAN – 18 MAY

It was a warm morning in New York. Arlene Thomas tried unsuccessfully to stifle an enormous yawn. It started Victor Dezner, Katie Keller, Mark Reynolds and Anna Milani yawning as well and that raised a good laugh.

'Sorry, guys,' said Arlene.

'No worries, darling, we're all exhausted,' said Victor.

The yawning episode had broken a tired silence in the boardroom of Dynamic Communications. Most of the staff had been working twelve-hour days for two weeks now, weekends included. The partners, Victor and Katie, had been working eighteen-hour days and had taken rooms at the Plaza Hotel, half a block south, to save on the commute and for somewhere to crash.

'Don't know about you folks, but I'm just going on adrenaline these days,' said Katie Keller.

'Absolutely,' agreed Victor.

Now that they were so close to the launch, they were beginning to get that tingle of excitement. Another buzz had been the bitching and moaning among their competitors about the amount of TV, radio and advertising pages they were booking. The gossip-rich bars and coffee shops in the area, from Fashion

Avenue to midtown Madison, were awash with wild speculation as to what Dynamic Communications was up to. Had they landed some new accounts? Or stolen key accounts from another agency? Another bonus for Dynamic was that Arlene Thomas, its principal buyer, had been able to screw an extra five per cent discount out of the newspapers and magazines because of the volumes she was buying up. That would add nicely to the standard fifteen per cent discount on advertising expenditure that the newspapers, magazines and some TV and radio stations paid back to the advertising agency, and would go straight to the bottom line.

Wow, Victor Dezner had thought, if Yamoura and BurgerFantastic keep spending like they're shaping up to, this could make us the No. 1 agency in New York in two years.

He wondered if they should maybe think about selling the business in a year or so while the name was strong and increasing market share. He couldn't keep working at this pace. He knew that Katie Keller was having similar thoughts.

'Okay, boys and girls,' said Victor, slapping himself across the face to perk himself up. 'TV advert. How are we looking?'

'Good,' said Katie. 'The daytime version will start first, then we'll shoot a new version every few months. Radio advert sounds great, thirty seconds, ties into TV campaign, same messages, same soundtrack.'

'Okay,' continued Arlene, opening another file. 'Outdoor advertising's good to go on Friday, starting with postering of the first hundred and fifty billboards on the island.'

Mark Reynolds whistled. 'One hundred and fifty sites?'

'Yep. And we're adding in every electronic site we can grab on a good traffic route, good retail pitches and in the locations Yamoura ordered.'

Mark frowned. 'Why those specific locations?' he asked, having a quick look down the list. 'They seem kinda random?'

'I don't know,' she shrugged, 'but if Yamoura want it, they get it.'

'Absolutely, Arlene, great work,' said Victor.

'Thanks, guys. Now, full newspaper and magazine campaign starts Friday week also, the first of June. Everything using the healing colours of blue and white.' She shoved copies of the advertising schedules for the next six months across the table and they all took a moment or two to scan them.

'Mark, I.T., what's the latest?' asked Victor.

'Sure, Vic, we're on track with the SuperVerve website – going live on Friday and ready for a lot of hits from that campaign. The usual soft, warm, professional and caring feel. It draws the consumer in, gives them a good feeling. Plenty of emotion. Within a minute or so, they'll be convinced that SuperVerve is the answer to all their problems,' he chuckled.

'Awesome, Mark,' said Katie appreciatively.

'Absolutely,' said Victor. 'And Anna? Any update?'

'Ladies and gentlemen,' Anna said in a mock announcer's tone, 'I am pleased to confirm that at 11 p.m. yesterday, I signed contracts with Max Sherry, agent for Christopher White of the Knicks and Ricky Morgan of the Giants.'

'Wa-hey!' cheered Victor and Katie.

Anna went on. 'Christopher White is box office. He's a real hot item for New York's basketball fans – all six feet four inches of him. He's the complete blond-haired, blue-eyed, all-American hero.'

They all cheered.

'Aye, and in case you've missed it, he's currently pictured on a thirty-foot billboard outside Madison Square Garden, home of the Knicks.'

More cheers.

She grinned at her colleagues. 'And, after a bit of a struggle, I got Ricky Morgan too. He's currently rated the most valuable player with the New York Giants. Just twenty-five years old. He's the quintessential black kid from the Bronx made good. Big street cred with the younger sports fan and black demographics.'

'Anna, you could hardly have come up with two better known names in the city.' Katie Keller beamed.

'Yeah, I'm pleased. Ricky Morgan had some reservations over endorsing a burger, says it's not a healthy image, but I got him over the line. Money talks.'

'How much?' asked Victor.

'Two million dollars each for a one-year campaign, plus an option for another year at one million bucks.'

Victor Dezner let out a long low whistle.

'These guys can practically name their own price at the moment,' continued Anna. 'Christopher White is going on the SuperVerve campaign. Apparently, he was plagued with stomach trouble until he discovered SuperVerve last week. And Ricky Morgan – turns out he couldn't run ten yards until he discovered how much energy BurgerFantastics gave him!'

They all laughed again.

'We've got a half day's filming time with both of them next week. We reckon we can get their TV and radio adverts in the bag within ten days.

'And,' Anna went on, 'I've got a strong commitment from *The Times* editorial side. They'll give us a half-page interview on Saturday week, lifestyle-type piece on Christopher White, how he stays healthy, etc. – we'll work in SuperVerve. And a week later we're going to give them an exclusive interview with Ricky Morgan. They nearly took my arm off. We'll get him to talk about BurgerFantastic, how the burgers are such an important part of his diet and lifestyle, so on, and so on . . .'

'Fantastic,' said Victor, punching the air with his fist. 'Guys, we are on fire here! Well done everyone. Now let's ram these campaigns home!'

24

NEW JERSEY

The KLM 747 cargo plane seemed to hang in the clear blue sky a minute or so after its wheels had lifted off runway 22 at Newark International. It was particularly hot for late May. The winds were coming from the south, raising New York's temperature by maybe ten degrees. When the southerlies blow at Newark, the aircraft switch to runways 22L and 22R, on a bearing of two hundred and twenty degrees. That takes departing aircraft within half a mile of the newly named BurgerFantastic plant.

Takar el Sayden stood in the parking lot, looking over the main gate at the giant plane. If I took a photo right now, it would be perfect for a corporate brochure, he thought ruefully. Just one shot would capture the big bright red and yellow BurgerFantastic sign at the gate, with the jet seemingly suspended over it. As he turned away to walk towards the office entrance, he realised he hadn't noticed the jets for years – just like everyone else who worked under the flight path. Why was it that he had noticed that plane today? He had a deepening sense of unease. Everything felt wrong. *C'mon, Takar, try and work through this.*

'Hi, Carol,' he said as he forced a heavy-hearted smile in the direction of his receptionist.

'Hi, Takar,' she replied cheerfully. 'Warm today.'

'Sure is – southerly winds,' said Takar, putting his foot on the first step up to his office.

'Oh, Mr Ali's waiting for you in your office. He said he was early. I knew he was the first appointment in your schedule so I showed him on up.'

A weariness came over Takar. Damn this guy, over twenty minutes early! Always catching me off guard.

'I hope that's okay?' said Carol, concerned at his expression.

Takar recovered his composure. 'What? Oh yeah, sure, it's fine, Carol.'

The man with the scars was sitting in one of the two chairs facing Takar's desk. He turned as Takar entered but didn't stand up.

'Good morning,' he said in that cold monotone voice.

'Mr Ali, I believe,' said Takar, taking his seat behind the desk, 'but I'll bet that's not your real name.'

'Names are unimportant, Takar. What is important are our actions,' said Ibrahim Fallah.

Takar did not reply. Through the window over his adversary's head he could see another white jet angling skyward. *Weird – I've never noticed a plane out of that window before either.*

'To business,' said his visitor, straightening in his chair. 'The good news, Takar, is that my superiors are very pleased with progress and with your cooperation. I am to reiterate that you and your family will be rewarded and not harmed, if you continue to assist.'

Takar sighed.

Fallah continued. 'I gather that your rebranding is going well?' he enquired, as he cocked a thumb over his shoulder in the direction of the new sign at the front of the depot.

'Yes, over one hundred new signs already up on my restaurants. New logos on menus, napkins, you name it. A pile of promotional material will be delivered to the restaurants on Wednesday and Thursday.'

'So that will all be in place for the start of the advertising campaign on Friday?' asked Fallah.

'Yes,' replied Takar, 'TV, radio, newspaper advertising, the whole lot starts on Friday.'

'Excellent, excellent.'

'If you say so.'

'And the funds in the bank are more than adequate?'

'So far, no problem. The advertising agency sent me invoices last week, which I've paid. The new signage is costing nearly a million dollars.'

Fallah nodded. 'The fifty million in instalments should be adequate for our first year. If funds come under pressure, let me know at once.'

'I will, don't worry.'

'And so, the final piece in the jigsaw,' said Fallah. He bent down and unzipped the front pouch on a black suitcase on wheels. He produced what looked like a glossy brochure.

'Now, my information is that the two vats in which you prepare your sauce every night are Alfa Laval models – five-hundred-gallon capacity vats of jacketed stainless steel.'

As he opened the brochure, Takar realised he was looking at a copy of the liquidator's sale catalogue from when they had bought the plant. *Where the hell do they get all this stuff?*

'In the case are fourteen plastic bags. Each bag contains five pounds of powder. You will empty one bag into each vat every night. I will bring you fourteen bags every Monday morning. You can keep them in your office. Just make sure each vat gets one bag per night.'

Takar nodded.

'Again, I want to reassure you that the powder is harmless. If you wish, every week, I will myself taste some powder from any bag you nominate.' As if to prove the point, Fallah opened the clip seal on one of the bags and scooped a crooked fingerful into his mouth.

'My friends will be buying burgers every day in your restaurants and testing the sauce. If there's no powder,' he paused, 'then Tasha, Farah and Jasmin die. Followed by the rest of your family.'

Takar stared at him and clenched his fists. He forced himself not to say anything.

Fallah continued. 'Please start with these two bags, on the last night of this month. So that all the sauce that goes out of here from the first of June has the powder in it.'

Takar nodded. He knew he had to obey. If some smart way out of this ever occurred to him, well, he'd deal with it then. For now, he was trapped.

*

Back in his apartment at the New York Metropolitan Library on Fifth Avenue, Ibrahim Fallah smiled at himself in the mirror. These were the best of times. He ran a finger over the deep scar on his right cheek. That had been worth it. A piece of hot shrapnel from the exploding Russian tank had seared his cheek as he leaped off its turret. As he jumped, he had heard the screams of the tank's four Russian crew as their bodies were shredded with shrapnel from the two grenades he'd dropped down their top hatch. After the Russian army crawled out of his country, he returned to his life as a man of literature at the library. It was a lonely and quiet life, but he found fulfilment among his books and in his studies of Islam.

His many years of quiet, law-abiding existence in New York made him an ideal 'sleeper' – someone who could blend their normal lifestyle with their terrorism, without raising suspicion. He kept himself to himself. That was one of the secrets. When the order had come from his old comrade Baddar Mussan, al-Qaeda's chief of intelligence, he had been thrilled. He hadn't enjoyed killing the old man in the factory, but it was a heavy responsibility to serve in this battle against the West, and the West's war on his brothers in so many countries.

His days were particularly busy now. As well as his work at the library, he had a new routine. As instructed, he had bought a nondescript white Toyota delivery van from a dealer in New Jersey, using fake ID of course. As promised, a book of dockets had arrived in the post, authorising collection of supplies of cephalosporin antibiotic, in both tablet and freeze-dried powder form, from the Yamoura logistics building. It was located on the Transworld Corporate Park in Queens, close to La Guardia airport, where all Yamoura's products were flown in. The guys at the warehouse simply scanned his docket, got a quickly scribbled signature and helped him load the van with the correct product. His was just one of dozens of trucks and vans that turned up there every day to collect stock. He used the same ID when collecting stock as he had when buying the van. *You just couldn't be too careful. The most stupid small details could derail a really good plan. What if I backed the van into someone else's at the warehouse? The warehouse guys might check driver's details from the licence tag. What if the name didn't match his signature on the collection dockets? Yes, I need to concentrate over every single detail.*

His orders were to build up a stock of the powder and tablets in his garage. Every Monday morning, he would be bringing fourteen bags of powder to Takar el Sayden at the factory in Newark. The tablets were for the dumping. Any chance he got during the week, he'd do some surveillance on el Sayden's wife and pretty daughters. Nice family. It would be a pity to kill them, as he suspected that he would eventually have to do. He always took a few photographs to give to el Sayden, together with the latest photos of his family in Tripoli, which arrived in his Dropbox account every week or so: that kept Takar on his toes.

25

MANHATTAN – 1 JUNE

Mrs Esther Wolfowitz was pissed off. She felt pissed off most of the time these days. *You work your ass off for fifty years, and for what? You raise a son and then he hardly ever calls!* She pressed the *on* button on the TV remote. Now, most of her days were spent in her small two-bed apartment, in a block full of retired people on Jay Street. The main interests in their lives were their illnesses, and she was no different. Though she still had Sidney, she supposed, as she heard her husband turn the key in the front door.

Sidney Wolfowitz shuffled in to the kitchenette, just as he did at 10.15 a.m., seven days a week, and took a loaf of bread, a carton of milk and *The New York Times* out of a plastic bag. At about 10.28 a.m., Mrs Wolfowitz knew that he would shuffle into the lounge with two cups of coffee and four slices of toast on a tray. He would hand her a cup of coffee and two slices on a plate and make some comment about the weather. He would then sink into the other armchair and, with a heavy sigh, he would open the newspaper. They would then watch Dr Phil, Rikki Lake, Oprah and Jerry Springer re-runs – or rather she would try and watch while Sidney annoyed her with his tut-tuts and grunts. *Is this what I survived Auschwitz for?* she sometimes asked herself.

Dr Phil turned perfectly on cue and looked out at his viewers. 'And we'll be back to see if Bruce did get through the week without beating his kids – right after these messages.'

Sidney Wolfowitz tut-tutted. Esther Wolfowitz sighed. A picture of a retired couple in a badly lit apartment came on their screens. These people were unhappy, just like them. The voiceover said in a weary tone, *'Are you feeling tired? Do you suffer from headaches, bowel or stomach problems? Do you sometimes wish you had more energy?'*

The screen now showed the couple chatting with an earnest and honest doctor, who nodded and smiled as he handed them a prescription. The voiceover and the screen both brightened – *'Then all you need is SuperVerve.'* The screen showed an attractive, smiling pharmacist, handing a box of SuperVerve tablets to the delighted couple.

'SuperVerve is clinically proven to alleviate bowel and stomach problems, headaches and listlessness. Get your energy back. Get SuperVerve.'

The advertisement cut to a new scene where the beaming elderly man was now energetically pushing his laughing grandchildren on two swings. The camera panned across a neat garden to where the grandmother sits relaxing on a comfortable garden chair. She is beautifully dressed, smiling and chatting with family members, while a daughter, or daughter-in-law, tops up her glass of wine. The sun is shining. Grandmother catches her husband's eye, he winks at her and she waves back.

The upbeat voiceover declares, *'SuperVerve – putting the verve back into your life. Ask your doctor if SuperVerve is suitable for you.'*

Wow, thought Esther Wolfowitz. She glanced over at Sidney, who also seemed to be impressed. 'Maybe we should find out more about that, dear?' she said.

'Yeah, sounds good, it's even in *The New York Times*,' he replied, turning the broadsheet towards her and tapping on a full-page colour advert. The bright blue and white SuperVerve logo beamed out at them and there were the same laughing faces of those grandparents and their families.

'We'll ask about it at the clinic,' said Mrs Wolfowitz. 'I was thinking of calling in there anyway. I haven't been feeling great.'

'Sure. Let's do that, dear. I'll come with you. Oh, I didn't show you these,' said Sidney, as he half stood to take something out of his trouser pocket.

'What is it?'

'Well, it looks like there is such a thing as a free lunch.' He handed her a coupon, as he squinted to read the print on a bright red and yellow flyer, with a picture of a succulent beef burger. *'BurgerFantastic – home cooking without the hassle. Buy one get one free, with this coupon.'*

'That looks like a good deal,' said Esther Wolfowitz, studying the advert, but struggling to read the print. 'One for you and one for me.' She paused and looked into the mid-distance. 'BurgerFantastic. Yeah, there's one of those down near the clinic. Let's try it out.' Then, raising her voice in exasperation as her husband shuffled towards the kitchen, 'Sidney, Sidney where have you put my glasses this time?'

She found them later in the fridge. Exactly where she had left them.

*

'So, Anna girl, like what did you say then?' Cindy asked as she and Anna checked their make-up in the restroom at Dynamic Communications. Anna had been updating Cindy on her only date with John Wyse, since the dinner at Le Cirque.

'I said I'd love to go out again but that I was really busy on these projects at work and could he leave it for a week before calling me. It's hardly even a white lie, I've got so much on.'

'Good move, girl. I'd push it to two weeks. Maybe even three.

You'll work him into a frenzy. Best way to make sure of landing him long term.'

'Jeez, Cindy, I hope you're right. I don't wanna blow this.'

'Trust me, Anna. Don't get used. Hey, he didn't say if he had any more good-looking detective pals looking for a real energetic mystery woman, did he?' Cindy giggled, scrunching a palmful of gel through her spiky red hair.

'Just his best buddy Cabrini that you met. He's great fun – life and soul of the station apparently. And separated.'

'Nah. He drinks way too much. Been there, done that, dated those guys. I do prefer to date married men though, they're so predictable.'

'Oh, how's that?' said Anna, inspecting her lipstick.

'There's no more potent mixture than a married man who feels he's not getting enough action at home, and the old four, three, two. Always works.'

'The what?'

'The four, three, two. Four drinks, three compliments, and two big tits. Never fails!'

Anna had to hold on to the side of the sink, she was laughing so much.

'So, those cops?' Cindy continued. 'Do they hang out a lot at that bar where we met them?'

'Harry's – yeah. It's near the police station, and it's near John's place too.'

'Oh, where does he live?'

'New block on Eldridge Street – not that I've been inside it.'

Hmmm. Harry's and Eldridge Street.

'Hey, I'd better get goin', Cindy. There's a few of us going out for lunch – they're waiting in reception. You wanna come along?'

'Yeah, sure, I was gonna have a sandwich at my desk, but I'd love to get out.'

'Cool, come on then.' Anna grabbed her handbag and rushed out to where four of the girls were waiting.

'Come on, Anna, we're starving.'

'Sorry, guys, where'll we go?'

'What about this?' said Sonya, handing her something over the reception desk.

Anna looked at the coupons in her hand and read aloud, 'BurgerFantastic – home cooking without the hassle. Buy one – get one free, with this coupon. Hey, that's one of our clients.'

Sonya smiled. 'A whole bunch of coupons got dropped into reception this morning.'

'Well, okay then,' said Cindy, opening the door, 'so let's take them up on their offer. There's a BurgerFantastic just down the street.'

'Hey, I'm all for supporting the clients, but it'll be caesar salad for me,' Anna said, patting her flat stomach.

*

At about the same time as Anna and her colleagues were heading out for lunch, Mr and Mrs Wolfowitz were walking half a block north to their doctor's clinic, near the intersection with Harrison Street. Sidney Wolfowitz walked slower than his normal pace, so that his wife could keep up. His twice-daily walks to the newsagent and convenience store were keeping him pretty fit. Mrs Wolfowitz wasn't happy.

'And David never visits. You'd think he'd have more respect for his mother, after all we've been through? Sheesh!'

'But he was here last weekend, darling,' said Sidney gently. 'We had lunch.'

'Don't talk nonsense, Sidney,' she shot back. 'You trying to make me sicker than I am? He hasn't been in New York for a year.'

They reached the surgery of Dr Ian French and took their seats in the busy waiting room.

'Mrs Wolfowitz, Dr French will see you now,' smiled the receptionist through the hatch.

'Oh, thank you,' she said, standing up slowly. She made her way towards the doctor's surgery. Dr French was waiting at the door. She liked Dr French. He always made her feel much better. They both sat down.

'And what seems to be the problem, Mrs Wolfowitz?'

'Well, doctor, I have very bad irritable bowel, stomach cramps and headaches,' she replied. 'Oh, and a lack of energy,' she added.

'And how long have you had these stomach cramps?'

'Oh, a long time, doctor.'

'And do you have diarrhoea, Mrs Wolfowitz?'

'Oh yes, from time to time. And sometimes I feel bloated.'

'Would you mind lying up on the examination table, Mrs Wolfowitz? I'd like to have a look at your tummy.'

Mrs Wolfowitz heaved herself up on to the table and lay on her back. Her very ample stomach settled in various directions.

Dr French worked his way around her stomach, pressing gently. From time to time Mrs Wolfowitz released a little groan.

'Yes, certainly seems to be a bit tender. Okay, Mrs Wolfowitz, you can sit back down.'

As she tucked in her blouse and sat down heavily in her chair, Mrs Wolfowitz said, 'You know, doctor, I've been hearing that SuperVerve tablets are really very good for this type of thing. What do you think?'

'Well, they would certainly be helpful for any inflammation of your intestines. We don't want it turning into colitis. It may be that you've picked up a persistent bug. That could also explain your headaches and generally not feeling well.'

He finished taking her blood pressure. *150 over 90, not too bad for an overweight eighty-something.* He checked her temperature, which was normal.

'Right, Mrs Wolfowitz,' he said, typing her name into his computer to open her file. 'So,' he scanned down the screen, 'you were last with me a month or so ago, when you had that bad cold and cough. And we gave you some doxycycline for a chest infection.'

'That's right – that cleared up fine – but this bowel and stomach problem's really getting me down.'

Dr French moved his mouse to open the screen where he

would record today's visit. He had a brand-new mouse mat that morning – the pharmaceutical reps were always dropping them in. This one had a bright blue and white logo and the strapline, '*SuperVerve – Working with doctors in alleviating gastro-intestinal problems, headache and listlessness.*'

Okay, now SuperVerve, he thought, that's cephalosporin, isn't it? He knew there was a leaflet on SuperVerve in his drawer. He pulled it out and read it. *Yep, straightforward cephalosporin, that should work.*

'Okay, Mrs Wolfowitz, I'll write you a script for SuperVerve. Take two tablets immediately, followed by two per day for a week. I'll give you a repeat prescription in case it doesn't clear up straight away,' he said, tearing off the script and handing it over.

'Oh, thank you, doctor.' Mrs Wolfowitz beamed.

Fifteen minutes later, Mr and Mrs Wolfowitz walked into the AppleDay Pharmacy on Harrison Street. Sidney bought eggs, milk and orange juice while Esther waited for the prescription to be filled. They got a twenty dollar bonus on their AppleDay Pharmacy loyalty card. Mrs Wolfowitz asked for a glass of water in the store and swallowed her first two SuperVerve tablets.

Funny, I feel better already, she thought. 'C'mon Sidney, let's go get lunch.'

Esther Wolfowitz clutched the brown paper bag containing the SuperVerve tablets, in their bright blue and white packet, as they walked to the BurgerFantastic restaurant six doors away. They ordered one BurgerFantastic, two fries and two coffees. Sidney proudly handed over his coupon and they received another BurgerFantastic – free. They sat in a corner booth.

'*Hit me baby*,' pumped out of the sound-system, as Sidney consumed his first, and Esther her second, large dose of cephalosporin that day.

*

6 JUNE – 11 P.M.

'Shit,' muttered Takar el Sayden. He was taking two bags of powder out of the case when one of his rings snagged on the plastic and a stream of white powder poured out onto the carpet. *What the hell is this stuff?* he asked himself for the hundredth time. He scooped some powder off the floor onto his finger and licked it off. Same as always: tasteless. If there was any smell at all, it was a vague smell of some medicine he remembered from when he was sick as a boy. He scooped a little more into his mouth. He waited. He could hear his watch ticking as he kneeled there and waited for another minute. He felt absolutely no reaction to the powder. No effect on his brain, no sickness in his stomach. *What the hell is all this about?*

Takar decided he'd better get on with his orders. He put two of the bags into a white plastic sack, which he carried down the office steps. He pushed open the door into the production area. *Lucky the sauce vats are at the office end of the building.*

There were thirty-five or so production staff on duty for the night, scattered around among the equipment, mass producing food for the early morning deliveries to New York's two hundred and fifty-two BurgerFantastic restaurants. The staff were well used to seeing him in the factory at night and wouldn't take any particular notice. He walked across the spotlessly clean sealed concrete floor to the nearest vat. It towered above him, almost to the full height of the building's twenty-five-foot eaves.

Shit.

He put the sack down and quickly doubled back to the door into the production area. Rows of hooks covered the wall. Most of them were empty. He took a white coat and hat from the top left hook, which was marked with the initials *T.S.* One thing the staff *would* find remarkable would be to see the boss not sticking to his own rules on hygiene. He pulled on his hat and coat, picked up one of the bags of powder and began climbing the steel staircase, which wound its way upwards to the top of the vat. *How ridiculous. Here I am wearing a hat to prevent a hair falling into any food and I'm about to empty five pounds of some goddam powder into the sauce.*

He reached a steel platform at the top, opened the hatch and looked into the slowly revolving, pale liquid. He emptied the contents of the bag into the middle of the creamy mass, which was gently thickening as it blended. He stuffed the empty bag into his coat pocket, descended the steps, and repeated the process in the second vat. He had decided that if anyone questioned what he was doing, he would say he was adding a brand-new secret ingredient. His staff would readily believe that, as other burger chains made a big deal about the 'secret ingredients' in their sauce.

Takar el Sayden left by the front door and got into his car. He drove slowly, on the way back to their friends' party, thinking hard about the last few days. He had badly underestimated the amount of beef and buns he was going to need. By Saturday afternoon, on just the second day of the rebranding launch, the computer in the depot was showing that some restaurants would run out of burgers by Sunday evening. He made a mental note to increase his orders for burgers and bread buns by another thirty per cent and to see how it went. He pulled up outside his friend's house, where he had been at a fortieth birthday party with Tasha. She was used to his quick trips to the depot at short notice, to sort out some problem or other. But she was becoming suspicious. She had confronted him that morning.

'There's something going on, Takar, and I don't like it,' she said. 'You are becoming withdrawn, secretive. Are you having an affair?'

'No, no, of course not, I promise.'

'There is definitely something on your mind. Is there something wrong with the business? I never understood why we had to start selling beef? You know many in our families would not appreciate killing cows outside the Halal tradition.'

'I'm sorry, love. I know I have been distracted. I will be okay again soon. Always remember that I love you and the girls, more than anything.'

He would have to be very careful. What if she gets a private detective to keep an eye on me? That al-Qaeda bastard might spot him and think I've tipped off the police.

★

MANHATTAN – 7 JUNE

The heavy blades of the slowly rotating fan cast a flickering shadow across the fourteen white coats in the conference room. The coats belonged to a selection of the consultants and department heads at the Patrick J. Brock Memorial Hospital on Broome Street, near the financial district. The meetings were arranged by management to review any issues that had come up the previous week. They were marked in the schedule as 'Patient Care Review'. The doctors knew that their main purpose was to give the administrators an early warning of any patient problem that might lead to a lawsuit. On a bad week, when there was a risk of litigation, a lawyer or two in dark suits would attend and anyone remotely connected with the case got the fifth degree.

'Quiet one today, thank God,' muttered Dr Conrad Jones to Dr Valerie Mahler, the head of the Accident and Emergency unit, who was perched on a table top to his right.

'Amen to that,' she replied. 'It's bedlam down there after that bus crash last night.'

Irene Sefton, the senior hospital administrator, who had been running the hospital for over twenty years, raised her voice.

'Okay, that's just about it, guys. Coupla smaller items – remember to get your leave requests in early by email to me, so we can coordinate things a little better this year.' She peered reproachfully over her clipboard. They all nodded.

'Also, I've got a note here from the finance guys. Apparently Yamoura Pharmaceuticals are supplying their cephalosporin at half the cost of the other companies' brands. So, under our economic prescribing policy, that's what the hospital will be stocking – so no point looking for any other brands. Okay, everyone happy?'

Fourteen grunts and nods, eager to get back to business.

'Thanks for your time, have a good week,' said the administrator, as she closed her clipboard with an efficient snap.

'Sounds like Yamoura are buying some market share,' said Conrad Jones to Valerie Mahler as they walked out the door.

'Sounds like someone left a machine on all night in Tokyo.' Valerie Mahler grinned as she hurried off down the corridor.

26

THE VILLA AT SAITON – 8 JUNE

'Gentlemen, we may have a perfect launch,' said the silver-haired Lumo Kinotoa as he, almost absentmindedly, moved a pawn on the chessboard at the centre of the table forward one space. There were broad smiles all round at the weekly meeting of the Chess Club. Unusually, this meeting had been moved to a Friday night, as Tsan Yohoto had suggested that it would be most useful to review the first full week of their plan.

'And Tsan,' asked Kinotoa, 'you are not too concerned about this detective you met at the dinner with Dynamic?'

'No, not really, Lumo.' Tsan Yohoto took Detective Wyse's Fifth Precinct card out of his pocket and frowned at it. 'I mean, it can't be ideal, to have a detective so close to our marketing team. But the beautiful Miss Milani has no clue about the real strategy behind our marketing, so I can't see what difference it makes if her boyfriend is a cop.'

Lumo Kinotoa nodded and looked at the others.

Kazuhiro Saito grinned. 'I'm sure Detective Wyse has more than enough on his plate, keeping Miss Milani satisfied, in between catching muggers.'

'I'm not so sure about all this,' said Dr Naga, frowning. It wasn't often that he disagreed with the majority view and his colleagues paid attention when he did.

'Obviously, you met him, and I didn't,' Naga continued, 'but it all seems too close for comfort to me. Sometimes, when one puts enormous effort into devising a plan, it can be a little loose end, which seemed innocuous, that causes everything to unravel. I think we should at least keep a close eye on him, so that if he needs to be eliminated at short notice, our homework will be done.'

There was a pause while everyone took this in. Then, after discussing options for another ten minutes or so, Tsan Yohoto summarised their conclusion.

'Very good. We will ask our al-Qaeda friends if they can have Detective Wyse watched, and gather information on him: where he lives, his routine, his friends, etc.'

All those around the table nodded solemnly.

'Lumo, you will please send a message?'

'Of course, Tsan.'

'Thank you. And so, back to the main agenda.'

'Okay, gentlemen, let's summarise the state of play after one week,' said Lumo Kinotoa.

He and his fellow conspirators moved closer together around the top of the table – Dr Naga, Kazuhiro Saito, who was tucking into a sandwich, and, of course, Tsan Yohoto. All four had files and writing pads in front of them.

'Kazuhiro, your marketing campaigns – can you summarise the launch?'

'Of course.' Saito nodded, swallowed quickly and looked down at his notes. 'Firstly, the BurgerFantastic launch has gone exactly according to plan. All two hundred and fifty-two restaurants were rebranded in time and the newspaper and radio advertising is underway. The "buy one get one free" promotion is a big success. Apparently, all the restaurants were about fifty per cent busier than usual. Twenty-four of them ran out of burgers on the Sunday, but that's been corrected.' He looked up and they all nodded.

He continued, 'The information from our friends in Afghanistan is that the restaurant owner, el Sayden, is fully compliant and reliable.' Saito raised his eyebrows. 'Not surprising, given that they killed his uncle in order to focus his attention. Anyway,' he said, 'he puts the cephalosporin in the sauce vats every night. As we requested, every week or so, Tsan, you will receive a letter from al-Qaeda's man in New York. Inside will be some leaflet or other. In the centrefold, will be a small scoop of sauce taken from a BurgerFantastic. Enough, Tsan, I'm sure, for you to test that our restaurant owner continues to add the antibiotic.'

'Yes.' Tsan nodded. 'Thank you. I need only a small amount.'

'What about consumption numbers?' asked Kinotoa.

'Well,' Saito said. 'These are popular and busy restaurants. Say, two hundred and fifty of them, each serving an average of one and a half thousand people every twenty-four hours. As there's a variety of food on the menus, let's say, conservatively, that one thousand of those customers have a burger. That's quarter of a million customers per day. That's one and three-quarter million burgers every week.'

'Excellent, excellent.' All nodded their appreciation.

'And, Tsan, on the medical side?' queried Kinotoa.

'Yes, all is going according to plan. Our logistics facility near La Guardia is well stocked with cephalosporin – tablets for the drugstores, tablets and intravenous fluids for the hospitals and supplies for our al-Qaeda friend. All supplies are double the labelled strength and every fourth tablet or IV bag is a placebo or dummy. This will help to provoke the erratic consumption patterns that will accelerate the build-up of resistance to the antibiotic.'

'And how about sales?' asked Kazuhiro Saito.

'Going very well,' responded Tsan Yohoto. 'In response to the TV, radio and newspaper advertising, our sales of SuperVerve cephalosporin tablets are up almost fifty per cent already. I expect that to increase steadily as the later phases of the marketing campaign are rolled out.'

'And numbers?' queried Kinotoa again.

'Well, we're only at the start, but if the evidence from other advertising campaigns holds true, I believe we can get seven or eight per cent of New Yorkers buying SuperVerve tablets.'

'My goodness, that seems a lot,' said Dr Naga, looking slightly surprised.

Tsan Yohoto smiled. 'Have faith in the God of advertising, Juro,' he said and Dr Naga returned the smile.

Lumo Kinotoa was drawing a margin down the right-hand side of his page and beginning to write in figures. 'Any other numbers, Juro?' he asked.

'Well, thirty-two hospitals with an average of four hundred patients per hospital, that makes twelve thousand eight hundred patients. If, say, five per cent are prescribed cephalosporin, that gives us another six hundred and fifty people consuming our cephalosporin products.'

'Excellent work,' said Kinotoa, writing the number in the margin.

'By the way,' continued Dr Naga, 'cephalosporin is also the standard antibiotic given to any patient undergoing surgery. So, because we're supplying our antibiotic to the hospitals at the lowest price, every single New Yorker having an operation is getting a nice strong dose of our product.' He looked around proudly at his companions.

'Excellent. Excellent,' said Kinotoa. 'And we understand the al-Qaeda man is making progress with our strategy of dumping tablets around New York?' he asked.

'That's right,' Kazuhiro Saito responded. 'Information from Afghanistan is that the dumping is well underway. Apparently, their man is dropping about twenty boxes in ten or so of our selected locations, every night.'

'Numbers?'

'Harder to be exact on this, as we don't know how they'll be dispersed, but with one thousand tablets per box, by twenty boxes, by ten locations each night, that's another two hundred thousand tablets every day. I don't know, maybe another four thousand consumers? The main thing is that they're out there, and someone's taking them.

'Okay, gentlemen,' said Kinotoa, totting up the figures in the margin. 'So, from BurgerFantastic we have already one point seven five million new consumers of cephalosporin. From prescriptions, already over one hundred thousand and set to rise rapidly, seven- or eight-fold. In the hospitals, six hundred and fifty, and perhaps another four thousand consumers each week from the van drops. Gentlemen,' he said again, as he sat back in his chair, 'we have already achieved an extra two million regular consumers of cephalosporin antibiotic in New York.'

There was a satisfied silence and they each looked from one to another in delight.

Tsan Yohoto broke the pause, with his low, quiet voice.

'My friends, we have done well. We are tipping the balance. I'll go back to New York soon and keep an eye on things.' Dinner with Miss Anna Milani would be a nice bonus. 'I'm looking forward to watching the Americans dig their graves with their own medicine.'

27

MANHATTAN – AUGUST

'Jonathan, please don't make me ask you again,' pleaded Sandra Phillips.

Six-year-old Jonathan hung his head. 'Sorry, Mom,' he said, as he scooped three more pieces of chocolate-flavoured breakfast cereal onto his spoon.

'Peter. Suzy has basketball practice at three. I'll collect her at four. Can you pick up Jonathan from daycare at three? You could leave him at Grandma's for a few hours and pick him up on your way home.'

Dr Peter Phillips hesitated. 'Yeah, sure,' he stammered, 'I'll get someone to cover for me at the clinic.' *Shit.* He'd been hoping to play nine holes after work. *Better play ball for now, though. Sandra's been giving me a real hard time recently.*

'Suzy, quickly please, honey, go put your lunch in your bag.' Suzy was kneeling on the floor, singing to an audience of her dolls.

'I'm gonna be like Adele, Mom,' she said.

'Course you are, honey, but you're gonna miss your ride.'

'Okay, Mom,' said her eight-year-old, leaping up enthusiastically.

Suzy is the only female in this house who remembers how to smile, her father thought grimly.

'Peter, can you *please* clean that damn fish tank tonight; it's stinking the place out.'

'Yeah, sure, no problem.'

'Jonathan,' Sandra snapped, 'for God's sake stop banging that spoon – Mom's got a headache.'

Jonathan reluctantly ceased his campaign to squash an invasion of chocolate-coated space invaders, before they overtook his army's base on the left-hand side of the bowl.

The atmosphere at the breakfast table was tense and strained. Just like our marriage, Peter thought. The alarm had woken him at 7 a.m. as usual. Lying in bed, he watched Sandra's chest rise and fall slowly and admired her long blonde hair, which flowed over the whole pillow. Even in sleep, her face was tense. But, as he watched his wife of eleven years, he became aroused. He put his arm around her waist, snuggled closer and began gently kissing her neck. Sandra woke immediately and glanced at her watch.

'Christ, Peter, no way, it's nearly ten past.' She removed his arm, swung her legs out of the bed and went out into the hall calling, 'Suzy, Jonathan, c'mon guys, rise and shine!'

Peter dropped his head back onto his pillow. *So much for that – not even a good morning.* Both he and Sandra could sense that their marriage was in trouble – drowning in a sea of pressure and stress. They seemed to have no time for each other, or for themselves, for that matter. No matter what he did, he couldn't make Sandra happy. Without saying it, they both knew they were keeping things going for the sake of the kids, and hoping that life would improve. Now, for the rest of the day, he had a clinic full of demanding patients to look forward to.

'Hey, Dad, don't forget your briefcase,' said Suzy, struggling to lift it up to him as he reached the door. He hugged his daughter and, as he pecked Sandra on the cheek with a 'Have a great day', he remembered the brochure he had meant to show her last night.

'Hey, honey, look at this,' he said as he took the glossy four-page brochure from his briefcase.

'Not now, Peter, you'll be late.'

'But this looks great, something to look forward to. Yamoura Pharmaceuticals are holding a convention in Tokyo, to coincide with the Olympics.' He pointed at the cover picture of passengers sunbathing by a pool, on the top deck of a luxury liner. 'All the way back on a cruise ship,' he added. 'And if it's anything like the way they looked after us at the Ryder Cup . . .' He trailed off, watching her face. Sandra had loved that trip.

She flipped open the brochure with its pictures of sandy beaches around an itinerary which included two 'medical conventions'. She spotted the quirky Tokyo Olympics logo, *Tokyo 2020.*

'Peter, for chrissakes. I can't think past the smell of the fish tank and what we're having for dinner tonight – let alone 2020!' She tossed the brochure on the hall table.

Sorry for trying.

'Have a nice day, guys,' she said, as she bent to kiss the top of Jonathan's head. 'See you this evening.'

Peter left the brochure where it was. *Maybe she'd look at it later. Anyway, there were plenty more at the clinic.* Bob Sanders had dropped some in with the research reports on the new cephalosporin product he was pushing. *What was the rebranded name? SuperVerve – Yeah, that was it. Jeez, I could do with a little verve in my life right now.*

★

Peter Phillips dropped Jonathan at daycare, leaving him with a giant hug and a high five, and arrived at the clinic on the corner of Second Avenue and East 23rd Street, just before nine. He made his way to his office through the packed waiting room, waving a greeting to Elaine on reception as he passed. 'Two minutes,' he mouthed, holding up two fingers in a peace sign.

Elaine nodded. She knew to give him a couple of minutes to gather his thoughts before unleashing a stream of patients on him.

He sat into his chair and booted up his Dell. Thirty-eight emails.

The first was from Eamonn Holmes, one of his partners at the clinic, sent to all the doctors at the practice and suggesting that they read the new research results on SuperVerve on the attached PDF, which had been sent in by Bob Sanders. Peter double-clicked and the SuperVerve logo burst onto his screen. Young, old, middle-aged, black, white, mixed race; they were all smiling. Peter sighed and closed it down. He'd read it later. Elaine tapped at the door and ushered in all two hundred and twenty pounds of Mrs Walton.

The doctor smiled as he stood up. 'Good morning, Mrs Walton.'

'Not much good about it from my point of view, doc,' she replied grumpily.

'Oh dear, what's the problem today, Mrs Walton?'

'It's my stomach, doctor, as usual,' she grimaced. 'I keep getting these cramps every couple of days. Then I get the runs. Then I'm okay for a day. Then it starts again. And I've got these aches and pains in my joints.'

Peter Phillips nodded. 'Yes, this really does seem to be going on too long.' Secretly, he suspected that Mrs Walton's staple diet of pizzas, chocolate ice cream and a daily bottle of white wine was the source of the problem.

'You gotta help me, doc – is there anything I can take?'

'Well, Mrs Walton, I think you may have a touch of colitis. It's an inflammation in your intestines. There is this new medicine for intestinal problems, which has been getting some great feedback. It's very good for settling the system and, apparently, it can also help you lose a little weight.'

Mrs Walton's eyes lit up. 'Sounds great, doc.'

'It's called SuperVerve. I'll write you a script for a ten-day supply and let's see how you get on. It's got an antibiotic in it, so make sure you finish the course.'

'I will, doctor, don't worry.' She smiled as if she was feeling better already.

Peter wondered about a routine examination of Mrs Walton's stomach, then rapidly dismissed the thought. The waiting room was packed.

'There. I hope you feel better soon, Mrs Walton,' he said as he signed the prescription, 'and remember to try and keep to a nicely balanced diet.'

'I'll try, doc,' said Mrs Walton as she took the script gratefully and headed out the door. She stopped in the lobby at the new AppleDay Pharmacy touchscreen kiosk.

'Good morning, how may I help you today?' asked the pharmacist who appeared on the screen.

'I have a prescription here, for SuperVerve.'

'Great. Just scan in your script and select your nearest AppleDay store and we'll have that ready for you in just a few minutes.'

'Oh, thank you.'

'You're welcome. Have a nice day, and thank you for shopping with AppleDay.'

In his office, Dr Peter Phillips glanced at the list of patients lined up on his monitor. Next up was Mr Williams. Seventy years old and fifty of those spent suffering episodes of bronchitis, strep throats and headaches. *Sounds like another candidate for SuperVerve.*

★

THAT NIGHT

Ibrahim Fallah flicked on the light in the garage at the back of the library. It had a loading door onto the back alleyway. This was where they took delivery of books, shelving, furniture or whatever. Scattered around the place were a few shelving units, a pile of broken chairs and some crates. In the middle of the garage were the white Toyota van and his brown Nissan. He climbed up into the van's driver's seat and pressed the button on his remote. The garage door slid open. He started the engine, reversed carefully out into the alley and two minutes later he was heading north on Hudson Street for the Bronx. It was almost midnight. He glanced in his rear-view mirror. He had left a corridor down through the back of the van so that he could use every single mirror. *Keep every option open, take no chances*. The rest of the van was stacked with brown cardboard boxes, each about the size of a shoebox. Each box contained one thousand SuperVerve cephalosporin tablets.

He had planned his route carefully. He took Fifth Avenue, south, as far as East 20th Street. He turned left and continued east until he was in the less familiar territory of the housing projects at Bedford and Stuyvesant, or 'Bedsty', as locals call it. He knew he would find what he wanted there. He turned right and passed the Stuyvesant Oval. This was starting to look the part. He was now surrounded by rundown apartment blocks, beat-up cars and boarded-up storefronts. There was a group of black males on every street corner. He passed another group of youths in their trademark hoodies, low-slung jeans and sneakers, who stood menacingly on the corner of One Gun Street.

Allah be saved, he thought, what had happened here to deserve that name?

He knew that the drivers of most vehicles moving around here at night were buying drugs. Most of the kids hanging around were both suppliers and addicts. The street got darker. Most of the street lamps were broken. He pulled into the kerb, slid his hand under his seat and grasped a wire handle. He pulled it slowly and heard a click and a thump behind him, as the trapdoor in the floor of the van opened and one box of cephalosporin tablets dropped into the gutter. As an engineer, it had taken him just six hours in the library's garage to rig that little apparatus. He checked his mirror and pulled back out on to the street. He dropped another box outside a vagrants' hostel near Williams Bridge and by 1 a.m. he had dropped twenty boxes around the Bronx. *Like dropping goldfish into a piranha pool*. He had to remember the approximate locations for his drops because his orders were to repeat the process as often as possible, in the same locations. He had been assured that the tablets were just regular medication. If the police stopped him he had appropriate documentation to confirm that he did part-time delivery work for Yamoura Pharmaceuticals. If the police were suspicious enough to test the tablets, they would turn out to be perfectly normal. So, he was untouchable. He didn't even need to carry any weapons.

He lifted a can of Diet Coke from the holder and took a swig, then headed south again for Queens, where he would drop another twenty boxes. The lucky finders wouldn't be sure what they had come across, but tablets had a value in these neighbourhoods. The SuperVerve branding would quickly be connected with the advertising. He turned on the radio, which was tuned to XM FM, just in time to catch the end of an advert for the new drug – '*SuperVerve – Putting the verve back into your life.*'

He turned left again and headed for Harlem. The familiar radio jingle for 'XM FM – Traffic and Weather for the Tri-State area' pulsed around the van. The 2 a.m. headlines told him that nine Muslim doctors working in the National Health Service in England had been arrested in connection with two failed car bomb attacks in London and one at Glasgow airport. A Jeep packed with explosives had been set on fire and driven by one doctor into the main entrance to the airport. The bomb hadn't detonated. The two occupants of the Jeep had been badly burned and several people injured. It was being speculated that the strike was a 'copycat' version of a similar attack by a group of doctors in 2007. That, too, had failed.

Bad luck, my brothers, thought Ibrahim Fallah. You didn't do your preparation properly.

*

MANHATTAN – AUGUST, TWO WEEKS LATER

'Jonathan, Suzy, everyone – come on, guys, keep together,' called Sandra Phillips as she ushered the excited group of kids along the sidewalk on Bridge Street. It was a beautiful sunny Saturday afternoon. It was Suzy's ninth birthday. Sandra had taken ten of Suzy's pals, plus a couple of Jonathan's, on a trip aboard the Navy's battle cruiser, *The Steadfast*, which was moored for the week near the

Brooklyn Bridge. After that, she'd let them run around for a while in Battery Park and she shushed them just long enough to say a prayer at the World Trade Center Memorial Fountain before going for some food.

'C'mon guys, keep up.' Goddamn it, where was Peter? Him and his damned golf. He was supposed to meet them off the ship. He'd better be at the restaurant. She was taking the group of kids for a meal before they went to see the latest animated film, at the cinema on the corner nearest Store Street. That was what Suzy had said she wanted and that was what her princess would get. Karen Patel, her closest pal from among the moms at Jonathan's daycare, had come along to help out. The chilled air inside BurgerFantastic was a welcome relief. The place was packed.

'Over there, ma'am.' The friendly manager pointed to a couple of free tables in the corner.

'Sandra! Suzy! Hi, guys.' Peter came rushing in, sweat pouring from his brow. 'Just made it, sorry, nearly late. How was the ship? High fives all round. Right, guys, let's get stuck into some burgers and fries!'

28

MANHATTAN – 20 SEPTEMBER

Professor Alan G.F. Milton strode across the busy lobby of the Waldorf Astoria Hotel on Park Avenue. He had practised walking with the backs of his hands rotated forward, like Presidents did. Makes your shoulders look bigger. He was wearing a navy pinstripe suit, a crisp white shirt and a plain red tie. *Showbiz, that's what this is*, he'd said to himself in the mirror that morning, as he carefully combed his thick, blond locks. *Got to look the part.* He was in New York to head up an information seminar on SuperVerve for an audience of New York doctors.

'Alan, Alan,' he heard a call from his left. He looked around and waving at him were Dr Cook, Professor Kolsen and Arlene Thomas. They were drinking coffee at one of the lobby tables.

'Hi, Alan, good to see you,' said Dr Cook. 'Have you met Arlene Thomas from Dynamic Communications?'

'No, I haven't had the pleasure yet,' said Professor Milton, clasping Arlene's hand in both of his own, 'but we spoke on the phone the other day.' Wow, great body, he thought, and he risked a quick glance at her ring finger.

'Nice to meet you, Professor, at last,' said Arlene.

Professor Milton shook hands with Professor Kolsen. 'Hi, Oscar, good to see you again.'

'Okay, gentlemen,' Arlene said, 'our seminar will be in the ballroom. We have it all set up and ready to go for 12.30. Why don't we go down and have a run through?'

'Sure, let's do that,' smiled Professor Milton, and, picking up their briefcases, they followed Arlene towards the elevator.

'You get that bonus cheque, Oscar?' Professor Milton quietly asked his colleague.

'Yeah, nice one. Two hundred grand in yesterday's post. Anton got the same.'

'Excellent. They seem to be very happy,' replied Milton. He had received a bonus of half a million dollars and a note hinting at plenty more to come if the SuperVerve success story continued.

Arlene held open the double doors into the ballroom and the three doctors paused to take in the scene. Over one hundred circular tables were laid out, cabaret style. Three magnificent chandeliers threw light in every direction, which sparkled off the crystal glasses on the tables. The stage was set with a large, cream leather couch, horseshoe-shaped around a glass coffee table.

Arlene steered them up on to the stage. 'Now, gentlemen, first I'll welcome the doctors, then the video takes about five minutes. Then I'll introduce you in turn to deliver your pieces and Professor Milton will close out. After you speak at the podium, please return and have some coffee at the table. I suggest we all sit fairly informally. No barrier signals in the body language, no folded arms. Legs preferably uncrossed, or crossed towards the audience please – we want to look "open". Don't let your hands drop below the level of the table – that can make you look suspicious. We'll do the Q&A from the couch – you'll all be individually miked as well.'

The three medics nodded attentively.

'I'll pick a moment close to 1.15 p.m. to finish up. I'll thank them for coming and get them moving into the next room for lunch. Everyone okay with that?'

'Awesome, Arlene, sounds A-okay,' said Milton.

'Good. After the run through, there's a seating area backstage for you and we'll get a little make-up on you, because of the lights. We'll be making a DVD of the event which we can send out to clinics and to the medical journals. We'll also put an edited version on the SuperVerve website so people can stream it.'

'Sounds great,' said Professor Milton appreciatively, confident that he was in the hands of a real professional.

*

The doctors were milling through the doors by 12.20 p.m. These big information seminars were usually well worth attending.

And no one does it better than Yamoura, thought Dr Peter Phillips as he handed over his invitation, chose a table and took a seat.

'Hi, Peter Phillips,' he said, introducing himself to four other doctors – all working in Manhattan clinics as it turned out. The brief seminar would conclude with lunch at 1.30 p.m. and 'an opportunity to network with colleagues', said the invitation. The lunch should be good too, thought Dr Phillips. Better not eat too much, though. He was due to play golf at four. The medical panel was certainly heavyweight – and all three on FDA approval panels, he noticed from their CVs. The full attendance was also bolstered by the fact that the seminar would qualify for two hours of 'continuing medical education', a requirement for doctors to keep abreast of new medical developments.

The ballroom was packed by the time the *Chariots of Fire* theme tune swirled around the room and the lights went down. Victor, Katie and Mark Reynolds from Dynamic stood at the back of the room behind the sound desk. All three felt that buzz of nervous excitement that goes with any big event. Victor Dezner nudged Katie and showed her his crossed fingers. Katie winked and crossed hers too.

'Break a leg, Arlene,' whispered Mark.

The music faded and Arlene Thomas, wearing a glamorous but professional black trouser suit and blue blouse, strode to the podium.

'Good afternoon, ladies and gentlemen, I'm Arlene Thomas and I'm facilitating our seminar today. Firstly, on behalf of Yamoura Pharmaceuticals, can I warmly welcome you all here and thank you for coming along.'

After a few moments of introduction, she nodded to the technician, and a giant screen burst into life with an expensively produced corporate video on the benefits of SuperVerve as reported by patients and doctors around the world.

Arlene returned to the podium. 'Yamoura have carried out extensive clinical trials on these newly discovered bonus benefits and asked an eminent independent physician, Professor Alan G.F. Milton, to assemble an independent panel of experts, to review that material. Firstly, Professor Oscar Kolsen, from Dallas University, will summarise his findings on early diagnosis.'

There was a polite round of applause and Professor Kolsen presented a fairly dull paper, with lots of charts and graphs on the big screen. He was followed by Dr Cook, who added his contribution on lifestyle illnesses and weight loss, in fifteen minutes.

Professor Alan G.F. Milton's paper was straightforward. From his team's rigorous review of the Japanese clinical findings, they were convinced that a more aggressive prescription regime of SuperVerve was leading to improved energy and quality of life as well as the alleviation of symptoms. Also, having taken expert advice on genetics from Professor Kolsen, he had no doubt that the findings would hold true for a western demographic.

The Q&A session went tamely enough. The only tricky moment came near the end.

'Professor Milton, Dr Caroline Kane,' called a voice from a table near the front. She was handed a roving microphone. 'Dr Caroline Kane, Manhattan,' she repeated. 'Thank you for your most interesting presentation. But, as I understand it, isn't this just the standard cephalosporin that we've all been prescribing for years? Why the name change? And don't we have enough trouble with developing resistance to antibiotics, without encouraging people to take even more?'

Professor Milton leaned forward on the couch. 'Thank you for your question, Caroline. Yes indeed, this is essentially a cephalosporin product. But one of the big messages for me is that we can get far quicker alleviation of a whole range of health problems by making earlier diagnosis. This rebranding also focuses on the extra benefits now discovered.' Even as he said it, Professor Milton thought it was a nice answer. *Probably worth a couple of thousand extra prescriptions next week.*

Recognising this as a strong closing moment, Arlene Thomas returned to the podium. 'Ladies and gentlemen, it's been a great session. Thank you so much again for your interest and support. Lunch is now being served next door.'

There was a burst of applause from the floor as the screen filled with logos and the *Chariots of Fire* music filled the room again. The not-so-subtle message of the Tokyo 2020 logo was picked up by most of the doctors present, who had already heard about Yamoura's convention in Tokyo to coincide with the Olympic games.

The lunch was superb, with the very best food and wine. On the way out of the dining room, a team of pretty young women handed every doctor a box containing the latest iPad, onto which information on SuperVerve had been loaded.

★

Not far away, Tsan Yohoto had asked a surprised Anna Milani to lunch at Spice Symphony on Lexington Avenue. Her bosses, Victor and Katie at Dynamic, had been a bit taken aback, but guessed it could only be a positive development. 'Getting closer to the clients and all that.'

'This is the best Asian restaurant I have found so far in New York, Anna,' he said, looking around at the busy tables. He got a delicious spark of pleasure from his visits to New York. *All these millions of people, and they have no idea that I'm propelling them to their deaths.*

'It's fantastic, thank you, Tsan,' replied Anna. She hoped that this wasn't going to be a prelude to him asking her to dinner, and pressing for a relationship. She had tried to talk about the SuperVerve campaign, but he told her he was more interested in her English upbringing and her views on American culture. The conversation was warming as he asked her about her family and growing up in the UK.

'Adam was his name. He was just eight,' she said. 'Leukaemia. I still think about him every day.' She was shocked to see tears suddenly flowing down Tsan Yohoto's cheeks.

'I don't believe it!' Yohoto said. 'One of my brothers died from leukaemia too. He was just eight also. His name was Horto. I also think of him a lot. Even after all this time.'

He reached for her hand across the table and she took it in sympathy as he told her all about Horto. This has really affected him, thought Anna, as Tsan dabbed tears from his eyes. He seems genuinely upset. He is actually really quite sweet, and a good listener.

Tsan then showed her a photograph of his twin sister and brother, who had also died young.

'So,' said Tsan wiping away a last tear with a smile. 'To happier matters. How is your Detective Wyse?'

And so Anna told him all about John Wyse and how they had met, and Tsan listened attentively.

29

MANHATTAN – 14 OCTOBER

Ricky Morgan pulled his baseball cap even lower over his eyes as he waited for the light to turn green. He blipped the throttle impatiently and sucked in the beautiful sound of the Ferrari's V12 engine as it roared an eager response. He switched his radio to HOT 97 ROCK. Opposite him, a giant digital screen was advertising Macy's to the traffic. A directional receiver on the screen detected that the radios in most of the vehicles stopped at the junction were tuned to rock and pop stations. The receiver's software did the rest and the screen quickly switched to an advert for Budweiser. The traffic light changed and in a haze of burning rubber, Ricky Morgan was up to one hundred m.p.h. in less than five seconds. *What a rush.* Not that he was in a hurry. They'd wait.

The sun was beating down on the fast-moving New Jersey Turnpike route to the Meadowlands complex and A$AP Rocky was pumping through the Ferrari's sixteen speakers. Ricky was on his way to the MetLife Stadium to shoot another TV commercial and life was good. He thought back to all the times he'd travelled out there on the bus from the Port Authority Station to watch his heroes at the old Giants Stadium. Never thought he'd be making the journey like this, to pick up easy money for smiling into a camera and talking about burgers. And it was great to be able to look after his mom's medical bills. *Jeez . . . hope she'll be okay.*

'Okay, folks, and . . . action.'

Ricky Morgan, in his blue and white Giants uniform, helmet under his arm, was sitting near the front of the east end stand. The camera was pointing downwards so that the playing field was in the background. Ricky turned slowly, looked into the camera and smiled.

'BurgerFantastic, for a fantastic life,' he said. He took a huge bite of the BurgerFantastic in his right hand, munched hard and winked into the camera.

'And . . . that's a wrap,' said the director.

'Nice one, Ricky,' said Anna Milani of Dynamic Communications, who was standing behind the camera. 'Just a few more photos while we're here and that's us finished.'

'Sure, no prob.' He glanced down at the burger in his hand. 'Hey, these burgers are really good,' he said. 'I'm gettin' to like them.'

The new TV commercial aired on eight New York satellite broadcast and cable stations, starting the third weekend of November. Sales at BurgerFantastic increased the following week by a further twenty-eight per cent and maintained an increase of twenty-one per cent. The Sunday after the first TV adverts were shown, the Giants were at home to Denver, in front of a full house. Over forty thousand people in the MetLife Stadium swamped the fifteen BurgerFantastic outlets around the complex for the 'Buy one, get one free' offer.

*

Christopher White grinned sheepishly as Jane Cash probed him about his love life. She was a natural comedian and the audience loved her questions. No wonder the *Jane Cash Show* on NBC got the highest ratings in New York. Jane caught the producer's signal. Two minutes to go. She turned up her charm by leaning towards Christopher White, New York's top basketball player, and a huge catch for her show. *Sure to boost the ratings even higher, and one in the eye for Jimmy Fallon. Better make sure he gets in the plug we agreed on.*

'So, tell me, Christopher, apart from all the hot women, what's your secret to staying really healthy and on top of your game?'

'Well, you know, Jane, it's really all down to a balanced diet and plenty of exercise.'

'But you can't always feel on top form?'

'No, sure, and to be honest, I did have a bit of stomach trouble for a while.'

'Trouble? Looks nice and flat to me.'

The audience laughed.

'No, I was getting cramps and headaches. And not feeling right on top of things. I wasn't making as many baskets either.'

'Oh, that doesn't sound like you . . .'

'Yeah, then my doctor put me on these new tablets called SuperVerve. They really helped me, so now I take them anytime I'm not feeling one hundred per cent.'

'SuperVerve?' said Jane.

'Yep, SuperVerve. As the saying goes, "Puts the verve back into your life".' The audience laughed again as he added, 'Puts the verve back into my game too.'

'Well, Christopher White, you sure are a super guy. And New York loves you.' The producer was counting down from ten. 'Christopher, thanks for being my guest. We'll see you tomorrow night, folks.' The floor manager whipped the audience up into thunderous applause and cheering, and the credits rolled.

Watching from the wings, Anna Milani could hardly contain her excitement. *That was a real winner. Yamoura will be delighted.*

★

SAITON, NEAR TOKYO – 5 NOVEMBER

Lumo Kinotoa was pouring a second cup of tea. The table was strewn with files, sheets of paper and printouts, scattered around the chessboard centrepiece.

'Lumo, the detective's girlfriend was telling me all about how dangerous his job can be. She mentioned that he has begun to suspect he is being followed for some reason,' said Tsan Yohoto.

'Do you think we should call off the surveillance? Or should we keep him under observation, Tsan?'

'I think we should continue to keep an eye on him, Lumo. But please tactfully warn our friends to be a little more careful.'

'I'll send a message after the meeting.'

Yohoto nodded. 'Now, back to business.'

'I believe the basketball player was very good on that TV show,' said Kinotoa.

'Yes, first class,' Tsan Yohoto responded. 'They were hoping for *The Late Late Show*, but apparently they wouldn't agree to the product endorsement. Dynamic are going to try them again later.' The conversation paused as Lumo Kinotoa took a sip of tea. He put his cup down delicately.

'Gentlemen,' he said. 'I have a concern about the next phase of the marketing of the SuperVerve tablets. We are making such marvellous progress on all fronts, but the weight loss claim for SuperVerve has always struck me as the riskiest with the Food and Drug Administration. I suggest that we leave well alone.'

There was a silence, which lasted for a good dozen ticks from the grandfather clock. Never before had there been a suggestion that they alter the plan. To do so would be to admit that their initial plan had a flaw, and that was hard to envisage.

Tsan Yohoto broke the silence. 'My great friend, Lumo. I appreciate your advice. But when you feel the momentum starting to help you throw your opponent over your back, you do not hesitate and allow him time to recover. We must not lose our advantage. We must push ahead on all fronts.'

*

ATLANTA CITY – 17 DECEMBER

Richard Allen, Senior Vice President of Dupitol Pharma, the multinational pharmaceutical giant, was pure Texan, fair-haired with a tanned six-foot-three frame. The monthly sales meeting with his twenty-five regional sales directors was not going well.

'For chrissakes, Tom, what's going on?' he asked, exasperated. 'It's a booming market,' he said to his sales director from New York. 'How can we be down over five per cent overall?'

'Well, Richard, I think it's all down to the losses in our cephalosporin sales.'

'What's going on?'

'Yamoura have cut the cost of their cephalosporin in half,' said a nervous Tom Jackson. 'So, under the economic prescribing policy, all the hospitals have to use their stuff. And they're flooding the city with this SuperVerve product, which is cephalosporin antibiotic, pure and simple.'

'So, what's the big deal?'

'They're claiming it cures every illness known to mankind. And they're throwing an absolute fortune at marketing the stuff. I've never seen anything like it.'

'What illnesses exactly?'

'Stomach cramps, bowel inflammation, chest infection – fair enough. Headaches – doubtful. More energy – very doubtful. Weight loss – I don't believe it.'

Richard Allen was incredulous. 'Weight loss! Haven't the FDA been asking questions yet?'

'Not that I can see. Yamoura seem to have US doctors in their pockets.'

'Humph,' grunted Allen. 'We should report them.'

'Are you joking, Rich? We're launching our own new female sexual dysfunction illness and cure next spring. Last thing we want is the Yamoura guys in the FDA blocking us.'

His boss hesitated. 'Yeah, you're right.'

'So, what's been the impact on our cephalosporin sales?'

'Pretty much one hundred per cent.'

'What does that mean?'

'Exactly that. We've hardly sold a gram of cephalosporin in New York for six months.'

'What the hell are they doing? They can't possibly be making money out of this.' Richard Allen paused, exasperation etched on his face. 'I know a couple of guys in sales at Yamoura. I'll see if I can find out what the hell is going on.'

★

NYPD HEADQUARTERS, MANHATTAN – 17 DECEMBER

'Paul Carter's office? Yeah, down that corridor, last door on the left.'

'Thanks.' John Wyse smiled at the secretary.

The last door on the left had a piece of card taped to it: *P. Carter – Profiling*. Wyse knocked.

'Come in.'

Wyse put his head inside the door.

'Hey John, how's it goin?' Paul Carter was stretched back in his chair, both feet on the desk, reading a book as big as a bible. He flashed Wyse a broad smile and jumped up to shake his hand.

'Come in, man, come in. You're welcome. Take a seat,' said Carter, indicating a couple of chairs. 'There's someone due for a meet but I should have a few minutes. Congrats again on your medal. And for saving our building!'

'Thanks, Paul,' said Wyse. City Hall had presented him with a Meritorious Police Duty medal for his role in preventing the truck bombing. Wyse had insisted that it be done without publicity. He sat down and took in the surroundings. The walls were lined with shelves carrying at least a couple of hundred neatly arranged books. Other than Carter's PC and the telephone beside it, there was little else in the office.

'This has to be the neatest office in the whole Puzzle Palace,' said Wyse.

Carter laughed. 'Just can't work with a whole load of clutter.'

'Hmm. Wonder what that would tell me if I was putting together a profile of you?' joked Wyse.

'Ha! Probably quite a bit. But I'm sure you didn't come up here to profile me. How are you doin' these days? I was kinda surprised to hear you decided to stay on, after our last conversation.'

'Yeah, so was I, to be honest.' Wyse shrugged. 'Dunno how Connolly talked me round,' he said, jabbing his thumb at the window, in the direction of the Fifth Precinct.

'I'd say he played the old "sense of duty" card? You know, duty to your colleagues, duty to the public, you're one of my best detectives – all that.'

Wyse smiled. 'You know, that's exactly what he went on about. How did you know?'

Carter shrugged. 'Smart cookie, Connolly. He's been around the block often enough to know how to size a guy up and work out his levers. Connolly coulda written a few of these books,' he said, circling a hand around the office, 'what with his life experience. So how goes it?'

'Lookin' up, I guess,' replied Wyse. 'Main event is this incredible woman that I've been dating. She's something special. But she's playin' things very slow. Keepin' a little distance.'

Carter smiled. 'Sounds like a smart girl to me, John. Nothing like a little mystery to keep you guessing.'

Wyse returned the smile. 'You're probably right, but it's a bit unusual in my book. You know, I've been seeing her for over six months and we haven't slept together. It's torture. Sez it's something to do with her upbringing and she'll let me know when the time is right.'

'Hmm. That's unusual all right. I'd say just hang in there, man, but mind yourself. Might be an old boyfriend pulling heartstrings or something. Play it her way. Take your time.'

'Yeah, you're right, I guess. You know, I still think about that stuff you said about leadership genes and all that. Guess I'll give all that a little time too and make a move when the time seems right.'

'Sounds like a plan to me,' said Carter. He opened the bottom drawer of his desk and took out a bottle. 'Water?'

'Yeah, thanks.'

Carter took two glasses off a shelf by the window and filled them. 'So how can I help you, John?' he said.

'Well,' replied Wyse, shifting a little in his seat, 'it's a bit awkward. This person has friends who wouldn't like me getting in the way. But I didn't know who else to come to for advice.'

'Try me.'

'Okay.' Wyse hesitated, took another sip of water and pressed on. 'Look, this is all unofficial and no names, but I'm worried that one of the detectives has a real big drink problem. But he won't listen to me.'

'Okay. So, you tried talking to him and he got angry?'

'Exactly.'

'Then he told you that he didn't have a drink problem, because all of his friends drink the same?'

'Right in one,' said Wyse, picturing some of the guys at the station.

'Bet they do too. Heavy drinkers hang out with heavy drinkers. Provides cover when the trouble starts.'

Carter sat forward on his seat. 'I'm afraid it's pretty simple, John,' he continued. 'I can't help you.' As if to emphasise the point, he firmly closed the cover of the book on his desk.

Wyse was taken aback. 'What, what do you mean, you can't help me?'

'I can't help you. You can't help him. And he can't help himself. So, we'd all be wasting our time.'

There was a tap on the door and a detective walked in.

'Oh, sorry.'

'No, no problem,' said Carter, standing. Just then, the telephone on the desk rang. Carter lifted it. 'Shit, sorry guys.'

The new arrival was hanging about at the open door, so Wyse stood to leave. Carter covered the mouthpiece with one hand and grimaced at him.

'Sorry, John,' he whispered. 'That's my advice. Walk away.'

John Wyse nodded, waved a thanks and let himself out of the office, feeling deflated.

Walk away, he says. But, how the fuck do you walk away from your partner?

★

19 DECEMBER

The tall blonde, in blue jeans and a sky-blue sweatshirt, kissed the guy in the overcoat as they sat at a picnic table and took out their Subway rolls. They were both laughing. Chatting away non-stop.

And obviously in love, guessed Detective John Wyse, who was sitting on a park bench in a sunny Central Park. Glenda was snoozing underneath the bench, recovering from the exertions of the walk, her telescopic legs spreadeagled in all directions. *I guess he's a lawyer or accountant and she works in a fashion store.* They kissed again, then turned back to the table to open bottles of Diet Coke. *I wonder if they'll still be together in a year? In five years? In fifty years?* Right now, he envied them.

Central Park at lunchtime was buzzing. Walkers, cyclists, joggers, skateboarders, roller-bladers, rich, poor, happy and unhappy, swirled around the paths and lawns, taking advantage of the crisp winter sunshine. The bark of a hungry sea lion from the zoo could be heard across the lawns. John Wyse's stillness on the bench contrasted with the frantic activity around him. He found himself feeling unsettled a bit more often these days. Kind of uneasy and thinking more deeply about his life. *Is this it? What is it really all about?*

He'd just been flicking through *The New York Times*. That had upset him too. On page three there was an article about the use of thousands of children as sex slaves in the Philippines. The writer said that over twenty thousand children had been thrown in jail, either arrested for their 'sex crimes', or because their parents were locked up. The big, frightened eyes of a six-year-old girl bored into Wyse from between the bars of her packed prison cell. *Fuck it, how can that happen?* The only guy who seemed to be fighting for the children was some priest, who kept getting flung in jail too. *Jesus.* He admired that priest guy. *Now there was someone making a difference with their life. Doing the right thing. That guy could sit back, at the end of his life, and know that he had done his best.* Wyse couldn't see that he would ever have that feeling. He was born. He partied. He was a good detective. He died.

He was doing fine at work, even if it bored him sometimes. He'd just retained his title as top marksman in the station at his bi-annual range tests. That felt good. He didn't have any money worries. He had lots of friends and had no problem finding girlfriends. He knew that women found his tall, dark looks attractive; not to mention the badge and the gun.

Why had he run a mile from the one relationship in his life that had begun to get really serious? Lisa and he had been in love. They'd lived together in his apartment for nearly three years. She had transformed the place from the quintessential bachelor pad into a real home. They had joked about getting married and having kids. But it had suited him to let time go by. No way was he ready for all that.

Then Lisa had moved out. The single guys at the station were delighted to have him back on the circuit. Cabrini had organised a party to celebrate his 'return'. He had felt sick the day that Lisa called him to say she had gotten engaged to Lawrence, the teacher she was living with. Big mistake. For now, despite his busy life and his busy surroundings, John Wyse knew that sometimes he felt lonely. *And lonely is a cold and painful place.*

He watched as the young couple stood up and the girl took the guy's hand as they walked away. They were laughing. *Yeah, me and Lisa. Big mistake.*

His thoughts turned to Anna. Beautiful Anna. There was something special about her. Something different. There had seemed to be a really strong connection between them, but then she had been a little cool again on the phone. He wasn't used to that with women. She had told him not to call for another week. He didn't know what to make of that. He knew the erratic hours that went with police work weren't helping their relationship, but she sure didn't seem to be making it easy. In his heart, he knew that he wanted to get closer to Anna. But that scared him too. *Maybe she is out of my league?*

Wyse sighed as he stood up. 'C'mon, Glenda, back home.'

While Glenda went through her yoga-like stretching routine, apparently a vital part of her transition from sleeping to walking, he picked up pieces of litter and stuffed them into the trashcan beside the bench. As he turned for the Columbus Circle Gate, he realised that Carter, the profiler, would have noticed that. 'Sense of duty,' Carter would call it. 'Always trying to do the right thing.'

Just wish I knew what the hell is the right thing for my life, right now. What's the right thing to do with my career? What's the right thing to do about Mike's drinking? And what's the right thing to do about Anna? Try and push things along – tell her that I love her? Or allow her the space she seems to need?

30

DUPITOL PHARMA, ATLANTA – 21 DECEMBER

'Hey, Bob, it's Rich.'

'Richie, you old dog, how's it going, buddy?' replied Bob Denman with a smile. He and Rich Allen went way back. They had met at college in Corpus Christi in south Texas, where they had both studied marketing. 'Straight A students in drinking beer and chasing women,' as Bob used to say. They had struck up a close friendship that had survived over the years, even while working for rival drug companies. While Rich Allen had progressed to the top of the North American marketing team at Dupitol, Bob Denman was based at Yamoura Pharmaceuticals, in the plush Americas Building on State Street, Washington. Bob's job was to coordinate the Yamoura lobbyists in Washington and to maintain his own good contacts with senators.

'You spent all those bonuses yet?' teased Rich Allen. It was rumoured in the industry that Bob Denman and a few of his peers had each received bonuses of up to five million dollars for their successful lobbying to legalise the advertising of prescription drugs in 1997.

'Not the whole lot, man, but Veronica sure is working hard on it.'

Rich laughed. 'Way to go, Veronica. And how are the kids?'

'All well, Rich. And your gang?'

'Yeah, all in good shape, thanks. Tim's going to do marketing down in Corpus.'

'Hey, following in the guru's footsteps.'

'Don't know that I'd be happy to see him in all of our footsteps, buddy!' They both laughed out loud.

'Hey, how can I help you, Rich?'

'Well, Bob, strictly off the record . . .'

'Sure, bud, as always.'

'I'm getting kinda puzzled about what you guys are up to in New York. Turns out we haven't sold a gram of cephalosporin up there in six months, cos Yamoura have grabbed the whole cake. What's going on, Bob?'

'Can't say I know for sure, Rich. Only story I've heard that makes any sense is to do with Tsan Yohoto's retirement.'

'Yeah, I'd heard he was phasing out.'

'He's due to retire next year. The guy's a legend. I'd say he'd be worth keeping there until he's a hundred.'

Rich Allen grunted. He was well aware of the esteem in which the pharmaceutical industry held Tsan Yohoto. 'So, what's going on?'

'Well, and this is only rumour, okay? I got this from a pal in Tokyo.'

'Right.' Rich Allen was getting impatient.

'Turns out Yohoto wants to bow out on a high note, leave a legacy to mankind etc., you know the routine.'

'Sure.'

'So, Yohoto announced this big benevolent gesture to supply the entire continent of Africa with free cephalosporin. Reckons he can save millions of lives by eradicating common infections.'

'Yeah, I read some articles on that.'

'Well, apparently every spare inch of capacity in Yamoura was put onto cephalosporin production. Every damn warehouse we have gets filled with the stuff.'

'Right, keep going.'

'Then it turns out there's a cock-up on the African side. Some of the regimes there won't take the stuff. Some of them will, but there are no doctors to prescribe it, or no infrastructure to get it out to where it's needed.'

'I'm with you.'

'So, the whole supply chain starts backin' up. Then it starts to interfere with shipping of our other products.'

'Okay.'

'Then the board decides to shift some of the cephalosporin by slashing the price and dumping it into New York. Some genius comes up with an idea to try some big marketing techniques to make the whole thing look like the best idea ever instead of an almighty cock-up.'

'So, it's a face-saving exercise to protect Tsan Yohoto?'

'That's how it reads to me, bud.'

'But they're throwing millions at the advertising.'

'Rich, we're talking Tsan Yohoto here.'

'What do you mean?'

'That's a whole lotta face to be saved.'

A pause. 'I hear ya.'

'My advice is keep your head down. Whole thing'll blow over in a year or so; in the meantime, find something else to replace your cephalosporin sales.'

Rich Allen sighed. 'Okay, buddy, sound advice.'

'And, Rich, usual rules – OTR.'

'You got it, Bob, off the record.'

★

THAT NIGHT

John Wyse stamped on his effects pedal as he came out of the guitar solo on 'Purple Rain'. He was filling in with the old band at a gig in the Bronx. Proper club. Loud and dark and a crowd that came for the music, boosted tonight by Christmas partygoers. He'd been a bit pissed off that Anna was working late again and couldn't make it, although she'd said she was disappointed. *This coulda been a great night out. Most of the guys have their girlfriends, wives, or whatever here, but not me. I changed my shift so I could go to her office party.*

When the band took a break, the routine was to gather outside the stage door, where the lane provided cool air and a smoking sanctuary. When Wyse stepped outside, the drummer and bass player were examining a brown cardboard box.

'What's up, guys?'

'Awesome solo, John. Still playin' like a god.'

'Dunno about that. But funny how it all comes back.'

The drummer opened the box and pulled out some smaller boxes. 'SuperVerve. What the hell's that? Look like some kinda tablets.'

'Where'd you get 'em?'

'Box was sitting in the lane. Just picked it up.'

'Maybe fell off a truck,' said Wyse.

A head appeared around the door. 'Guys. Three minutes.'

31

MANHATTAN – 6 JANUARY

'Superhero – let's fly!' Jonathan Phillips guided his black plastic Superhero across a lunar base constructed with french fries. 'Pow!' He fired two missiles from under the dragon's wings and nuked the alien hiding behind his burger.

'Watch it, Jonathan, mind your Coke,' said his mother. Sandra grabbed the drink as it slid towards the edge of the table.

Karen Patel at the next table raised her eyes to heaven. 'Never a dull moment, Sandra,' she said, nodding to the boys at her own table, who were also conducting a ferocious battle to the death, with their own Superheroes. Her daughter, Lauren, a budding supermodel, wasn't going to be seen dead with a plastic dragon Superhero, which had sparked a row among the boys as to who should get it. Lauren settled the dispute with a game of rock, paper, scissors, which Jonathan had won.

The BurgerFantastic storefront on East 22nd Street, near the intersection with Park Avenue, was covered in posters for their new promotion. *Free Superhero with every BurgerFantastic. Collect a free Superhero each week for ten weeks.*

'These are really good quality,' Sandra remarked, crunching a fry and picking up one of the plastic toys. 'Beats me how they make money giving them away free.'

'Guess it's all about volume,' ventured Karen.

'Well, we'd better get used to it, honey. Just nine more weeks of Superheroes to go!'

*

12 JANUARY

Her tongue rolled slowly over his. Her moist lips tasted of cherries. John Wyse felt like there was an electric charge running around his body and his head spun. He put his arm fully around her shoulder and pulled her body closer to his own. He could feel her breasts against his chest. They simultaneously broke away from the kiss and, noses touching, looked deep into each other's eyes. At that moment, neither could think of anything else.

'Wow,' said Anna Milani.

'Wow, back.'

It was three o'clock in the afternoon and they were sitting on a bench at the southern end of a frosty Central Park, near the Grand Army Plaza entrance. A friend of Anna's was exhibiting their paintings of mountain scenery at the Graduate Center Art Gallery on Fifth Avenue. Anna had invited John along and she was excited about how good they were. She particularly liked the one of some place called Jaji and he was contemplating buying it for her. His interest cooled when Anna reckoned that the price was about five thousand dollars.

They'd gone for lunch together, to the restaurant in the Four Seasons on East 57th. It was one of Anna's favourites as it did a great vegetarian selection. Wyse had the sole meunière and they shared a chilled bottle of Sancerre. It was Anna who suggested a stroll in the park. Funny, she was still playing it a little cool. She had gently declined his suggestion that they declare they were 'exclusive' now.

'John,' she blushed, 'thank you so much for asking. I have no intention, whatsoever, of seeing anyone else. I'm so happy that we met, but I don't want to mess things up by going too fast.'

She was going to some business function that night and he wasn't invited. And he was getting pretty tired of hearing about SuperVerve tablets and how awesome that Japanese guy Tsan Yohoto was. He was back in New York to oversee progress with the marketing campaign apparently.

'John, he is just so nice. He took me to this amazing Asian restaurant. He told me that Yamoura was very impressed with my work. Vic and Katie think it's great that he wants to spend time with me.'

'Hmmm.'

'But he's not coming on to me or anything. For God's sake, he's in his seventies. And the craziest thing is that he had a brother who died of leukaemia too. And *his* brother was eight just like mine. I think we kinda connected over it. His other brother and sister died young too. I think he's lonely.' She laughed. 'And he was interested to hear all about you too. Said he hopes you're taking proper care of me.'

'I do my best.'

'And you are the best, John.' She pecked him on the cheek. 'Anyway, he said we'll have to have another lunch sometime, somewhere I choose. I threw out a few ideas but he won't go anywhere where they're roasting meat. Doesn't like the smell of it. He said he's glad I'm a vegetarian.'

Wyse still had suspicions about that guy's motives with Anna. *What's a big tycoon like that doin' spending so much time with her? I'll be keeping a close eye on that fella.* Saturday night in Manhattan and he'd nothing arranged. He'd kept the night free, just in case their lunch date developed into a bit more. He had hoped that it would. He could feel himself falling in love. Pure and simple. Every few minutes, he found that he was thinking about Anna again. The way she looked. The chats they had. Her cute accent with its crazy expressions. She was completely different to any other girl he'd ever dated, not to mention the slow pace she was putting on their courtship. *Maybe that's the way they do it in England? Certainly not very New York.* As of now, the best option for tonight was a voicemail from Cabrini, suggesting they check out a party on Park Avenue. Same block as J-Lo apparently.

★

MANHATTAN – 15 JANUARY

'*New York Girl* has put its rates up again,' said Cindy over the desk divider.

'No way,' replied Anna. 'That must be like twice in three months?'

'Yeah – full-page colour's now over five grand. That's if you can get it.'

'What do you mean?'

'Haven't you noticed, girl? Ever since you guys started buying up space in every magazine in town, it's getting harder for the rest of us to get our usual spots in the women's mags. And they're tightening up on editorial.'

'Don't blame me, honey, I'm just hanging with the celebs,' teased Anna.

'Yeah, okay, but Arlene's buying up space like there's no tomorrow. She's booking every cover, back page, inside cover, centrefold that's goin'. It's getting, like, embarrassing, trying to tell our fashion clients that there's no space – cos Dynamic's already booked it!'

Cindy flipped over the magazine to show Anna the back cover. Anna picked it up and read the blurb aloud.

'Life in New York can take its toll on a girl, coping with the stresses and strains of work and relationships. We all need a little help from time to time. If you suffer from headaches, tummy upset or a lack of energy, SuperVerve can put you right back on top of your game. And SuperVerve tablets not only give you more energy, they have also been clinically shown to help with weight loss. Ask your doctor if SuperVerve is suitable for you. SuperVerve – putting the verve back into your life.'

'Sounds like we could all do with some of that!'

'You said it, girl,' chuckled Cindy. 'But why do these medical adverts always tell you to ask your doctor for more information?'

'That's cos the tablets are only available on prescription from a doctor,' said Anna.

Cindy raised her eyebrows and looked at the magazine again.

'Okay ... but if only a doctor can decide whether you need these, why promote them to the public?' she asked.

'Power of advertising, girl,' said Anna, tapping the side of her nose as she stood up, smiling. 'The patients ask for it, the doctors prescribe it. Keeps us all in a job!'

'S'pose so.' Cindy shrugged and tossed her copy of *New York Girl* into Anna's wastepaper basket.

'Hang on,' said Anna. She retrieved the magazine, shook it open over her desk and four coupons for BurgerFantastic fell out. She handed them to her friend.

'No point wasting these.'

'Guess not. Thanks,' said Cindy as she stuffed the coupons into her purse. 'How's Mr Detective?'

'Don't rightly know.' Anna shrugged. 'Saw him a few days ago for lunch. Nice day out. I'm doing what you say, so I haven't called or texted since. But he hasn't called me either. I think he's getting pissed off with the hard-to-get stuff. I know he's got some kinda do on Friday for a cop that's leaving. And I've been so busy ...'

'Don't you worry, honey. You're playing it perfectly.' Cindy smiled. *Excellent. Time to make my move.*

★

HARRY'S BAR, MANHATTAN – 18 JANUARY

John Wyse was getting drunk but he felt the tap on his shoulder and turned around.

'Hey!'

'Hey, John, how are you? It's me, Cindy. Fancy meeting you here again! What's going on?'

'Oh, it's a going away party for one of the detectives,' said Wyse, pointing behind him at the packed back room. 'I've just passed the guitar on to someone else. Having a breather.'

'Great, can I get you a drink?'

'No, let me get you one. What'll you have?'

'Vodka and soda, please. Hey, I'll grab that table over there if you wanna take a break?'

A couple of minutes later Wyse put the drinks down and sat opposite her.

'Cheers, John,' said Cindy, clinking glasses. 'You're looking great.'

'Thanks. You too.' He meant it. Cindy was certainly voluptuous. What was it his mother always said? The more cleavage a girl shows, the more business she means. By that measure, Cindy coulda been Donald Trump.

'Hey, you seen Anna recently?' he asked.

'Yeah, sure. We see each other at work a lot. But not so much just now. She's been caught up in some big projects.'

'Huh. Tell me about it,' said Wyse sarcastically. 'It's all I ever hear – too busy.'

'Oh, everything okay with you guys?'

'To be honest, Cindy, sometimes I wonder. There seem to be so many reasons that she can't meet up that I wonder if she really wants to. Sometimes I feel like I'm being messed around.'

Cindy looked down and, after a pause, took hold of his hand and looked him in the eye.

'John, can I be straight with you here?'

'Sure.'

'Look, Anna's a good friend of mine, but I don't want to see you getting hurt. So, this has to stay strictly between us. Can I trust you?'

'Of course,' said Wyse, his stomach knotting.

'She's seeing another guy.'

The words hit Wyse like a truck. He felt like vomiting. 'Fuck's sake. I don't believe it.'

'Yeah. I'm sorry, John,' she said, taking his hand and squeezing it. 'Some old boyfriend. It's been going on a long time.'

Wyse shivered. 'That makes me feel sick.'

'You need a drink,' said Cindy, waving at a waitress. 'My round.'

'Thanks. I'll join you on the vodka. Make it a double.'

★

'Hey, you could do with a coffee, John. C'mon up and I'll make you one.'

Wyse had agreed to share a cab with Cindy and they were stopped outside her apartment. Cindy threw open the door of the cab, leaned over and pecked his cheek. Her perfume was nice. She had been really kind to him as they hit the vodka together and he knew he was really drunk now.

'C'mon, John, it'll be good for you.'

As soon as they got into the living room of her small flat, Cindy took his hands, held his bleary gaze, pushed him gently against the wall and flicked her tongue in his ear. He didn't resist. She undid her blouse, unfastened her bra, and guided his hands onto her breasts. He felt himself stiffening, quickly.

Cindy undid his belt, lowered his boxers, kneeled down and took his cock in her mouth.

★

TWO DAYS LATER

Wyse was on the couch in his apartment, recovering from a night out with Cabrini. Even Cabrini, not generally noted for his sensitivity, had asked him what was wrong. Wyse hadn't told him what had happened with Cindy, and didn't plan to.

'Jesus, what a mess,' he said in the general direction of Glenda, who cocked an ear, grunted, and resumed her snoring. He couldn't believe that he had allowed himself to be messed around by Anna. And ending up with Cindy . . . Fuck. That was a mistake. Ridiculously, part of him felt guilty about it. She was Anna's friend. She'd definitely come on to him, but he hadn't exactly been fighting her off. Great sex, though. He'd have to sort that out now, too. It was nice of her to tell him what Anna was up to, but she just wasn't his type. First thing to do was restore some pride in the mess with Anna, without dropping Cindy in it.

He started on a text . . .

> Hey Anna. Been thinking a lot. The two of us are just too busy for this. We need to go our own ways. Best of luck. John

He would never end a relationship by text under normal circumstances. But she had lied to him, made a fool of him, and he didn't want to see her again. He felt sick about the whole thing. *Wonder what she'll make of that? Jeez, man, why do you care? I'm the victim here.*

32

21 JANUARY

Christ, she looks shit, thought Cindy as she handed Anna another tissue in the restroom at Dynamic Communications.

'I'm devastated,' said Anna, her mascara streaking down her cheeks. 'Just outta the blue. Said we're too busy. Let's go our separate ways.'

'Don't worry, hun. Everything happens for a reason.' *And I'm the reason.*

'But it felt so right,' Anna sobbed. 'I think I overplayed the hard to get part.'

'Well, whatever you do, don't go chasing after him now. Give it some space, see if he misses you enough to come back.'

Anna blew her nose. 'I guess so,' she snuffled.

*

That evening Wyse got a text.

Hey John, wow that was some night! Hope you're feeling better.

You wanna hook up this week? Cindy x

He replied.

> *Hey Cindy. Thanks for looking after me. Hope you're doing good. I'm gonna hibernate for a while and get over all this. John*

Sure, I understand. Take care of yourself. Let me know if you ever need any more Healing. lol. X

Cindy hit send. *He'll be back. They always are.*

★

9 FEBRUARY

It is extraordinary how readily the most bitter of enemies can get around to cooperating, once they have a common purpose.

Richard Allen, senior vice president, sales and marketing at Dupitol Pharma, was worried. He had no doubt whatsoever that his old college buddy, Bob Denman, had given him his honest appraisal of the situation in New York. But something didn't sit easily with him. He had poked around a bit and spoken to some of his contemporaries at the other drug companies. They had all noticed the heavy advertising spend by Yamoura and had seen their own cephalosporin sales evaporate. No one was too sure what was going on, but, because it was just one city, and just one product, at the low margin end of the business, the other companies seemed content to sit it out. What everyone was surprised at was that Yamoura were pushing new benefits for an old drug.

'I'm surprised the FDA aren't on it yet,' said Roger Flack at Xantlox Webber, in another 'off the record' call.

'Maybe they are,' said Richard Allen.

'Don't think so, Rich, woulda got out by now. Any event, it's not our job to do the FDA's work. And the last thing we need is

Yamoura objecting to our own advertising. That would ruin the game for everyone.'

Richard Allen still felt uneasy. He felt even more uneasy when his marketing consultants in New York called him back.

'Hey, Richard, Paul Schander at Big Spark.'

'Hi, Paul, any news?'

'Well, I've been making some enquiries. Naturally, we've seen the SuperVerve campaign. Pretty routine work by Dynamic Communications. Very big spend so far, and word is that it's producing the goods.'

'You can say that again.'

'You betcha, Richard, but you may not like this bit. Girl working here with us is good friends with a girl from Dynamic, who's involved in the campaign. I asked her to see if she could find out a little more. Word from there is that they can hardly sleep they're so excited about this launch. Inside track is that New York is just a pilot campaign and that they're gonna be rolling it out across North America.'

'Just for SuperVerve?'

'Don't know about that, but Dynamic are pulling every marketing lever as far as they can. And that means pushing advertising, celebrity endorsements, medical endorsements, doctors' incentives and pushing the FDA to the limit.'

'Hmmm.'

'I'll let you know if I hear any more, Richard. And don't forget we're here, as soon as you need us.'

'Yeah, no problem, Paul, and thanks for the feedback.'

Richard Allen sat quietly looking out his window at the Atlanta skyline. This was getting too big to ignore. His experience told him that it was the little things left unmanaged that caused the big trouble down the road. His gut told him that something was up. Yamoura were on a free run in New York. It was time to give them something to worry about.

*

Book Online

> The Empire State Building, at the intersection of Fifth Avenue and West 34th Street, is a 102-storey Art Deco skyscraper. Completed in 1931, the Empire State Building stood as the world's tallest building, until the completion of the World Trade Center in 1970. After the destruction of the World Trade Center on 9/11/2001, the Empire State Building once again stood proudly as New York's tallest building, until the completion of One World Trade Center. Book sightseeing tour tickets online.

Tsan Yohoto smiled. The al-Qaeda sleeper in New York certainly had a sense of humour. He was reading from a glossy four-page tourist leaflet that had arrived in his mail that morning. Tsan had instantly recognised the plain brown A4 envelope with the New York postmark. Every few weeks he received some brochure or other in a similar envelope. The first brochure had been an old one for the Windows on the World restaurant, on the top two floors of the WTC's North tower. The second had been an information leaflet on the Pentagon.

He opened the centre page of the leaflet and smiled again when he saw the blob of sauce, about midway up a photograph of the Empire State. He scooped the blob into a plastic container and buzzed his PA to send it down to one of the Yamoura laboratories for analysis. The result would be back the next day. As usual, he expected that it would include 'egg whites, cream, salt, milk, preservatives, colouring. And cephalosporin ...'

*

MANHATTAN – 21 FEBRUARY

Anna Milani had had the most miserable month of her life, certainly since her brother died. She threw herself even more energetically into her work, to distract herself, but she still couldn't help checking her phone every few hours to see if there was a message from John. As the weeks went by, she found herself thinking about him more, not less. She found herself thinking back over all their dates, all those great conversations and all the fun. It had felt so right. He was different. How could she hope to ever meet another man like that?

The more she thought about it, the more certain she became that playing so 'hard to get' had been a huge mistake. She knew where Cindy was coming from, and she was way more experienced than her, but John was too genuine. He was big and strong, but he was vulnerable too. He wasn't the type of guy you had to play games with. *Time to take action.*

★

22 FEBRUARY

Wyse noticed someone leaning against a car as he approached his apartment block. About fifty yards away, he realised it was Anna. *Whoa, what's this about?*

'Hey, John,' she said, standing straight as he got to her.

'Hey, Anna, are you okay? Didn't expect to see you here.'

'I was waiting for you.'

'Oh? What's up?'

Cards on the table. 'I've been missing you. Badly. Can we go somewhere and talk?'

'Eh, sure. Fancy a glass of wine?' Seeing her again had shaken him. His heart was fluttering. *Keep your wits about you, John. She looks amazing. She's lost weight, though.*

'C'mon,' she said as she linked his arm and led him towards the wine bar at the end of Eldridge.

★

It didn't take long to reconnect. Perhaps ten minutes. Sitting at the corner table, she got straight to it.

'John, I am so sorry. I have never missed anyone so much in my life. I messed you around. I was playing hard to get because I really wanted you. I thought it was the right thing to do. I overdid it. I know I was always buried in work and not around enough, but that's eased a bit and I'll balance it better this time. I've never met anyone like you before. Will you give us another chance?'

Wyse hesitated. 'But I heard you were seeing someone else?'

'What?'

'That's what I heard.'

'Who from?'

'Just kinda picked it up on the grapevine.'

Anna took his hand and looked him in the eye. 'John, I promise you, on my parents' lives, I have never seen anyone else since I met you.'

That was pretty convincing. Looking deep into her eyes, John believed her. Maybe Cindy had another agenda going. But better not mention Cindy, only gonna cause problems.

They held hands across the table and agreed to give it another go. Anna was trying hard not to cry, and Wyse felt a lump in his throat too.

★

27 FEBRUARY

Ah yes, there it is. Richard Allen took a deep breath and enjoyed the warm Californian air, as he left the arrivals hall at Palo Alto Airport. He joined the line for a cab. If there was one benefit that he still enjoyed after ten years with Dupitol, it was the winter sales trips to California and Florida. As most of the continent started to shiver, he would make sure to get in a couple of games of golf, in perfect weather. It used to be blood pressure treatments and depression that kept the tills ringing at Dupitol. Those sales were still great, but Dupitol and several others in the pharma-industry had hit pay dirt by flooding the country with the highly addictive, opioid pain relief medication. The doctors were doing their bit by throwing prescriptions around like confetti. With a hundred people a day dying from overdoses, the Drug Enforcement Administration was calling it an epidemic, and the legal class-actions were piling up. But the profits were so enormous that Dupitol would be well able to pay any damages or fines – in the unlikely event that anyone could prove any wrongdoing.

At the sales meeting that afternoon, Richard scanned the latest printout of regional drug sales. Hmmm, there it was. Way down the list in terms of profitability, but Dupitol's sales of Clafox, its branded cephalosporin product, were rock solid at 32% market share in California. Makes this New York thing hard to take.

He glanced at his watch. He was meeting Damian Nowoski at five.

*

The call to the Palo Alto headquarters of WordOutWorld had been unusual from the word go.

'Hey, Damian, how are ye? Rich Allen here at Dupitol Pharma.'

'Oh, hello, Rich, there's a surprise. To what do I owe the pleasure?'

'Hey, Damian, you know, our organisations have been kickin' the hell outta each other for long enough.'

'That's for sure.'

'And I've been thinkin,' you know, we're all only here on this planet for so long. We may disagree on a whole lotta stuff, but I don't see why we can't get along better on a personal basis.'

'I see,' said a bemused Damian Nowoski. Damian Nowoski was twenty-eight years old, with an IQ as bright as his piercing blue eyes. He had worked with WordOutWorld since he had graduated. WordOutWorld was a fiercely independent organisation, dedicated to protecting the principles of free speech, consumer rights and the environment. Staffed by a team of lowly paid but dedicated individuals, WordOutWorld was a major thorn in the side of industry and politics, whenever they saw abuses of power and privilege.

'You know, Damian,' continued Richard Allen, 'we know each other's names so well, yet we've never met and I'd like to change that.'

'Sure,' said Damian, a little hesitant. 'Sounds okay to me.'

'I'm in your area next week, Damian. Would it be convenient to meet up?'

'Sure, no problem. Why don't you drop into the office?'

'Well, I'd prefer to keep it casual, Damian, you know, off the radar. How 'bout a beer after work one evening, say Wednesday at five at The Bleachers?'

'Yeah, sounds fine to me.'

'Okay, Damian, nice talkin' to you – see you Wednesday.'

'Sure thing, Richard, see ya.'

Damian Nowoski let out a long, low whistle. *Something's up, Damian boy, something's up.*

★

Richard Allen wrapped up the sales meeting with the usual stuff about 'achieving new goals', 'living the values of the Dupitol family', and 'turning challenges into opportunities'. In the back of the cab he took off his tie and folded it into his jacket pocket on the seat beside him. He had been on a course once where he had learned that he should dress like the person he was meeting, in order to case the connection. He had seen photos of Damian Nowoski and he was damn sure he wouldn't be wearing a tie. A minute later he took off his gold cufflinks, put them in his pocket and rolled up his sleeves. He patted the bulging white envelope which was folded over in the inside pocket of his jacket.

'Hey, Damian, nice to meet you, man – hope you haven't been waiting too long?'

'No, just got here,' said Damian, returning the firm handshake. His thick curls were even longer than Richard Allen had expected, and he hadn't shaved for two or three days. He was wearing a Nirvana T-shirt, beach shorts and a pair of sandals.

'What'll it be, Damian?' said Richard Allen. 'I could murder a beer.'

'Yeah, Bud's good for me, man.'

'Two Buds it is then,' said Richard, waving to the barman. *Better have the same drink too.* 'Why don't we take that table over in the corner?'

After three Buds each, things hadn't exactly loosened up a whole lot. Damian Nowoski was getting a little bored. *When will this guy get to the point?* The waiter plonked two more bottles of cold beer on to the table in front of them. Just in time, Richard Allen stopped himself asking for a glass. After another few minutes of complimenting WordOutWorld, Richard Allen made a round trip the men's room, squeezed his long legs back under the table and decided to make his move.

'Damian, can we, like, go off the record here?'

'Sure, man.'

'You know, Damian, we've had our disagreements over the years. And I don't think we're ever going to agree on a lotta stuff.'

'I expect not,' said Damian, sensing they were nearing the action.

'And this whole area of advertising prescription drugs. I believe it's a fundamental principle of free speech and unrestricted access to information that's at stake. I truly believe that the American people are entitled to as much information as possible about how our industry can improve their lives . . .'

'Yeah, tell that to all the people who took Tranztok for their arthritis. To the ten thousand who are suing.' Damian sat up straight in his chair as he became more animated. 'It's abuse and illegal promotion by the drug companies and I don't like it. We're into disagreement territory, Rich.'

'Damian, in fact, we're into agreement territory.'

'Really?'

'Yes, really. There's a line in the sand that should never be crossed and, strictly between you and me, Damian, I think that line has been crossed.'

'Go on,' said Damian, eyebrows raised.

Richard Allen glanced around the bar. He took the envelope out of his jacket, which was hanging on the back of his chair, and slid the envelope across the table.

'Have a look at this later, Damian.'

'What is it?'

'Well, in short, it's a disgrace. And it could get out of control. You know Yamoura?'

Damian nodded. 'Of course.'

'Well, word is they're on a major marketing strategy. They're going to rebrand lots of old drugs, hype up some new Mickey Mouse benefits, advertise the hell outta them and make a fortune in the process.'

'Why do you think that?'

'Because, Damian, it's already started. They're running a pilot campaign in New York, promoting cephalosporin antibiotic like it was the key to eternal life. The stuff they're saying about it is,' he grimaced, 'frankly unbelievable.'

There was a pause.

'So why aren't the FDA down on them?'

'Ah, c'mon, Damian, you know the speed they move at. And Yamoura are clever. Because cephalosporin is as old as the hills, they didn't need a new approval to rebrand it. The FDA can only get them on their misleading advertising. And that could take for ever.'

'So,' Damian said, 'what you need is someone to start complaining loudly.'

'Very loudly.'

'Loud enough to force the FDA to look at it?'

'You got it, Damian.'

'And, for obvious reasons, Dupitol can't be seen to be breaking up the old boys' club.'

'Well, I wouldn't put it like that, but . . .' Richard sat forward in his chair. 'Damian, in that envelope is a copy of every advert they've run. There's a USB key with the TV and radio adverts on it. And there's copies of the promotional and back-up stuff they've been giving to the doctors.'

'Who wrote that stuff?'

'The usual, Damian. Three high-powered medics, who all happen to be on various FDA approval panels.'

'And on Yamoura's payroll?'

'I couldn't say, Damian.' Richard winked. 'Maybe you'd like to have a look at it with your guys, see if it's worth asking a few questions?'

'Yeah, okay, we'll have a look.'

'Cool. Call me on my cell phone if you need me,' said Richard, handing over a card. 'But let's keep it low key.'

33

THE VILLA AT SAITON – 15 MARCH

The Chess Club meeting hadn't had this much tension in the air since the presentation to its al-Qaeda friends almost a year ago. Once the formal weekly review meeting started, Tsan Yohoto interrupted the chairman to say there was something they must look at.

'Please proceed, Tsan,' said the chairman, somewhat surprised. Changes to the running order were almost unheard of.

Tsan Yohoto booted up the shiny laptop in front of him. He pushed it out towards the centre of the table where all four could see it. The lead article on WordOutWorld's website filled the screen.

ANTIBIOTICS NOW HELP YOU LOSE WEIGHT? DRUG COMPANY ADVERTISING HITS A NEW LOW

Damian Nowoski and Alex Pigot

Drugs multinational Yamoura Pharmaceuticals is pushing claims about its cephalosporin antibiotic brand SuperVerve beyond the bounds of belief. Yamoura, aided by slick New York marketing consultants, Dynamic Communications, is claiming new benefits from cephalosporin, including relief from headaches and listlessness. The Japanese multinational is also claiming that it has clinical proof of sustained weight loss being experienced by patients taking SuperVerve. On the strength of these new benefits, the brand is now being heavily marketed in New York. Our sources tell us that prescriptions for SuperVerve have increased by over 500% in a year! Has no one in the drug industry read about the growth of antibiotic resistance? For how long is the FDA going to sit on its hands and let this abuse continue? With global pharmaceutical sales now running at over $1 trillion per annum, this is big business. Come on, FDA, do your job – or is the problem that your guys are also employed by the drugs companies?

There was a silence. Then, 'Shit,' said Lumo Kinotoa.

'Certainly a quicker media reaction than we expected,' said Kazuhiro Saito.

'What's their circulation?' asked Dr Juro Naga.

'It's a web-based publication,' replied Saito. 'I read somewhere that they have a distribution list of about one hundred and fifty thousand. Most of the medical journalists subscribe and sometimes they quote WordOutWorld. Problem is, everyone in the FDA downloads it – they like to hear what's being said about them.'

'Has Bob Denman in Washington heard anything?' asked Lumo Kinotoa.

'Not yet, or he would have been in touch,' replied Tsan Yohoto, 'but I'll give him a call. He's listed as our company secretary at the Washington office, so any official communication from the FDA will go there.'

'Could this affect our plan?' asked Kinotoa.

Tsan Yohoto paused. 'Let me think. Curse them anyway. At the rate the FDA move, we can hope for another month or so before a query. Then we'll bury them in a paperwork response and string them out for as long as possible. They're probably going to look for the clinical trial results. We've plenty of data to bog them down. Then it's up to our Professor Milton and his panel to smokescreen them. Hopefully, one of his pals will be put onto any inquiry. With any luck, we should get another twelve months out of it.'

'So, we keep going?' asked Dr Naga.

Tsan Yohoto nodded firmly. 'We keep going. Gentlemen, this is just a little extra pressure. Lumo, let's review the numbers.'

'First, our Islamic friends tell me that their man hasn't missed one night of van drops in a year,' said Lumo. 'So that's holding steady at about four thousand regular consumers.'

'And the hospitals?'

'Very solid,' said Dr Naga, 'as expected. We have a rolling hospital population of about two thousand five hundred patients on our cephalosporin. We should soon see some early sporadic cases of cephalosporin antibiotic resistance in the hospitals.'

'How so?' asked Kinotoa.

'Well, I expect some cases soon where people will contract food poisoning from a routine source. They'll need hospitalisation, where they'll be prescribed our cephalosporin. Also, there'll be some other illnesses caused, where other strains of bacteria have increased their numbers, to take up the space left behind by the bacteria killed by the SuperVerve tablets. We'll get extra sporadic deaths, mostly in elderly people, but it won't be enough to alert anyone to the bigger picture.'

Lumo Kinotoa wrapped things up. 'Excellent progress, gentlemen. The only fly in the ointment is WordOutWorld. Let's hope we can stonewall them and the FDA until our next phase, when we start wiping out New Yorkers en masse.'

*

MANHATTAN – 26 MARCH

'It's just awesome,' Anna was telling Cindy. 'We're getting on really well!'

'That's great. I'm so happy for you.'

'Tell me more about this guy José you've been seeing.'

'Oh, he's cute. Fit, too – I met him at the gym.'

'Hey! How about a double date? We're going to the U2 gig on Friday. There was a mix-up with tickets and I've got two spare. Why don't you come with us?'

'Wow,' said Cindy. 'Fantastic. I'll check with José. Shouldn't be a problem.' *This is gonna be funny.*

*

'*It's a beautiful day.*' Bono held the swaying crowd in the palm of his hand for U2's encore. Anna was jumping up and down and singing her heart out. John Wyse was torn between looking at the stage and looking at his girlfriend. She was wearing what she called her 'rock chick' look: tight black leather trousers, black T-shirt, black leather jacket, black knee-high boots. She looked sensational. They had been back dating now for over a month and had grown increasingly intimate. He wanted and needed her, more and more.

He'd been taken aback when Anna, so enthusiastically, told him that she'd invited Cindy and some guy to come to the concert with them. Nothin' much he could do about it but keep shtum and hope it all went off okay. He was pretty sure that Cindy would be keeping shtum too.

The crowd streamed out of Madison Square Garden into a cold March night. The clamour of giant electronic screens promoting Coca-Cola, McDonald's, Nike, SuperVerve and upcoming concerts at the famous venue illuminated the bustling pavements.

'Oh. My. God,' said Anna, hugging Cindy. 'That was unbelievable! It was amazing having you guys with us.'

'Awesome. Thanks for the invite,' said Cindy, returning the hug. 'Okay, guys, where to? I'm starving,' she said.

'And I'm parched,' said José. 'Let's buy you guys a drink.'

'How about both?' said Cindy. 'Come on, food first,' and she pointed up the street to a brightly lit BurgerFantastic, near Macy's.

The two couples began walking towards the restaurant. As they waited at the lights outside Pennsylvania Station, José lit a cigarette, and Anna and Cindy found their attention grabbed by galloping horses on a screen in Macy's window. It was a Budweiser advert. As they watched, the camera on top of the Quivada screen calculated the distances between their eyes, noses and cheekbones. The computer decided they were both female, white and aged about thirty, and changed the screen to a SuperVerve advert – *Putting the verve back into your life.*

'Wa-hey, go SuperVerve!' cheered Anna, laughing with Cindy.

Not surprisingly, the BurgerFantastic restaurant was packed with U2 fans. John Wyse joined a line. 'BurgerFantastics, fries and coffees all round? Anna, your usual salad?'

'Yes please, we'll grab a table.'

'I'm paying,' said José, joining Wyse in the line.

Killian Desmond, the restaurant manager, thinking on his feet, had U2's 'City of Blinding Lights' blaring out over the sound system. Wyse made his way over to their table, struggling with a large tray.

'There you go, you said you were hungry!'

'Jeez, John, we'll never eat all that,' laughed Cindy.

'Hey, it was only fifty cents more to supersize the burgers – so I decided to treat you.'

Sitting opposite him, Cindy caught his eye and winked, as she slowly sucked on a straw. Wyse felt her foot touching his ankle. He moved his leg away and held Anna's hand on the table for a moment. *Jesus, Cindy, please don't cause a scene. Hopefully she can keep her mouth shut. Well, not always! She's enjoying playing with me here.* He put his arm around Anna.

In the background, Bono sang about not letting beautiful days get away. John winked playfully at Anna. *Don't worry, Bono, I won't.*

*

Over the years, John Wyse had learned that sex with a woman you felt a real connection with took you to a different place. And making love with Anna ranked as the most incredible experience of his life. After BurgerFantastic, they'd gone for a few drinks at Fitzy's, an Irish bar on 49th Street. 'May as well keep the theme going,' Wyse had said.

Fitzy's was also playing footage of a U2 concert on the screens around the bar. After a couple of drinks, Cindy and José had left. John took Anna's hand and squeezed it gently.

'Hey, baby, I'd love to bring you back to my place?'

Anna leaned over and kissed him on the lips. 'Sure, chuck.' They caught a cab back to his apartment on Eldridge Street. He made coffee in the small kitchen while Anna connected her phone to the sound system.

'Hey, John,' she called, 'you think U2 are good, you wanna hear this guy, Hozier.'

'Cool, go for it,' he said.

Anna chose Hozier's 'Better Love' and stroked Glenda's head as she snored in her bed.

John felt the butterflies in his stomach as he took her coffee mug from her and put it with his own on the floor. He leaned forward, put his arm around her and pulled her close. They kissed, deeply and longingly, feeling the desire build. Suddenly, Anna pulled away.

'Phew, it's hot in here,' she said.

For a moment, John was worried. He needn't have been. Anna reached down and began pulling her T-shirt out of her leather trousers. She slowly lifted the T-shirt over her head, revealing a very sexy, black lace bra. Wyse stood up and scooped her into his arms. Hozier's honeyed voice followed them through the open door as he carried her to his bedroom.

Some better love, but there's no better love . . .

Anna locked her arms around John's neck and kissed him as he laid her on the bed. Lying beside her, Wyse cupped her ass and pulled her tighter against him. Anna moaned, rolling over onto him.

Wyse had dreamed of this moment, many times, and had thought about how he would make their lovemaking slow and gentle. Those thoughts exploded as Anna swiftly unbuckled his belt, pulled his jeans down and took his cock in her hand. Hozier added a pulsing drum, like a heartbeat.

That ever has loved me, there's no better love . . .

She slipped out of her underwear as he flung his shirt away and struggled out of his jeans. Naked, she took his breath away.

'Quick, John, I want you,' she whispered in his ear. She wrapped her long legs around his hips and pulled him closer. Wyse's head spun in a whirlpool of desire, intense like he had never felt before. He flipped her over onto her back and Anna moaned and arched as he entered her.

Darling, feel better love, feel better love . . .

Their intensity built, faster and faster. She was biting her lip, her eyes closed, thrusting against him, deeper and deeper as she began to come. Wyse was transfixed. Her beautiful face. Her passion.

'Baby, baby,' he moaned. 'Look at me.'

Anna's eyes fluttered open and they looked deep into each other's souls as he exploded inside her.

Feel better love . . .

★

About fifty yards down the street, Ibrahim Fallah had just pulled in to watch Wyse's apartment from his brown Nissan. He could see that there were two people in the apartment from the shadows moving around behind the net curtains, but not enough to identify them. Then the lights went out.

Looks like he's got company. Probably some girl staying the night. Maybe I'll kill her, too. Confuse things a little. Make it look like a double mugging gone wrong.

He tensed as a police car drove down the street. On the side of the car he read *1800-COPSHOT–$10,000 Reward*. It was the free phone reward line for information about any shooting of a police officer. If there was one thing the police department would throw all resources at, it was the murder of one of their own. He would have to be very careful.

*

WASHINGTON – 12 MAY

Click. The trunk of Bob Denman's 7 Series BMW closed gently after the porter had lifted in his clubs.

'See ya, Tim,' he waved, as his golfing companion, Senator Tim Willis, reversed out of the space beside him at the Army and Navy Country Club near Arlington National Cemetery. His cell phone rang as he opened the car door.

'Bob Denman.'

'Hullo, Bob, Maurice Chadwick at the FDA.'

'Hey, Maurice, how are ya?'

'Good, thanks. Hope I didn't catch you at a bad time?'

'No, no worries, I just made sure I lost on the eighteenth to one of your bosses.'

'I won't ask.'

'What can I do for you, Maurice?'

'Just thought I'd give you a heads-up, Bob. There's a bit of a stink kicking up here over one of your products.'

'Oh, what's that?'

'SuperVerve, this cephalosporin brand that you're marketing in New York.'

'And what's the problem?' said Bob Denman cautiously.

'WordOutWorld have been questioning the claims you're making in your advertising. You must have seen it?'

'No,' said Bob, playing dumb. In fact, he received weekly briefings on every media mention of Yamoura or one of its products. He'd been expecting a call.

'Well, it's on their website. Anyway, I've been told here to make some enquiries with you guys. Just thought I'd let you know there's a letter on the way – you know the routine.'

'Yeah, sure, Maurice, I appreciate that. I'll give you a call when I've seen it.'

'Okay, Bob, keep it on the short grass.'

'You betcha.'

34

MANHATTAN – 7 JUNE

Mrs Esther Wolfowitz groaned as she pulled her knees up towards her stomach. *Jesus, what a cramp.* She put her hand to her clammy forehead. She was drenched with sweat. Sidney snored beside her. She needed to get to the toilet, fast. She sat up and swung her legs out of the bed. She groaned again as a searing cramp doubled her up. *Jesus, this is bad.* Dizzy, she just made it onto the toilet before she suffered a massive episode of diarrhoea. She wiped the sweat off her forehead. That was to be the first of four trips to the bathroom that night. Sidney snored through the whole lot. Christ, you wouldn't want to be dying, she thought as she looked at his peaceful expression. She sipped some water from the glass on her bedside locker and eventually got back to sleep at 5 a.m.

'Morning, honey, here's your tea.'

Esther stirred as Sidney put a cup of tea and a plate with two slices of toast, down on her locker.

She groaned.

'What's wrong, honey? You're normally awake by now.'

'Jesus, Sidney, didn't you hear me during the night?'

'Can't say I did, honey – what happened?'

'I've got really bad diarrhoea, worst ever.'

'Oh no, I'm sorry to hear that, dear,' said Sidney, looking concerned.

Esther very slowly propped herself up on the pillows, sipped some tea and ate half a slice of toast. Thirty seconds later, she was scrambling out of bed and rushing for the bathroom.

★

'Hello, Dr French's surgery.'

'Hello, it's Sidney Wolfowitz here. I wonder if the doctor could come and see my wife – she's ill.'

'Oh dear, Mr Wolfowitz, what seems to be the problem?'

'Well, she has really bad diarrhoea. She's sweating and she's just started vomiting. There's no way she can get to the clinic.'

'That's no problem, Mr Wolfowitz. Dr French has a couple of house calls to make after the surgery. He'll call by at about six o'clock.'

★

'Ow, ow!' Three hours later, Mrs Wolfowitz almost leaped off the bed when Dr French gently pressed her abdomen.

'Oh dear, you certainly are very tender. We'll have to get you sorted out. Do you think you could have eaten anything that might have caused this?'

'She had beef burgers at our son's barbeque at the weekend,' offered Sidney.

'That could well be the problem then,' said Dr French. 'I think you have food poisoning, Mrs Wolfowitz. You have it pretty severely, and we don't want it becoming toxic, so I'm going to get you on to an antibiotic. That'll sort you out in a couple of days. And I'm concerned that you're dehydrated. It's important that you take these.' He handed Sidney a box of six sachets of electrolytes powder. 'These will help replace the fluids and minerals you're losing. Drink plenty of liquids, but best not to eat anything for the moment.'

Mrs Wolfowitz groaned. 'That won't be a problem, doctor.'

'Here's a few cephalosporin tablets to get you started. Take two straightaway and then two, three times a day. Mr Wolfowitz, can you get the prescription tomorrow?'

'No problem, doctor,' said Sidney. 'Glad I had the chicken!'

★

THE NEXT DAY

David Wolfowitz answered the phone at his house in Connecticut. It was his neighbour.

'Hey, David. How you doing?'

'I'm good, Eleanor, thanks. And you?'

'Not so good. Been really sick the last coupla days. Jim too. We're a bit better now, but the doctor thinks we have food poisoning.'

'Oh no!'

'Yeah, he asked us did we have anything that mightn't have been fully cooked, maybe a barbeque? We both had those kosher beef burgers at your house and I'm just wondering . . .'

'Shit. I hope it's not that. Me and Jacqui have been fine.' Then David remembered that they'd both had the chicken. 'Eleanor, thanks for the heads-up. I'll ring around and see if anyone else is sick. I'm glad you're starting to feel better. Say hi to Jim.'

Ten minutes and three phone calls around the neighbourhood later and a stunned David Wolfowitz needed no more confirmation. Everyone who had had the burgers at his barbeque was sick. One was about to go to hospital. A call to New York added to his distress. His mother had eaten the burgers and she was sick too.

★

'Please ask him to come as quickly as possible,' pleaded Sidney Wolfowitz, 'she's really bad.'

'Don't worry, Mr Wolfowitz, I'll make sure that Dr French is there within thirty minutes,' replied the receptionist, picking up the urgency in the old man's voice.

Almost twenty hours after his last visit to the apartment on Jay Street, Dr Ian French found himself pressing on the same doorbell.

'Thank God you've come, doctor,' said Sidney Wolfowitz, as he opened the door.

Esther Wolfowitz's condition had deteriorated considerably. She lay white faced on the bed and was barely able to acknowledge the doctor. Her forehead was wet with sweat. Her antibiotic tablets were on her bedside locker, beside a glass of water. Dr French swiftly checked her blood pressure and took her temperature. One hundred and three degrees.

'She's been on the toilet nearly non-stop, doctor. And she told me there's blood coming out too,' said her anguished husband.

'Has she been taking her tablets?'

'Yes, doc, I make sure of it. But she's vomiting as well, so I don't know if they're staying down.'

'Mrs Wolfowitz, we're going to get you into hospital for a few days to get the antibiotic and some fluids into you intravenously.'

Mrs Wolfowitz nodded and groaned.

'Don't worry, you'll be fine. It's just that this food poisoning bug has gotten the upper hand.' Dr French started writing a quick note to the emergency department on his headed notepaper. 'Query food poisoning from beef? Severe diarrhoea, sweating. Blood in stools. Prescribed cephalosporin 100mg 3.D. Re-examined today. Temp. 103°. BP 100 over 60. Dehydrated. Regular vomiting. Query septicaemia. Dr I. French.'

He handed the note to Sidney. 'I'm going to call for an ambulance. Make sure you give this note to the hospital staff when you get there.'

'Sure, doc.' Sidney stroked his wife's hand. 'You'll be fine, honey. Quicker we get some fluids into you the better.'

Four minutes later Dr French had confirmation that an ambulance had been despatched from the Patrick J. Brock Memorial Hospital, about five minutes away on Broome Street.

'Jeez, honey. At least you're gonna be outta that hospital a lot quicker this time.'

Esther Wolfowitz closed her eyes tight and nodded. She would never forget the months she had slept on a mattress there, making sure her beloved son David survived his illness.

35

15 JUNE

At the Yamoura Pharmaceuticals office in Washington, Bob Denman spotted the Maryland postmark and the label addressed to 'The Company Secretary, Yamoura Pharmaceuticals'. He hardly needed to open the envelope to know what the letter – on its expensive headed paper – said.

> **Re: Federal Food, Drug and Cosmetic Act and Related Regulations**
>
> Dear Sir/Madam,
>
> On behalf of the Authority I am required to advise you that the Division of Drug Marketing, Advertising and Communications wishes to inquire into the advertising of claimed benefits to patients consuming SuperVerve tablets. Copies of sample advertisements are enclosed, together with text of broadcast advertisements.
>
> In accordance with normal procedures, the inquiry will be

assisted by an Advisory Committee of three suitably qualified independent medical practitioners, not, as yet, nominated. You are now required to provide the Authority with all available scientific evidence to support the advertised benefits, including expert medical reports, safety statements and clinical trial results.

We look forward to having your cooperation throughout this inquiry. Please write to the undersigned and formally acknowledge receipt of this communication.

Yours faithfully,
Maurice Chadwick,
Regulatory Review Officer
Division of Drug Marketing,
Advertising and Communications.

'Hmmph,' snorted Denman. *Usual guff.* He flattened the letter down in his scanner, saved it as SuperVerve/FDA, clicked *forward*, selected Yohoto's email address and hit *send*.

*

At the Chess Club meeting two days later, the letter was the main item for discussion.

'So, we are agreed, gentlemen,' said Lumo Kinotoa. 'We should demonstrate that we are taking the matter very seriously, but we will delay everything as best we can.'

'Yes,' said Dr Naga. 'We write back with promises of our full and enthusiastic cooperation, our sincere belief that any inquiry will completely vindicate our advertising, blah, blah.'

'No,' said Tsan Yohoto, 'that's letter number two. Our first letter should thank them for their interest in our product, but point out that cephalosporin is already FDA approved.'

'But they know that,' said Dr Naga.

'Of course they do,' Tsan Yohoto smiled, 'but it will add another two weeks to any inquiry, while they circulate our letter and someone writes a response.' Now they all smiled.

★

PATRICK J. BROCK MEMORIAL HOSPITAL, BROOME STREET, MANHATTAN – 16 JUNE

Irene Sefton, the hospital administrator, was running her usual Monday morning review meeting with the Heads of Departments. As usual, the room was packed, with most of the doctors having to stand.

'Okay, guys, good morning, thanks for your attendance, hope you all had a good weekend,' she sing-songed. 'All righty – item one, last seven days, any unusual patient events or complaints?'

After no one else volunteered anything, Dr Conrad Jones, who was sitting on the edge of a desk near the back, put his hand up.

'One from my side, Irene,' he said, and then looked down at the open chart on his knee. 'Mrs Esther Wolfowitz, eighty-two years old, admitted on the eighth, suspected food poisoning, diarrhoea, vomiting, dehydration. Prescribed IV fluids and antibiotics. Slight improvement for two days on fluids. Died Saturday 3 p.m.'

'Okay, Conrad. She was fairly elderly; why your particular concerns?'

'Her son's a lawyer from Connecticut. He was there when she died. Took it very badly. Got aggressive with the house doctor. Said that another person who got food poisoning from the same barbeque was hospitalised in Connecticut and discharged in good shape, three days later. Says he's going to sue our ass.'

'I see, thanks for alerting me. You happy with our procedures?'

'Yeah, I've reviewed the file. She came in through the ER, by ambulance. Looked like a routine food poisoning. Letter from referring doctor. Responded to fluids, stool culture confirmed e-coli infection.' He flicked through the file. 'Temperature stayed high. She became very toxic. No response whatsoever to IV cephalosporin. Looks like she died of peritonitis.'

'Valerie?' the administrator enquired of the Head of ER. 'You happy with the procedures on admission?'

'Yes, Irene, one hundred per cent. I've read the notes, spoken to everyone.'

'So, thanks for the warning. Make sure you keep your files safe. We'll wait for the autopsy report.' As the doctors shuffled out at the end of the meeting, Valerie Mahler walked alongside Conrad Jones.

'That's sad, that poor lady. Apparently, her son was shouting that she didn't survive Auschwitz to die from food poisoning in a New York hospital. You think he'll litigate?'

'Nah.' Conrad Jones shrugged. 'He told one of the nurses that he was the one who cooked the burgers. I think he's got enough on his mind.'

*

'It's not your fault, David. How were you to know? You were such a good son to her. Always visiting. Always calling.'

Sidney Wolfowitz was distraught. His sobs echoed around the kitchen as he sat hunched and red-eyed over the table. David hugged his dad tighter, tears streaming down his face.

'C'mon, Dad. You've hardly eaten in two days, let's get out. It'll do you good.'

Sidney numbly agreed and five minutes later David still had his arm around his dad's shoulders as they walked, teary eyed, to the nearest BurgerFantastic.

*

Dr Peter Phillips stood up to greet a new patient. 'Hi, Ms Sheperd. Take a seat. How can I help you?'

'Hi, doctor. Call me Cindy.'

'Sure, Cindy.' Smiling. 'Are you feeling unwell?'

'No, doctor, to be honest I'm fine. It's just that I've been struggling with my weight and I could do with a little help.'

'Okay. Do you mind if I take your blood pressure and do a few little tests?'

'No problem.'

'Can you please step on the scales? And I'll check your height.'

After a few questions about Cindy's diet and lifestyle, Dr Phillips concluded that his patient was perfectly fit and well, although perhaps a few pounds overweight.

'You're in good shape, Cindy. I wouldn't be worrying. A little less fat and sugar in your diet will get that cholesterol number back into the normal range.'

'Thanks, doctor. I've been hearing a lot about these SuperVerve tablets and how they can help with weight loss. Do you think I could try them?'

Peter Phillips hesitated for a moment. *Yet another SuperVerve prescription. There's far too much of this antibiotic sloshing around, and God knows how it's supposed to help with weight loss. Still. If I don't write the script I'll lose a new patient. And Yamoura will move on to some other product before long. And there's that trip to Tokyo . . .*

'Sure. I'll give you a prescription for repeats up to six months, if you feel you need them. Always finish the course and take the tablets at regular intervals.'

Five minutes later Cindy was heading for the drug store on the corner.

36

6 AUGUST

Will you look at that, thought Professor Alan G. F. Milton as he stole another look at the breasts of a student jogger in the car park of the University of Washington. *Nineteen, twenty? Got to be at least a 34E!* He opened the door of his new Porsche Boxster and flung his briefcase onto the passenger seat. He got another glance at the equally bouncy rear of the jogger as he fixed his hair in the rear-view mirror and then his cell phone rang.

'Professor Milton speaking.'

'Professor Milton, how do you do. This is Tsan Yohoto in Tokyo. Can you talk?'

'Yes, yes, I'm in the car.'

'Professor, as you know, we are delighted with our SuperVerve progress in New York. Your work has been most helpful.'

'Why, thank you, Tsan.' *The one and a half million dollars has been most helpful too.*

'We have just another nine months or so to go with our New York pilot programme. We are most keen to complete the work and there is, of course, the potential of final bonuses, depending on sales.'

Professor Milton's heart soared.

'Unfortunately, we have the slight nuisance now of an FDA inquiry. Some nonsense about our advertising.'

Professor Milton's heart sank.

'We're going to need your help. We've given the inquiry all the clinical trial data and they need you and your team to meet with a panel of doctors at the FDA. You know, the usual routine.'

Professor Milton's heart sank further. *Christ, this is all I need.* He'd sat on a few approval panels over the years, but he wasn't too keen on being questioned about his own reports.

'Of course, Tsan. I'd be glad to help,' he offered.

'We're fixing a time with them for the meeting. I'll email you the names of their doctors – I don't recognise any of them.'

'Great, thank you.'

'We're not in any rush to get this underway, as I'm sure you understand, Professor. So, I suggest you alert Professor Kolsen and Dr Cook. I feel it highly unlikely that the schedules of three such important men will allow for an inquiry meeting for at least a month.'

'Highly unlikely, highly unlikely,' Milton agreed.

'We'll speak again soon, Professor. Goodbye,' finished Tsan Yohoto.

Professor Alan G.F. Milton let out a heavy sigh and frowned at himself in the mirror. *An FDA inquiry. I've a real bad feeling about this. Better call the boys.*

*

'Hey, lass,' said Anna Milani, 'it's not so long since you were, like, giving out about that stuff.'

'If you can't beat 'em, join 'em,' said Cindy as she downed a SuperVerve tablet with a mango and passion fruit smoothie. It was half eight on a bright morning in Manhattan. Cindy and Anna were in the juice bar in the Newlife Fitness Club on West

43rd, opposite the New York Times building, and just a couple of minutes' walk from Dynamic Communications. They tried to work out together at least twice a week, starting at 7.45 a.m., which usually saw them showered and at their desks before nine.

'So, how's Mr Detective?' asked Cindy.

'Oh, he's great. It's been real nice being together for the summer. He's taking me to meet his parents soon.'

'Woohoo!' said Cindy, mock punching Anna's arm. 'Getting serious.'

'Maybe.' Anna laughed. 'How are things with José?'

'Huh. All over I'm afraid. The usual "this isn't working" speech.'

'Aw, Cindy. I'm sorry,' said Anna, reaching over to give her a hug.

'Don't worry. Plenty more fish in the sea and all that.' *Maybe it's time for another slice of Mr Detective? Sounds like he's thinking of settling down. A lotta guys like a last fling.*

'Hey, guys, can I join you?' Liza, a sassy lawyer, another regular at the gym, pulled in a stool.

'Sure, lotsa room.'

Liza put her glass of fresh orange juice down, opened her handbag and took out a packet of SuperVerve.

'You still got those stomach problems?' asked Cindy, nodding at the packet on the table.

'No, that's okay now,' said Liza, pushing her thick curly hair back into a bobble. 'The SuperVerve did the trick. But now they've discovered they also help with long-term weight loss. In Japan, apparently, and there aren't many fat people over there.' She swallowed a tablet and flinched as the tangy orange juice sparked her taste buds. 'You guys should know – you do the advertising!'

'Yeah,' replied Cindy. 'Seems to work too. I'd say about half the girls in the gym are taking them.'

'You're right there,' said Liza. 'You want one, Anna?'

'Me? No thanks, I'll just stick to the smoothies and the exercise,' said Anna, smiling.

'Well, I'm gonna take all the help I can get,' said Cindy, taking her own packet of SuperVerve out of her bag. She swallowed a tablet, then stood up and examined her outline in a mirror. 'Got to counteract all those BurgerFantastics!'

37

FOOD AND DRUG ADMINISTRATION, MARYLAND – 16 OCTOBER

In a conference room on the third floor of the Lincoln Building, things were not going well for Professor Alan G.F. Milton and his team of Professor Oscar Kolsen and Dr Anton Cook. The FDA had put together an Advisory Committee to review the SuperVerve advertising. It was chaired by Professor Svetlana Kozlova, a professor at Harvard, and assisted by Dr Nicola Oliver and Dr Jacob Deller. Professor Milton was happy enough about the two doctors on the FDA panel. He'd seen them at several Yamoura events and they were probably on the company payroll. Professor Kozlova, on the other hand, had a reputation as a maverick and had been critical of prescription drug advertising in the past. An old-style medic, she had over forty years' clinical experience. Her stern expression was heightened by her habit of frowning over her black spectacles, which perched heavily on the bridge of her nose.

The three Advisory Committee members sat on one side of a large table, littered with files and pieces of paper. Opposite them, for three uncomfortable hours, were Professor Milton and his team.

Professor Kozlova glowered across the table. 'Professor Milton, we've been through your clinical trial evidence. It all happens to have taken place in Japan and the reports are signed off by Dr Juro Naga. I presume he will assist us here with our inquiry?'

'Oh, yes, Professor, naturally.'

'And these various other Japanese doctors who were involved in the clinical trials – will they also be made available to us?'

'Certainly. Once they have sufficient notice.'

'So, Professor, what you are saying is that your team reviewed the findings of the trials in Japan and effectively "localised" them for the US market?'

'Yes, that's it, Professor. As you know, our team has huge experience in this area. Professor Kolsen and Dr Cook also helped me in concluding that the results in Asia would genetically hold true for a North American population. I myself have specialised in the ear, nose and throat area for almost thirty years.'

'Indeed. So, gentlemen, to keep it simple, what we have here is a long-approved antibiotic, namely a cephalosporin, and Yamoura claims to have discovered these new benefits for patients taking it now?' said Professor Kozlova.

'Yes, that's an accurate summary.'

Kozlova sighed heavily. 'Professor, doctors,' she continued, looking them each in the eye, in turn. 'Even at this early stage, having reviewed the papers, I have to say I am greatly concerned about the claims being made about headache relief. And claiming long-term weight loss – using data for patients recovering from just about everything from bowel inflammation to urinary tract infections to strep throats … just seems extraordinary.'

'Professor, it's all absolutely legitimate, a real breakthrough,' replied Professor Milton, aware that Professor Kolsen beside him was fidgeting. 'I have no doubt that when your team has had enough time to fully review all the evidence, you will be more than satisfied.'

'We'll see about that,' said Professor Kozlova, closing her file firmly. 'This whole thing stinks to me. Gentlemen,' she said, glaring at all those around her, 'we'll be taking this further.'

★

Tsan Yohoto was struggling to remain calm. Bob Denman was on the phone.

'My man at the FDA called. Off the record. Apparently, Milton got fried. We got the worst possible chairperson in Kozlova. Word is they're going to go through all of the clinical trial reports, challenge them line by line, interview our researchers on methodology, and then throw the book at us.'

'What will happen then?' asked Tsan Yohoto, the anxiety clear in his voice.

Bob Denman sounded worried too. 'My source thinks we're almost certainly looking at a warning letter. And that requires us to cease all advertising. They may even require us to re-advertise, to correct any previous misleading statements. Apparently, Kozlova is saying it's the worst case she's seen since they jumped on Lamiton and Pravatsil.'

'How long have we got?'

On the other end of the line, Bob Denman sighed. 'Can't be sure, Tsan, but not long. Two, three weeks at most.'

★

FIFTH PRECINCT STATION – 15 NOVEMBER

Wyse was walking through the public office, heading for the stairs, but his route was partly blocked by a local woman with a small dog on a lead, who was talking to one of the officers about a cardboard box, which was on the counter between them. The officer put his hand into the box as Wyse squeezed by with an, 'Excuse me.'

The officer was asking, 'Where did you find it?'

'Over at Baruch. Just laying there in the morning when I come out. Not there last night when I walked the dog.'

Wyse would have kept going but a flash of blue and white packaging caught his eye as the officer pulled out a smaller cardboard box.

'Huh. SuperVerve,' read out the officer.

'Can I see that?' said Wyse, taking the packet. *500mg cephalosporin tablets*. 'Were they just on the street?' he asked.

'Yes,' said the woman. 'I thought I should hand them in. Maybe there's a reward?'

'Don't know about that,' said the officer.

'Funny,' said Wyse, peering into the box to confirm that it was filled with more boxes of SuperVerve. 'That's the second time I've come across these tablets turning up in the street. Mind if I hold on to a packet?' he asked the officer.

'Be my guest,' was the reply.

'Thanks.'

Strange. These are the tablets Anna's company is advertising. I'll definitely look into this. If there's some kind of illegal trading going on, maybe I could earn a few brownie points for Anna with those Japanese guys. And a few brownie points for myself.

Back at his desk, Wyse called an old friend at the Office of the Chief Medical Examiner on East 26th Street. 'Hey, Dan, John Wyse. How you doin'?'

'Hey, John. I'm fantastic. Buried in evidence, from car parts to body parts. How can I help?'

'I was hoping you could take a look at some tablets for me. SuperVerve.'

'Oh, the ones Christopher White says are helping him make all those baskets?'

'That's them. I've had some boxes cropping up in strange situations. Just thought I'd check 'em out. See if they're real. Might be some counterfeiting going on.'

'No problem, John. But there's a couple of weeks' backlog on non-urgent stuff.'

Shit. 'Dan, I'd really appreciate you bumping me up the line on this. For old times' sake? I've got a bad feeling about these tablets.'

'Old friends are best, John. Send 'em over and I'll see what I can do.'

*

16 NOVEMBER

'Options, gentlemen?' Lumo Kinotoa was chairing an emergency meeting of the Chess Club. It had been arranged at short notice, following another call from Bob Denman in Washington. The four Chess Club members were sitting anxiously in the study of Tsan Yohoto's apartment. The atmosphere was tense.

'We're running out of options,' said Dr Naga. 'I can offer to go and meet this Advisory Committee in Maryland and bluster it out. Might get another couple of months out of it. Problem is, if they start contacting researchers down the line, there are doctors' and technicians' names on the list who were never involved in any scientific work on SuperVerve.'

'We can hardly risk that now,' said Kinotoa. 'We could blow everything at this stage.'

'There is another option,' said Kazuhiro Saito. 'We could change the style of our adverts for the last six months of our campaign.'

'How do you mean?' asked Dr Naga.

'The adverts we've been running, both print and broadcast, have been what they call "Product Claim" advertisements.'

'What does that mean?' asked Naga.

'It means the advert mentions both the medical condition and the name of the drug to cure it, in the same advert.'

'So?'

'So, that type of advert is FDA regulated. However, we could switch now to what they call a "Reminder". For example, where we name our product, SuperVerve, but don't say what it's used for. Or, we can advertise the symptoms or conditions we can treat, but without naming the product. We can say "Consult your healthcare provider for information", or something similar.'

Dr Naga was puzzled. 'Yes, I can see that we have established our brand strongly enough now that the public will make the connection between the symptoms and SuperVerve. But, what's the point?'

'The point, Juro, is that "Reminder" adverts and "Help Seeking" adverts are completely outside FDA control. They can do nothing about them.'

'Ah,' said Dr Naga. 'Very interesting.'

There was a long silence while everyone thought. As usual, it was Tsan Yohoto who reached a conclusion first.

'Gentlemen, we are running out of options and running out of time. Our plan is in jeopardy, but we have come too far to risk losing everything. The critical thing now is to maximise and sustain the numbers – about three million – who regularly take cephalosporin.' He paused, and looked around at his friends. 'Gentlemen, we must accelerate our plan. We will deflect the FDA by writing to them and undertaking to withdraw our advertising, as soon as practical. In the meantime, we throw everything into maximising sales of SuperVerve and BurgerFantastic over the next fortnight. My friends,' he paused again and looked them each in the eye, 'we will begin infecting the burgers with e-coli in two weeks. The first of December!'

38

NEW JERSEY – 19 NOVEMBER

Takar el Sayden was anxiously spinning his gold rings. He was well settled into this damned routine. The weekly meetings with 'Mr Ali'. The nightly emptying of the white powder into his vats of sauce. *It obviously was harmless or something would have happened by now.* But his life was unravelling so fast that he felt out of control. His wife Tasha had insisted they attend marriage counselling. She said he had become more and more withdrawn, wasn't as relaxed with the girls and was obsessed with the business. He wasn't communicating with her any more. He hadn't taken a holiday in eighteen months. She wanted him to see a doctor. He knew that she was right. With tears in her beautiful eyes, Tasha had told him that this year could be their last together. *But what could he do?* And then, a different type of meeting this morning – maybe this nightmare was coming to an end? Ibrahim Fallah or 'Mr Ali', as Takar knew him, had turned up at his office, as usual, at 9.20 a.m.

'Good morning,' Mr Ali said quietly, 'I have this week's powder here in my case.'

Takar el Sayden nodded.

'Takar, you have done very well. My superiors are pleased. You will be glad to hear that our relationship may be coming to a close a little earlier than expected.'

Takar's eyebrows arched and his heart leaped. *Maybe this is good news?*

'My superiors have decided to end their experiment soon. For the moment, you must continue to put the powder in the sauce. But you must go tomorrow to see the advertising people at Dynamic Communications.'

Takar remained silent.

'My superiors want to finish this experiment ... with a bang, you might say. An extra five million dollars has been credited to your account at the Bank of America.' He handed over a slim envelope.

'This contains, on one page, your instructions to Dynamic Communications to step up advertising and promotions of BurgerFantastic for one more month. You can spend the five million. For the last few weeks, there will be a special promotion – the ninety-nine cent BurgerFantastic.'

'What!' exclaimed Takar. 'We might as well give them away!'

'It is a last push, to reinforce your new market share. You are to advise all staff that they will each be required to work overtime for at least two weeks. You should hire extra temporary help.'

Takar shrugged in resignation. 'Whatever.'

'You also need to step up your security precautions from now on. Make extra certain that the vats are cleaned very thoroughly, every day, straight after the night-time production. Also, when you have finished with the plastic bags, you should take them off the premises and dump them.'

'Okay,' said Takar. 'But we're gonna be overrun trying to keep supply going at that price.'

Fallah stood up and said calmly, 'Just sort it. And then, very soon, it will all be over.'

*

Ten minutes later, Ibrahim Fallah was smiling to himself as he drove east towards Manhattan from Newark.

'Turn right onto McCarthy Highway,' instructed the voice on the GPS unit mounted on his dash. He was taking the opportunity to divert into a beaten-up housing project close to the airport, to drop a few boxes of SuperVerve out of the bottom of his van. *There we go.* There was a gang of teenagers hanging out beside a liquor store. He drove fifty yards past, pulled into the kerb, checked his mirrors and grinned, as he heard the box drop gently onto the street.

There was a fresh momentum to his orders from Afghanistan. Apart from the new instructions to Takar el Sayden, he had been told to maximise drops of SuperVerve in the target areas. He had taken two weeks' leave from the library and now, every day, he collected a vanload of tablets from the warehouse at JFK. He then spent his days and nights driving around New York, dropping off his cargo. He was also keeping an eye on Detective Wyse whenever he had a chance. *Yes*, he thought as he drove, *something big's going to happen very soon. I must be careful. No mistakes.*

★

At the offices of Dynamic Communications in Manhattan, Victor Dezner could hardly contain his excitement. *Pop* – the cork exploded from the top of a bottle of Bollinger and ricocheted off the boardroom ceiling. All the company's forty staff had crowded in and everyone cheered loudly.

'Guys, this is what makes it worthwhile. Working with such a talented and dedicated team.' Victor kept filling glasses as Katie Keller took over.

'So, the great news is, we have two of the three nominations for Campaign of the Year *and* a nomination for Agency of the Year, in the New York Advertising Awards. And it's all down to your hard work. Guys, we are all over this city.'

'Cheers,' said a beaming Anna Milani, as she raised her glass.
'To SuperVerve,' said Katie.
'To BurgerFantastic,' said Anna.
'Absolutely,' said Victor.

*

FIFTH PRECINCT STATION

'John. Dan Strzempka.'
'Hey, Dan. You get a chance to look at those tablets for me?'
'Sure thing. They're pure grade cephalosporin antibiotic all right. And the packaging looks genuine. But funny thing is . . .'
'Yeah?'
'Must have been some problem in the factory. The dosage is wrong.'
'Whatcha mean?'
'The packaging says 500 mg tablets, but the strength is twice that.' Dan paused. 'Plus, some of 'em are, like, placebos.'
'What?'
'Yeah. Literally starch and water. No active ingredient. Musta been a faulty batch. It's genuine cephalosporin all right, but if anyone took them they'd be getting very erratic doses.'
'Oh.' John was lost for words.
'I'll email you the report. You want me to do anything else, John?'
'No, thanks, Dan. I'll look into it.'
'All right, man. Take it easy.'

*

'Shhh, Asif, keep your voice down.' Karen Patel glared across the living room at her husband and pointed at the ceiling. A rare row had broken out between them and she didn't want Lauren or Ryan, who were asleep upstairs, to hear it. It was unusual for Asif to get home midweek, but a software problem he'd been sorting out in Chicago had been resolved ahead of schedule. Their original plan for a quiet, romantic night in together had gone unexpectedly off the rails, after they got the kids to bed and uncorked a bottle of wine. They'd turned the TV off and Celine Dion's heart was going on and on in the background.

'I'm concerned about Lauren,' Karen had said. 'This damn cold she has seems to be going on for ever. And her throat is sore too.'

'You worried about the musical?' asked Asif.

'You bet I am.' Their daughter was taking the lead role in the school production of *Frozen*. Lauren not only looked the part, but her singing voice was stunning for her age. Her heart was already set on being an actress or a singer.

Asif topped up their glasses. 'Maybe you should take her to the doctor?'

'Yeah, I know. It seems to be just a cold, but maybe they can give her something.'

'Mmm.' Asif sipped his Chardonnay. 'Maybe it's just me, but has she put on a bit of weight recently?'

Karen nodded. 'You know, I think you're right. Maybe she's eating too much junk, what with the stress of the rehearsals?'

'Yeah, maybe, but Ryan's got heavy too. I think they're eating too many of those damn BurgerFantastics. Jeez, how many times a week are they having them? Three? Four?'

'Huh. I'd like to see you try and tell them they can't go. All their friends eat there too.'

'Well, maybe they should be getting more fish and chicken and vegetables and stuff.'

'That's easy for you to say, Mr SuperChef. You're not stuck here all week, running around in circles and trying to fit in meals. You cook for them.' Karen crossed her arms and glowered at her husband.

'Hey, relax, honey, it's an observation, not a criticism.'

'Well, it sounds like a criticism to me.'

There was a long, tense silence. Asif broke it.

'Okay, honey, how about I promise to cook the main meal, here, on either Saturdays, or Sundays? I'll go out in the mornings and get some fresh ingredients.'

'Yeah, okay then, that sounds good,' Karen said, a tear in her eye. She wasn't used to any conflict between them.

'And in the morning,' Asif added, 'we tell the kids, no more BurgerFantastic for a month.'

'It's a deal. I'll try and get them back on some healthier stuff. And I'll take her round to the surgery after school,' said Karen, blowing her nose in a tissue. The conflict in the air had eased, but any plans for romance that night had followed Celine Dion onto an iceberg.

*

The next day, Dr Peter Phillips recognised the name on the schedule on his screen. *4.15 p.m. Lauren Patel.*

'Hi Karen, hi Lauren, how are you?' he beamed, standing up to shake their hands. 'According to my kids, you're gonna knock 'em dead in *Frozen*, Lauren. Next stop Broadway, I'd say.' He bent down, lowered his voice and whispered, 'Just don't forget your old friends when you're accepting your first Oscar, eh?'

Lauren smiled. She liked Dr Phillips.

'So, how can I help you, guys?' he asked.

'Well, Peter, you know it's *Frozen* that's getting us real worried. Lauren's got this cold, a runny nose, headaches – and now her throat's a little sore.'

'Oh dear. Let's see if we can sort that.' Dr Phillips smiled, noting Lauren's watery eyes and reddish nose.

'Okay, Lauren, let's have a look.' He checked her temperature with an electronic thermometer placed in her ear. 'Ninety-eight, that's normal. Alrighty, open wide.' He looked carefully into her mouth and throat. 'Say *Aaaah*.'

'Aaaah.'

'Hmmm.' Not much going on there. No inflammation. No redness. No spots. He felt her glands. They seemed fine. 'That sore?'

'Nope.' She shook her head.

Peter Phillips looked into Lauren's ears through his otoscope and then checked her blood pressure. *110 over 70. All normal.* Then he listened to her lungs through his stethoscope. *Clear as a bell.*

He sat down again and looked at mother and daughter.

'There's no sign of any infection at all. How long have you been feeling poorly?'

'Just a few days,' said Lauren.

'I think you've just got a bad cold, honey. If you can keep yourself warm and drink plenty of liquids, I think it'll blow over in a couple of days. You can take an aspirin if the headache's bothering you.'

Karen was disappointed. 'But, Peter, the musical's so close. What if she's just at the start of something and it gets worse? We won't have time to fix it. She could miss the whole thing.' Peter Phillips saw the anxiety in her face. 'Isn't there something you can give her, just to be sure?'

He decided to keep her happy. 'Sure, sure. It could be that there's a little strep throat coming on from all that singing. I can give you an antibiotic, just to make sure we keep on top of things.'

'Oh, thanks,' said Karen, relieved that this visit would be worthwhile.

'Take two of these tablets, three times a day,' said Peter Phillips, writing out a prescription. 'Remember, it's an antibiotic, so don't stop taking them, just cos you feel better. Make sure you take all the tablets.'

'Thanks so much, Peter, you're a pal.' Mother and daughter smiled as Karen took the prescription. 'Say hi to Sandra – I'll probably see her tomorrow at the school.'

'Sure thing,' said the doctor, returning the smile. 'See you on Broadway, princess.'

★

Anna Milani and Tsan Yohoto were sipping coffees after lunch in the Park Hyatt.

'We are so delighted with the success of the SuperVerve campaign in New York – not least thanks to your work, Anna – that we're going to accelerate the expenditure in this last phase.'

'Fantastic, Tsan, that's great news. It's been such an exciting campaign to work on.'

'And how is your Detective Wyse keeping? Still treating you well, I hope?'

'Oh, John's great, thanks. Not seeing enough of him, it's been so busy.'

Yohoto nodded and smiled, and Anna went on.

'Funny, he told me the other day that he's come across a couple of big boxes of SuperVerve. He thought at first they'd been stolen. Maybe there's a black market in them? Or even counterfeit? Anyway, he got them checked and some of the dosages are wrong. I said I'd tell you in case there was a faulty batch?'

Tsan Yohoto kept his coffee cup to his mouth, hoping it would disguise the blood rushing from his face.

39

THE CHESS CLUB, SAITON – 23 NOVEMBER

The light from the antique chandelier glinted off the silvery hair of Lumo Kinotoa, the chairman of both Yamoura Pharmaceuticals and the Chess Club. Tsan Yohoto looked across the table at his oldest friend. *Yes, Lumo was starting to look older than his seventy-six years. There was no doubt that the pressure and strain involved in implementing this great plan was taking its toll. The hand of fate rested upon their shoulders. Within weeks they would have achieved a full and fitting revenge on the Americans for the deaths of their families and the humiliation of their country.*

Lumo Kinotoa savoured the last mouthful of a cucumber sandwich and washed it down with a sip of tea. He was tired but he summoned up his strength again. He preferred to keep their decisions unanimous, but a rare argument was developing.

'So, back to this Detective Wyse, Tsan,' he said. 'You are convinced that he poses a real threat?'

'Yes, Lumo. Anna, his girlfriend, told me he had come across some boxes of SuperVerve. Must be some of the ones that were dumped. Apparently, he thinks he's doing her a favour by poking around to see if there's some illicit trade going on. He had a box analysed and told her that some of the dosages were different than stated on the packet. He's getting too close for comfort. He's still low risk, but at this stage we can't afford any slip-ups.'

'But, Tsan,' said Kinotoa. 'I think it is an unnecessary risk. What if one of al-Qaeda's sleepers gets caught? It could draw attention to our whole plan.' He raised his eyebrows to Kazuhiro Saito and Dr Naga, inviting their opinions.

Saito sighed. 'I have to take Tsan's advice. He's the one who has met Wyse and is much closer to all of this.'

'I'm inclined to agree,' said Dr Naga. 'Obviously, there are risks associated with all options, but our plan is Tsan's brainchild, and I trust his judgement.'

Tsan Yohoto rammed home his advantage. 'For once, Lumo, I must disagree with you completely. My instinct tells me that Detective Wyse is becoming too much of a danger. Please tell our friends in Afghanistan to have him eliminated, as soon as possible.' *Pity to upset Anna. But I can't risk jeopardising the plan over a detail like her feelings.*

Kinotoa nodded. 'As you wish, Tsan. I will send the request after our meeting. Now, gentlemen, back to the main business. Tsan, final numbers?'

'My friends,' said Tsan Yohoto with a smile. 'We now have over three million New Yorkers saturated in cephalosporin. The city has been primed for large-scale antibiotic-resistant infection. We have reached the tipping point. It is now a question of how many of them we can infect with our e-coli bacteria before BurgerFantastic is identified as the source and closed down. You can be sure that they'll waste a lot of time testing meat all over New York before anyone thinks of checking the sauce. Once the hospital wards are packed, I'm sure our curtain swishing strategy for spreading the infection will increase the death toll even more.

'After that, the numbers that die is up to God.'

'And Allah,' said Lumo Kinotoa with a grin.

'And the curtain swishers,' added Dr Naga.

★

After evening prayers at the Al Jahada Mosque on Side Street, the Bronx, a few members of the congregation were sipping herbal tea and chatting quietly with the spiritual leader of the mosque. They knew he was al-Qaeda, and they had all been influenced by the teachings of al-Qaeda in their formative teenage years. It was from this group that Ibrahim Fallah had carefully selected his two recruits. They recognised him approaching as the group began to break up.

'My friends.' He smiled, and laid a gentle hand on the shoulders of the two young Muslims. 'It is time to start your work. *Inshallah.*'

Ibrahim Fallah had researched their backgrounds carefully, and had subtly assisted in their ongoing radicalisation. Their families were al-Qaeda supporters and they could be trusted to cooperate and to maintain absolute discretion. This radicalisation process was carried out secretively, as it would be abhorrent to the vast majority of those attending the mosque. He drove them in his brown Nissan to the back of the library. In silence, the two recruits took in the neatness of the garage there, the stacks of chairs, shelving units, a workbench, tools and a musty smell of oil. There was now a second white van parked inside.

'My friends,' continued Fallah in his quiet voice, 'the elders have decided that your work must begin.'

The two recruits listened, wide-eyed.

'Please tell us how to proceed, Ibrahim?' asked one.

Fallah pointed at the second white van. 'This is for you. I have added some lettering on the sides.' The six-inch high, navy blue words *Hospital Maintenance Services* clearly indicated the van's new status. 'You will pose as hospital maintenance staff. You will pretend that you are working for a company which supplies and maintains curtains – the type you see around beds in hospitals.'

They nodded.

'You do not need to understand your work. The most important thing is that you open and close as many curtains in the hospital wards as possible – starting with the Emergency Rooms and then working through as many wards as you can.'

'But why?'

'As I said, do not concern yourself with why. Even I do not have that answer. We must trust the wisdom of our leaders. Inside the van are some hospital bed curtains, screens on wheels and a toolbox. You simply walk into the wards, pushing the screen on wheels and then begin to adjust nuts on the curtain rails around the beds. Always pretend to test your work by swishing the curtains around each bed a couple of times. Don't linger. There's lots of wards to get through.'

Compliant, the two recruits nodded.

'In the van, you will find two white coats. Inside each coat is a fake ID for an employee of a hospital maintenance company – in case a security guard challenges you.'

'Where do we keep the van?'

'You should leave it here when you are not using it. On the driver's seat is a set of keys, a key for the garage door and a remote control. The van is perfectly legitimate and you are insured to drive. Also, on the passenger seat is a map of the five boroughs, on which is marked the hospitals you are to concentrate on. Take the next few days to familiarise yourselves with the locations, the best places to park and the best routes to get from one to the other.'

'How often do we visit each hospital?' asked one.

'Try to get around each hospital as often as you can. Vary the times that you call. If you go to one hospital during the day, go after 8 p.m. the next time. The nurses and security guards generally work eight-to-eight shifts. It will minimise any risk of suspicion.'

'Yes, Ibrahim, we understand.'

'In approximately ten days, I will contact you with instructions to start. I will see you every few days at the mosque and you can advise me of any problems. And, of course, you must never speak to anyone about me, or about your work,' he concluded.

Both of them nodded earnestly. 'Of course, Ibrahim.'

Ibrahim Fallah embraced his new recruits and then drove them back to the mosque. As they said a quiet goodbye, one of the conspirators puffed out his cheeks.

'Phew. This gets real in ten days.'

'Best look at those maps then,' was the reply.

★

'Peter, it's lookin' real good for Tokyo 2020,' said Bob Sanders.

'Hey, that's great Bob,' said Peter Phillips, as he knocked back his fresh orange juice as they sat at the counter at the Delish Juice Bar on Broome Street, near his clinic.

'Yep, we're drawing up the likely list for the conference over the next couple of months. So, we're givin' it, like, one last push.'

'Sure, sure,' said the doctor, getting the message.

'And the SuperVerve launch has gone so well – word is they're gonna shoot the lights out with this trip.'

'Awesome.'

'So, see what you can do, buddy, over the next couple of weeks – I'd love to see you at those Olympic Games.'

Yeah, thought the doctor grimly. Dr Peter Phillips, USA. Gold medal for prescribing SuperVerve.

40

1 DECEMBER

Every newspaper and magazine published in New York that day contained a full-page advert:

The Two-Week Wonder!

Every BurgerFantastic Just 99 cents

BurgerFantastic – Home cooking without the hassle

Every billboard and electronic display that Dynamic Communications could beg, steal or borrow contained the same message. A new radio advert was quickly put together and pumped out twenty-four seven on New York's twenty-seven local stations. With the leftover budget, Dynamic decided to re-run the adverts with Ricky Morgan, which had worked so well last year.

The manager of McDonald's on Wall Street shook his head as he read the advert while travelling to work on the subway underneath Manhattan. *Doesn't look like McDonald's will be selling too many burgers for the next coupla weeks. At this rate, BurgerFantastic are gonna beat our record of twenty thousand burgers sold from one outlet, in a day.*

★

Takar el Sayden drove towards the BurgerFantastic production facility at Newark. Things were changing, all right. Mr Ali had come to see him the previous day. He'd promised him that the 'experiment' was nearly over. He'd given him a fresh set of photographs of his smiling daughters, standing in line for the latest kids' film. Was it his imagination or did the powder look slightly different this time?

By early lunchtime that day, every one of the two hundred and fifty-two BurgerFantastic restaurants in New York had a line of up to fifty people, waiting for a table or a takeaway. 'Boss, we need more staff, it's crazy,' shrieked one of his managers into Takar el Sayden's cell phone.

'Just keep going, see what you can do,' he replied. Same advice he gave to almost every manager that day.

★

MANHATTAN – 8 DECEMBER – 6 P.M.

'Peter?' Sandra was calling him, almost as soon as he got the front door closed. 'Peter?'

Dr Peter Phillips leaned his golf bag against the wall under the stairs and followed his wife's voice into the kitchen.

'Hi, honey,' she said. 'Good game?' She was smiling warmly and that made him glad. Sandra had seemed happier recently and things had been going much better between them. Quite why, he didn't know, but it sure felt good.

'Yeah, great, thanks, won it on the seventeenth with a birdie. You woulda been proud of me! Well?' he said, pecking her on the cheek.

'Sorry to bring you back to basics, Tiger, but the clinic said Mr Walton's been on. Says his wife is very sick and can you go round.'

'Aw, shit!'

'And I've had to put Suzy to bed, she's got diarrhoea. And now

Jonathan's getting cramps. Will you go up and have a look at Suzy?' asked Sandra.

'Sure, on my way.' He tapped lightly on his daughter's door.

'Come in, Dad,' she said. She managed as big a smile for him as possible. She was propped up in bed, listlessly watching a movie on her laptop.

'Hey, princess,' he said, kissing her forehead. 'What's going on, honey?'

'I've got these real bad, like, stomach cramps, Dad. And diarrhoea. Worst I've ever had.'

'Oh dear, my little princess.'

'But Mom says the worst is over, Dad. I just need to drink lots of water.'

'Good old Mom – she's right there.' He put his hand on her forehead. 'Okay, honey, you don't seem too hot. I've got to go out and see a patient. I'll come up and see you again in an hour or so.'

'Okay, Dad. Love you.' Suzy smiled weakly.

He grabbed his briefcase and reached Mrs Walton's apartment about fifteen minutes later. Her worried husband opened the door. 'Boy, am I glad to see you, doc, she's not good.'

Mrs Walton was flat on her back in bed, a packet of SuperVerve on the locker.

'She started with real bad diarrhoea, doctor, a couple of days ago,' Mr Walton gabbled. 'Then she started running a temperature. She's been vomiting as well, most of today, and shivering.'

Dr Phillips carefully examined Mrs Walton's abdomen, which was very tender, and took her blood pressure. *Ninety over fifty. Shit, that's toxic. Temperature a hundred and three degrees. Is that a rash?*

'Mr Walton, did she eat anything unusual recently? Shellfish? Pâté? A barbeque?'

'No, no, just her usual routine.'

'Has anyone that she's been with fallen sick as well?'

'Not that I know of.'

'I think she's got food poisoning. It may have become septicaemia. We need to get her onto IV fluids and an intravenous antibiotic. She's not going to keep tablets down. I'm going to send her to the hospital by ambulance. She'll be back to normal in a couple of days.'

'Jeez. Okay, doctor, thank you.'

Three minutes later an ambulance was on its way from the Patrick J. Brock Memorial Hospital. But Peter Phillips returned home to find that Suzy had deteriorated and his wife was feeling so weak that she was lying on their bed.

'Jonathan's downstairs, will you check on him?'

He found Jonathan lying listlessly on a beanbag in the den, beside his toy drum kit.

'Hey, Dad. I was practising my drums, cos Suzy's gonna let me be in her band, when she gets to be like Adele. But then I felt too sick.'

Peter Phillips stroked his son's brow, noticing that his soft brown curls were damp with sweat. 'Hey, that's okay, soldier,' he said and he kissed his son on the back of his neck. He gently scooped his little boy up in his arms. 'Now, let's get you up to bed.'

*

9 DECEMBER – 8.30 A.M.

'It's Sandra for you on line two.' Dr Peter Phillips had just sat down at his desk when the call came through.

'Peter, they're both much worse. Suzy's vomiting and there's blood in her diarrhoea. And Jonathan's doubled up crying.'

'Okay, honey, try and keep calm,' he said; the distress was clear in her voice.

'Will I give them something to stop the diarrhoea?'

'No, that could make it worse. I think they've caught some bug and it's got to go through their system.'

'It's not that, Peter. There's something going on.'

'What do you mean?'

'I rang Jonathan's daycare to say he wouldn't be coming in.'

'And . . .?'

'They said that over half of the kids are out sick.'

'Uh, oh.'

'Yeah, and it's the same at Suzy's school. The principal told me that every time he puts the phone down it rings again. And every call is another parent saying their kid is sick.'

'There's just some bug going around that's hitting the kids.'

'Maybe, but I'm not feeling so good myself. Hey, I'd better go, Suzy's calling.'

'Okay. I'll get back home as quickly as I can, but the waiting room's packed.'

One hour later, Dr Phillips had seen five patients in a row, all with diarrhoea and bad stomach cramps. *What the fuck's going on?* he wondered as he leaned back in his chair. Then he had an idea.

'Patrick J. Brock Memorial Hospital,' answered the receptionist.

'Can you page Dr Conrad Jones for me, please.'

'Certainly, caller, one moment.'

He held for about thirty seconds and then he heard the familiar voice.

'Hey, Conrad, it's Peter Phillips here.'

'Hey, Peter, how's that old swing?'

'Just about gets me round.' The doctors were both members of the same golf club, but Peter didn't want to chat about golf.

'I'm a little concerned here, Conrad. I've got a clinic full of patients with severe diarrhoea. My kids have it, too, and apparently half of their schools are out sick too. Are you seeing anything strange at the hospital?'

'I've just finished rounds, Peter, and I haven't heard anything new. Hang on and I'll try Valerie Mahler at the ER.' Within a minute he was back on the line.

'Peter, looks like you're on to something. Valerie says it's like a war zone down there. A lot of patients being referred in by doctors – mostly with severe cramps, bloody stools, vomiting and dehydration.'

'Jeez, any idea what's going on?'

'No, but they've started alerting the public health authorities.'

'Wow – it must be some real bad bug or virus.'

'Yeah, I'm sure we can get it sorted, but they're starting to run outta beds.'

'Gotta go, Conrad, talk to ya later, buddy.'

'No problem, man. And keep that left arm straight.'

*

That evening, Detectives Cabrini and Wyse were heading south on Fifth Avenue, passing the Guggenheim Museum, when Wyse abruptly interrupted Cabrini's views on Beyoncé vs. Rihanna.

Wyse put his hand up. 'Sssh. Mike, listen.' He turned up the volume on the police radio.

'What did you say he was dropping, twenty-two?'

'Up in Harlem. Coupla boxes fell outta a white van. We opened 'em up. They're some kinda tablets called SuperVerve. Looks suspicious to me. He's maybe ten blocks ahead of us on Fifth. Southbound. Traffic's real slow here, though.'

'You get a tag?'

'Nope. White Toyota van.'

'Okay. All cars. Anyone near Fifth and 70. Eyes out for a white Toyota van. Southbound. Suspicious activity. Stop and search.'

'That's more of those SuperVerve tablets, Mike. Let's get this guy and see what he's up to. Hold the siren. Let's see if we can tail him.'

'You got it.' Cabrini dropped into second gear and pulled out to overtake a bus as they passed the Apple store. Then, as they passed Trump Tower, Wyse exclaimed.

'That could be him. About three blocks. Going pretty quick.'

Cabrini increased speed, closed the distance on the van and broke a red on 54th, provoking a salvo of horns. A block ahead,

Ibrahim Fallah's heart skipped a couple of beats as he noticed the Crown Victoria in his rear-view mirror.

Cops. Fuck. Will I let them stop me and try and talk my way out of it? Instinct kicked in. As he sped past St Patrick's Cathedral, the lights ahead at the junction with East 50th turned red. Nearly back at base. *If I can just stay far enough ahead of them.* As the traffic started crossing from both sides, he floored the accelerator and shot through the junction. Eighty yards back, Cabrini weighed up his options. There was a gap opening up on the right . . .

Wyse roared, 'Watch it, Mike!'

At the last second, Cabrini spotted a stroller emerging from behind a truck, being pushed over the crossing. He stood on the brakes, pulled the steering wheel left and the car went into a long broadside slide, tyres howling in protest. The woman turned to face the noise and screamed a torrent of angry Spanish as the Crown Victoria shuddered to a halt, six feet from her and her baby.

'Fuck me,' exhaled Cabrini.

Beside him, Wyse had pulled the door handle off the inside of the door, as he gripped it through the skid. 'Fuck me is right, Mike,' he said, showing Cabrini the handle clenched in his hand. 'Good stop.'

'Bit too close for comfort,' said Cabrini, wiping sweat from his forehead. 'But we lost the van.'

'Don't worry. We'll get him soon enough. God knows what that guy's doing.'

★

Perfect. Ibrahim Fallah saw the junction snarl up behind him and took a quick right into West 48th Street and then an immediate left into Avenue of the Americas. Then he ducked left into East 42nd and ninety seconds after leaving Wyse and Cabrini trapped in his wake, he was driving under the electronic door into the garage at the rear of the Metropolitan Library. He sat quietly in the van for a few minutes after the door had closed behind him.

Phew. That was close. Why are the cops following me? Did someone spot me dumping the tablets? And that old Crown Victoria looks like the one that Detective Wyse drives. The sooner I kill him the better. Tomorrow night should be perfect.

41

MANHATTAN – 10 DECEMBER

There was just no doubt about it. *I love this girl,* John Wyse said to himself. She's incredible.

His mother was right. 'You'll know it when it happens,' she had always said. He thought he had 'known it', with Lisa, but the timing was wrong and he had screwed it up. Sitting in the kitchen of his neat apartment, he took another pensive sip of instant coffee and felt the hot liquid warm his throat. With curious timing, 'At Last' by Etta Jones was playing on the radio. That was the first song that he and Lisa had slow-danced to. Five years later, no matter what he was doing, all it took was the first few bars of the song and he could still smell Lisa's perfume. He made his decision. *Time to act, John Boy. I'm not gonna mess up again.*

His pulse quickened every time he heard Anna's voice. He got a sick feeling in his stomach if she didn't return a call on the same day, even after so many months of dating.

He'd been out to meet her family in New Jersey. Nice folks. Kinda quiet. She'd come down to Washington to stay at his parents' house, for their wedding anniversary. 'Separate rooms,' his mother had insisted, smiling.

'Wow, don't let her go,' his dad had whispered. And John knew he wouldn't.

He booked Emilia's on Union Square again, their favourite Italian restaurant. *And the venue for our very first date.* Massimo had done them proud, organising the best table in the house. And his usual complimentary bottle of champagne. Wyse got there early, read the menu six times and still couldn't remember anything on it.

He felt her presence without looking up. The atmosphere in a room changes when ten or twenty people all spot something amazing at the same time. Anna attracted an increasing number of admiring glances as she gracefully allowed Massimo to take her coat. She was dressed in a simple black dress, to just above her knee. She looked even more striking than usual, in particularly high heels. She wore a pearl necklace and pearl earrings. Her face seemed to illuminate the whole restaurant, her beautiful sallow skin, that easy smile and those stunning, intelligent green eyes. She walked like a supermodel to his table.

'Hello, gorgeous,' she smiled at him.

He could hardly eat his dinner, his heart was pounding so hard. He chose his moment after the cheese plate.

'Yes! Of course.' With a shaky hand, she took the single diamond ring from the blue Tiffany's box. Her eyes were sparkling, damp with tears.

'Oh my God, John, it's so beautiful.' She leaned over and kissed him.

John had tears of happiness in his eyes too. Massimo spotted his moment and ducked in with two fresh glasses of his best Bollinger. A few people at the tables around them spotted what was going on and began to clap and raise their glasses to toast them.

'Hey, baby, what about moving into my place soon?' said John, as they took a cab back later.

'I'd love to, honey,' said Anna, her head resting on his shoulder. She kissed him. 'Just give me a week to get organised. It would be lovely to be together for Christmas.' They were silent for a while, both enjoying the moment. After a while, Anna whispered in his ear.

'John.'

'Yes, baby.'

'I love you, very, very much. You make me so happy. I'm the luckiest woman in the world.'

His heart surged and electricity seemed to crackle through his whole body. He looked down into her eyes and held her gaze.

'That makes me very happy, baby. I love you too.'

But, as their cab headed towards Wyse's apartment, Ibrahim Fallah was choosing a parking space near by.

*

Ibrahim Fallah decided that he would use his Glock pistol to kill Detective John Wyse. *Pity, one of my favourites, and I'll have to dump it. But I'll need something with plenty of punch. And it's untraceable.* His monitoring of the detective's apartment block had given him a good idea of the layout, and he knew exactly which apartment Wyse lived in.

The front door and lobby are too public. Too well lit. I'll get in through that door from the service yard, go up the stairs, pick the lock and wait inside for him. The old burglary gone wrong trick again. The message from Afghanistan was to make sure and get it done. If one of his girlfriends comes back with him, I'll kill them too. I'll use the silencer.

There were no lights showing from Wyse's apartment. Fallah parked his brown Nissan well down the street, away from streetlights. When there were no cars or pedestrians in view, he pulled on a pair of black leather gloves, walked to the service yard entrance and climbed over the gate. He stood for a moment in the shadows and put his hand on the gun in his pocket. There was no sign of anyone about so he began to walk towards the service door into the building. The next thing he felt was an excruciating pain in his calf, as a dog sank its teeth into him. Fallah stifled a scream and clubbed at the dog with his gun. The dog yelped, let go and scuttled behind some bins.

'Aaaaah. Shit.' Fallah looked down at his leg, which was already pumping blood into his trousers. *Shit. A goddam dog. That doesn't bark.* He climbed back over the gate and limped heavily to his car. *I'll try again soon. Might have to do it on the street.*

★

Anna woke earlier than usual. The first traces of sunlight were filtering around the curtains. She looked at John, who was in a deep sleep, and smiled. Trying not to wake him, she eased herself out of the bed and tiptoed, naked, across the timber floor towards the bathroom. Passing through the living room, she whispered, 'Hi Glenda.' Glenda, who was nursing a sore head, opened one eye, gave a half flick of her tail, grunted and went back to sleep. Anna closed the bathroom door quietly, had a pee, washed her hands and appraised herself in the mirror. She cupped her left breast. *Blimey, are my boobs bigger? No, don't think so. I'm imagining it.*

She felt her right breast. *Was her nipple more sensitive than usual? Maybe it was from that night of passion with John? What an evening it had been. Engaged to be married!*

She'd been taking her pill like clockwork, so surely she couldn't be pregnant? Then again, their wild lovemaking must be pushing the limits of any contraceptive! She stifled a giggle.

Jesus. I can't be! What would my parents say? And how would John react? He'll be fine with it, surely. Talk about life taking over when you start making plans. I'd best get a pregnancy test kit. Give it another few days though.

Anna went back to the bedroom and slipped under the duvet. Wyse stirred, turned over, put his arm around her and fell back asleep. Her heart was thumping and her mind raced, as the noise of traffic built steadily from the street. *I can't be. Could I?*

42

MANHATTAN – 11 DECEMBER – 10.15 A.M.

The Center for Disease Control and Prevention has its headquarters in an eight-storey, 1970s office block on Catherine Street, on the southern end of the island, near the financial district. The administrator, Dr Kim Scholler, was having a hectic morning and had just called her boss, Brian Holzman, at the Department of Health and Human Services.

'Brian, this is big. Of the thirty-five hospitals in the metropolitan area, fourteen have reported that they're overrun with possible food poisoning cases.'

'Jesus. Okay, Kim, let's watch our procedures on this. Does it look like food poisoning to you?'

'You know, that's one of the first things you're going to suspect, but the numbers look way too high. And it's too widespread. We've got multiple cases centred on Manhattan, but there's plenty coming in from New Jersey, Queens, Brooklyn – all five boroughs.'

'Could be an airborne infection then?'

'Yeah, or something in the water supply.'

'Let's go Code Red,' Holzman decided. 'We invoke full alert procedures to the hospitals, doctors and the public. Keep the public announcements nice and calm – we don't want a panic.'

'Okay.'

'I'll notify the National Institute of Allergy and Infectious Diseases.'

'Okay.'

'And the Office of Emergency Management. And you get the hospitals to send as many blood samples and stool samples as they can to the labs. Quicker we can find out what this is, the better.'

*

11.00 A.M.

At the Patrick J. Brock Memorial Hospital, the administrator, Irene Sefton, had called an emergency meeting of the department heads. The atmosphere in the room was charged with tension.

'Guys, thanks for coming. As you know, we've invoked our emergency plan. I'm cancelling all leave and calling in all staff on leave. As of now, we have no available beds. ER is overfull and we have,' she hesitated and looked at her notes, 'forty-seven patients on trolleys in the corridors, or in chairs, awaiting admission.'

'And it's getting worse, Irene,' chipped in Valerie Mahler. 'The ambulance dispatcher tells me they've a three-hour delay on calls, partly because they can't get patients out of the ambulances and into ER. We've run out of trolleys.'

Silence.

'Jesus,' said someone down the back. 'This is unheard of.'

'Okay, the Center for Disease Control and Prevention has issued an alert for New York State. All the hospitals are reporting a similar level of admissions, so it looks like it's something in the water supply or possibly airborne.'

'Any deaths?' asked Valerie Mahler.

'No, thank God. So far, we have a big chunk of the population presenting at a similar stage of illness. I've checked the National Diseases Surveillance System and there's no fatalities reported.'

She grimaced. 'Hopefully, it'll stay that way.' She referred again to an email printout on her clipboard.

'Priority now is to get as many samples as we can to the labs. Problem is, it's gonna take another two to three days until we know exactly what we're dealing with here. Until then, treat every case as you see fit.'

*

2 P.M.

The open plan second floor of the Fifth Precinct station on Elizabeth Street was packed with plainclothes and uniformed officers. Word of the wave of illness had reached the station.

Sergeant Jim Connolly had called the meeting.

'Listen up guys, looks like this city's got a crisis.' He had their immediate attention. 'One – we've got gridlock around all the hospitals. Sullivan, Rodisky – I want a traffic management plan for our precinct in operation by 4 p.m. Keep the routes to the hospitals clear.

'Two – there's nothing like a crisis to make the bad guys think we've got our eye off the ball. All leave cancelled until further notice.'

There was a groan around the room.

'I'm authorising full overtime rates.'

A small cheer.

'Leonard, Peters: I want a plan for increased protection on all the banks, galleries, you name it. Anywhere our gangster friends might take a pop at.'

Peters nodded. 'On your desk in an hour, sergeant.'

'Three – the Center for Disease Control's office in Manhattan just happens to be in our patch at Catherine Street. They've set up a task force there which is gonna be workin' around the clock on this. They're lookin' for a law enforcement presence on the team. They're also looking for help securing public utilities, public buildings – whatever places they think they may have to shut down and search for germs, or whatever it is they're lookin' for. Cabrini, Wyse, you go see what you can do to help.'

'On it, sergeant,' said Wyse.

'I want to be kept in the loop on everything, twenty-four seven until this is sorted. Ain't no one gonna say that the Fifth wasn't right on its game.'

'Hmmm – there's a change of scene,' said a grinning Cabrini to Wyse as they tramped down the old wooden stairs. 'All the crap you talk, this diarrhoea thing could be just your scene!'

John Wyse punched his buddy's shoulder. 'Let's get round there.'

As they walked down the steps of the station, out of the corner of his eye, Wyse spotted a man ducking around a corner, further down the street. Dark. Swarthy. Middle aged. It could be nothing, but his instinct told him he was up to no good. If they'd had the time, he would have gone back to see what the guy was up to.

43

2.45 P.M. – THAT DAY

Cabrini drove the unmarked Ford Crown Victoria towards Catherine Street for their first meeting at the Center for Disease Control and Prevention. Most of the detectives' cars had been upgraded to Ford Fusions, but Cabrini still had the Crown. Wyse reckoned that Sergeant Connolly probably shared his opinions on Cabrini's driving. Cabrini, however, was in observant form today and, after a few minutes, said,

'Hey, John, don't turn around, but check out that brown sedan about ten cars back.'

Wyse lowered himself in the seat and got a glimpse of a brown car in the wing mirror as it nipped in behind a van.

'Got it. What about it?'

'Noticed it behind us comin' outta Elizabeth. It's made every turn we have. Good way back, but I think he's following us.'

'What you wanna do?'

Their minds were made up for them when the Nissan made a sudden turn off into a side street.

'You get the plate?'

'Nope.'

'Wanna go back?'

'Nah. It's probably nothing. Guess we'd better get our asses down to the disease control place.'

Accelerating in the opposite direction, Ibrahim Fallah grimaced. He had spotted Wyse moving around in the seat to get a look at him in the mirror. *I need to back off a little. These guys are smart.*

*

At the Center for Disease Control and Prevention, Wyse and Cabrini showed their badges and were taken up to the incident room, which was in crisis. Dr Kim Scholler quickly introduced the detectives to the team. They wouldn't remember all the names, but there were several medics and a senior guy called Burt Dilzman from the Office of Emergency Management. At least a dozen people were already sitting around the large boardroom table in the conference room when Wyse and Cabrini pulled two chairs in at one end and sat down.

Dr Kim Scholler continued speaking. 'The crucial thing is that we identify what we're dealing with as quickly as possible. Most of those affected started displaying symptoms last Sunday morning. Problem is, until the virus or bacteria, or whatever it is, has been identified, we don't know how big this is going to be.'

'How do you mean, exactly, doctor?' asked Bill Fulzer who was representing the FDA.

'It's all down to the incubation period, Bill. For example, some bacterial infections will become obvious, say, twenty-four hours after someone has been infected. With other infections or viruses, it can take a week or more before the person actually gets sick.'

'So, we don't know whether the people who are sick contracted this on, say, Saturday, or Saturday week ago?' asked Fulzer.

'Exactly,' replied Dr Scholler. 'And, not wanting to cause unnecessary alarm, but if, for example, this bacteria takes a week to make you sick, and if people were exposed to it, say this day last week . . .'

Bill Fulzer got the point. 'Then, what we've got now may be only one seventh of the people who have been affected.'

'Or less than one seventh, if people are still being infected,' Dr Scholler added.

'How do you mean?' Fulzer asked.

'Problem is, we don't know what this is yet. People may be getting infected as we speak. The two crucial bits of info we need are: what's the bacterium or virus, and then how did so many people get exposed to it? We've sent a questionnaire to all the hospitals so they can record patients' movements over the last fortnight.'

'If you'll pardon the pun.' Cabrini couldn't resist it.

Kim Scholler frowned. 'Thank you, detective. I mean, where everyone has been, where they ate, what buildings they've been in, so we can try and find a common denominator. Jack, your side?'

Burly Jack Barrett was the 'no nonsense' head of the Municipal Water Division, based at the city's Pollution Control Plant on Wards Island, just over the Triborough Bridge from Manhattan.

'We've tested every single reservoir and pipe we got, doctor. Still got results coming in from the labs but, so far, clean as a whistle. We'll keep at it, but I don't think it's our water.'

'Jack, thanks. Chuck?'

Chuck Taylor was with the Department of Pollution Control.

'Same story here, Dr Scholler. We're taking hourly air quality samples in the five boroughs. Nothing to report, apart from the usual crap.'

'Thanks, Chuck – please continue to take hourly readings until further notice.'

She let out a deep sigh and said, 'My money's on a food poisoning event. I'm amazed how high the numbers are – and how sick people are. It looks like something that's particularly virulent. Most of the cases so far are here in Manhattan, but we've plenty in the other boroughs. We're looking for a common denominator, so we've got teams checking out the different meats in the factories that supply the restaurant chains and caterers. Next step is to check the restaurant chains. Meanwhile, every lab we've got is running cultures on stools and blood being passed by patients in the hospitals located closest to them. Depending on the strength of the infection, it's going to take time for the cultures to start producing useful information. However, if people are still being infected, then every day that goes by, the situation will only get worse. The first lab reports are due in to us from about 2 p.m. –'

She stopped as the telephone in front of her rang.

'Excuse me, everyone.' She picked up the handset and nodded her way through a one-way conversation.

'That's my people upstairs,' she said, hanging up. 'They're inputting feedback from the hospital questionnaires and looking for any cross-matches.' She paused.

'Folks, this may be our breakthrough. We already have about one thousand patients who were at the game at the MetLife Stadium last Sunday week. That's a real big coincidence.'

She stood up and addressed Wyse and Cabrini at the opposite end of the table.

'Detectives, we need the stadium shut down immediately. I want a ring of steel around it. No more traffic, in or out. We need a police escort out there for my lab technicians.'

'You got it,' said Cabrini, stepping to the side of the room and punching the speed dial on his cell phone.

'Everyone else, you know what to do. We lock the stadium down, check all the kitchens, toilets, air handling, seats, anything that people came into contact with.'

Everyone started pushing back chairs and standing up.

'People, this situation's gonna move real fast. Let's have all the heads of departments back here at five o'clock.'

*

Cabrini flicked on the siren and emergency lights as he drove them back towards the station. The traffic was chaotic. Over the radio the police dispatcher told them that ten cars were already on the way out to the stadium.

'Always said a lotta crap comes outta the Giants,' quipped Cabrini. 'What's she talking about air handling for?'

'Not sure. Might be Legionnaires' disease?'

'We're not in the middle of the freakin' desert here, John.'

'Nope, but you've got that wrong, bud. It's not some kinda tropical disease.'

'Ain't it?'

'Nah, nothing so dramatic. About thirty years ago, there was a convention or some kinda reunion for ex-Legionnaires, some hotel in Philadelphia.'

'Yeah?'

'So, they all got real sick. Most of them died.'

'So? Did their old war diseases all flare up together?'

'Nah, there was some kinda virus in the air con unit. Got pumped into all their bedrooms, wiped 'em out.'

Cabrini grinned. 'So, if it had been a convention of shoe salesmen, then Legionnaires' disease would be called "Shoe Salesman's disease"?'

'I guess so.'

A pause.

'Doesn't sound quite as dangerous, does it?' said an amused Cabrini.

Wyse frowned. 'Mike, this whole thing's getting interesting. Let's go out to the stadium and see what's goin' on.'

44

NEW YORK – 12 DECEMBER

Enrica Rodriguez balanced her sleeping two-year-old daughter Kayla on her hip as she pulled the door of her Ridgefield bedsit closed. It was 6.50 a.m., still dark, and very cold.

'I'm sorry, honey. I know it's not fair.' She hated this horrible routine of pulling her sleeping daughter out of her bed every morning, just so she could get her into the crèche as soon as it opened. She felt guilty about leaving her kid all day, but the most important thing was trying to hold on to her new job with the Department of Health. As a single mom, what else could she do? And Kayla's father had turned out to be a user. No maintenance again this month. *Asshole!*

At least the Department's head office wasn't too far away, just across the George Washington Bridge on 168th Street. Once she had given Kayla a last sad hug at the crèche, it was just a few stops on the subway. The next few days were going to be crazy busy though, with this suspected food poisoning. They were all being promised overtime, which she needed badly, but she was going to need a lot of help from her mom and her asshole ex, if she was going to work late.

At the office, Enrica collected a few packs of plastic containers, plastic bags, what they called 'standardisation workbooks', labels and thermometers. She had been assigned to check out a sample of BurgerFantastic restaurants. Ideally, you were supposed to get as wide a geographical sample as possible, but she had a plan to inspect maybe six restaurants that day, and to finish up in Upper Manhattan, close to the office – and to home.

At 9 a.m. her cell phone rang. 'Enrica, you're not returning my calls. Your rent is five weeks late.'

'I'm so sorry, Mr Dickersen. I'm working overtime now and I'll have it all for you, end of next week. Promise.'

'This is your very last chance, Enrica. If you don't pay, you're going to have to leave. I have my own costs to cover.'

'I promise. I won't let you down again.' *Jesus, give me a break.*

Her first call was to the BurgerFantastic restaurant on West 165th Street. It was packed with customers. She walked around the counter. 'Hi,' she said, showing her ID to a member of staff. 'Can I see the manager please?'

Five minutes later she was in the cooking area, being shown around by the manager, who was well used to Department of Health inspections.

'My priority today is to take away some samples,' she said. 'I won't be doing a full inspection.'

'Sure. No problem,' said the manager. 'Take anything you like. And if you're hungry, then lunch is on us.'

'No need for that, thanks.' *Against the rules anyway.*

Enrica had a quick look around the kitchens and the storage area. *Spotless as usual.*

She began taking the temperatures of pieces of chicken, lamb, pork and beef burgers in the cold holding area, and then again after cooking. She was testing a cooked burger, *155 degrees, A-okay,* when her phone rang. *At last.* She took the call.

'Pablo.'

'Wassup, baby?'

'What's up is I need to work late. I need you to pick up Kayla at seven.'

'Oh, sorry, baby. I can't do that. I got sumthin' on.'

'You gonna tell me you got a job?'

'No. Just plans. Know what I mean?'

'Like plans to start paying maintenance for your daughter?'

'Don't be like that, baby. You know I'll make it up when I get a job.'

'Whatever.' *Jesus.* She ended the call and tried her mother. Straight to voicemail.

She ticked a few boxes on the FDA workbook and put samples of meat into plastic bags. She sealed them and started writing out labels for each bag. Her phone rang.

'Ms Rodriguez. I'm with the New York Gas Company and I'm afraid we're going to have to cut off your supply if your account isn't paid.'

Jesus Christ. 'I'm sorry. I'll have it at the end of the month.'

'I hope so, Ms Rodriguez.'

She tried her mother again. Voicemail. *Shit!*

She decided to put samples of lettuce, tomatoes, cucumber and pickles in bags too. Then she repeated the routine in five other BurgerFantastics in midtown that day and brought the samples to the analysts, or the 'disease doctors' as they are known at the Department. She just made it to the crèche by 7 p.m. to pick up Kayla.

45

13 DECEMBER – 10 A.M.

'No, no! Please God, no!'

Suzy had managed one last weak smile to her father, as her organs started shutting down. Peter Phillips' anguished howls echoed around the Cedars Ward at the Patrick J. Brock Memorial Hospital. After the doctors had confirmed that she was dead, Peter Phillips sat for an hour, holding his daughter's hand and stroking her long blonde hair, which framed her deathly pale face on the pillow. Eventually, Dr Conrad Jones and one of the nurses came back and opened the curtain on one side of the bed.

'Peter, I'm so sorry, we tried everything.'

'How the hell could this happen, Conrad?'

'I'm sorry, Peter, I just can't be sure yet. We threw everything at it. Nurse,' he nodded a 'go ahead' to the nurse, who began removing the intravenous fluid line and the antibiotic line from the dead girl's arms.

'She got something really, really virulent, Peter. Very toxic. We got her straight on IV cephalosporin, but she just kept deteriorating. Her kidneys packed up. She had a septicaemic shock. I've never seen a ten-year-old who didn't respond to treatment like this. We'll have to wait for the autopsy to see what it was.'

Tears streamed down Peter Phillips' crumpled face as he kissed his daughter on the forehead.

'What now, Peter?' asked Conrad Jones, putting a comforting arm around the doctor's shoulders.

Peter Phillips shook his head slowly. 'I don't know, Conrad. Do I tell her mother? She's on the eighth floor. And she's not in great shape. And my son Jonathan's in the paediatric unit. Jesus, are *they* going to be all right?'

After he had led the broken-hearted father from the ward, Dr Conrad Jones went back to the dead girl's bed.

'Thanks, nurse,' he said as he helped her remove the heart monitors. 'Ask the porters to take the girl to the mortuary. As quickly as possible. By the sound of it, we've got about fifty people waiting for the bed. Oh, excuse me,' he said, as he stepped backwards through the curtains and onto the toe of a maintenance worker, who was fixing the curtains on the next bed.

*

CENTER FOR DISEASE CONTROL AND PREVENTION – 3 P.M.

'Two point two billion!'

'That's what it says.'

'Surely that's gotta close them down?'

Chuck Taylor, head of the Department of Pollution Control, was reading aloud from a CNN.com newsflash on his laptop, as they waited for the meeting to start.

'Drug giant Dupitol Pharma to pay record two point two billion dollar fine to resolve criminal and civil liability for fraudulent marketing of pharmaceuticals, the Justice Department announced today.' He skimmed down the report. 'Promoted drugs for use on certain ailments or at dosages that were not approved by the FDA.'

'Jesus,' said Jack Barrett from the Municipal Water Division.

'Dupitol subsidiaries also pleaded guilty to a felony violation for misbranding their products with intent to defraud or mislead.'

Taylor kept reading from his screen. 'Justice Department said Dupitol salespeople created sham requests from physicians, asking about unapproved uses of certain drugs. The information was then mailed to doctors. Dupitol also entertained doctors at luxury resorts as a way of encouraging them to prescribe its drugs.'

'Stinks to high hell,' said Barrett, shaking his head.

Taylor continued. 'Justice Department said Dupitol provided kickbacks to healthcare providers to encourage them to prescribe several of their highest selling drugs. The settlement includes a provision for eight whistle-blowers at Dupitol Pharma who will share one hundred and twenty million dollars.'

'But that fine! That's gotta put them outta business.'

'Doubt it, guys,' said Bill Fulzer from the FDA, leaning across. 'Two point two billion – that's about two weeks' revenue for Dupitol.'

Dr Kim Scholler interrupted by tapping her glass with her pen and the buzz of conversation died down.

'Let's get going, folks.'

She waited while everyone pulled in their chairs and topped up their coffee cups.

'Thanks, everyone. Same team as yesterday, but I'd like to introduce you to two new faces. First, Professor Samuel Ghent. The professor is with the Infectious Diseases Society of New York.' She nodded to the thin, greying man of about sixty, wearing a red and blue bowtie, in the chair alongside her.

'Professor, briefly, can you tell us what you do?'

'Sure, Kim, glad to be on the team. You may have heard about us before under the acronym IDSNY. We established in New York back in ninety-three. Basically, we're a grouping of physicians, researchers, etc., who specialise in infectious diseases. We help with the response to any public health crisis and act as a conduit between the City's Department of Health and ID specialists. In addition, we advise government on bio-terrorism threats.'

'Thanks, professor, glad to have you along. Everyone, things are moving fast. Detectives,' she addressed the opposite end of the table, 'thanks for your quick response at MetLife Stadium, but it may have been a wild goose chase. We checked the food concessions equipment and everything's clean. We haven't found anything else suspicious out there either, and our systems are now alerting us to the fact that we also have large numbers of patients who visited Radio City, the Empire State Building, the Rockefeller Center, Ground Zero, you name it. So, unless we shut down the whole city . . .?' She let the question hang in the air. No one responded. 'Then we need to look somewhere else for clues.'

Kim nodded to the second new member of the team.

Charles Steelman was about forty, with curly brown hair and a white, open-neck shirt. He was sitting about midway down the table. He smiled and nodded to the various faces looking at him.

'I decided to call Charles in as well because of certain developments,' Kim said. 'Dr Steelman is director of the Foodborne and Diarrhoeal Diseases Branch of the Center for Disease Control. Charles?'

'Yes, hello everyone. The major development is that we now have multiple early reports back from the labs, based on stool and blood samples from the hospital patients. It's pretty certain now – we're dealing with a massive e-coli infection.'

His words were met with a few nods around the table, together with a few glazed expressions.

'Please go on, Charles,' prompted Kim.

'Well, as you know, it's a classic food poisoning bug. Unfortunately, it looks like we're dealing with an Escherichia coli O157:h7 bacteria, which is right at the most virulent end of the scale. Our labs are continuing with what we call a DNA fingerprinting process, which will give us more information on exactly what we have, but that's going to take another two to three days.'

Detectives Wyse and Cabrini, and the rest of the group around the table, were listening intently.

'So, what are the implications of this e-coli bug?' asked Chuck Taylor from Pollution Control.

'The good news is that it's treatable,' replied Dr Scholler, 'even though it's at the tougher end of the spectrum. The bad news is that e-coli has about the longest incubation period of all the foodborne bacteria. E-coli toxins are produced in the large intestine, rather than higher up, so the symptoms are slower to appear. Symptoms can develop after a couple of days, but it can incubate for a week or so before someone gets sick with it. There were hundreds of people infected, and some killed, by e-coli at Jack in the Box restaurants a few years ago and the symptoms took a long time to show.'

'So, people might still be picking it up?' asked Chuck.

'Yes, I'm afraid so. And, as of now, we don't know the source. We're looking at all the food manufacturers, the catering companies, the meat processors, the restaurant chains, all the usual suspects. To some extent we're overwhelmed by the numbers. We still have multiple cross-references for patients – places they've eaten, places they've visited, mass produced foods they've consumed . . .'

There was a silence.

'This,' continued Kim Scholler in a downbeat tone, 'is going to get worse before it gets better. We've been collating reports from the hospitals all day. We now have over five hundred deaths from this infection.' The atmosphere in the room chilled by about twenty degrees. 'Most of them are in Manhattan, but one hundred or so are spread around the boroughs.' She turned to look at the bowtied professor beside her. 'Professor?'

'I've been looking at the morbidity reports and doing some profiling. It's showing what I would have expected for a virulent infection at this stage.'

'Which is?' prompted Dr Scholler.

'Well, pretty much all of the fatalities are among those with weaker immune systems, for example, young children and the elderly, or anyone on chemotherapy. To be specific, forty-five per cent of the deaths are children under eight. About forty per cent are adults aged over seventy. I'll bet that the other fifteen per cent are HIV positive, with compromised immune systems.'

'And, Dr Steelman, now that we know what we have, what is the advised treatment?'

'Our advice is that you attempt to rehydrate the patient, rebalance electrolytes, try and prevent organ damage. We don't try and stop the diarrhoea – it's usually better to let the toxic matter get out through the system. Normally, you wouldn't rush into antibiotic treatment until there's evidence of blood loss and toxicity. However, we're getting a lot of that in this case and most of the hospital patients have been put on intravenous cephalosporin since yesterday.'

'Why's that?' asked Detective Wyse.

'It's about the best antibiotic we can throw at this,' replied Dr Steelman. 'The drug of last resort, we call it. Forty-eight hours on cephalosporin and rehydration should bring the patient around.'

'Should?' asked Cabrini.

'Well, given the numbers we're dealing with, first question is: do we have enough cephalosporin? I've sent an alert to all the hospitals confirming the e-coli O157:h7 analysis and they all need more cephalosporin. Looks like we'll be okay, though – the main supplier has a good stock in the city, but . . .'

'But?' prompted Wyse.

'I must say,' Dr Steelman continued, 'I am very concerned at the numbers we are handling. And the early morbidity rate, though, as the professor explained, fatalities are currently confined to groupings with weaker immune systems. This is a very nasty bug we're dealing with. It could get much worse before it gets better.'

'And,' finished Dr Kim Scholler, 'we still don't know the source.'

46

HARRY'S BAR, MANHATTAN – LATER THAT EVENING

Health Crisis in New York – Is it something we ate? New York's Hospitals are overrun and over one thousand people have died. I'm Randy Tyler for Fox News. More, after these messages.

Harry had turned up the volume on the TV and most of the people in the bar had paused to watch the 7 p.m. news. Detectives Wyse and Cabrini were sitting on their usual barstools and had a good view of the television. They had briefed Sergeant Connolly on the day's events, before clocking off.

'Okay, boys, stay with it,' had been his reaction. Cabrini had suggested a quick beer on the way home and Wyse had agreed. Anna was working late.

'Jeez, buddy, hope the hospitals can get on top of this quickly.'

'Shhh.' John Wyse pointed at the TV. Dr Kim Scholler had appeared on the screen.

'Yes, Randy, the public health authorities are on high alert. We're dealing with an outbreak of e-coli food poisoning. The hospitals have been fully informed. We haven't yet identified the source, so for the moment we're asking everyone to ensure that all food is very thoroughly cooked.'

Next, Fox News switched to a story in Syria. IS extremists were threatening to behead another six hostages. Harry turned the TV down again.

'Fuckin' assholes,' said Cabrini. 'Two more beers, Harry,' he called as he stood up and made his way to the restroom.

John rubbed his eyes and yawned. He was tired. He focused on the TV again.

'And there's even talk of a Nobel Prize nomination for humanitarian work.'

There was some Japanese guy on the TV. *Hey, isn't that . . .?*

'Tsan Yohoto's Yamoura Pharmaceuticals have spent millions of dollars shipping free supplies of cephalosporin antibiotics in a mission to eradicate disease in famine-stricken African nations.'

The camera cut to show a long line of emaciated figures waiting to get access to a field hospital. The next scene showed the tiny, limp body of a three-year-old girl being bundled up in a blanket and placed in a shallow grave by her mother.

'And this little girl is just one of thousands to die, because she had no access to medicine or clean water. Her mother has buried all six of her children, just like this.'

The mother's sunken brown eyes gazed pitifully up at the camera. John Wyse had a lump in his throat. *Jesus, that's awful.*

'And Tsan Yohoto's benevolence hasn't done the Yamoura share price any harm at all. Today in Tokyo, Yamoura are up five per cent on the Nikkei. For Fox News I'm Andrea Mortimer in Darfur.'

Wyse took a sip from a fresh bottle of beer. *Good to see there's some decency left in the world. Just shows, I must have misjudged that guy, Yohoto. Must tell Anna. She must know about it, though?* He frowned. *Cephalosporin – isn't that the same stuff that –?*

His thoughts were loudly interrupted by Mike Cabrini, sitting back heavily onto his barstool, as he invited Smith and Williams to join them. 'Four beers, Harry,' he shouted. Then noticing Wyse's expression, 'Hey, John, why so serious?'

'Mike, see that cephalosporin stuff, that they're giving away free in Africa.' He cocked a thumb at the TV.

'Yeah,' said Cabrini, gulping his beer.

'Isn't that the same stuff they were talkin' about today at the meeting?'

Cabrini paused and then launched into his infamous impression of Huggy Bear, from *Starsky and Hutch*. Eyes wide, he faced Wyse and said in a hugely exaggerated, African-American accent, 'It's all shit to me, brother. Don't make no difference if it's black or white! High five!'

Wyse couldn't help but join in the laughter.

'Hey Harry, where are those beers?'

★

THE VILLA AT SAITON

'*Omedetou.*'

'And *omedetou*, to you, Tsan.'

Tsan Yohoto had called a breakfast meeting to review progress. The four members of the Chess Club stood in front of the plasma screen in the drawing room of Lumo Kinotoa's villa. The clinking of glasses rang around the room as, triumphant, they raised glasses of sparkling water to each other. Lumo Kinotoa had sat a bottle of champagne in a bucket of ice on the table.

'We will leave the champagne until after the meeting,' Tsan had said when he arrived.

'We are nicely on track,' he continued. 'Today, Monday, is the ninth day since we started adding e-coli to the sauce. The hospitals in New York are overwhelmed. The Public Health Authorities have identified our e-coli bacteria and are beginning to realise how virulent it is, but now they think they can cure their people with cephalosporin.'

'So, what do you think will happen next, Tsan?' asked Kazuhiro Saito.

'Apparently they started large-scale intravenous cephalosporin treatment today. But as their patients are totally resistant, we will see a big upturn in the number of deaths from tomorrow.'

'And for how long do we continue infecting the sauce?' asked Saito.

'For as long as we can, my friend. How are the BurgerFantastic sales?'

'Still very strong at about two million per week – and rising. The ninety-nine cent special ensured thousands of new fans! So, gentlemen,' said Saito, excitedly, 'every day potentially buys us close to three hundred thousand victims.'

'Excellent, excellent,' said Dr Naga, rubbing his hands together, his thin face breaking into a smile.

'Any news from our al-Qaeda friends?' asked Kazuhiro Saito.

Lumo Kinotoa responded. 'They say there hasn't been a clear chance to kill the detective yet. He must be smarter than we thought.'

Tsan Yohoto interjected. 'We can tell them to leave Wyse alone for now. We're past the tipping point – so there's not much he, or anyone, can do now. Please also tell them that they can cease the van drops of SuperVerve; those tablets have done their job. Tell them to concentrate on the curtain swishing in the hospitals!'

Pop – the cork exploded out of the bottle and Lumo Kinotoa tried to stop the champagne frothing on to the carpet. They moved back to the end of the room and stood in front of the huge plasma TV. The four men hugged and cheered each other as they sat watching minute-by-minute coverage of the disaster unfolding in New York. All the US networks had now switched to nonstop coverage. The Fox News reporter was talking earnestly into the camera from the familiar position at the railings in front of the White House.

'Government officials now put the death toll at close to five thousand. The President has declared a state of emergency for New York. Troops have been sent into Manhattan to prevent any breakdown in public order. Behind me, the President's officials are working around the clock in an effort to beat this public health disaster. Just as Mayor Giuliani re-opened the theatres on Broadway, two days after 9/11, the President is encouraging New Yorkers to continue with their daily lives with bravery and dignity. Some senators are saying that the government is not doing enough and seem to have learned nothing from New Orleans. I'm Tom Broden for NBC News, the White House.'

'Our revenge is in play.' Dr Naga laughed. 'Oh, how they deserve it! More champagne, Tsan?'

'No thank you,' said Tsan Yohoto, who was looking at the black and white photograph in his hand. 'Please send a message of thanks and congratulations to our colleagues in Afghanistan. Now I must go and see my mother.'

★

MANHATTAN – 10 P.M.

John Wyse and Anna were snuggled into each other on the couch in his apartment.

Wyse said, 'So, it was on the TV. A story about Tsan Yohoto saving thousands of lives in Africa, by donating free medicine.'

Anna prodded him. 'There ya go. I told you he was a great guy.'

'Hmm. Maybe I misjudged him. Anyway, it turns out that the antibiotics that he's giving away are the same type they're using here to fight this food poisoning. Isn't that weird?'

Anna shrugged and clicked the remote. 'I'd like to see that interview. Should be on again soon.' Wyse pulled her closer and inhaled the smell of her perfume. He kissed the back of her head.

'Mmmm' was her response. Then after a silence, 'You know John, I've been thinking. And I'd like to ask you a favour.'

'Sure, honey.'

She turned to face him. 'You know we both want to have kids in a few years. When the time's right?'

'Yeah?'

'If we have a boy, can we call him Adam?'

'After your brother. Of course. It's a beautiful name.'

Anna's eyes moistened as she kissed Wyse and squeezed him tighter. She had never felt so complete.

'John. I love you.'

*

Ten miles away, Dr Peter Phillips sat in the darkness of his kitchen with an open bottle of whiskey in front of him. He was on his third glass. He stared blankly through the window into the garden. There was Suzy's swing, moving gently backwards and forwards in the breeze. His beautiful girl was dead. His wife and son were in hospital. The doctors had assured him that they had identified the infection, had started Sandra and Jonathan on the correct antibiotic, and had sent him home to sleep. He jumped as his cell phone beeped to alert him to a message. He slowly thumbed the buttons to read it. It was from Elaine at the clinic.

> John, where are you? Clinic is overrun. Several patients have died – Mrs Riccini, Mrs Walton. Please call urgently.

He sighed heavily and dropped the phone on to the table.

Poor old Mrs Walton and her endless complaining. And Mrs Riccini.

And then he thought of her six children. And then he thought of his own daughter, Suzy. He thought that he could see her now, on the swing in the garden, her long blonde hair blowing in the wind. Singing like Adele. Smiling her beautiful smile. And then he cried.

47

PATRICK J. BROCK MEMORIAL HOSPITAL, MANHATTAN

'Well you'd better get the damn lawyers in, cos this stinks to hell.'

An exhausted Dr Conrad Jones angrily threw two medical charts back onto the desk of Irene Sefton.

'All right, take it easy, we're all doing our best. Let's keep calm and work this out.'

Ten minutes earlier the furious doctor had banged into the hospital administrator's office, holding two fresh reports from the hospital lab. Two teenage brothers, Karl and Mike Johnson, who had been badly smashed up in a car wreck, had been making good progress, following multiple surgeries for broken bones and lungs punctured by crushed ribs. Both, however, had deteriorated rapidly over the previous three days and were now seriously ill with septicaemia. The doctor had immediately suspected a post-op wound infection, or internal bleeding. The lab reports in his hand, however, were now telling him that both boys had a toxic e-coli O157 infection.

'For chrissake, Irene, they've been in our wards for over a month, so whatever happened, they've got this in our hospital. Have we checked out our own damn kitchens?' he asked, exasperated.

'C'mon, of course we have, you know that. The whole damn city's down with food poisoning.'

'I knew we shouldn't have put so many patients on the wards. But how the hell is this e-coli spreading around the wards so quickly?'

'I don't know, I'm not the doctor here.'

Conrad Jones opened the door to leave.

'Look, Conrad, we're all under huge pressure right now. I'll get your wards cleaned again and I'll try and get the contractor to put on another cleaning shift. They're already maxed out on overtime. And you can help by getting *all* of the doctors to wash their hands in between treating patients – they're the biggest offenders on the wards.'

'Thanks, Irene,' he sighed. 'Either way we're screwed, you know. We can't have patients coming in here with broken bones and dying from a food poisoning bug. From something they didn't even eat!'

PART THREE

FALLOUT

48

BURGERFANTASTIC DEPOT, NEWARK – SUNDAY 15 DECEMBER – 6 A.M.

'Perhaps ten more days, my friend. I promise you, maximum ten more days.' Ibrahim Fallah spoke calmly, from his usual chair in Takar el Sayden's office. 'And then you will never see me again.'

Takar el Sayden was slumped in his chair and he didn't show any reaction to his visitor's words.

He is close to breaking point, thought Fallah. He has definitely lost weight and he looks exhausted. I must be careful with him.

'There is more powder in my case, Takar. It is vital that you keep up the routine – two bags in the sauce every night.'

'Don't you know what's going on in this city?' snarled Takar el Sayden. 'There are people dying from food poisoning. If this damn powder is behind this . . .'

'Do not threaten me, Takar,' said Fallah firmly. 'I assure you that our experiment has nothing to do with events in the city. How could it? We have been conducting our experiment for eighteen months now. Without any effects. And you have seen me take samples myself. You have my word. Just ten more days.'

Takar el Sayden was far from convinced. His adversary shoved his customary envelope full of photographs of Takar's family across the desk.

'Such cute little girls, Takar. I would hate to have to harm them. Stay calm. Courtesy of BurgerFantastic, you are now an even richer man. Ten more days and you and your family can enjoy your money in peace.'

'Bastard,' spat out Takar el Sayden.

*

CENTER FOR DISEASE CONTROL AND PREVENTION – 7.45 A.M.

Dr Kim Scholler was sitting, ashen faced, at the head of the conference room table, as the rest of the Task Force came into the room. She had been in her office since six, reviewing reports from the hospitals and fielding panicked calls from hospital administrators. Her words hung in the air for what seemed an age.

'It's a meltdown.'

No one dared to break the silence. Eventually the bowtied Professor Samuel Ghent, who had taken up his usual seat to her left, broke in quietly.

'Perhaps, Dr Scholler, you would let us have the numbers?'

Kim Scholler looked down at a pile of printouts in front of her and read from some notes she had made. 'I regret to say that we now have over ten thousand deaths reported. And rising.'

'Jesus fucking Christ!' blurted out Chuck Taylor from Pollution Control. There was a shocked silence in the room. Jack Barrett from the Municipal Water Department had his head in his hands. Again, Professor Ghent tried to move things along.

'Dr Steelman,' he said, addressing the CDCP's Doctor of Foodborne and Diarrhoeal Diseases. 'What's happening with the treatment?'

'Professor, my team is in touch with all of the hospitals. They're all saying they can't take any more admissions. They've got car parks full of people trying to get admitted.'

'So, what are they doing?' asked Detective Cabrini.

'For now, they're just sending them home,' replied Steelman. 'The big problem is that the first influx of patients is not responding to antibiotic treatment – if anything, they seem to be getting worse. We're seeing patients becoming very toxic, very quickly. A lot of them are developing septicaemia and we're getting deaths from peritonitis, meningitis and kidney failure.'

'So, what do we do?' asked Professor Ghent.

'We just keep throwing the antibiotics at it and hope that this starts to turn around,' said Steelman. 'Luckily, we've secured a good supply line of cephalosporin.'

Dr Scholler broke in, 'Professor, any views?'

The professor sat back in his chair and said calmly, 'Well, I'm not given to dramatics, but the doctor's use of the word "meltdown" is not unreasonable. We've DNA fingerprinted this damn bug and there's no doubt that all the patients have caught the same thing. We'll have more information on it over the next thirty-six hours. Certainly, the question of antibiotic resistance might arise, but it's too early to say.'

'What's that?' asked Detective John Wyse.

'The bacteria are learning how to fight off the antibiotics,' said the professor. 'It's potentially a massive problem – we'll have to keep an eye on it.'

Dr Scholler took control again.

'Worst-case scenario, this is going to multiply, because we still haven't identified the damn source. I've spent most of the morning on the phone to Homeland Security in Washington. They're about to push the button on the National Response Plan. There's a crisis meeting there in one hour. They want me, Professor Ghent and Dr Steelman there ASAP. Detectives,' she addressed Wyse and Cabrini, 'we need a police escort and a helicopter to Washington.'

'On it,' said Cabrini, heading out of the room, cell phone in hand.

'The rest of you, for now,' she continued, 'keep looking for the source. And keep calm. The Mayor's office is looking for a statement. Last thing we want is complete panic.'

*

Detectives Wyse and Cabrini blinked and turned their backs to the cloud of dust kicked up by the police department helicopter. The pilot gently raised the collective with his left hand, then eased the cyclic forward with his right, and the powerful machine carrying Dr Scholler, Dr Steelman and Professor Ghent clawed its way out over the Hudson River, from the helipad on 84th Street. The police escort for the six-block journey from the Center for Disease Control had proved essential, as the gridlock around the city's hospitals had snarled traffic across the entire island. The two detectives turned again to watch the helicopter bank to the southwest towards Washington. A three-hour drive would be cut to forty-five minutes.

'Hope those guys come back with some answers,' said Cabrini, glumly.

'I've got a real bad feeling about this, Mike,' replied John Wyse. 'Like this is completely new territory.'

'Hope you're wrong, pal. C'mon, let's get back to the station,' said Cabrini, as they turned towards the car.

'All right, but I wanna stop off for a coupla minutes and say hello to Anna.'

'Ain't you seeing enough of her, man, now you're living together?'

'Well, yeah,' said Wyse, as he sat back into the passenger seat, 'but we've both been workin' so hard, last few days, we only seem to cross paths for an hour or so. I just wanna make sure she's okay.'

'All right, man,' said Cabrini, switching on the siren. 'Where is it? Times Square?'

'Yeah, Broadway and 43rd.'

They skirted around Ground Zero, in the shadow of the Freedom Tower, and headed north on Broadway.

'You've got it bad for this girl, John – I can tell,' said Cabrini with a grin.

'You betcha, Mike – this is the one.'

★

The elevator pinged as Detective John Wyse reached the eighteenth floor of the Paramount Building, overlooking Times Square. Cabrini had parked the car on yellow lines and had gone for a coffee in the Starbucks across the street.

'Hi, Sonya,' said Wyse as the Dynamic Communications receptionist looked up.

'Hi, John,' she replied, flashing him a smile. 'Not here to arrest anyone I hope?'

'Not today.'

'Take a seat, John, I'll let Anna know you're here.'

Wyse sat into a white leather chair and casually picked up a copy of *Time*, which was on top of a small pile of magazines on the coffee table. The front cover caught his eye. There was a full cover picture of Tsan Yohoto, Anna's client, with the heading:

Can This Man Save Africa?

Huh. Maybe we could do with him here, right now, to save New York. He flicked to page five to read the story.

> Tsan Yohoto, Japanese businessman and philanthropist, has been nominated for a Nobel Prize for his humanitarian assistance in Africa. The soon-to-retire giant of the pharmaceutical world inspired his corporation, Yamoura Pharmaceuticals, to spend millions of dollars in providing free cephalosporin antibiotics to disease-ridden nations in Africa.

Yep, there's that cephalosporin again.

'Hey, John.' Anna's voice interrupted his thoughts. She quickly crossed the room to him. She was wearing a pair of perfectly fitting blue jeans and a plain white T-shirt. As always, she looked gorgeous.

'Hi, honey,' he said, kissing her on the cheek. 'Hey, you see your client's on the cover of *Time*?'

'Yeah, isn't he fantastic? Must be great to be able to make a real difference in the world. Come on in,' she said. 'I was just having a sandwich at my desk.' She led him in through the open-plan office.

'Hey, you can sit there,' said Anna, indicating Cindy Sheperd's empty chair at the next desk. 'Cindy's out sick.'

'Oh?' said Wyse, sitting down. 'Has she been sick long?'

'Few days – and, like, six of the other girls. They've all got this food poisoning thing. We heard that Cindy had to go to hospital. I'm worried sick about her. It's weird without her – the place is like a morgue.' Then, nodding her head at her own heaped desk, 'and I've been flat out in here. So, what's up, babe?'

'Just worrying about you, honey.' Wyse looked around him, lowered his voice and said, 'Keep it to yourself for the moment, baby, but this food poisoning thing is gettin' outta control.'

'Really?'

'Yeah. All the hospitals are full. They're gonna have to start moving people outta state.'

'Wow, that's heavy.'

'Yeah, just be real careful what you eat.'

'That's one advantage of being a vegetarian,' said Anna, smiling. 'Want some?' And she offered him half a salad sandwich.

'Yeah, thanks,' he said, reaching across. 'Haven't eaten since real early.'

'You still on for the big dinner tonight?' asked Anna through a mouthful of salad.

'Tonight, yeah . . .' Christ, he'd forgotten all about that.

'Don't tell me you'd forgotten, John. It's the advertising awards at the Waldorf!'

'Yeah, I know. Looking forward to it.'

'Wait till you see my new dress. Katie told me and Arlene to go and spend what we liked. She says we've gotta look our best for the winner's podium. She reckons we're gonna sweep the boards.'

Anna took another bite of her sandwich and nodded to the right. 'Take a look out the window.'

John stood up and walked the ten paces or so to the window overlooking Times Square. Directly opposite him and dominating the Square were two enormous electronic screens – side by side on the Bank of America building. The blue and white screen read:

SuperVerve – putting the verve back into your life

The red and yellow flashing sign beside it read:

BurgerFantastic – Home cooking without the hassle.

99 cent offer for one more week

'Hey – I see what you mean! That's your Japanese guys, isn't it? And your burger chain?'

'Yessir, and only the two biggest marketing campaigns in the history of the city, that's what,' said Anna, wiping salad cream off her upper lip. 'Completely blown everyone outta the water and both campaigns using my celebs,' she said, proudly. She lowered her voice and pointed left. 'Katie and Vic are in the boardroom, practising their acceptance speech.'

'And does all the advertising work?' asked Wyse.

'Does it work? Take a look to the right.'

John Wyse went back to the window and looked further down into Times Square. On the opposite side of the street was the ubiquitous bright red and yellow BurgerFantastic sign. Below it was a line of about thirty people waiting to get into the restaurant.

'Suppose it's not too hard when you're giving them away for ninety-nine cents,' he said. 'How does that make sense in terms of a profit?'

'All about market share I suppose,' said Anna, shrugging and chucking her napkin in the wastepaper basket.

'And why these two huge marketing campaigns at the same time?'

asked Wyse. 'Is there some connection between BurgerFantastic and SuperVerve?'

'No.' Anna shook her head. 'Not that I ever heard. It's just coincidence I guess.'

'So, the SuperVerve campaign has worked, too?' he asked, sitting down again at Cindy's desk.

'Oh, you betcha. Half the city's taking them. There, see for yourself,' she said, pointing at a packet of SuperVerve on Cindy's desk. John Wyse picked up the familiar blue and white box with the smiling face of a slim young woman on the front.

'SuperVerve – Putting the verve back into your life,' he said, reading out some of the words printed on the packet. He turned it around in his hands. There was the smiling girl again. He read out the small print:

'Manufactured by Yamoura Pharmaceutical Corporation. Contains forty-two 500 mg tablets of cephalosporin.'

More of that antibiotic. It's everywhere. Isn't it bad to be taking too many antibiotics? Maybe that's why Cindy's sick?

The door into the main office suddenly burst open with a bang and Sonya the receptionist ran in. There were tears streaming down her face.

'Anna, Anna!' she called out.

'Jesus, Sonya, what is it?' asked Anna.

'It's Cindy!' Sonya cried out. 'She's dead.'

49

THE PENTAGON – 12 NOON

The tables are certainly getting bigger, thought Professor Ghent glumly. There were at least twenty people around this one, several in military uniform, and a swarm of assistants buzzing in and out. Every piece of paper brought into the meeting and circulated brought worse news as the death toll in New York mounted rapidly. The city's hospitals were clamouring for somewhere to start sending body bags.

One hour into the meeting the Director of Homeland Security had made his decision. 'People, we're activating the National Response Plan. We're heading for fifty thousand dead.' He turned to his deputy director. 'Press all the buttons. Inform the President's office. Get the army, navy, FBI and CIA heads in here. Issue a press statement emphasising the need for calm.'

'Yes, director, right away.'

After two hours of further debate and with the body count piling up, it became clear that even opening every other hospital and nursing home within range was not going to be sufficient.

'Central Park it is, sir,' said General Farrington. 'We can have a field hospital under construction there within twenty-four hours. We can give you up to five thousand beds and stretchers there.'

'You're going to need a lot more than that,' said Professor Ghent.

'Then fill every park in New York!' barked the director. 'This is going to make New Orleans look like a picnic.' He turned to his deputy director. 'What's the White House position?'

'Everyone appealing for calm, but keen to be seen to be reacting quickly. Encouraging everyone to keep as much normal business going as possible – good for morale and all that. But there's talk about quarantining the city. No decision though.'

'Christ. Don't think we need to do that yet.' He looked around the room and found no response. 'Any funding issues?' Nobody spoke.

'Folks, to summarise, we're not going to cut off Manhattan and we're not going for a mass evacuation. We're reluctantly going to move more people into hospitals in other states because you don't think it's overly contagious . . .'

'No, yes, well – it's not ideal,' said Dr Charles Steelman. 'E-coli is not a classically airborne infection, but the hospitals are reporting a surprising amount of cross contamination.'

'What do you mean by that, exactly?' asked the general.

'Patients who were already in hospitals, without food poisoning, are getting sick from the e-coli too. They're catching it from the food poisoning victims. It's almost as if there's something spreading the infection around the wards. We'll need to issue an even stronger directive to the hospitals on hygiene. It's vital that the hospitals try and stop this infection from spreading. Fist bump protocols, no handshakes, the whole lot.'

'Okay. Do it,' said the general.

'And,' Steelman added, 'we need a public announcement to maximise hygiene precautions: make sure you wash your hands, particularly for kids in crèches, nursing homes, no unnecessary visits to hospital – all that stuff.'

'But why the hell can't you find the source?' asked the director, not bothering to hide his irritation.

'It's because of the numbers, director,' replied Dr Kim Scholler.

'We've got too many common denominators. Our staff are testing the food producers and restaurant chains twenty-four seven and still haven't found anything. They'll all have cleaned their equipment by now and overheated the cooking equipment to kill any infection.'

'So, we may never find it?' snapped the director.

'Perhaps not. Let's just hope there's no new infections going on.'

'And that the antibiotics start kicking in soon,' added Dr Steelman.

The Director of Homeland Security sighed. 'Hope,' he said, 'is one thing I don't like depending on.'

*

MANHATTAN – 12.15 P.M.

John Wyse had comforted Anna as best he could. Eventually, she sent him away saying she would stick around with the rest of her colleagues, who were all equally distraught. He hugged her tightly again and kissed her tear-streaked face. 'Okay, baby, I'll see you later. And don't forget, I love you.'

'I love you too. See you at home,' she sobbed as she squeezed his hand.

Cabrini was driving them towards the station on Elizabeth Street. Wyse told Cabrini the news about Cindy and they sat in silence as Wyse grappled with feelings of shock laced with guilt. *Okay, can't do anything about that now. Gotta focus on the main issue here.* The gridlocked traffic gave him plenty of time to think.

'You know, Mike, I've got a real strange feelin' that there's a lot more going on here than we think,' said Wyse eventually.

'How do you mean?'

'All this food poisoning stuff and the antibiotics. I wish I knew more about it. Something feels off.'

'Not really our job, buddy, but I know just the girl who can help you with all that.'

'Yeah? Who?'

'My little sister, Maria, that's who. She's one of these fancy microbiologists or whatever they're called. Spends her whole time wearing a white coat in a lab, I know that.'

'Really? Where does she work?'

'She's at the St Vincent's University Hospital – it's off the Henry Hudson Parkway.'

'Can we go see her?'

'Sure, why not? I'll call and make sure she's there.'

*

Cabrini swung the car onto Riverside Drive and they headed uptown for St Vincent's.

The bright overhead lighting sparkled off rows and rows of glass test tubes, glass cases and light boxes. There were a lot of computer terminals too. Wyse had never been this close to a working laboratory before. The lab assistant tapped on a high window and Maria Cabrini waved to them, as soon as she heard the knock. She came out through a double set of heavy doors and began taking off a blue facemask, a hairnet, a white coat and blue plastic shoe covers.

'Hi, guys, sorry for the delay. We have to keep the inner lab as clean as possible.' Finally, she was finished. Detective Cabrini gave his sister a hug, then wrinkled his nose as a waft of air from the laboratory reached him. 'Jeez, sis, I thought labs would smell all clean and sanitised?'

Maria Cabrini smiled. ''Fraid not, Mike. Don't forget what we're working with in there.'

'True. Hey, sis, this is my buddy, Detective John Wyse, the guy I told ya about.'

'Maria, nice to meet you. We're trying to help out with this food poisoning crisis and I thought you might be able to assist me.'

'Yeah, sure, it's certainly keeping us in overdrive.'

'What's involved?'

'Well, pretty much every lab in New York has a big backlog of cultures from patients. We've had a whole lot of samples coming in here from Chinatown.'

'And what have you found?'

'We've fingerprinted the DNA – the bacterium is definitely e-coli O157:h7 – it's very virulent. And very toxic. It's spreading like wildfire.'

'Why can't the doctors stop it spreading?'

'It could be that the cephalosporin antibiotic needs another day or so to get on top of it . . .'

'Are they using the right drug?'

'Sure. Cephalosporin's known as the antibiotic of last resort for this kind of thing. Let's put it this way – if the antibiotics don't work, we're into a cholera or bubonic plague scenario.'

'Well, from what we're hearing today, there's people dying like flies,' replied Wyse. 'It's already outta control.'

'I know, if I was in charge,' she said, 'I would be getting very worried about mass antibiotic resistance.'

'Which is what?' asked Wyse.

'It's my area of research,' she continued, 'and it's a ticking time bomb that no one is paying enough attention to. Put it like this – there's a war going on between the bacteria and antibiotics. And the bacteria are winning. In my view, it's a bigger threat to us all than global terrorism.'

'How's that?'

'Well, because we've been consuming too many antibiotics, and for too long, the bacteria have learned to genetically mutate, so that the antibiotics can't kill them. And now the bugs have learned how to fight off lots of different antibiotics. MDROs we call them – multi-drug resistant organisms. Then there's all the antibiotics in livestock and farmed fish going into the food chain. Even soaps now are "antibacterial".' She mimed the quotation marks by crooking her index fingers. 'Our own bodies are teaching the bacteria how to fight off the antibiotics. It's all messing with Mother Nature, big time, and eventually she bites back.'

'If you're right, can this problem be fixed?' Wyse asked.

She grimaced. 'As far back as 1978 the American Academy of Science predicted that antibiotic resistant e-coli would develop and would be untreatable. And they were right. The World Health Organisation is calling it a global crisis. There's over seven hundred thousand people a year dying from antibiotic resistant bacteria. And it's getting worse. They're predicting that we won't have any antibiotic that works for urinary infections in four years. And we've had some resistant strains of e-coli for years now. That's my speciality,' she said. 'I'm analysing some cultures right now. Wouldn't surprise me if this bacterium turned out to be not sensitive, that is, resistant, to cephalosporin.'

Wyse was shocked. 'But if the problem's that bad, why don't we hear more about it?'

Maria Cabrini shrugged. 'Dunno, guess it's a bit like global warming – everyone's waiting for someone else to solve it. And, if everyone thinks it's not going to happen while they're around . . .'

'So, is that what we've got in New York – mass antibiotic resistance?'

'Could be,' she said. 'It's a huge outbreak and it sure looks like something tipped the balance and let the bacteria get on top.'

★

1 P.M.

All TV and radio stations interrupted their normal schedules with a newsflash. The Mayor of New York was standing at a podium on the steps outside City Hall.

'A state of emergency for the State has just been declared by the President,' he said. 'The army will shortly begin constructing field hospitals in the five boroughs. Our sympathy is with the very,

very many who have died, and with their families.' The Mayor paused, bit his lower lip and continued,

'I appeal to my fellow New Yorkers to remain calm. Please stay in the city and please observe the hygiene information notices. We will try to go about our daily lives, as best we can.'

He looked into the camera. 'My fellow New Yorkers, in the same spirit with which we fought back after 9/11, New York will defeat this latest crisis. God Bless New York.'

The death toll was now believed to be more than seventy-five thousand people.

*

Outside the laboratory at St Vincent's University Hospital, Cabrini had lost interest in the conversation between Wyse and his sister and had wandered back outside to the reception area. Wyse, however, was keen to learn more.

'What happens when someone who's consumed too much cephalosporin gets infected with e-coli?'

'Well, that person's system is already going to have antibiotic resistant bacteria in it. So, when the e-coli bacteria arrive in the stomach and bowel, the resistant bacteria already there are going to get much worse. The resistant bacteria are going to teach all the other bacteria how to fight off the antibiotics too. It's a real mess. The infection gets outta control and poisons the patient.'

'And what if someone wanted to deliberately infect a lot of people with e-coli?'

'I suppose they'd have to put it in the water supply or in the food chain. Something that lots of people eat.'

'Like burgers?'

'No, wouldn't work, cos cooking the burger would kill the e-coli.'

'Oh.' Wyse was silent.

'Although, if it was like the Taco Bell outbreak –'

'Remind me, what was that again?'

'A few years ago, lots of people got food poisoning around the same time, from eating in Taco Bells all over northern States. People got very sick.'

'So, it was the meat?'

'No, like I said, it couldn't have been cooked. The e-coli turned out to be on one of the vegetables, which were added after the meat was cooked.'

'Ah, right. So,' Wyse spoke slowly as he processed his own thoughts, 'if someone wanted to cause the most damage by giving people food poisoning, they would pick people who were already antibiotic resistant? And they'd mostly be resistant because they'd been taking a lot of antibiotics?'

'Yeah,' she said. 'That's not how a scientist would put it – remember, it's the bugs that are antibiotic resistant, not the people. But same thing in the end.' She paused. 'Jesus ... Sorry. To answer your question, I guess you'd have to make sure that a huge amount of the population had taken lots of antibiotics.'

'How often?'

'Oh, fairly regularly, I guess, and probably over a couple of years. Look, John,' she said, glancing at her watch, 'I've enjoyed the chat, but we've a big backlog of samples in there.'

'Oh yeah, sorry. But one more question,' he said, wondering if he sounded like Columbo. 'If you wanted to get lots of people to take cephalosporin, and then e-coli ...'

'Put it in the food chain,' she said, pulling on her lab coat and hat.

'But not in burgers because of the cooking?'

She shook her head.

'So, something added after, like ... a sauce or something.'

'That's quite a conspiracy theory, detective,' she said, winking as she disappeared back into the lab. 'Call me if you need any more.'

*

Mike Cabrini was in the reception area, leafing through a magazine. He stood up when Wyse emerged.

'Hey, John, whaddaya make of that?' he said, showing Wyse the cover of *American Pharmaceutical*. Wyse read aloud from the cover story headline: *Arthritis drugs and Viagra now dominate marketplace.*

Wyse looked quizzically at Cabrini.

'Well,' said Cabrini, 'don't you think it's a bit funny?'

'How so?'

'These drug companies,' said Cabrini, keeping a straight face, 'they spend half their time trying to get the stiffness outta people . . . and the other half trying to get the stiffness into people!'

Wyse looked at his pal and gave up trying to keep a straight face.

'C'mon,' he grinned, throwing the magazine back on the table. 'We've got work to do.'

50

1.10 P.M.

The police department pilot used the roof of the New York Police Museum as his horizontal reference as he settled the helicopter onto the helipad on Pier 6. A police escort whisked Dr Kim Scholler, Professor Samuel Ghent and Dr Charles Steelman back to the Center for Disease Control and Prevention. The National Response Plan, the country's all hazards approach to managing domestic incidents, had been activated. Washington would now coordinate the response on all fronts, to include Homeland Security, emergency management, law enforcement, emergency medical services and public health. The Manhattan team had been asked to return to the Center for Disease Control and Prevention and to keep Washington updated on casualties. They were to return to the Pentagon that evening, to attend the next meeting. Kim Scholler's face went a deathly white as she scanned through the printouts from hospitals in New York and adjoining states, which were laid out on the conference room table.

'Gentlemen,' she said to the other doctors, 'we are now at over one hundred thousand dead. And the influx of new patients is rising.'

*

As Dr Scholler broke the latest devastating news, Detectives Wyse and Cabrini were returning south along the Hudson Parkway from the meeting with Maria Cabrini. Wyse was deep in thought and Cabrini knew better than to interrupt him. The police radio told them that streams of heavily laden cars were beginning to back up from the entrance to the Lincoln Tunnel toll. Wyse spotted that some of the drivers were wearing surgical facemasks. *Looks like we may have the beginning of an unofficial evacuation here.* They were suddenly flagged into the kerb by a motorbike cop.

'What's this about?' said Cabrini. The answer was clear as soon as a convoy of over one hundred army trucks crossed the George Washington Bridge in front of them, coming from New Jersey into Manhattan. Once across, the convoy turned south for Central Park.

The cop waved them on again but, just after Cabrini crossed the junction, Wyse shouted, 'Stop!' and slammed his hand on the dashboard.

'Sorry, Mike,' he said to the startled Cabrini. 'Quick, turn around and go back to your sister.'

Maria Cabrini was concentrating hard, peering down the lens of a microscope, when she was distracted by a rapid knocking on the glazed partition.

What the hell now? She sighed and went back out through the double doors, removing her facemask as she went.

'Look, guys, I'm kinda busy –'

'Sorry, Maria,' interrupted Wyse. 'Just one thing.'

'Okay.'

'You remember when we came in here first?'

'I'll never forget it.'

'Why did you say that you had got a batch of samples from Chinatown?'

'Cos that's where they're from, presumably?'

'But why? Surely you get the samples from the nearest hospitals? Mount Syracuse and Elm Park are right beside you. Chinatown's way down the island.'

'Well, they're all Chinese, the samples we got.'

'How do you know?'

'From the DNA fingerprinting. All the bacteria samples we got contain human DNA from Chinese people. So I guessed we got Chinatown.'

'Could they be Japanese?' asked Wyse.

The researcher frowned. 'I suppose they could,' she replied. 'They're definitely all Asian – I just assumed Chinatown. It's unusual.'

'Could you tell Japanese from Chinese DNA?'

'Not too sure. I could check up on that. It's easy to distinguish, say, Asian from Caucasian or African, but differentiating Japanese and Chinese might be tough. Not my area. It would be a break though from endlessly confirming e-coli in stool samples. Why do you say Japanese?'

'Just a hunch. What are you working on at the moment?'

'Like I said earlier, if this e-coli bacterium has learned how to fight off antibiotics, and we lose cephalosporin altogether, we're in big trouble. We may be already. I'm starting to think about options. Above my pay grade, though.'

'So, is there no way to make antibiotics work again?'

'It's trial and error really. A good example is penicillin. When penicillin became available after the war, it was seen as the "miracle drug" – the answer to all our problems. But after years of overuse of penicillin, some staph and strep bacteria appeared that could resist penicillin. But scientists discovered that by adding clavulanic acid to penicillin, it became effective again against the bacteria. So, these days, one of the most popular antibiotics prescribed is called Augmentin – which is simply penicillin plus clavulanic acid, which allows it to outflank the bugs.'

'Gotcha. And do you have something that could make cephalosporin work again?'

'I may do,' Maria said cautiously. 'I've been experimenting with a prototype over the last few months and my tests are showing a new effectiveness for cephalosporin, when I add a particular combination of acids. But it needs months more testing.'

'If your hunch is right, we don't have months. Can it work immediately?'

'Perhaps, but it's a gamble.'

'Can it be mass produced?'

'Yeah, simple enough,' she said. 'I've got the formula – any lab can do it.'

'I think you should be dusting it down, Maria,' said Wyse, frowning as he shook her hand and turned to leave. He looked back at her.

'Thanks, Maria. Can you please keep your cell phone on after hours?'

*

2.05 P.M.

He's rigid with shock, thought Dr Conrad Jones.

Dr Peter Phillips was staring blankly at the bedside curtains around his wife's bed. Conrad Jones had pronounced Sandra Phillips dead five minutes earlier. One hour before that, in a ward three floors lower down at the Patrick J. Brock Memorial Hospital, Conrad Jones had watched as Peter Phillips lay on his son's bed, hugging Jonathan's small, dead body and stroking his sweat-matted curls. The little boy's hand was still clutching a black Superhero toy dragon.

'I'll leave you here for a few minutes, Peter,' he said, standing up. Peter Phillips didn't even notice him leave. Dr Conrad Jones, too, was reeling from shock and exhaustion. He had been working around the clock. He stepped out into the ward, closing the curtains behind him. The ward looked like something from a battlefield. The hospital had reluctantly taken the decision to double up the number of beds in each ward, accepting that this increased the risk of cross infection. The ward now contained sixteen beds, packed together. Three other patients had been shoved into the ward on trolleys. All patients were on IV cephalosporin and IV fluids. And all appeared to be dying. Struggling to get between two trolleys and a bed were two maintenance crew, pushing a curtain on wheels.

Jesus, what's the point in banning visitors from the hospital to reduce the risk of infection and still let maintenance guys in to fix curtains?

Annoyed, he strode to the nurses' station at the end of the ward, picked up the phone and paged Irene Sefton, the hospital administrator. She came on the line after about twenty seconds.

'What's up? Any good news?' she said wearily.

'No, but I'm wondering why we have a maintenance crew in here fixing curtains when we hardly have room to breathe?'

'We don't have a maintenance contract for the curtains. Old Joe does that.' Old Joe was the legendary seventy-four-year-old janitor, the only person still working in the hospital who had been there from its opening day in 1969.

'Old Joe does it? Then why are there two people banging curtains around my ward?'

She responded irritably. 'I have no idea, but it doesn't seem like the biggest problem in the world right now.'

Conrad Jones turned around to face back down the ward. The maintenance crew had vanished.

*

As they drove their white van out of the hospital's service yard, one of the curtain swishers turned to the other. 'So you're okay for another run this evening?'

'Yeah. Turns out I'm free tonight. We can go back to some of the same ones we did today. They're in such a state they're never gonna notice us.'

'Yeah, you're right. But you know what, there's a lot more going on here than we know about. All these people dying. Tonight's run, I'm gonna bring my gun. Just in case.'

51

ST VINCENT'S UNIVERSITY HOSPITAL – 2.22 P.M.

In her busy laboratory, Maria Cabrini was analysing organisms identified in the first batch of stool samples. They had known for a while that they were dealing with an e-coli O157:h7 and now she was looking at it more closely. She popped another two Tylenol and fought her tiredness. *No room for mistakes.*

A few days earlier, she had started growing bugs from the stool samples on culture plates, which take a day or two to develop. Then she had begun identifying the infections using a Maldi-Tof mass spectrometer. She had also been loading blood samples from patients into a Bacti-Alert machine, which would help to identify infections. At the bottom of each tube was a nutrient 'culture media' to accelerate the growth of any organisms in the samples. Maria Cabrini had inserted fifty glass tubes into fifty slots in the machine.

The numbers of bugs must be low, she'd thought, as the days had passed and the Bacti-Alert machine hummed away peacefully, without alerting her to any developing organisms. It was after she returned from her lunch break that day, that she got her first surprise. All fifty orange lights were flashing their rhythmic alert.

Fifty out of fifty! She tapped her colleague on the shoulder.

'Hey, Chris, take a look at this!'

Chris Davison swivelled around on his chair and paused to take it in. 'Wahey! We could save a few dollars on a Christmas tree with that!'

Since then, Maria had been carefully analysing the cultures. She shook her head and frowned at the fifty printouts on her desk.

'E-coli O157:h7, resistant to cephalosporin.'

'E-coli O157:h7, resistant to cephalosporin.'

'E-coli O157:h7, resistant to cephalosporin ...'

Stated all fifty.

She put her hands over her face. Full-on antibiotic resistance, on a large scale. *Jesus, this is gonna be bad. Better double check those tests. And I'd better check and see if there are any other antibiotics this damn bug is resistant to.*

*

It was 2.30 p.m. and Wyse and Cabrini had resumed their drive back to the station from the visit to Maria. They had just turned left into 155th Street when John Wyse, who had been deep in thought, suddenly shouted again.

'Here, stop!'

'Jeez, John, what's with all the shouting?' said Cabrini, putting his hand over his right ear. 'Can't you give me a little more notice?'

'Quick, over there, pull up.'

Cabrini manoeuvred into a space outside the BurgerFantastic at 232, 155th Street. He had barely killed the engine when John jumped out and disappeared into the restaurant.

'Jeez, don't mind if I do,' said Cabrini, chucking the 'Police on Duty' badge into the windscreen and hurrying after his buddy. Wyse was at the end of a line of about ten people waiting to be served.

'Christ, John, I'm starving too, but can't we calm down a little?'

'Sorry, Mike, just a bit distracted. I'm buying.'

'Won't argue with that, bud, I'm going for a cigarette,' said Cabrini, heading back outside. Wyse reached the top of the line. 'Two BurgerFantastics, two large fries, two coffees to go, please.'

'Sure thing, sir,' said the young server. 'That'll be six dollars please.'

Six dollars? thought Wyse. How the hell? Then he remembered that the burgers were just ninety-nine cents each. He put the money on the counter and watched as the restaurant worker took two freshly cooked burgers off the grill and placed them on two bread buns. Then she added some lettuce, gherkin, onion and tomato. Lastly, she picked up a large white plastic container and squirted a creamy sauce on top of the salad, before topping off with another bread bun. She boxed the burgers, added them to John Wyse's cardboard carryout tray and slid them across the counter.

'Have a nice day.'

'Thanks. You too.'

Wyse left the restaurant. Cabrini was flicking his cigarette butt into the gutter and was pleased to see him returning with the food.

'Thanks, John, good choice.'

Wyse put the tray on the hood of the car and handed a coffee and a packet of fries to Cabrini.

'Thanks, bud.'

Wyse put a coffee and a bag of fries for himself on the hood. Cabrini put his hand out to take a burger but Wyse spun around without giving it to him. 'Come on, Mike, gotta go.'

Cabrini was standing, open-mouthed, with a fry in mid-air, halfway to his mouth.

'Aw, John, for fuck's sake, what's going on?'

'Quick, Mike. Can you drop me back to the station, and then take these burgers to Maria?'

'Sure, but they're gonna go cold.'

'Not to eat. Ask her to check the sauce for e-coli. Urgent. I'm thinking these BurgerFantastics might be the cause of all this.'

Cabrini gaped at him. 'Sure, no problem.'

'And, for God's sake, don't eat them.'

*

2.52 P.M.

Cabrini had driven just half a block east on 155th when he had to stop at a red light at the junction with Broadway. It was a pleasantly bright Manhattan afternoon. Wyse marvelled at how the streetscape could look so relatively normal, in the midst of the disaster enveloping the city. The famous New York fighting spirit was on display. Just as the city had refused to yield after 9/11, it would be 'business as usual' for most New Yorkers, no matter what. But the traffic seemed to be getting lighter, as some businesses on the island began to shut down and office workers stayed at home. Two teenage kids in Giants T-shirts and caps came walking past, carrying large red and yellow BurgerFantastic bags. Wyse lowered his window and, flashing his badge, called the kids over.

'Hey guys, Police. I strongly advise you not to eat those burgers.'

The lights turned green and Cabrini hit the gas, shaking his head. The two dumbfounded teenagers were left staring.

'What the hell? Thought this was supposed to be a free country?' said one.

*

3 P.M.

Cabrini pulled in tight against the kerb outside the police station on Elizabeth Street. The rest of the drive back from the University Hospital had been uneventful – Wyse deep in thought and Cabrini beginning to worry about his colleague's stability. As soon as the car stopped, Wyse jumped out and ran up the steps to the front door of the building.

'Christ, here we go again!' said Cabrini watching him. He found a couple of fries, which had dropped down beside the gearshift, and crunched them, enjoying the salty taste. Could do with a beer now, he thought as he pulled out and headed back to his sister. The uneaten BurgerFantastics were on a cardboard tray on the seat beside him.

Back at his desk, Wyse nudged his mouse and his screen flickered into life. *Yamoura Pharmaceuticals,* he entered. *Search.*

'World leader in pharmaceutical manufacturing, multinational, Tokyo based, 55,000 employees, share price rises, Tsan Yohoto, charismatic leader of . . .'

Blah blah.

He went back and entered *Tsan Yohoto.* He hit *enter.*

'Tsan Yohoto, charismatic leader of Yamoura Pharmaceuticals, nominated for a Nobel Prize for humanitarian aid . . . free cephalosporin . . . Darfur . . .'

Wyse clicked on *Biography.*

'Tsan Yohoto, born 1940, Hiroshima, Japan, Chief Executive of . . .'

John Wyse sat back in his chair and whistled a long low note.

Hiroshima, 1940. So, he'd have been five.

Wyse thought for a moment, then picked up his phone and punched in 1-1-8-0 for directory enquiries. 'Hi, you got a number please for BurgerFantastic, like a head office or a depot or something?'

A delay. 'Sir, I got two, maybe three hundred different addresses, all classified as fast food restaurants. Nothing else.'

'Thanks,' said Wyse, hanging up.

He thought for a moment and then called out into the busy open plan office. 'Hey, what was BurgerFantastic called, like a year or two ago?' There was no response from the roomful of busy detectives.

'Bad time to start a quiz, John,' said Sergeant Jim Connolly, as he walked past.

'No, wait, I remember,' said Hanson, looking over a partition.

'*Quick 'n' Tasty*, that was it. Always thought the food tasted better then. And why the hell did they change the name?'

John Wyse gave him a thumbs-up and redialled directory enquiries. This time he got an answer.

'Quick 'n' Tasty, Head Office and Production Facility, Basin Street, Airport Business Park, Newark.'

John scribbled the address on his pad, then got back on his computer and googled BurgerFantastic. He opened the top story, which was an article from *The New York Times*.

> BurgerFantastic, the New York restaurant chain, has eclipsed McDonald's, Burger King, Pizza Hut and all the other fast food outlets in the Greater New York Metropolitan area, with the mother of all marketing campaigns. Over the past eighteen months, BurgerFantastic has maintained an unprecedented campaign of promotional offers and TV and radio advertising, which have sent sales into the stratosphere. BurgerFantastic founders and main shareholders are husband and wife team Takar and Tasha el Sayden. The couple arrived in New York from Tripoli, Libya in 1992.

Libya, thought John Wyse. *Isn't that where the Pan-Am bombers came from?* He leaned back on his chair, closed his eyes and concentrated for several minutes. He was oblivious to the hum of conversation and ringing phones around him. He sifted carefully through the mountain of new information in his brain. *Jesus, were they really trying to flood New York with antibiotics?* He challenged his intuition, again and again, until he could think of no new angles. This medical stuff wasn't his area. He could make a complete fool of himself and waste valuable time. Tens of thousands of lives could depend on what he did next. Would he act, based on a hunch, or play it safe and keep his head down? He thought about Cindy, and all the other people who were dead or dying. Then he remembered what Tsan Yohoto had said to Anna. 'I'm glad you're a vegetarian.' *Now it made sense!* He thought back all those months ago, to the conversation in the car with Paul Carter, the police profiler. *What's the right thing to do?* He let his chair fall forward and he opened his eyes, his mind made up. *Okay, John, time to show some leadership*. He got up and strode towards the door.

'Come on, Mike,' he said, spinning Cabrini around, just as the weary detective was about to come in the door. 'We're going out again.'

'Where now?' said Cabrini, turning and jogging after him.

'BurgerFantastic,' called Wyse back down the corridor.

'I thought you didn't like them?' shouted Cabrini.

'I'll tell you all about it in the car.'

52

3.32 P.M.

With the siren screaming, Wyse and Cabrini were making rapid progress across the Upper West Side.

'Head for Newark, Mike,' said Wyse as he entered the BurgerFantastic depot address into the GPS unit on the dash.

'Okay, buddy, but isn't it about time you started telling me what the hell you're doin'?'

'Yeah, sure. Here goes . . .'

Wyse's theory took them as far as Newark Bay.

'So, you ain't got no proof?' Cabrini was looking bamboozled. 'But you're thinking this whole thing could be a terrorist attack?'

'That's it, Mike. If I can get any proof, I'm gonna have to alert Homeland Security – the bio-terrorism guys.'

'Jeez – not so sure it all stacks, John. But Maria said she'll check the sauce on that burger for e-coli, pronto.'

Cabrini killed the siren about half a mile before they reached the industrial estate. A spattering of rain freckled the windshield and Cabrini flicked the wiper stalk. A large sign at the entrance to the estate told them that Basin Street was the second left. Cabrini pulled into the BurgerFantastic car lot, slowly. It was reasonably full but they got a visitor's space near the door.

'Okay,' said Wyse. 'I'm not expecting trouble, but be ready.'

They walked into the reception area and Wyse flashed his badge to the receptionist.

'Hi there, do you mind if we have a look around?'

'Not at all . . . is there something wrong?'

'Nah, just routine, can we go into the food production part?'

'Sure, no problem . . . it's that door down there,' she said, pointing. 'I'll get one of the production managers to show you round.'

Three minutes later, Cabrini exploded with laughter as he watched Tammy Ward, the production manager, fit a white hairnet onto Wyse. A moment later it was Wyse's turn to smile as Cabrini got his white coat and hairnet.

'All right, John, that's enough. Deal is, no one hears 'bout this in the station.'

'Okay by me, pal,' said Wyse, slapping his buddy's palm.

'Just mind you don't slip on that floor, detectives,' cautioned the production manager, pointing at the white tiles. Just a few steps into the depot, the view was dominated by two gleaming steel vats, rising almost as high as the factory roof.

'What are those, Tammy?' asked Wyse.

'They're the sauce vats, detective, for the burgers.' Walking closer, Wyse saw that there were steps around each tank, leading to the top.

'You wanna go up?' asked Tammy Ward, following Wyse's gaze.

'Nah, it's okay.'

Wyse's eyes followed the steps back close to the ground, where four heavy steel pylons supported each vat. Close to the bottom step, Wyse noticed a small brass plate. He leaned closer to read it.

Manufactured in Sweden by Alfa Laval.

Wyse straightened up slowly and closed his eyes.

'You all right, bud?' asked Cabrini.

'Mike.' There was a pause. 'You remember that murder; that

old guy? 'Bout two years back – in that old factory. The body was beside a steel vat, like this, only smaller.'

'Oh, yeah, sure, South Street. The factory used to be for Quick 'n' Tasty.'

'That's it. Who was that guy?'

'Christ, can't remember his name. We never got the perp. Think the old guy was foreign, though. Where was it he was from? Libya. Yeah, that was it. Libya, for sure.'

John Wyse stared blankly at the top of the vats again.

'John – you seein' stars or something?'

'No, but I'm startin' to see a whole lot more dots that need joining up. I think that murder may have been a whole lot more than a burglary gone wrong.'

Wyse put his hand inside his jacket and switched the safety catch on his gun to 'off'.

'Okay, Mike, eyes wide open.' Wyse waved over to the production manager who was standing further down the factory. 'Tammy, hey Tammy,' he called.

'Everything okay, detectives?' she asked, walking over.

'Sure, but we'd like to see Takar el Sayden.'

'Oh, I'm afraid not, guys. Takar is on vacation.'

'When did he go?'

'He was here in the production facility at about 5 a.m., I believe. He's often here during the night. As far as I know, he left and picked up his family and they caught a real early flight.'

'D'you know where they've gone?'

'Sure,' replied Tammy, with a smile. 'Back to the old country. Tripoli.'

★

4.05 P.M.

'Police and troops have quelled an outbreak of violence and looting in Harlem,' said the news announcer. *'Twenty-two people have been*

injured, three of them seriously. This is Chris Danson for XM FM, on another dark day for New York.'

★

Wyse frowned and turned down the volume on the radio as they drove back into Manhattan. Black clouds were beginning to darken the skyline.

'National Guard fully deployed, bud,' said Cabrini, pointing at six soldiers in full riot gear at the junction of Broadway and 145th. As they made their way uptown, it became clear that troops were being positioned at every major intersection. Both detectives could sense an atmosphere of high tension descending on the city.

Wyse called Dr Kim Scholler and got put through after a short delay.

'Doctor, it's Detective John Wyse. What's the latest?'

'It's bad, detective, real bad. Completely out of control. Death toll's going to be close to a million at the rate we're going.'

'Jesus.'

'And we still haven't found the source. Only positive news is that the numbers of new infections presenting are down a little to about a quarter of a million every twenty-four hours. The bad cases are being bussed out to other states, now that the system's completely overrun. There's no point in pretending otherwise.'

Wyse was doing the math. 'So, every hour that goes by, over ten thousand more people get sick?'

'That's about it, detective.'

Wyse hesitated, and then gambled. 'Doctor, are you sure you've checked out BurgerFantastic?'

'Oh, sure, John, we've had teams in all the restaurant chains, in their kitchens, in their suppliers. Complete blank. There's well over two thousand fast food joints in the city, so they're an obvious suspect. We'll have checked all their meat products – beef, chicken, pork, etc. For sure, they've all cleaned everything thoroughly by now, but we're still getting infections, so it doesn't look like it's a restaurant chain.'

'Doctor, can you go back and check the vats that they make the sauce in for the burgers?'

'The sauce? At BurgerFantastic? Why?'

'A hunch. Please trust me. The central depot in Newark. The Airport Business Park.'

'Well, okay, I'll send a team back in there.'

'Do you need police backup?'

'No, we're fully authorised to enter. Unless you think we do?'

'Shouldn't be any problems, but I'll send a couple of cops out to help.'

'Okay,' said Dr Scholler, a little hesitantly.

'And, doctor. Please call me as soon as you hear anything.'

*

5.05 P.M.

'John? This is Kim Scholler.' Wyse was at his desk at the station, and had been stretched back in his chair, deep in thought, when the call came.

'Kim, any news?'

'Just got a call from our team. They're on the way back in from the BurgerFantastic depot.'

'Yeah.'

'Technician said it's so clean you could do an autopsy in there. We checked the vats they blend the sauce in. Everything's been thoroughly cleaned today, of course – just like all the other places. Our guys have taken samples and swabs and we won't be sure until they run the tests. But they can usually smell trouble a mile off and they think it's clean.'

There was no response.

'John, you there?'

'Yeah, sorry, just thinking.'

'I'll let you know if anything develops.'

One minute later, the detective rapidly redialled Dr Scholler's cell phone.

'Doctor, it's John Wyse again.'

'Is everything okay, detective?' she said, surprised at the excitement in his voice.

'Send them back.'

'What?'

'Send them back.'

'Where?'

'To BurgerFantastic. Send your team back to BurgerFantastic. But tell them to look for cephalosporin, not e-coli.'

'What?' she said incredulously.

'Look for cephalosporin – in the vats they make the sauce in, but also in the boss's office, the whole place –'

'Detective,' she interrupted. 'This is very unusual. Our teams are under extreme –'

'Dr Scholler – please, please trust me, just one more time?' He sounded desperate.

'Well, okay, detective, one more time.'

★

5.45 P.M.

'John? This is Kim Scholler. The place is covered with it.'

'With what?'

'With cephalosporin powder.'

'Bingo.' Wyse thumped his desk.

'At least, we believe it's cephalosporin – we'll tell you for certain when we get it to the main spectrophotometer. There's traces on the boss's desk, in the carpet, on the office stairs, the steps up to the vats – the place is alive with it.'

'Kim, thanks. Can you get someone to drop a sample of it to a technician called Maria Cabrini at St Vincent's?'

'The University Hospital?'

'That's the one. Thanks, and call me when you're certain.'

'Detective, what's going on?'

'Doctor, I'm no scientist, but I think we may have to take one hell of a gamble. When's your next team meeting?'

'We're leaving for Washington in twenty minutes. The meeting's been moved to the White House.'

'Okay. Don't go without me. I'll call.' Wyse hung up. Twenty minutes. That's about another three thousand infections. Gotta move fast.

*

He got straight through to Maria Cabrini.

'Maria, John Wyse. There's some powder on its way in to you from the Center for Disease Control and Prevention. Make certain for yourself that it's cephalosporin. Real fast.'

'Sure thing. John, I'm starting to get some really weird results from analysing this bacterium. This e-coli infection is resistant to cephalosporin, and it looks like it's multi-resistant too. It's also resistant to the carbapenem antibiotics – and I'm talking *super-resistant*. It almost looks manufactured. Nothing the hospitals throw at this is gonna work. I'm gonna run the tests again and –'

Wyse interrupted. 'No time for that. I want you to put all your formulae and stuff for this prototype in your bag and be outside the hospital reception at 6.30 p.m.'

She agreed hesitantly. 'And there's an e-coli infection in the sauce on those burgers that you sent over with Mike.'

'That's it.'

'John, what's –'

'No time for questions. Front door, 6.30 p.m.'

*

Wyse grabbed a handful of magazines and newspapers from desks around the office. He shoved them into a large brown folder as he ran out through the ground floor of the police station and jumped into the unmarked police car. With one hand on the steering wheel, he hit the speed dial for Cabrini's cell phone.

'Mike?'

'Yo.'

'I've taken the car. I need you to trace any vehicle registered to a Takar or Tasha el Sayden. S-A-Y-D-E-N. Once you know what it is, I think you'll find it at Newark Airport – whatever terminal goes direct to, or connects to, Tripoli.'

'And?'

'Bring a police forensic team with you. Get them to check out the vehicle for cephalosporin powder. And anything that has an e-coli bacteria in it. Start in the trunk. Call me if you get a result.'

'Okay, where are you?'

'I'm going to the White House.'

'What?!'

'With your sister.'

'What?!'

'Don't worry – call me as soon as you can with any results. Don't forget now: cephalosporin. And e-coli.'

*

Almost as soon as John Wyse ended his conversation with Cabrini, his cell phone beeped twice. He glanced down.

> Hi baby. Hope you're okay. Awards dinner cancelled. Hanging with office guys. All v sad. Luv you. Laters. Anna xxx

With one thumb he texted a reply:

> Luv you too babe. See you tonight xxx

53

6.20 P.M.

The blades on the giant black and white helicopter were already turning as John Wyse screeched up to the helipad on Pier 6. Ducking his head low, he climbed into a rear seat. Dr Kim Scholler, Professor Ghent and Dr Charles Steelman were already on board. The pilot was craning his neck to check that he had fastened his seatbelt. Wyse gave him a thumbs-up, the pilot pulled in the power and the powerful machine lifted smoothly skywards.

Wyse pulled on his headset and began talking to the pilot whilst gesticulating left, towards the north. The pilot got on the radio and was cleared for an alteration to his flight plan. The first Maria Cabrini knew of the change in plan was when the helicopter dropped into a thunderous hover over the lawn in front of St Vincent's. Three minutes later, she was strapped in beside Wyse and the helicopter was over the Empire State Building, on the forty-minute flight to Washington.

★

Six miles northwest, the first of an expected capacity crowd of eighty-three thousand people were arriving at Meadowlands, by car and bus, for the game at the MetLife Stadium. The Giants versus the Chicago Bears had an 8 p.m. kick-off. Ricky Morgan was the only player from the Giants who was in hospital. The NFL, in conjunction with the Public Health Authorities and the Mayor's office, had decided that the game should go ahead, despite the disaster enveloping the city. 'Let's try and keep morale up,' the Mayor had said.

About three miles out, the Patel family were in high spirits as they headed towards the game in their Chrysler Voyager. Asif and Karen, with Lauren and Ryan in the back, were all wearing Giants' shirts and caps. Lauren was wearing a novelty red, white and blue Giants' wig. *She even manages to look fabulous in that!* thought her dad proudly. Lauren had gotten over her cold in time to wow the audiences as Princess Elsa in *Frozen*. Asif and Karen were counting their blessings that their kids had avoided the sickness which had hit about half of their classmates. With the city in chaos, they still hadn't heard that Sandra, Suzy and Jonathan Phillips had died the previous day.

'Look, Dad, there it is!' squealed an excited Ryan, pointing at the distinctive shape of the oval, steel-grey stadium on the skyline ahead.

The staff were opening up at the fifteen BurgerFantastic franchise outlets at the stadium, and getting ready for a busy night ahead. Asif and Karen had agreed to relax the ban for one night only.

⋆

Mukhtar el Maswar, the mullah of the village of el Kohl, could hardly speak for excitement. He had received word that some very important visitors had returned to the caves near his village. As requested, he had brought three of his men on horseback, laden with provisions. He had gladly accepted the invitation to stay for the magnificent meal. Now, here he was, sitting on a rug under a canvas awning, with a group of the top al-Qaeda leaders, eating date and nut sweets and drinking freshly brewed coffee. The mood was festive. Mussan, their communications expert, had set up a battery-powered laptop with a satellite link, connected to a sixteen-inch screen and there were loud cheers and laughs as the men watched the devastation unfolding in New York on US TV stations.

'What a magnificent plan,' said el Maswar, shaking his head admiringly.

'Yes – *The Manhattan Project* is what our Japanese friends call it,' replied a beaming Kiyo Arai.

He raised his small coffee cup in triumph. 'To Tsan Yohoto and our friends in Tokyo.'

54

7.15 P.M.

The President of the United States of America dropped his chin onto his chest and clasped his head in his hands. He was sitting at his desk in the Oval Office. On the right-hand side of his desk was the vice president. Seated in front of them, in a rough U shape, were the heads of the dozen or so government departments which manage America's National Response Plan. The atmosphere was tense, depressed, and angry.

'A hundred thousand people dead so far,' said the President quietly, shaking his head. 'And the very best brains in this government are telling me that, one – this is going to get worse. It may reach a million. Two – that you still don't know what's causing it, and three – that our hospitals can't cure it?'

Nobody in the room answered and nobody dared to catch the President's eye. There was a gentle knock on the door and an aide ushered in Dr Kim Scholler, Professor Ghent, Dr Charles Steelman, Detective John Wyse and Maria Cabrini.

'Excuse me, Mr President. This is the medical team from the Center for Disease Control and Prevention in New York.'

'You may have to change the name of your organisation, doctors,' said the President, grimly.

'And this is Detective John Wyse, New York Police Department and Ms Cabrini is a technician at St Vincent's University Hospital in Manhattan.'

The President waved a tired hand at a few empty chairs on his left. There weren't enough for everyone, so Wyse and Maria Cabrini stayed standing.

The vice president spoke. 'Detective Wyse, I believe you have something to contribute?'

'All suggestions welcome,' said the President. 'I haven't heard any good news in a long time.'

John Wyse's knees were shaking as he took a couple of steps forward on the deep, gold carpet and faced the President.

'Mr President, I'm a detective, not a doctor. I was assigned to assist the CDCP in Manhattan.' He paused.

'Go on,' said the President.

Wyse cleared his throat. 'Mr President, I believe we have been looking at this whole thing the wrong way around.'

'How do you mean?'

'Everyone has assumed that this is a, let's say, routine public health issue, that's got out of control. And we've been assessing it from that viewpoint only.' Wyse swallowed and continued. 'Mr President, I believe this whole disaster is a deliberate terrorist attack.'

The President raised his eyebrows in surprise. There was a shuffling of feet around the room and a couple of nervous coughs.

'Well, well, Detective Wyse, and what makes you think that?'

'Mr President, it's kinda hard to explain but please bear with me. I'm going to go through it backwards.' Wyse had planned his approach during the helicopter journey.

'Go ahead.'

'Okay. Now, one of the reasons we haven't found the source is because of the sheer numbers of people infected. Our systems couldn't cope and there were too many options to investigate. The terrorists counted on that. We seem to have had well over a million people infected in the last week or so. That's huge. I think that looks deliberate. Despite the normal routine checks of our water supply, air and food supply, nothing turns up. The food manufacturers, the suppliers, the restaurant chains, etc., clean their equipment and because we can't pin it down, we get stuck.'

The President nodded.

'Yet,' Wyse continued, 'every day sees new patients turning up with infections. But the incubation period for the bug must be about the same for everyone, so that means that new infections continue to happen every single day. That also looks deliberate to me.'

'Okay, detective, so who's doing it?'

Wyse scrabbled in the brown folder under his arm and pulled out a copy of that day's *New York Times*. He opened it on page three and displayed a bright red and yellow advert for BurgerFantastic.

'Home cooking without the hassle,' read the President. 'Ninety-nine cents for every BurgerFantastic. Ninety-nine cents? That's *giving* them away.'

'Mr President, this company has undertaken the heaviest marketing campaign ever seen in New York, over the last eighteen months. They've spent tens of millions. They sell more burgers than anyone. Heading for three million a week. That easily gives us two million-plus infections.'

There was a pause.

'But why,' asked the vice president a little impatiently, 'if they can infect over two million people in a week, would they bother doing all this marketing for eighteen months?'

'Firstly,' replied Wyse, 'they wanted to build up the customer base to the highest possible number. Secondly,' he hesitated for a moment, 'and this is where it gets a bit complicated . . .'

'Go on.'

'I believe they were putting an antibiotic in the burgers for those eighteen months.'

'An antibiotic?' said the President incredulously. 'Look, detective, this is all sounding a bit off the wall –'

'Mr President, please hear me out?'

The President saw the desperation in Wyse's face. 'Okay, but keep it quick.'

'Mr President, the whole reason that this has gotten so bad is that the hospitals can't treat the patients. The antibiotic doesn't work any more. That's because, for over eighteen months, the terrorists were putting the antibiotic into the burgers. Then, they chose their moment and switched the antibiotic for an e-coli bacterium.'

He scrabbled again in the folder and pulled out a handful of newspapers and magazines.

'Look, Mr President,' he said, flicking through a selection of adverts for SuperVerve. 'There has been another massive marketing campaign for this drug – SuperVerve. In New York only. Half the city's taking it. The campaign coincides with the BurgerFantastic campaign. And they're by the same advertising agency.'

The President read through one of the adverts. '*SuperVerve – putting the verve back into your life.* Hummm,' he said, putting the newspaper down. 'So, what *is* this SuperVerve?'

Wyse answered quickly. 'Mr President, it's more of this cephalosporin antibiotic. It's exactly what the sick people need to cure their food poisoning. Problem is, the population's already been deliberately used to accelerate this antibiotic resistance. The people may have been conned into taking cephalosporin by all this advertising. New Yorkers have been buying the antibiotic in the drug stores and getting it, without knowing it, in the burgers from BurgerFantastic. So, we're sitting around waiting for the antibiotics to work and, Mr President,' Wyse was breathless now, 'I don't think they're going to.'

The President leaned forward on his chair. He looked enquiringly to his left at the group of medics. 'Doctors?'

Dr Kim Scholler nodded slowly. 'Medically, it's entirely plausible, sir.'

Professor Ghent added, 'Antibiotic resistance is a ticking time bomb – it looks like something may well have accelerated this.'

The President sat back in his chair and looked at the selection of faces around him.

'So, who's behind BurgerFantastic?' he asked.

Wyse replied, 'It's owned by a Takar el Sayden. His retired partner was murdered about two years ago. That may have been to keep him quiet.'

The FBI and CIA directors both started writing. Wyse noticed and added, 'He's gone. He flew out of New York with his family this morning. We found traces of cephalosporin powder all over his office. And in his car.'

'Where has he gone?' asked the CIA head.

'Tripoli. Libya.'

The President and vice president exchanged glances.

'And SuperVerve? Is there a connection?' prompted the vice president.

'Yes,' said Wyse. 'Yamoura Pharmaceuticals. They're a huge multinational drug company. Japanese. The boss is a guy called Tsan Yohoto, in Tokyo. Mr President, he was born in Hiroshima and he was five years old when we dropped the bomb. His brother and sister were killed. This could be him taking revenge.'

The CIA head turned to the President. 'Revenge is a dish best served cold. I believe that would fit the Japanese mentality. And where is this Mr Yohoto, at the moment?' he asked.

'Just gone on vacation too, apparently,' said Wyse. Cabrini had made a few calls for him.

'So, Detective Wyse, if your theory is correct, what do you think we should do?' asked the President.

'Sir, first thing is, I suspect that the e-coli infecting was being done by el Sayden at BurgerFantastic. He was putting it in the sauce blender before the sauce got sent out to the restaurants. So, only good news is, I think the infecting's stopped. The exception to that,' he said looking around him, 'is last night's batch, which is being consumed as we speak. I suggest you shut down BurgerFantastic straightaway and broadcast warning messages on TV, radio, social media.' People all around him were furiously taking notes. 'Starting, I suggest, by alerting big venues.'

'How do you mean?' asked the vice president.

'For example, the Giants play the Chicago Bears at Meadowlands in about thirty minutes from now. The Mayor's been saying the game should go ahead, in honour of the dead. There's probably over eighty thousand people there. There's fifteen BurgerFantastic concessions around the stadium. You could get thousands of new infections there in the next hour –'

'Do it!' The President jumped to his feet. 'Throw everything at it, police, army, shut down every damn outlet they have!' People began scurrying from the room. The President sat down again and took a long drink of water. 'So, Detective Wyse, if you're right, we've identified the source. But we still have the dilemma of how to deal with those who've been infected.'

'I believe I am right, sir. But there's more. This is where you really need the doctors, but can I introduce you to Maria Cabrini.'

The President nodded at Maria, whose knees trembled as she stood, slightly behind John Wyse.

'Ms Cabrini is a microbiologist at St Vincent's University Hospital. She may have the answer to the food poisoning.'

The President raised his eyebrows. 'Ms Cabrini?'

'Thank you, Mr President.' She took a tentative step forward. 'Yes. I have been researching antibiotic resistance for some time. I've been developing some prototypes to make antibiotics effective again against the bugs that have learned how to resist them. One of those is for cephalosporin. I was given stool samples from the hospitals. Like everyone else, I'm running cultures, but, I believe we're looking at a particularly virulent strain of multi-resistant e-coli. And super toxic. If Detective Wyse is right, and millions of New Yorkers have already been saturated with antibiotics, then, the antibiotics we're doling out in the hospitals are probably just making things worse.'

'Jesus,' said the President, looking around him in exasperation. 'When we get these bastards . . .'

'It's a big gamble, sir,' continued Maria Cabrini, 'but I think we have to instruct the hospitals to stop prescribing cephalosporin until we reconfigure the cephalosporin with this combination of acids.' She pointed at her briefcase, then continued. 'I've got the formulae, everything we need in here. We need to get it into mass production, quickly. If my test results follow through, the cephalosporin will become effective again and, in forty-eight hours or so, patients will begin to recover.'

Again, the President looked enquiringly in the direction of the doctors. Again, Scholler, Ghent and Steelman all looked at each other and together slowly nodded their agreement to the President.

'It's feasible,' said Professor Ghent. 'Only other option is to wait and hope.'

'Never liked that option,' said the President. He sat silently for thirty seconds, eyes closed as he rubbed his temples. Then he stood up again. 'Okay, doctors, go do it. We can't risk this getting any worse.' The medical experts all hurriedly left the room together, taking Maria Cabrini's briefcase with them. There was no time for handshakes or goodbyes.

The President sighed. 'Well, Ms Cabrini, Detective Wyse, let's hope you've cracked this. If so, this country owes you one hell of a debt of gratitude. Those sons of bitches. Imagine,' he said, turning to his vice president, 'poisoning us with our own medicine, our own cure.'

'Mr President,' Maria Cabrini interrupted nervously. 'There's one more problem. I discovered that there is a component of human DNA in the bacteria. It's from a person of Asian descent. It must have been deliberately added. If it's from this Tsan Yohoto, then . . .'

'Yes?'

'We may have another longer-term problem.'

Wyse interjected. 'This Tsan Yohoto, sir, he survived the atomic bomb at Hiroshima, so he must have been exposed to radiation.'

Maria continued. 'His immune system will have been compromised. He will be at a higher than normal risk of developing leukaemia.'

‘So?’ said the President, shrugging and looking puzzled, ‘can’t say I feel too sorry for him.’

‘Sir. He may have deliberately passed on that risk to every one of the New Yorkers who were infected by burgers from BurgerFantastic. We won’t know for years.’

The President was incredulous.

‘Aw, for chrissakes,’ he said, throwing his pen down on the desk. ‘Go catch these bastards,’ he snarled in the direction of the directors of the FBI and CIA.

55

The flight back to Manhattan, in rain and wind, seemed to take just five minutes, as John Wyse and Maria Cabrini excitedly recounted the events of the last few hours. The medical team had stayed behind in Washington to coordinate the new medical response. Wyse was dropped off at the helipad on Pier 6 and a few minutes later he was walking in the front door of the Fifth Precinct station. Maria accepted the pilot's offer to drop her back to the hospital. As she looked down on the spectacular, illuminated skyline of a Manhattan that had been devastated by sickness, she wondered if she would ever be able to joke about the day she made the commute by police helicopter.

Back in the Oval Office, the President of the United States was standing at the window, very still, and staring blankly across the gardens towards the Lincoln Memorial. The vice president was sitting on a chair, his elbow resting on the President's desk. Everyone else had left and the room was quiet. Eventually the President spoke, without turning away from the window.

'The Manhattan Project,' he said. There was a silence.

The vice president hesitated. 'I beg your pardon, sir?'

'The Manhattan Project,' repeated the President, quietly.

‘Yes, of course, sir. I remember. That was our codename for the secret project to develop the bomb we dropped on Hiroshima.’

The President turned around and looked grimly at his right-hand man. ‘And just look at Manhattan now. I suspect,’ he glanced down at the name he’d scribbled on his notepad, ‘that Mr Tsan Yohoto remembered that too.’

*

8 P.M.

The beauty of the MetLife Stadium is its easy access.

‘Come on, Dad, hurry up, we’ll be late! Come on, Mom.’ Ryan Patel, almost sick with excitement, had practically dragged his parents through the car lot and onto the first of two escalators leading to the back of their seating area. The family stepped off the escalator into the oval-shaped concourse which runs along the back of the stands. All around this area, fast food restaurants, Coca-Cola stalls and bars clamour brightly for business.

Standing to the left of the door into one of the washrooms, Police Officer Earl Finch was having a good time. A shift at the Giants games was always welcome. There was rarely any trouble, apart from the odd drunk or pickpocket, and, by standing on the first couple of steps into the seats, he got to see most of the game. For free.

Officer Finch frowned as he tried to interpret the message crackling through on his radio. He pressed ‘*transmit*’.

‘Say again please, over.’ He listened again as the message was repeated, more slowly. His frown turned incredulous. He looked to his left where a long line of fans were eagerly waiting for their ninety-nine cent BurgerFantastic. At the top of the line, a man in a blue Giants shirt was paying for his family’s meal. Leaving the counter was a very pretty young girl, wearing a novelty Giants wig. Her dainty hands were dwarfed by the supersized BurgerFantastic, which she was holding in a paper napkin. She started to raise the burger, to take a bite.

'Hey,' shouted Officer Finch, striding urgently towards her.

But the girl couldn't hear him over the noise.

'Hey, there!' The burger reached her lips and she began to open her mouth. Officer Finch turned his last few steps into a dive and the punch he threw split Lauren Patel's lip, as her BurgerFantastic flew into the face of the astonished BurgerFantastic manager.

*

9.07 P.M.

John Wyse sat down wearily at his desk, his head spinning. He was collecting his thoughts ready to brief Connolly when the burly sergeant suddenly appeared beside him.

'Yo, John, there's a rumour goin' around they've found the source of this damn food poisoning. You gonna tell me about it anytime soon?'

'Sure, sergeant. It's complicated.'

'Okay, but before you do, there's a call just come in from a Dr Conrad Jones at the Patrick J. Brock Memorial. Says they've got two people over there posing as maintenance crew. Thinks they're up to no good. You and Cabrini wanna take it?'

'Yeah, no problem.'

'Okay, the doc says he'll be waiting around the back entrance.'

'I got it,' said Wyse, standing up and automatically patting his left upper chest to confirm his gun was holstered. He speed dialled Cabrini, but Mike's phone was off. He ran down the stairs to the first floor and used the radio to try the radio in their car. There was no response. He jogged back up the stairs. 'Anyone seen Cabrini?'

'Can't raise him,' said Connolly, shaking his head. 'Haven't seen him since he took a late lunch. He's not answering his cell. Smith and Williams are AWOL too. If those fuckers have gone on the beer, just when we need everyone we've got –'

'Maybe they're sick?' Wyse interrupted, doubting himself, even as he said it. *Jesus, Mike, don't let me down now. Of all times.*

'Some chance,' grunted Connolly. 'Anyway, no time to lose. I'll sort those clowns later. Take Carroll.'

'Kevin, come on,' said Wyse, beckoning the young Irish detective.

★

9.09 P.M.

Conrad Jones had spotted them again, stepping into an elevator at the other end of the corridor, *pushing their damn curtain on wheels.* They went up, he observed, as the floor numbers lit up, in turn, over the elevator door. Even though they were wearing white coats, hats and facemasks, Conrad Jones was sure they were the same two he had seen twice before. Goddamn, we've enough to be doing right now, he thought, taking down all the cephalosporin lines in a hurry, without any more distractions. But he had a feeling there was something strange about these two. The policeman had told him that two detectives were on the way. Conrad had said he would meet them in the service yard at the back.

★

9.12 P.M.

Wyse drove. He killed the siren a block from the hospital and drove quietly into the service yard. Most of the yard was taken up with a dozen or more black hearses, in a line outside the mortuary. There were a few cars parked on the left, and a white Toyota van, with *Hospital Maintenance Services* displayed on the side.

'There he is,' said Kevin Carroll, pointing at Conrad Jones who was wearing a white coat and standing outside a door marked *Deliveries*.

Wyse pulled in and, a minute later, the doctor was taking them to the service elevator.

'Two of them,' he said. 'Third time I've seen them messing around with curtains in the wards. Except I checked and we don't have an outside maintenance contractor for the curtains.' He hit the button. 'They went to the top floor,' he said.

They stepped out into the lobby of the twenty-second floor and paused to look through the glass doors into the Elms Ward.

'There they are, look,' said Conrad Jones in a low voice, opening the door wide and stepping into the long, rectangular ward. They walked slowly between rows of tightly packed beds and trolleys on either side. The maintenance crew closed the curtains around the last bed in the row and started heading for the door at the far end.

'I think they've seen us,' said Carroll.

'Police, stop!' called out Wyse.

The two figures hurried out through the door at the far end, leaving their curtain on wheels behind them.

'Let's go,' said Wyse, breaking into a run. Four seconds later, he was pulling open the door. The two suspects were about twenty paces away, walking fast along a long narrow corridor. Wyse and Carroll began to jog after them.

'Stop. Police. Stop. Now!' shouted Wyse. The two figures ahead of them began to run and so did the two detectives. The two white coats disappeared around a corner and Wyse and Carroll drew their guns as Wyse flattened himself against the wall and peered around. The fugitives were halfway along another long corridor, sprinting now. Wyse and Carroll rushed after them.

'Stop. Armed Police!'

The escapees had reached a door at the end of the corridor. One of them grabbed the handle. It was locked. He spun around with a gun pointing at Wyse and Carroll, who dived for the floor and fired three shots each, in rapid succession. The two figures in white coats crumpled to the ground. The detectives dashed the last five yards and stood over the bodies. Carroll kicked the gun on the floor out of reach, which was unnecessary, given the large hole in the gunman's forehead. Wyse's target was lying face down and a bright red bloodstain was soaking through the back of the white coat, between the shoulder blades. The figure convulsed two or three times.

'Easy now,' said Wyse, pointing his gun at the fugitive's head, the face partly covered by a surgical mask which had slipped upwards. He slowly turned the body into the recovery position, on its right side. There was no resistance. 'Easy now.' He pulled down the facemask and his heart froze with shock. Staring up at him were the dead eyes of Anna Milani, his fiancée.

56

EARLIER THAT DAY, BUT EVENING IN TOKYO

'Tsan, my beautiful boy,' said Saina Yohoto. 'I am so excited to go flying with you to see the stars. What a wonderful idea. I am a very lucky old woman. But I am worried, you look so very tired.'

Tsan Yohoto smiled. It was amusing to have a woman in her nineties worry about your health. And to be referred to as a boy, when you are in your seventies. *Mothers will never change.* Before the flying trip, he had taken Saina to her favourite restaurant, Bunkyo, near the National Museum.

'Do not worry, my darling mother,' he replied. 'It has just been the strain of arranging my departure from Yamoura. And there has been a lot of work in connection with this.' He tapped his finger on the picture of himself on the cover of *Time* magazine, which lay on the table. He had been telling her all about the great progress they were making in Africa.

'My son, I am so proud of you. You and I have survived a lot together. But I think we can be proud of our efforts to bring healing and goodness into a dangerous world.'

'Yes, Mother, and I thank you again, with all my heart, for everything you have taught me and for giving me the confidence and strength to pursue my goals in life.'

'Thank you, Tsan, such beautiful words. I am sure that your father and Kendo and Lita are proud of the work we have done since they died.'

Tsan took the photograph of Kendo and Lita from his jacket pocket and gave it to his mother. He held her hand and they both felt tears in their eyes.

*

Thirty minutes later, mother and son were in Tsan's Lexus LX heading south of Tokyo on the Daiichi-Keihin freeway.

'Soon we will be closer to those stars, Mother,' Tsan said, pointing at the gathering twilight, and she smiled. He pressed the *play* button on his steering wheel and a waltz soothed through sixteen speakers. Strauss was his mother's favourite composer. Forty-five minutes took them to the northern outskirts of Yokohama. He was glad to note that it was a clear sky, as he took a left at a signpost for the Yokohama Flying Club. They were now driving due east, towards the sea. The security guard raised the barrier and saluted when he recognised Tsan Yohoto. The small private airfield was deserted. Tsan drove around the back of the hangars. *Yes, there she is. Good, they left the extra fuel.* He carefully helped his mother up the step into the plane and fastened her seat belt.

'Hold tight, Mother,' he joked, kissing her as he gently helped her put her headphones on. Then he used the seat belts to strap two of the four-gallon containers of aviation fuel into the back seats, placing the other two in the rear footwells. Tsan Yohoto climbed into the pilot's seat, turned the key in the Cessna's ignition one stop and checked that the tanks were full, as per his instructions. He started the engine and confirmed that they could hear each other through their headphones. After a two-minute warm up, he taxied out on to runway 07. *No need for radio calls. There is no one in the tower at this time of night and we're outside the zone of controlled airspace around Tokyo's Kokusai Kuko airport.* He opened the throttle wide and, ten seconds later, the wheels of the Skyhawk SP left the tarmac.

*

They crossed the coastline at an altitude of one thousand feet, heading due east. The Pacific Ocean lay ahead, flat and calm. His mother was transfixed by the beauty of the sparkling sky.

'You're right, Tsan, you really do feel much closer to the stars when you are flying.'

Once over the ocean, he turned right and took up a southwesterly heading. He allowed his height to climb as he crossed land again and they gasped at the splendour of Mount Fuji, soaring into the sky away to their right. He broke out over the ocean again near Osaka and then followed the coast, on his right-hand side, for another hour or so. Then his whole body began to tense.

The screen in front of him was now showing the town of Kure ahead, which was where he had lived with his mother after the bomb. Kure marks the edge of a headland and, after that landmark, Tsan Yohoto banked sharply right. Into Hiroshima Bay. His heart began to beat more quickly. He tried not to tense up on the controls. He checked his compass and turned slightly more to the right, to pick up an exact, north-northwesterly heading of two hundred and ninety degrees. His eyes filled with tears. He wanted to be on exactly the same heading as the Yankees in the *Enola Gay* as they had approached Hiroshima from Tinian Island.

'Mother, I have great and important news to tell you.'

'Are you okay, my son?' Saina had noticed the tears in her son's eyes.

'Yes, Mother. This is a very important day for us. I have finally managed to take our full revenge on the Americans.'

'What do you mean, Tsan?' Saina said, her voice faltering.

'I have been working on a great plan for many years now. All those deaths in New York – many, many thousands of them. That is my work.'

Saina's eyes widened. 'What?'

'Yes,' Tsan said proudly. 'I tricked them. I tricked them into taking too many antibiotics, then I waited until the antibiotic resistance developed and last of all I gave them an infection that they cannot cure. My work is a fitting tribute to father and Kendo and Lita, and now we can join them to celebrate.'

Saina, barely able to comprehend what she was hearing, said, 'Tsan, what are you saying? Are you mad? You cannot have killed all those people. It is murder!'

Tsan's face crumpled. 'Mother, surely you must feel proud of me? This is my dream fulfilled!'

'Tsan, this is no dream. It is crazy!' she shouted. 'Take me back. Stop this madness!'

Tsan, shocked, shook his head. 'No, Mother, it is too late.' *How could she not be delighted with my work?*

'Tsan. Stop. Stop. Please stop!' His mother was now beating his side with her hands, but it was futile, and she soon simply sat in paralysed horror.

The tears flowed down Tsan's face as a voice crackled over his headphones.

'This is Hiroshima Control. Unidentified aircraft on two nine zero degrees heading to Hiroshima, please declare your identity and your intentions.'

In the tower at Hiroshima's Kuko Airport, the controller had noticed the blip on his screen approaching Hiroshima's airspace from over the bay. He tried again.

'Hiroshima Control to unidentified aircraft over Hiroshima Bay. You are entering controlled airspace. Declare your identity and intentions.'

Tsan Yohoto did not reply and turned the volume on his radio down. He needed to concentrate. Suddenly, he cried aloud, 'Ah, there it is!' as the lights of Hiroshima appeared in the distance. He checked his heading again. Two hundred and ninety degrees. *So, this was how the murdering bastards saw my city, before they destroyed it and my life. Before they killed my father, my brother, my sister.*

He blinked away his tears and gasped again at the instantly recognisable view of the city. A navigator's dream, he thought, grimly. *The river, that is what they would have looked for.* North of Hiroshima, the giant River Ota splits in two, and then divides again and again through the city until it bursts into the harbour in seven parallel channels, visible in the air from miles away. Tsan could imagine the *Enola Gay* navigator doing a last check of the river on his chart, before they dropped the bomb. A bomb they had thought it amusing to nickname 'The Little Boy'. Tsan Yohoto was sobbing uncontrollably now and he thumped the door beside him in fury and despair. The tears in his eyes distorted his vision, as he flew on over the city centre.

'Hiroshima control to unidentified aircraft over Hiroshima city. Identify yourself immediately and declare intentions. If you have radio transmission failure, turn on your transponder and squawk seven six zero zero. Over.'

Tsan Yohoto barely heard the increasingly alarmed voice in his headphones as he flew over the city, recognising landmarks. There were still some large empty plots, which had not yet been redeveloped.

Away to his right he noticed green navigation lights rising from the direction of the airport and turning towards him. *Probably a police helicopter. Time to move.* He banked away to the southwest, maintained his altitude of one thousand feet and checked on the GPS that he was on course. A few minutes later, he was over the southwestern suburbs. He slowed up to about seventy knots then reached back and unscrewed the lids on two of the fuel containers behind him. He dropped the lids into the footwell and began looking at the ground.

'Hiroshima Control to unidentified aircraft. Identify yourself. Exit the control zone immediately.'

His mother summoned up the last of her energy and began to lash out at him again. 'Tsan, Tsan,' she cried. 'My son, please stop!'

Suddenly, Tsan Yohoto's heart almost exploded. He could see it. The park. The park. The park where they had been playing when the Yankees dropped the bomb.

Now he was a little boy again. He was lying on the ground, screaming in pain. His head spun in shock. Mother was beating his back. He was on fire. Why? Mother beat out the last of the flames and held him tight on the ground. He could hear Mother's heart pounding in her chest. Together, the little boy and his mother turned around to find Kendo and Lita on the swings. The smell of burning flesh filled his nose.

In the cockpit of the plane, Tsan cried out. He could see swings in the park. He flung the control column forward and put the aircraft into a steep dive, aiming directly at the swings. The smell of burning flesh grew even stronger. He screamed aloud. His mother was screaming too.

'Yankees, this is one "Little Boy" you're never going to forget!'

The aircraft shuddered in protest and the wind howled past as the speed built and built. As the park filled his view, Tsan could see Kendo and Lita's charred bodies on the swings. Backwards and forwards. Backwards and forwards. Backwards and . . .

EPILOGUE

Thirty minutes after the meeting at the White House, all two hundred and fifty-two BurgerFantastic outlets were shut down. By the next day, the first supplies of cephalosporin, newly constituted by Maria Cabrini's formula of acids, were being delivered to hospitals throughout New York and the adjoining states. Twenty-four hours later, doctors began to report an improvement in patient symptoms. A further thirty-six hours later, the tipping point had been reversed and hospitals began discharging patients, while fewer patients were presenting with new infections.

One year later, a full Congressional Inquiry was complete. The final report stated that 122,086 people died as a result of poisoning with e-coli O157:h7, which had initially proved untreatable owing to antibiotic resistance. The first recorded victim was Mrs Esther Wolfowitz, a pensioner of Apartment 68, 9012 Jay Street, Manhattan. The last recorded death was Ricky Morgan, aged twenty-five, a football player with the New York Giants. The Inquiry concluded that the cause of the outbreak was deliberate infection with e-coli O157:h7 and that the motive was terrorism.

A powerful Senate Committee of Inquiry was established to investigate Detective John Wyse's theory that the epidemic was caused by the deliberate acceleration of antibiotic resistance in

New York, prior to the introduction of the e-coli bacteria. Despite thousands of hours of investigation and cooperation between various government agencies, it was found that this theory could not be proven. The presence of cephalosporin particles at the BurgerFantastic factory, while suspicious, was not conclusive. Furthermore, there was no formal report before the Inquiry by the Food and Drug Administration into the alleged misleading advertising of SuperVerve, as Yamoura Pharmaceuticals had withdrawn the campaign voluntarily.

The FDA was praised for its intervention in the case.

(Maria Cabrini was of the view that the FDA inquiry probably forced the perpetrators to introduce the e-coli bacteria earlier than they had planned. Had the population continued to consume cephalosporin at the same rate for another six months, she believed that the epidemic of infection would have been completely overwhelming. Also, she suggested, the terrorists had been rushed into introducing the e-coli in December, rather than the following summer. The warmer summer humidity would have increased the survival and transfer of bacteria and would have caused even more deaths.)

However, the Committee of Inquiry did direct the FDA to formally reassess the country's vulnerability to widespread antibiotic resistance.

At private committee level, Maria Cabrini proffered her theory that Tsan Yohoto had deliberately added his own DNA into the infecting organism in order to increase the incidence of leukaemia in New York. This theory proved difficult to investigate, as a sample of Tsan Yohoto's DNA was needed in order to compare it against the bacteria. Tsan Yohoto had been killed in a plane crash in Japan and his body had been completely incinerated in the subsequent fire. An enquiry was made as to the availability of DNA from any relatives of Tsan Yohoto. It was reported that Tsan Yohoto's only relative was his mother, Saina Yohoto. Unfortunately, she had died in the same crash as her son and, in accordance with his will, what very little remained of their bodies had been cremated and their ashes scattered in a public park in Hiroshima.

E-coli O157:h7 was discovered in the sauce containers in all the BurgerFantastic restaurants on the day they were closed. It is believed that these were all from the last two vats of sauce, which had been infected the previous night. The prime suspect for the deliberate infecting of the sauce is Takar el Sayden, the BurgerFantastic owner and the Inquiry held that his motive was terrorism, in collaboration with persons unknown.

The file on the murder of Abdel Moamer, the founder of the Quick 'n' Tasty restaurant business, remains open. It is not known whether he was aware of the plot. Detective John Wyse offered the view that he had been murdered, either because he would not take part in the conspiracy, or to put pressure on his nephew, Takar el Sayden, to cooperate.

A request was sent to the Libyan authorities asking that they cooperate in returning Takar el Sayden to the US, to assist the investigation. The Libyan government respectfully pointed out that the evidence was flimsy and that they doubted if Mr el Sayden would receive a fair trial, given the media coverage of the events. An extradition warrant was served but is not considered likely to have much chance of success. Takar el Sayden now lives with his family near Tripoli and is reported to be a very wealthy man. The BurgerFantastic company was closed down permanently and the Newark production facility freehold and the restaurant leases were sold by the liquidator, in one lot, to a national pizza chain.

Yamoura Pharmaceuticals continues to thrive. Following Tsan Yohoto's death, his old friend, the silver-haired Yamoura chairman, Lumo Kinotoa, was appointed as *daitoryou* or chief executive.

Dynamic Communications have continued their profitable growth. They were never accused of any foul play in connection with their marketing campaigns for SuperVerve and BurgerFantastic.

Professor Alan G.F. Milton was issued with a verbal warning by his colleagues at the Food and Drug Administration, concerning the thoroughness of his work in the SuperVerve case. Two months later, a senior lecturer unexpectedly entered Professor Milton's study one evening, shortly before the end of term exam results. Professor Milton was sitting on the edge of his desk, receiving oral sex from a blonde twenty-two-year-old student, who had been concerned about her grades. Two weeks later, following a university inquiry, he was fired from his position as Professor of Otolaryngology. The following day, his wife Sylvia threw him out of their house and filed for divorce.

Dr Peter Phillips never worked again as a doctor. He moved to Miami, and worked for three months in his brother's car hire business before committing suicide.

One week after the White House acted on his colleague John Wyse's theory, Detective Michael Cabrini was called into Sergeant Jim Connolly's office at the police station. Already in the room were the police department lawyer and a police doctor. Sergeant Connolly told him that they were of the opinion that his alcohol abuse was seriously affecting his work and went on to list a number of examples. The final straw had been his non-availability to assist Detective Wyse in confronting the curtain swishers at the hospital. (It transpired that Detective Cabrini had gone for lunch at Harry's and had met Detectives Smith and Williams, who were discussing problems in their marriages. He decided to have a beer, and 'one thing led to another'.) Detective Cabrini accepted that this was a dereliction of duty. He was suspended and given two options – either an inquiry would be held into his conduct and he would probably be dismissed, or he could choose to stop drinking and enter an addiction treatment centre, with the full support of the police department.

Detective Cabrini entered the six-week residential programme at the Cedars Rehabilitation Institute in Brooklyn. Cabrini described the experience as 'life-changing' and subsequently remained sober. Six months later, his wife Liz invited him back into the family home in New Jersey. A few months later, he retired from the Force and now works as a qualified addiction counsellor.

Detectives Smith and Williams, who were both on final warnings about their drinking on duty and unreliability, refused the option of attending rehab. They were both fired and now work as security guards at a New Jersey mall.

The Inquiry considered the roles of Anna Milani and her fellow 'curtain swisher' Muhammad Fattar Attabak. The Inquiry concluded that there was insufficient evidence to prove that they were trying to spread infection by manipulating curtains in the wards. Instead, it was proposed that they were observing conditions in the hospitals and reporting to persons unknown.

Wyse and Cabrini later pieced together a few of the clues. Milani is a common Iranian surname, and it transpired that her family were Sunni Muslims, originally from Iran. ('You always said her eyes reminded you of a Persian cat,' Cabrini told him, half joking.) Anna was born and reared in Leeds, in the north of England, where she had come under the influence of a group of radicalised al-Qaeda supporters, as did a number of her peers who were involved in the London tube and bus bombings, and the second Glasgow airport attack. Later, Wyse remembered the day of their first kiss in Central Park. She had brought him to see her friend's paintings. He realised now that the one she liked most had been of the mountain setting for the Battle of Jaji, Osama bin Laden's legendary defence of a training camp known as 'The Lion's Den'. And he wondered if her Muslim faith accounted for her refusal of sex until well into their relationship. Wyse remembered all those 'projects' she was working on, at unusual hours – perhaps they had nothing at all to do with Dynamic Communications.

Homeland Security discovered a diary kept by Anna Milani, under a pile of magazines in her bedside locker. John Wyse was shown her last entry, which was on Saturday 14 December, the day before she died.

I love John so much it's scary! Pretty sure I'm pregnant, but haven't done the test yet. OMG! People are dying from this food poisoning thing. It's awful. Cindy's out sick too – hope she's okay. Very worried. Tired doing this curtain swishing thing, and keeping it from John. Don't know what the point is? I need to get out of it as soon as I can, but I can't risk anything happening to them at home. Stuck for now.

Maria Cabrini was awarded a Presidential Citizens Medal, for her role in reversing the catastrophe. She accepted a post as a researcher, specialising in antibiotic resistance, at the National Institute of Allergy and Infectious Diseases.

Detective John Wyse was granted two weeks' compassionate leave and counselling, following the death of his fiancée. He stayed with his sister's family in Malibu, where he spent most of the time walking on the beach contemplating the shocking events, with the voices of the dead echoing through his head.

He was invited to a private lunch with the President at the White House, together with his parents, where the President praised him for his detective work and his leadership in bringing an end to the crisis. The President presented him with an Excellent Police Duty award.

John Wyse was delighted to accept an offer of a new position with the Joint Terrorism Task Force with a brief 'to encourage lateral thinking and to assess the USA's ability to predict and react to terrorism threats of a non-traditional nature'. Unknown to him, a covert Homeland Security team is currently keeping him under surveillance, because of his link to Anna Milani. On Saturday night next, he is having dinner at Mike and Liz Cabrini's house. The Cabrinis have also invited Mike's sister, Maria.

Ibrahim Fallah continues in his position of chief librarian at the New York Metropolitan Library on Fifth Avenue. The maintenance crew's van was never connected to him. Along with hundreds of others who attended the same Bronx mosque as Anna Milani and her fellow curtain-swisher, he was routinely checked out by police and no suspicions were raised.

He subsequently received new instructions from Afghanistan

and now spends most of his spare time carrying out surveys of the Manhattan subway system. What he doesn't know is that Lumo Kinotoa, the chairman of the Chess Club, has drawn on his learning as a military historian to conceive a new strategy. That plan would soon see Fallah involved in an extraordinary new plot, which would bring widespread terror to western cities.

ACKNOWLEDGEMENTS

I learned the hard way about antibiotic resistance, after losing my legs in a fire, aged twenty. I have managed to do very well on my new prosthetic legs, but I am walking around on skin that has been grafted from other parts of my body, and it is not as strong as normal skin. Every now and then I will get a cut or a blister and I usually manage my way around that with plasters and antiseptic creams. However, if I'm unlucky, or doing too much walking, the wound will become infected, and that's a different level of problem. The solution was always to take a course of antibiotics, and within forty-eight hours or so, I would see a significant improvement. I could usually even keep walking while the wound healed.

Thus, I frequently took antibiotics throughout the 1980s and 1990s, with great results. However, everything changed in the early years of this century. I developed a routine-looking skin infection and took a course of antibiotics. The infection got worse. I took an extended course of antibiotics. The infection got worse. I was prescribed different types of antibiotics. They had no effect. My familiar skin infection had learned how to resist the antibiotics. I had to spend long periods in a wheelchair. It took extended treatment with different antibiotics, and a new skin graft, to eventually solve the problem. Thankfully, it's almost ten years now since I had any infection and I've learned to avoid them by taking greater care with my prostheses and adapting my lifestyle.

I would like to thank Dr F.X. Keane, consultant (retired), at the National Rehabilitation Hospital, Dr Nicola Ryall and Dr Jackie Stowe, also of the National Rehabilitation Hospital, for their great help and advice over the years.

Dr Colm Power in Wicklow, and my microbiologist friend who prefers to remain anonymous, have given me invaluable assistance with medical detail. Early drafts of the book read more like a medical textbook than an entertaining thriller, and microbiologists will spot where I have used artistic licence to help keep some of the medical issues understandable. Any mistakes are down to me. But the premise remains true: the more antibiotics we take, the more antibiotic resistant bacteria will develop.

A number of other medical professionals helped me in writing this book. They share a deep unease about the entire system by which medicines are prescribed to patients, but preferred not to be mentioned.

Dr Paul Carson and Glenn Meade, authors of many worldwide bestsellers, have been of enormous help to me, both in practical terms, and as an inspiration. I am very grateful for your time and encouragement.

Tim Palmer, P.J. Cunningham, Cliodhna O'Donoghue, Kate Egan, Tom Mooney and Michael McNulty were my 'test readers' and provided great encouragement and skilled critiques. Thank you all very much, for helping me to bring this story to life.

Security and defence analyst Declan Power helped with a question on the Middle East and any mistakes in that area are mine.

Thanks to Bolton's finest, Chris Bogle, for some north of England dialogue for Anna, such as, 'Best look at those maps then.' (Did you spot the clue?) Thanks also to marketing expert Ronan O'Driscoll, Art O'Leary and Paul Dunne for coming up with lots of suggestions for brand names. Mary Stoner in Dallas double-checked a few American terms for me.

Thanks to Vanessa Fox O'Loughlin and the Inkwell Group for good advice, and particularly to Afric McGlinchey, for a great first edit, which made all the difference in getting published.

My huge thanks to all the team at Black & White Publishing, for believing in my book and helping to make it as good as it can possibly be. Particular thanks to Graham Lironi, who was great to work with as a sharp-eyed editor, and who added lots of ideas too.

If you're interested in looking deeper into the drug approval process and marketing phenomenon, the FDA website is a rich seam of information. Just like Tsan Yohoto, you can register and they will email you copies of their reports and warning notices to the pharmaceutical companies, as they're published. The reference to the fake drug site, Havidol.com, is factual.

Finally, I would like to thank the police officers of the First and Sixth Precincts, Manhattan, and especially the Fifth Precinct, for their courtesy and helpfulness in answering endless questions and for letting me hang around and observe. New York's finest!

ABOUT THE AUTHOR

Paul McNeive lost his legs in a fire aged twenty, and this life-changing experience and what happened to him on his road to recovery inform his debut novel, *The Manhattan Project*. In a highly successful career, Paul was the managing director of Savills, Ireland, and is now an international motivational speaker, a columnist for the *Irish Independent*, was the world's first double amputee helicopter pilot and is an ambassador for the Douglas Bader Foundation. He is also on the board of Ireland's National Rehabilitation Hospital.

Visit paulmcneive.com.